Justin McCarthy

Paul Massie

A Romance

Justin McCarthy

Paul Massie
A Romance

ISBN/EAN: 9783337347888

Printed in Europe, USA, Canada, Australia, Japan

Cover: Foto ©Andreas Hilbeck / pixelio.de

More available books at **www.hansebooks.com**

PUBLISHER'S NOTICE.

THIS story was published in England, anonymously, and was very successful. It received from the Press most flattering notices, and had a wide sale. All of which was very pleasing to the Author, as its success was purely the result of merit, and was not influenced by the Author's brilliant reputation as a novelist and essayist. It is now, for the first time, published in this country, and over the Author's name, at his own suggestion.

The following notices appeared in the London "Pall Mall Gazette" and "Saturday Review":

(*From the Pall Mall Gazette.*)

"This book has the very unusual merit of uniting, without incongruity, the interest of romantic incident with the interest of striking sketches of natural character. . . . We have here all the usual elements of a sensational novel, and we have actors who are neither puppets nor monsters, but specimens of ordinary humanity, and the sensational incidents serve only to develop the naturalness of the characters. . . . We may say that altogether we have not read many books so full of promise as 'Paul Massie.'"

(*From the Saturday Review.*)

"This is the story of 'Paul Massie,' the latest romance of the sensational kind, and we think it exceeds in merit the greater number of its predecessors. The story is well told, and the style is bright and effective. The sketches of the various foreign refugees are good, and the characters of Salome and Mrs. Massie are well drawn and well contrasted. . . . There is much keen discrimination of character throughout the book generally."

CONTENTS.

PAUL MASSIE.

PROLOGUE.

TO help towards the understanding of the story about
to be told, something in the nature of a preliminary
chapter or prologue is necessary. This story, be it observed, is called a romance. If, therefore, any reader should
hereafter be inclined to grumble because in the course of the
following chapters he may meet with incidents or people, or
even mysteries, the like whereof do not encounter him every
day, when he takes his walks abroad, or rides to the Bank
on his omnibus, let him not say that he has not been fore-
warned. Perhaps what he may read here is none the less
true for being called romance ; but even if it be untrue
and impossible, it at least shall have the merit of presenting itself from the beginning frankly and without false
pretences.

One glimpse into events occurring a whole generation
before the opening of our story will perhaps be a convenient means of anticipating some conjectures and questions.
We hold up a torch for a moment to illumine a group
in a far background of the picture, and then pass on.

Seven or eight-and-twenty years and an ocean divide
the scene of the prologue from the scene of the romance.
A night of almost tropical heat lies upon the landscape,
and the principal object we see is a villa of Spanish-con-
struction, in the midst of neglected but still beautiful
grounds on the outskirts of a town in a disturbed country.

If it were day, one might see that a vast and noble mountain-peak dominated the scene ; the region all around was rich with orange-orchards and cotton and maize, bedecked here and there with the wild rose, and made musical by the tinkle of unnumbered streamlets.

One of the windows of the villa was open, and a light streamed from it on the balcony. In the room within a fair-haired Englishwoman, young and timid and tearful, half in passion, half in fear, was bidding farewell to one she was never to see more. He whom she was urging to go, yet by her very entreaty compelling to stay, was dark-haired and dark-eyed, with sallow cheeks, a lithe sinewy form, and tender caressing ways.

A charming love-scene, no doubt. Sweet young hearts about to be rudely rent asunder. Romeo and Juliet on the shores of the Gulf of Mexico.

A door opens suddenly, and another woman stands in the room. She is fair and English, like the first ; to whom, indeed, she bears a striking resemblance. But there is decision in her manner, and strength of character in her expression.

"For shame !" she says in a stern tone ; and the pair of lovers fall asunder, and one of the pair looks aghast. A great actress has been seen to look just so when the screen is flung down and she stands a discovered Lady Teazle.

"How did you dare to come here?" asks the severe intruder, turning upon the young man.

He was disconcerted, but not abashed. He began, in broken English, and with a wonderfully musical voice, some inflated platitude about love daring everything ; but she cut him short with a look of the most absolute scorn.

"Love !" she said. "Love, that steals in at night like a robber"—he smiled—"to destroy that wretched girl ! like a robber and a coward !"

"Nay, Madame Massie—pardon ; not a coward. I

care not for my life; I have shown it once and again. If I were a coward, I were not now here. And I only came to say the one farewell—the very last."

The other lady now plucked up a little courage, and came forward:

"Indeed it is true, Agnes," she said. "He, Leon, has not been five minutes here. I did not know of his coming; I did not let him in: he climbed up by that balcony. He might have been killed. And he was going away the moment, the very moment you came in. Perhaps we shall never see him again." Her tears came anew.

"Have you no pity?" asked Leon, looking again at the elder sister, and this time speaking in French, which, though still a foreign tongue to him, was far more familiar than English. "You are not—you cannot be—hard of heart: you so young, so fair, so *incomprise;* nay, more than misunderstood—"

"Deserted, you were going to say," she calmly added. "Yes, deserted by my husband; else you were not here now. But though deserted by my husband, not deserted by my principles, by my conscience, or by God. I can still protect myself and *her.* Go, Leon. You are not heartless or wicked, I know. Go, and never, if you have a man's honor, look upon her again."

"It is not likely," he said with emotion, "that we shall meet ever more. She soon returns to Europe—is it not?— and I—I follow my star. But you do me justice; I am not bad. I love her—yes, do not stop me—I must say it, even to you; and I cannot wish that we had never met. Adieu! Will you not give me your hand?"

"No; if we meet again, perhaps I may give it to you then. Now I can only think of the danger you have brought upon her weakness. Good-by."

He then turned to the younger sister. The elder put her arm on her shoulder to draw her away. Leon seized the girl's hand, and pressed it to his lips. Then he quickly drew something from one of the fingers, kissed the hand again, sprang into the balcony, looked back for the last time, and was gone.

That was truly the last time the sisters saw him in life. Next day his body, pierced through the heart by a pistol-bullet, was found in a little plantation outside the limits of the grounds belonging to the house. A card was found thrust under his vest, and on it were some words in English. Those who discovered the body could not read the writing; but the card was brought to Agnes Massie. Self-controlled as she was, she nearly swooned as she read the words:

"Done in fair fight.—PAUL MASSIE."

CHAPTER I.

EARLY in the month of February, a few years back, the Massies of Seaborough-house, Seaborough, were expecting a visitor, whose coming was anticipated with no little anxiety and curiosity. If a stranger could have looked into one of the rooms of the house where this story opens, one wild and wet night at the time just mentioned, he must have perceived at a glance that the occupants of the apartment were waiting in expectation of somebody or something to arrive. The Rev. Eustace Neale Massie, rector of Seaborough parish and owner of Seaborough-house, was walking up and down the room, every now and then looking at his watch : occasionally taking up the *Times*, and glancing for the twentieth time over the leading articles on the American question, the coming Budget, the expected Church-rate debate, and the policy of the French Emperor. His mother, Mrs. Massie, was looking silently and anxiously through the half-opened curtains into the wild dreary night. Lydia Massie, her daughter, lay on a sofa, and sometimes tried hard not to yawn. Sarah Massie, second cousin and bride-elect of the clergyman, was occupying herself in making up papers and letters for the post. Dinner had been kept waiting for some time—an unusual occurrence in Seaborough-house, where the inmates were generally ruled by a punctilious regularity.

"Perhaps he will not come to night," said Mrs. Massie, closing the curtains and turning away. "I almost wish he did not ; it is so wet and wild. How cold it grows!" She drew a shawl round her shoulders and took a chair

1*

close by the fire. She shuddered, indeed, as if with cold, and looked anxious and uncomfortable.

"Cold, mamma ? I think it is rather warm; and I don't believe he is coming to-night," said her daughter, who was unmistakably tired of waiting. "The dinner, I should think, will be cold enough."

"He is certain to come," said the clergyman decisively.

"But the weather—such winds!" suggested Mrs. Massie.

"He has made voyages a good deal longer in weather a great deal worse," replied Eustace. "I don't suppose a few hours of the Channel would distress him much, or put him in fear."

"One thing certain," said Lydia, "is, that if he should not come, mamma will never sleep to-night. I can see that her mind is filled with dreadful visions of wrecks, and orphan boys flung ashore tied to broken spars. I am sure she only sees in cousin Paul an interesting blue-eyed child, who deserves our pity because he has been sent out into the wide world, travelling all alone without his governess."

"I think he is coming now," said Sarah Massie, looking up from her papers. "Somebody certainly is; I have heard the sound of wheels these some moments."

"Sarah has ears like Jessie Brown, or Jenny Jones, or whatever her name was, at Lucknow," said Lydia. "I am sure I heard no sound but the wind."

The sound of wheels, however, soon became quite distinct. Then the gravel before the hall-door was heard to crash under a carriage. Eustace ran out.

"Eustace, take care of yourself," said Lydia. "You will certainly take cold, if you go to the door without hat or coat."

Sarah followed the clergyman, to make sure that he did not rush too rashly, and without protection, into the jaws of night. Mrs. Massie had risen when the sound of the wheels was first heard; but she sat down again, and looked very pale. Indeed, she visibly trembled. Lydia gave a quick glance at herself in the mirror, and prepared to receive a visitor in becoming attitude.

Voices were heard outside in eager friendly talk; and then Eustace and Sarah Massie reëntered the room, conducting the long-expected visitor, the cousin to be seen for the first time.

"Mother," said Eustace, "here, at last, is our cousin Paul."

"Stay," said Lydia in a tone of sudden alarm; "mamma is not well."

Indeed, the moment the new-comer presented himself within the threshold of the room, Mrs. Massie's agitation reached such a point, that she sank back in her chair, turned perfectly white, and seemed to become positively unconscious. There was for a moment so much alarm that all courtesy of welcome, all interchange of greeting, was forgotten. Only for a moment, however. Mrs. Massie almost instantaneously revived, and although still in somewhat of a tremor, advanced and gave her nephew an affectionate greeting.

"Mamma is so nervous," said Lydia, "and has not been very well lately; and then she so alarmed herself about the weather and the danger of crossing the Channel."

Mrs. Massie added a few gentle words about her nephew's resemblance to his poor dear mother, and the emotion which was called up by seeing him and by the memories which were thus brought to her mind. Paul had then some opportunity of offering a formal greeting to the family, and did not neglect the privilege of kissing both his fair cousins. Sarah received him with frank and friendly welcome. Lydia on the other hand turned her eyes upward, and endeavored to look slightly alarmed.

Paul Massie was not like any of his relatives in personal appearance. Mrs. Massie was pale, although not thin, —rather plump indeed,—with soft blue eyes and thick fair hair. Her daughter was strikingly like her. Eustace was a handsome dignified young man of some six-and-twenty, with white forehead, soft auburn curls, and luxuriant auburn whiskers cut in the approved clerical fashion, delicate complexion, small hands and feet, graceful figure—almost a model High-Church clergyman in appearance. The new cousin had nothing of the family type or tinge. He was rather tall, very muscular and sinewy; slender, save for his broad chest and shoulders. He had thick black hair, had neither beard nor whiskers, but wore a long moustache drooping below his chin on either side. His face showed a complexion of almost tropical darkness. Sun-scorched and worn, he looked several years older than Eustace Massie. He would have had a grave and perhaps even melancholy expression, but for the restless glitter of his black eyes. He was entirely unlike what Eustace at least expected to see. The graceful clergyman stole side-glances of amazement at the new-comer, and looked as if he found it no easy task to repress a shudder.

But Eustace was all polite welcome. He presently took his cousin away to show him the arrangements which had been made for his accommodation.

"You only passed through France, I suppose?" remarked the clergyman, as the pair were leaving the room.

"Passed through?" replied Paul. "I had to remain four, nearly five months in Paris."

"But you never told us?"

"No; I feared to alarm you; and I knew that my detention could not last long."

"Your detention?"

Paul laughed. "Yes," he replied; "I was in France as a prisoner. I can tell you all in five minutes; it is not a long story."

"I like our cousin very much," said Lydia, when Eustace and Paul had left the room. "He will create quite a sensation at church next Sunday. He looks like Don Cæsar de Bazan. I wish he had not frightened poor mamma, though.—Better now, mamma, are you not?"

But the mamma made a very faint and wan attempt at a smile. She left the room presently, her eyes brimming over with tears.

This was Paul Massie's first visit to England. Born in Vera Cruz, he had been brought up principally in the United States, receiving such education as he had in one of the State colleges. He had had some training in a great New York shipping house, and being quick, clever, and energetic, was sent to establish new branches of the firm's trade in California, in Australia, in Russia, and in India. He had been nearly all over Europe, had spent at different times months and months in Paris, but had never crossed the English Channel to see the country which he always called his home, after the genial, loving fashion of people who hail in any way, however distant, from the old land. None of the Massie family ever came to see him. He had himself only a faint memory of a fair grave woman, whom he now assumed to have been his mother; but he had never seen his father. Evidently his uncle the late Mr. Eustace Massie never had any wish to look upon his nephew. The nephew always understood that there had been some family quarrel about a marriage, and troubled himself no farther on the subject. He had led a happy, varied, active life, which suited his energetic, restless temperament. He was not a thorough business-man by any means, but he had perhaps a sort of genius for developing new branches of commerce, and discovering fresh unexpected fields of enterprise, which might be made profitable by the patient, careful labor of others. The death of his uncle left him the inheritor of a considerable sum of money; it procured him, too, a pressing, brotherly invitation from his cousin Eustace (now a man of some fortune) to pay England and his family a visit, with the view, perhaps, of settling in the old country altogether. At the time the invitation reached the New World, Paul was once again in Mexico. The letter followed him from New York to New Orleans; from thence to Vera Cruz; and, not finding him there, it fell into hands which took care of it, and when Paul was attainable once more, forwarded it to his address. For while Paul was in Mexico there suddenly turned up the famous Mexican expedition of England, France, and Spain, to obtain satisfaction for wrongs done to European subjects. Paul was thoroughly Mexican in his views; and when England and Spain had drawn back, and France proceeded alone on a path of avowed and ostentatious conquest, he abandoned his commercial mission and joined the Mexican forces. He had for some time been a friend of the brave and ill-fated General Zaragoza, and under that gallant soldier (too early cut off) he accepted a commission. His military career was very short; he was made a prisoner before Puebla, and conveyed with many others to France. It was while lodging in Paris, under a sort of honorable custody, that he at length received the news of his uncle's death and cousin's invitation. He understood that the ban which kept him out of the Massie circle was at an end; that it had died with his uncle. His captivity was not difficult to bring to a conclusion, and he came to England.

Paul and his kinsfolk were very happy the first night of his visit. The two young women enjoyed his conversation immensely, and the Rev. Eustace was pleased, puzzled, and amused. Paul had the fresh, unconstrained manners of one who has gone much about the world and mixed with all sorts of people. He certainly wanted that which an English drawing-room would call manner; but he showed an originality and a variety in his style and his conversation which would probably have proved a great deal more attractive to most women, and to all rational men, than the conventional urbanity and cold grace of regular social life. Eustace Massie became more and more reconciled to his cousin, although he would not perhaps have much liked the bishop, or even the dean, to be one of the party. Paul could talk of everything and every place,—of India, Persia, and the Greek islands; of the Crimea, where he had actually arrived in time to see the great day of Balaklava; of Mexico and Texas, and Santa Anna and General Scott; of Juarez and Zaragoza and General Forey. He could explain the most difficult points of the American question to Eustace, who, like every respectable English clergyman, was given to political discussion. He sang and played—sang Spanish songs, French songs, and had he been asked or encouraged, could even have sung negro melodies. But Eustace heard in silent grief that his cousin was a believer in spiritualism, mesmerism, and other abhorred superstitions; and Mrs. Massie was not pleased to learn, that when left to himself her nephew hardly ever desisted from smoking.

CHAPTER II.

A MESSAGE FROM THE SEA.

MRS. MASSIE sat in her bedroom alone. She was quite dressed, and was seated in an arm-chair before a bright fire, which seemed just now to have little power to warm her pale cheeks and shivering form. She had once been a beautiful woman, and indeed was still too young to part with her claims to beauty. Fair, soft, now somewhat inclined to plumpness, she betrayed a peculiar character of weakness and indecision about her pale blue eyes and her sensitive, tremulous lips. She was a woman to be happy and sunny in happiness and the sun; to shrink up and wither before the first chilling blast. Adversity is a medicine which people are rather fond of recommending indiscriminately as a panacea for their neighbors. Like other medicines, it only agrees with certain constitutions. There are nerves which it braces, and nerves which it utterly shatters. There are people whose good qualities shine brightest in the darkness, like the ray of a diamond; but there are others whose virtues are only brought out by the light, like the colors of a silk. Mrs. Massie's nature shone in the light of serene happiness. She was loved by her son and daughter; and she was happy while they were near her, and peace was around them. Thus they had lived since the death of her husband.

Had her married life been unhappy? People supposed so. Her late husband had been a little wild in his youth; but the utter break-down of his elder brother's conduct and chances would have made him the good boy of the family and his father's favorite, only for his sudden and secret marriage. This led to quarrels: and he was only too glad to get the chance of making a career by endeavoring to turn to account some property the family had long possessed in Mexico and California, and which his elder brother had utterly failed to manage. His young wife (a stranger to Seaborough) had followed him to Vera Cruz. She was accompanied by her sister—Paul's mother, as people afterwards learned. Mr. Massie did not prosper much in Mexico : but his father soon died, and left him in trust the family property, which was considerable. So Eustace Massie the late came back to England. But he was broken in health, and led a sickly, complaining, indeed morose and maundering kind of life ; letting the estate and all about it fall into neglect, and displaying commonly the very worst of his temper to his wife. There was nothing very distinct to be said against him, but people did not like him ; and there was a vague notion that he was a harsh, unkind, and jealous husband. Those who visited the house saw indeed no greater unkindness than was conveyed by somewhat cynical manners, and an objection to go into society, or to permit his wife to go there. At all events, Mrs. Massie rather withered under her husband's influence, and concentrated all the love of a very loving soft nature upon her children,—thereby rendering Mr. Massie more cynical still.

One person in the world Mr. Massie never would hear mentioned, and that was his nephew Paul. This was the more surprising, as there was a double relationship. Mr. Massie's wife's sister, unhappily for herself—for all parties —met Mr. Massie's elder brother in Mexico. The latter was a handsome, wild, reckless ne'er-do-well, whom his father exiled to the management of the Mexican property, after he had sold out of the army here somewhat in disgrace. The exile did not manage the property, but joined Santa Anna; and during the short interval between one revolution and another, found means to fall in love with Mrs. Massie's sister, and persuaded her to marry him. They had not been long married before he deserted her altogether, and disappeared. His wife never saw him again, and it was supposed that he must have fallen in one of the thousand revolutionary conflicts of which Mexico became for years the cockpit. Paul was born after his disappearance, and during the absence of Eustace in California. Soon the sisters, who had up to this time kept together, separated. Eustace Massie brought his wife back to Europe, and her sister went to live in the United States, where she applied herself to the bringing up of her boy. She died while he was yet but a child, having written with her dying hand a letter bequeathing the care of him to her sister and brother-in-law.

Now every one who talked of the matter in Seaborough said that Mr. Massie had for some reason forbidden his wife to hold any communication with her sister during the later years of the latter's life; and that even her dying appeal did not induce him to do more than make formal provision, through an agent, for the child's education and maintenance in America. It was undoubted that Mr. Massie did not accept with willingness, or discharge with energy, even the formal and technical duties of guardianship. It must be owned that although there was sincere sorrow when Mr. Massie's breaking health at last broke altogether, the house became much more cheerful after his death. The air seemed clearer when his melancholy footfall could no longer be heard echoing for hours as he paced slowly up and down the long hall: when his voice no more reproved or sneered or maundered by the hearth. Yet every one supposed that his marriage had been one of love, at least on his side.   But people remarked too that throughout the different branches of the family of the Seaborough Massies, the sons of every second generation were always good for nothing, and were certain to have a wild youth followed by a broken-down manhood and an early death.

The night of her nephew's arrival, Mrs. Massie sat, as has been stated, in her room alone.   She had been very happy all the evening, after the first sudden shock and burst of involuntary tears.   She had engaged and joined in the bright vivacious conversation, and had listened in wonder and admiration while Paul poured out his rapid, dashing, sometimes even brilliant talk.   Now that she was alone, the tearful mood seemed to have come back again. Was she thinking of her lost husband?   Was she thinking of the sister sleeping in a far-off western grave—the sister with whom she had made the dreary voyage to New York, and the long journey over prairies and mountains, and through half-built towns and among the log-huts of scattered settlers ?   Surely Mrs. Massie was not thus mourning even for her sister ; for indeed they hardly got on well together in life, the one being gentle and rather weak, the other strong and perhaps rather stern.   Or did the coming of her nephew merely sadden her because it so inexorably recalled days of youth and scenes lost sight of since youth ? Those Mexican days were a period of struggle, which, if not very hard, was yet trying to a gentle, orderly nature; and Mrs. Massie had no great cause, one might think, to remember them with any regret.   Certainly the coming of her nephew, disturbing as it did the tranquil current of her monotonous life, had affected her spirits to a degree which she could not resist.

After awhile she rose and looked out of the window, vacantly, upon the leafless boughs and the moonlit lawn. Suddenly a sound struck upon her ear, which, although only caused by the opening of a window, startled her.   A shadow fell across the balcony, which ran along the front of the house immediately under her window.   She looked out, and saw a man's figure on the balcony, just before the room which had been given to Paul Massie. Instantly she put out her light.

What she saw ought not to have been very startling even to her ; and when the explanation of it appears, it will show itself less startling still. But it produced upon Mrs. Massie all the effect of some ghastly supernatural visitation. It was merely the lithe form of a sinewy young man descending from the balcony to the lawn by clinging around one of the light iron supporting pillars. It was no robber or murderer, for the figure was that of Paul Massie. The young man's face was turned towards Mrs. Massie's window, and his black hair, dark complexion, and gleaming eyes, were clearly visible just for an instant—for the duration of a flash of lightning. His mode of getting down to the lawn was a little irregular, but there was nothing very frightful in the action. It must have been something about the look, the features, the position, something recalling a painful or fearful memory, which alarmed the lady who happened to look from her window. For she literally started back—almost sprang back, and hardly kept down the scream which was rising to her lips. She buried herself in her chair once more, and covered her face with her hands. She spoke to herself in a broken kind of way, as weak nervous people when affrighted often do. "It was his very look," she murmured,—"his very look ! just like that night. I was happy, nearly happy, until this poor boy came here ; and now I am wretched ! "

Thus she groaned, weeping, for a few minutes repeating her half-articulate words over and over again. When she had recovered a little from her passion of fear or grief, she approached the window once more, and looked timorously out. But the object of her sudden emotion was gone. There was no human form to be seen anywhere on the quiet lawn.

"I could not have been mistaken," she murmured. "It was not fear or fancy. I am not going mad."

Nothing could be simpler or more easy of explanation than the cause of the unexpected appearance and descent which Mrs. Massie had found so full of terror.

Paul Massie's room was on the same floor with that of his aunt, and looked, like it, upon the balcony, which ran along the whole front of the house, and, supported, as has been said, by iron pillars, formed the roof of a veranda. Beneath was the lawn, once waste and dreary, now freshened up, trim, well cared for, and bright. The tastes of the Rev. Eustace Massie all led to neatness and smooth finish. Small regard for the picturesque had he where the picturesque was not consistent with the clean and the orderly. Everything around and inside Seaborough-house now indicated its change from the careless ownership of the sickly, cynical, melancholy man to whom the present occupant had succeeded. Below the wall of the demesne ran a line of rugged strand, on which this night the surf was dashing heavily. There had been a sharp gale, and although it had nearly passed away, the sea still chafed and heaved, and broken clouds drifted across a watery moon. It was a cheerless, cold, wet spring night, drawing on towards midnight; and the moon shining out now and then upon white waves, or shingle, or patches of sodden grass, gave but a more dreary aspect to the scene. Paul Massie, when he got to his room, might surely have gone to bed and rested in comfort, after weeks of a sort of half-disguised incarceration. But he did not. He might, had he owned the proper amount of sentiment, have "flung himself" into a chair, and thought of the beaming eyes of his cousin Lydia. But he did not—his life had been too rough and active and varied to encourage much of the sentimental in his nature. He simply lit a cigar—a strong, pungent, full-favored, one might almost add, able-bodied Havana—and smoked. The enjoyment was delicious, but the smoke soon began to perfume the room terribly.

"This will never do," thought the *novus hospes*. "My aunt will never endure me if I begin in this way the very first night. These curtains are very pretty, and I daresay costly; and I have not had the society of relatives so long that I can afford to be expelled from it all at once."

He was not afraid of February night air, not being in the habit of taking cold. So he put on a wideawake, opened the window, and stepped out on the balcony, carefully closing the window behind him to prevent the smoke from getting in again.

It was very pleasant despite the cold, and the sound of the surge was fascinating to Paul. He was in a restless mood too, partly caused by the novelty of being for the first time in his life "at home," and his uncertainty as to whether the long desired situation would suit him after all. He thought it would be very agreeable to smoke by the edge of the sea. So he bit his cigar tightly, pressed his hat firmly on his head, and unhesitatingly committed an act which his clerical cousin would hardly have done to procure himself a bishopric. He stepped over the balcony, clung round one of the pillars, and slided easily to the ground. Then he strode rapidly down the lawn, and made for the sounding sea. As he descended by the pillar, he thought he observed light in one of the windows; but it was immediately extinguished.

Paul soon reached the strand, and walked slowly along the edge of the sea. He was in a kind of dreamy delight. He looked vacantly along the shining track of light which sparkled on the waves, and his eyes lost their restless glitter, and became calm and melancholy. There was something very odd about this man's eyes. That restless glitter just mentioned was not always pleasant to look upon. In general the story-teller's comments upon the eyes of his hero or heroine are a bore, and an unpardonable, unnecessary bore, because every reader takes for granted the lustre and the beauty of the orbs in question. Bright eyes, even if only green, like Becky Sharp's, are positively the one essential which the most audacious innovator among novelists has never dared to disregard.

Of late we have had plenty of ugly heroes and heroines;
heroines not very young or externally very attractive;
heroines who were not fashionable or romantic, or touch-
ingly poor, or deeply wronged, or even in certain instances
scrupulously virtuous; heroes with red whiskers and large
feet; stupid heroes and heroes with dreadfully vulgar
names. We have had for heroes the consumptive, the
insane, the inane, the hunch-backed, the lame, and the
blind; the tailor, the shoemaker, the groom: we have
absolutely abandoned most of the dear old conventional
tracks chalked out by precedent for the heroic and the
romantic. But what novelist has yet ventured to give his
heroes and heroines, when he left them the enjoyment of
sight at all, any eyes which were not bright? In real life
it may be that there are some good, gifted, and even
heroic men and women, whose eyes only beam with a dull-
ish lustre. There have been poets of late the fine frenzy of
whose eyes was concealed by blue spectacles; nor has our
own age been without daring adventnrers and renowned con-
querors whose organs of sight showed scarcely more brilliant than the proverbial boiled gooseberries. But heroes
of this kind have not yet had their physical realities all
acknowledged in romance; and therefore, as Paul Massie
is the hero of a romance, it might be assumed that rational
readers would understand him to be endowed, *ipso facto*,
with eyes of the regulation brightness. The peculiar glitter of his eyes has only been mentioned because the peculiarity really has some sort of connection with the clue of
the mystery which, it has already been acknowledged, does
somehow lie along the foundation of this story.

Paul Massie walked slowly along the edge of the shore,
smoking. It had been a week of storms and wrecks; and
stray fragments of timber still came floating in almost upon
every surge. Only the evening before a fine bark had
gone down within sight of some rocks, the peaks of which
might almost be discerned from where Massie now walked.
Paul continued his promenade, until it brought him to a

long sharp promontory of bare rock, which ran far out into the surf. At this point he might very well have given up his midnight ramble and turned back. But who comes to a barrier without desiring to see what is on the other side? Paul chose to scramble over the wall of rock, wet and slippery though it was. He had no great difficulty in getting over, and he leaped down upon the sand of a little creek, where the water flowed less noisily in. Here he found that he was not alone.

A few paces off, showing darkly in the moonlight, close to the edge of the strand, he saw the stooping figure of a man, bent over some object which his form concealed. The man started hastily up as Paul leaped on the sand, and Paul could see plainly enough that the object he bent over was a corpse.

Paul approached rapidly, and the man got up.

"It's no use," said the latter, in a tone of embarrassed gruffness—"she's dead."

So she was; quite dead. Evidently the sea had tossed ashore in this little creek one of the many victims of yesterday's wreck—from which so few had been saved. Paul looked down upon the body of a woman, well-dressed, black-haired; the black hair clinging round her like seaweed.

"She came ashore just now," said the man in explanation; "just with the turn of the tide. I thought she might be alive; and I did my best to bring her to; but she's as dead as a stone, ain't she, sir?"

"Quite dead, poor creature," said Paul, looking down at the ghastly face and the long lank hair. "No use leaving her to lie here; we must have the body removed somewhere out of this. But I say, my friend," Paul suddenly said, looking up at the man, "are you a fisherman or a sailor?"

"No, I ain't," was the gruff reply.

"Have you nothing at all to do with the sea?"

"Nothing at all."

"I thought as much. You must know very little indeed of the sea, if you supposed that woman could be still alive after lying in the water since yesterday's wreck."

"How was I to know it was yesterday's wreck?"

"There was no wreck since yesterday. Do you live here? If you do, you must have known that."

"Supposing I do and supposing I don't, what then? What does it matter? I live where I like. I suppose it's no affair of yours. If you know all about her, look after the body for yourself."

He turned away whistling.

"Don't go just yet," said Paul; "I should like to know what you have been doing with this body."

"You don't fancy I have been murdering the woman?" said the man, turning round with a defiant and very unpleasant sneer.

"No, I don't. I can see well enough that the woman has been dead of salt water these twenty-four hours; but I do suppose that you've have been robbing her."

"Do you? Where's your proof then? I'm as much above robbery as you are, or any damnation foreigner like you."

"That's a magnificent diamond ring you have on your finger, my friend," said Paul. "Pray where did you get that?"

The man suddenly thrust his hand into his pocket. Paul as suddenly seized his wrist, and, despite his struggle, drew the hand completely out. Yes, there was a very remarkable ring on one finger; a central diamond set in a circlet of small brilliants.

"I'll take my oath," said Paul, "that ring once belonged to that dead woman."

"No, it didn't," replied the other fiercely. "My sweetheart lent it to me, if you want to know. But what the devil does it matter to you?"

"Just that I must know who you are before you go. This body must be removed, and we must see who owns this diamond ring your sweetheart gave you."

Paul's antagonist was a young man, tall and strong, with shoulders a little stooped and rounded. He was a hulking fellow, looking an indescribable compound of groom, blacksmith, and fisherman ; a sort of figure almost always to be seen lounging about the doors of public-houses at sea-ports and watering-places. He had a face which was not ill-looking, but certainly was unpleasant ; light eyelashes, sandy, scrubby whiskers, a heavy lower jaw, sharp white teeth, and eyes which always wandered away to the sea or the shore or the sky, or anywhere from the face of a questioner. These were the chief characteristics, of the person with whom Paul was thus brought into unexpected collision. The man was sinewy and powerful ; he suddenly disengaged his hand, thrust it into a breast-pocket, and in a moment the blade of a knife gleamed in the moonlight.

"What's to hinder me," he said in a savage under-tone, " from driving six inches of this into your ribs ? Let me go, I tell you—you had better ! What's to hinder me from having your life ? "

"Only this," replied Paul, suddenly seizing the threatening wrist with one hand, while he flung his other arm across his antagonist's chest, and with a movement of indescribable rapidity, in which one arm and knee were brought simultaneously into action, he bent the man backwards in a position almost exactly the reverse of that which is familarly described as chancery. The wrist which held the knife Paul wrenched forcibly round until the weapon clattered on the stones. The fellow struggled powerfully, but in vain. Paul kept the hold he had got for some seconds.

"That," he said very coolly, "is a lesson for nothing for you. *That* is the reason why you cannot have my life —at least when you give me warning of danger. You need not struggle—I could hold you there for half an hour. If I don't keep you any longer so, it is only because I don't want you to learn the trick and practise it at some honest man's expense. That will do; you may go. I don't want your name now. I shall know you again."

"You'll know nothing bad of me," said the other, getting on his feet, and slowly rubbing his strained limbs, while he endeavored to smooth his face into a good-tempered expression. "My name's Jem Halliday, and you're about the strongest gentleman I have met in this part of the country. I'm not from here myself, no more than you. You've a powerful grip, wherever you came from. May I take my knife? I'm a bad-tempered chap sometimes, but I never meant to hurt you. I needn't have gave you warning if I did—you said so yourself."

He picked up his knife and put it in his pocket. Paul began to think he had been rather abrupt in his suspicions and actions, and felt half ashamed of his impetuosity. Still the diamond ring gleamed even now with a very sinister lustre on the coarse hard finger of Mr. Halliday.

"We must have something done with this body," said Paul, looking down at the drowned woman. "Is there a village near?"

"Just up the cliff a bit, and the public-house will be open yet. I'll go up and send some one down."

"Do," replied Paul; "I'll wait here. Stay—you smoke? Have a cigar."

Jem took a cigar from the extended case, lighted it with the fire of Massie's Havana, and after two or three heavy puffs, uttered the satisfactory ejaculation, "Prime!"

"You're a stranger here, sir?" observed Halliday, while still bringing his cigar into full play. "Come from over sea, perhaps? Can I show you some of the place to-morrow?"

"Thank you," replied Paul, still not quite certain about his companion. "I am staying with my cousins—yonder, at Seaborough-house."

"A cousin of Mr. Massie, sir?"

"Yes."

"Then you're Mr. Paul Massie, perhaps?"

"I am."

"Thankee, sir ; glad to see you."

Had Paul been paying a close attention to the expression of Halliday's face, he might have seen a singular blending of surprise, cunning, and satisfaction depicted in it. But he paid little heed, and there was nothing surprising in the fact of his name being known to Halliday. Seaborough was a small place, and half the parish might have known beforehand the name of the rector's expected visitor.

Halliday went up the cliff. He stopped a little, and looked back every now and then, and chuckled queerly, noiselessly to himself : "Well, of all the games," he muttered, "this does beat! Paul Massie, Esquire, here!" and he thrust his hand into his jacket-pocket; "and Paul Massie, Esquire, there!" and he jerked his head backwards in the direction of the strand, and softly chuckled again. He soon reached the height of the cliff, and presently disappeared.

Paul paced slowly up and down beside the dead body. He had nearly forgotten all about the diamond ring—the cause of his recent struggle. He had now to wait some considerable time, and the night was cold. The excitement of his little adventure having long since exhaled, it became dreary and cheerless work the standing sentinel over a corpse on a wet strand ; and Paul almost wished he had not chosen to enjoy his cigar outside the precincts of Seaborough-house. He had had many odd adventures in his career, and had stood sentry, during his short campaign as a Mexican volunteer, where there were corpses enough within sight, and living enemies more than enough within hearing. But the presence of this one corpse now filled him with a chilling and ghastly sensation. He was a stanch believer in spiritualistic influences and mesmeric forces, and had many faint shadows of Mexican superstitions still floating vaguely over memory and mind. Every time that in his narrow walk he turned round, it seemed to him as if

the body had taken a new position : sometimes he thought
he saw the eyes open, and look sadly at him; sometimes
he fancified that a voice of melancholy warning, wild and
sad as the wind which was now dying over the sea, murmured his name. He will never, perhaps, get over the
superstitious notion that some mysterious influence exhaled
from that dead body upon Seaborough beach, and appealed
to his intelligence and sympathies in vain.

It was a great relief to him when at last there came
down the cliff a village police-officer and a couple of coast-
guardsmen. Paul gave up his charge, and promised to
call next day at the magistrate's or coroner's office to state
all he knew about the finding of the body. He did not fail
to mention his suspicion about the diamond ring, which,
forgotten for a moment, now again came back to him.
Halliday's not having returned chiefly recalled his doubts;
and on putting one or two questions regarding him, Paul
received answers which confirmed his original suspicions
as to the antecedents and the doubtful character of his
late antagonist. Official report described Mr. Halliday as
an idler—perhaps a smuggler; certainly a ne'er-do-well.
Great civility was shown to Paul when he explained that
he was a relative of Mr. Massie of Seaborough-house.

Two o'clock in the morning as Paul looked at his watch.
Quite time to return, and steal as quietly as he might into
his bedchamber. Happily for him the Massies kept no dogs
and no gamekeeper, and took little heed of village stories
about poachers and robbers. He had therefore no need to
fear a night alarm and the contents of a hasty blunderbuss.
He made his way quickly enough along the strand, where
the receding tide had left the long seaweeds all bare. He
clambered over the wall of the demesne, and threaded his
way in moonlight and shadow to the house ; climbed the
slender pillar again, and got upon the balcony. He peered
in through the window to make sure that the room was his ;
and at the first glance he fancied, nay felt almost certain,
that he saw a figure there which suddenly crossed the floor

1*

towards the door and disappeared. Yet it was his room; the window was unfastened; the embers of the fire were burning down; his luggage was stowed in one corner; a cream-colored volume of railway reading he had bought at the terminus of the Northern line in Paris lay upon the table. So he entered, fastened the window, drew the curtains, and determined to get to bed at once and have a good sleep.

Tired though he was, that sleep did not come soon; nor when it came, was it deep and dreamless. His arrival and his night's adventure had excited his mind, aud however the weary body pleaded for rest, the aroused imagination refused to settle into quietness. For hours he was haunted by half-waking dreams, in which dead women brought him ghostly messages from the deep; white figures entered his room with noiseless and spectral tread, drew aside the curtains of his bed, bent over him and whispered unintelligible words into his startled ear. Once or twice the illusion retained so strong a power over him that he leaped out of bed, broad awake, and searched the room, and tried the lock, which he had himself made fast. All was as it had been. No sound was to be heard except, from without, the distant moan of the waves on the shore. He returned to bed, again to be vexed by goblin messages and melancholy female forms, now in some confused manner seeming to glide through the brilliant mazes of Mexican woods, and surrounded by ever-dissolving groups of dusky figures; half-waking dreams of a wearied man on whose mind a very slight surprise following so much novelty had acted with unwonted power. Paul heeded them little, except as regarded the irritating wakefulness to which they so often recalled him. At last he grew less and less conscious of their power; the phantoms and the forests were no longer provokingly clear, but faded into a dim dreamy background; then sank away altogether, and he fell fast asleep.

CHAPTER III.

SEABOROUGH AND SALOME.

PAUL MASSIE might well have been excused, even by the most inveterate and objectionable advocate of early rising, if he slept until an advanced hour of the following morning. When he had thoroughly awakened, and obtained a complete consciousness of where he was (which was not achieved until after some moments of vague and hazy conjecture), he raised the blind and looked out of the window. The morning, or day, was fresh, crisp, and bright, and the rime of a hoar-frost had not yet wholly left the boughs of the poplars and the glass of the conservatory. He saw the figure of Mrs. Massie pass across the lawn and enter the house. He looked at his watch; it was eleven o'clock. In a few minutes he had dressed, and was hastening to the breakfast-room, wondering whether he was guilty of keeping the family waiting. Only Lydia was in the room, looking bright, fresh, and pretty. She gave him a warm greeting.

"Every body is gone," she said. "We knew you were tired, and did not think of having you called. Mamma is not very well, and has not left her room. Eustace and Sarah have gone into Seaborough to find out all about the wreck, and whether any body has been saved. I am sure I hope somebody has been saved; don't you, cousin Paul? I may call you Paul, may I not? Eustace is so good; whenever anything of the kind happens, he can never rest until he is on the spot. Sarah has gone with him, of course; he likes her to be with him. Eustace and Sarah are engaged, you know. So I remained at home to keep you company."

Was Paul rather awkward in expressing his delight? In truth, he was a little puzzled. Mrs. Massie he had just seen entering the house, shawled and furred ; yet he was now told that she could not leave her room. "White lies, I suppose, are permitted to fashionable people," thought our Mexican *ingénu;* "but if I were a clergyman, they should not be told in my house." The Massies were not at all fashionable people ; but they were, in their calm and easy gentility, the nearest approach to fashion Paul had known.

"Don't thank me," Lydia broke in upon his thoughts ; "and don't feel flattered ; for I really wanted to go with Eustace ; only he would not let me. He asked me if I meant to leave you all alone the first morning of your coming ; and when I said, 'Couldn't Sarah stay?' he made no answer. Indeed he doesn't think I am as useful as Sarah ; and he is quite right. Eustace likes us to be very useful—'efficient' is his word."

"I don't believe I shall get on well with my cousins," Paul was thinking all this time. He plunged into conversation, however ; and once started, kept briskly on. They conversed about the weather, the place, the wreck, London, Paris, music, and anything else that offered. Paul began to feel rather genial and pleasant under the influence of his fair breakfast-maker's vivacious talk. A pretty girl must be very uninteresting indeed if a *tête-à-tête* with her does not animate a young unmarried man. Lydia was able to say something on every subject ; whether she understood the matter—which was not always, or did not understand it—which was very often.

"What an adventurous life you have led ! " she remarked. "You will find it dreadfully dull, living here ; this place is utterly commonplace. Did you ever read Disraeli's *Ixion in Heaven* ? No ! Well, Ixion writes in Juno's or somebody's album (you must write something in my album, cousin Paul), 'Adventures are to the adventurous.' But I am sure Ixion could never have discovered any adventure in Seaborough."

"And yet," said Paul, "I have not been here twenty-four hours, and I have had a sort of adventure already."

"You! an adventure here! Why, you have not crossed the door-step yet—outwards I mean."

"No, I have not exactly crossed the door-step; but I have been to the sea." Paul told his little adventure, which was not much after all; and added, that he must presently go into the town to complete his share of the story.

"Pray take me with you, and I will show you the way. It is only a few minutes' walk; and I like being a guide."

Paul was quite delighted with the companionship.

"I shall be ready in five minutes," said Lydia.— "Alice" (to a pretty, dark-haired girl who had been waiting at table, and coming into and out of the room), "give Mr. Massie the *Times*. It has come; I saw it in the hall just now."

Paul had quite time to range over all the news, political, social, and maritime, in the leading journal; to glance at the points of the articles; to observe with what astounding inaccuracy localities were described in the Mexican telegrams, and in what he would have called the "editorials," before Lydia again made her appearance. Paul put away the paper, walked up to the fireplace, and having looked at the pretty little *bijou* of a. clock which stood there, and found that if it was right his watch must be dreadfully wrong, he glanced into the large, somewhat old-fashioned mirror above it, and saw the smiling face of his cousin reflected there. By the expression of her eyes she seemed to say that she had caught him in the act of admiring himself—in which she certainly was mistaken. Possibly she stood a little to be admired herself. In her walking-dress—furred, shawled, petticoated in the manner most charmingly "suitable to the season"—she was quite worthy of a more enraptured glance than that which she received. In the matter of feminine dress, at least, Paul was a very savage.

In the matter of masculine dress he was not a D'Orsay, and he presently put on a rough poncho and a wideawake,

But he was a remarkable-looking man, and therefore Lydia liked the idea of walking into the town leaning on the arm of a brown-cheeked stranger, with a Spanish moustache, whom she might introduce on the way to any chance friend as her cousin from Mexico.

They had a pleasant walk over the crisp lawn, and then along the frosty road, one side of which was almost entirely open to the cliff. The sea heaved beneath, no longer stormy, but not yet calm.

Seaborough town, or village, was not exactly a seaport, and not exactly a bathing-place, but it was a kind of blending of two failures. It might have been a seaport, only that so very few ships found it worth their while to come there, except as an occasional and very precarious refuge —*statio malefida*—against stress of weather. It might have been a bathing-place, only that people somehow did not find out its attractions generally, and passed it eastward and westward to get to more fashionable and crowded, or even to more peaceful and secluded places ; for if it was not fashionable and full even in August, it was not lonely and peaceful even in December. It had photographers' shops and Paris bonnet-shops with plate-glass windows— at least, it had two of the latter establishments—and a Young Men's Christian Association, where lecturers from London addressed audiences on the discovery of America, John Bunyan, the Planetary System, Popular Novelists, and Tennyson. Its walls were frequently placarded with programmes of entertainments in which Mr. and Mrs. Walter de Lancy illustrated by lecture, piano, and song the Minstrelsy of Scotland, or the Naval Victories of England. It had its controversial meetings and lectures ; its announcements of orations on the crimes of the Popes and the Mysteries of Iniquity ; on the other hand, its proclamations of philippics against Luther and Henry VIII. It had sometimes, but only rarely, and in the very best season, its theatrical company, or perhaps its circus. It had a bookseller who kept a circulating library, and had published a

2*

guide book containing a good deal about the principal families of the locality, and, among the rest, about the family of the Massies,—for which reason Lydia always kept a copy, and often studied these particular passages,—and containing also a list of subscribers in the beginning, the list comprising every one in or near the town whose name, or whose estate, or whose shop, or any of whose relatives and friends found honorable mention in the body of the work. There were views sold in this and the stationer's shop; views separate or on the top of letter-paper,—"the Harbor of Seaborough," "Seaborough Pier," "Ruins of Seaborough Abbey," "Townhall, Seaborough," etc., etc. In summer there were a few bathing-boxes wheeled out upon the edge of the sea, and a German band occasionally played at evenings on the gusty pier. The principal street ran along the crest of the cliff over the shore; and through every lane, and indeed through every window on the seaward side, the passer caught delicious glimpses of the water in summer, and of dreary wild waves in winter. There was only one pretentious street in the town, the remainder being rather squalid and rickety, made up of boatmen's and fishermen's cottages, small public-houses, dingy, doubtful looking tenements with "Board and Lodging" on little signs over their windows, some rope-makers' and block-makers' workshops, and a few dismal, very dismal, tea-gardens.

There was, further, an indescribable aspect of smuggling about the whole place, and many of the inhabitants had an odd way of haunting the strand at queer hours, and looking anxiously out seaward. People who carried on no particular business that any one could observe succeeded in making fortunes somehow; and there was invariably an overwhelming popular resistance to any attempt at the introduction of that part of the Towns' Improvement Act which relates to the lighting of the streets with gas. Even a Library and Museum Rate, feared and hated by the community, they would gladly have endured rather than the detested gas-lighting innovation. There were rarely any public assemblies, except religious tea-meetings and the gatherings of the Branch Missionary Association. In ancient days Seaborough had been highly reputed for sound Protestantism and wrecking. Legends ascribed to its ingenious inhabitants the oft-told story of the lame horse with the lantern sent stumbling along the strand, to beguile the mariner into the delusion that he beheld a floating light, and might port his helm with safety. A dash of the slave-trade too had once highly flavored the commercial pursuits of Seaborough; and when, on the outbreak of the American war, a vehement pro-northern lecturer came to the town and denounced the horrors of slavery, the bulk of the population, still remembering the pursuits of other days, regarded his allusions as personal, and rising in their might, they mobbed him. Perhaps when it is remarked that the men who did not keep shops seemed to have nothing whatever to do all day long but to lounge at the doors of public-houses, even when not able or not desiring to enter and pay for drink, enough will have been said to convey to the intelligent mind a reasonable notion of the outward social aspect of Seaborough.

It was into this promising abode of men that Paul Massie and his cousin walked through roads lightly covered with frost and by little icy pools, where urchins endeavored to find surface hard enough for sliding, and failing in the attempt, tried to get fluid space enough to swim boats.

"You will find it very dull in Seaborough," said Lydia; "it is very little better than this even in summer. I thought it dreadful when I came back from school in Paris. Don't you love Paris?"

"I don't quite think that I do. I feel delighted when I enter it, and quite happy for a few days or weeks. But somehow it wearies me after awhile."

"Perhaps you cannot easily make up your mind to stay anywhere. I am sure I could not, if I were a man. But I think I should like to live in Paris best.　Where did you live in Paris?　Our school was in the Faubourg St. Germain.　Such a fine old house, with a court and a great gate : some great person—a king, or a dauphin, or a duke —lived there once."

"For me," said Paul, smiling, "I think when in Paris I generally find myself living in Bohemia, and herding among the Bohemians."

"Bohemia?　What is that?　Is there a place called Bohemia in Paris?"

Paul had many a time been drawn by his affinities, led by his star, into the heart of wild Bohemia, and had often shaken the hot hand of the last brilliant chieftain of the dispersing Bohemian bands—the generous, reckless, good-for-nothing, gifted Henri Mürger.　But he entered into no description of his Paris life.　The Massies had never heard of Mürger ; and if they had known anything about him, would as soon have associated with the lieutenant of the Forty Thieves as with the friend and companion of such a personage.

His cousin soon ran on to other questions about Paris, which exacted only very brief, and generally negative replies.　Did he know the Duc de Millefleurs?　No, he didn't.　Had he never met the Marquise de Turlupin?　No, he hadn't.　Had he never attended any of the receptions of Madame de Vieillenoblesse?　Never.　Had he never met the brilliant and eccentric Princesse de la Tour d'Ivoire?　Never met, never heard of the lady in his life. Surely he must have known Lord Cowley, the English ambassador?　Well, yes, he did—a little.　In fact, application had been made to Lord Cowley about him when he was brought to Paris a Mexican prisoner, and Lord Cowley had offered to use his influence for him, if Paul would petition the Emperor and declare himself a British subject, which Paul declined to do ; but, on being released, he had felt bound to call and thank his lordship.

Lydia began to think her cousin a very odd sort of

person. Any difficulty with the constituted authorities only suggested to her mind a participation in burglary. She began to fear that this was not at all the sort of cousin she had expected; whom she had pictured as wild, handsome, and romantic, but likewise very genteel, and mixing always in the best society. Paul had not the least idea that he was sinking so rapidly in her estimation.

As they passed through the street they met two ladies who had just stepped out of a carriage, and were going from shop to shop of the few pretentious establishments in the town. These were two of the very persons to whom Lydia had but a few hours before longed to present her foreign cousin; but she changed her mind, or her heart failed her. She only bowed and smiled a smile of the sweetest friendship, and passed on.

"Who is that with Lydia Massie?" said one lady to the other, as they stood upon the threshold they were about to cross to look after our pair.

"I don't know at all," the other replied; "a distinguished-looking man too."

"Handsome, I think. He looks like a Spaniard. Perhaps he will marry her."

Ladies, it may be observed, generally talk of the gentleman marrying the lady. They always seem to assume that the woman is to be married whenever, and only whenever, the man chooses to have her for his wedded wife. Men, on the other hand, commonly throw the right and responsibility of choice upon the lady.

Presently a light pony-carriage, drawn by two pretty gray animals, drove up and passed Lydia and her cousin. In the carriage sat two ladies, one of whom held the reins. Paul had only a glimpse of them as they passed, but could see that she who drove was younger than the other, and wore a pretty Amazonian hat and feather. As they passed she looked fixedly at Lydia. Lydia looked in return, and seemed first surprised, then doubtful, then confused, and then saluted with a blush the lady in the carriage, who returned the salute with a graceful bow. The lady in the carriage seemed as if she were inclined to stop the ponies ; but Lydia passed on, and the carriage went its way likewise.

"So you know some of our people?" said the elder lady in the carriage.

"O yes; I know the Massies well enough. I knew them better long ago. My dear Mrs. Charlton, it's no secret—I was a governess there once. Lydia grows a very pretty girl. I have not seen her for some years."

"Her brother is a handsome man. I wonder who can that person be—the foreign-looking gentleman with her."

"I presume it is her cousin Paul. I am quite sure it is. He comes from Mexico. I have heard of him."

"Is he likely to marry her?"

"I don't know. I have been told that he is rather a remarkable man ; and I don't think Lydia has any brains."

The carriage disappeared. We follow it no farther just now. One of its occupants at least we shall often meet again.

It was necessary for Paul to visit the coroner's court, to give such very slight and unimportant information as he could contribute touching the finding of the drowned woman's body. Lydia had to make some purchases in the town, and she offered to wait for him at the music-shop. Paul easily found the place where the inquest was to be held. When passing one of the many alehouses on the way, he saw his friend Halliday lounging at the door, and the latter made an awkward kind of bow in token of recognition.

"Found drowned." There was no other verdict mortal jury could arrive at. The woman had been drowned, and then washed ashore, and there was an end of her. She seemed by her face to have been English, and her clothes were English in make and material. There was no means of identifying the body, except indeed the initial "L" upon some of her garments ; nothing more. There had been

two vessels wrecked within the past few days off the coast :
one a small brig, none of the crew of which had been saved ;
the other a passenger-ship from New Orleans to London,
some of the crew and passengers of which were safely
housed in the town. Some of the latter attended the
inquest, but were unable to give any information about
the woman. It did not seem to matter much ; the sea
would soon, no doubt, wash in other bodies as well, and
this first dead waif of the deep would be forgotten. It has
been said that Paul was tinged with much of superstitious
fancy. He had felt persuaded that something affecting
himself was to arise from the incident which flung this
corpse across his path the very first night of his arrival in
the long-looked-for home. He felt dissatisfied and disappointed when it became evident that all clue to the identity
of the dead woman seemed lost forever. As he came down
the stairs of the house where the inquest had been held, he
jostled against Halliday.

He rejoined his cousin, who had not had long to wait
for him. As they passed through the street, they presently
met Eustace and Sarah. Eustace came eagerly up to Paul,
and made many inquiries as to how he had slept, and how
he felt, and so forth ; and apologized for having had to
hurry out of the house the first morning after his arrival.
The wreck and the distressed condition of the poor people
who had been saved fully explained the necessity for his
leaving home so early.

"I ought to have gone with you," said Paul ; "I might
have rendered some assistance. I feel quite ashamed of
having been so lazy and sleepy."

"Nay," interposed Sarah, "but you were doing good
by stealth while we were asleep. We heard all about you
this morning, and how you were trying to save a poor
drowning woman among the rocks last night."

"Come now," said Lydia, "you never told me a word
of that. Then you were quite a hero. I thought you only
found the poor creature's body washed ashore."

"That was indeed the whole story," Paul replied; "there wasn't a shade of the heroic about the affair. I went out on the strand to smoke, and I stumbled over a living man and a dead body. That was the adventure, and nothing more."

But they would cling to the heroic aspects of the story, and would have it that Paul had performed some wondrous feat of personal daring. Lydia in especial thought this quite delightful, and pressed involuntarily the arm which she was pleased to believe had battled with seas and winds the night before in striving to rescue endangered womanhood. Paul was again romantic and charming in her eyes.

While the clergyman and the ladies were engaged in showing Paul some of the remarkable aspects of the town, and the cliffs and the sea, Lydia suddenly bethought her of one of the morning's incidents.

"Eustace," she exclaimed, "I have news for you. Do you know who is in town? Do you know whom Paul and I met this morning?"

"No, indeed—who was it?"

"Guess. I will give you three guesses."

"My dear, I couldn't guess anything; Sarah will guess for me."

"I don't think it needs much guessing," said Sarah. "I am sure I know already."

"Then have you seen her?"

"Yes, we have seen her."

"And Eustace too?"

"Certainly; Eustace too."

"What, Eustace—you actually saw her? How did you bear it?"

"My dear, of whom are you speaking?"

"O, come, you know very well. Of course I am speaking of Salome. Paul and I met her this morning,—an old flame of my brother's, Paul,—and she looked charming. Such a pretty hat and feathers; and such sweet gray ponies! I declare she hasn't grown a' day older. What did you think of her, Paul? Was she not pretty?"

"Really I had scarcely time to observe, I saw only a feather and two bright eyes. I might have observed the lady more closely if you had given me warning in time."

"But I never knew she was in town until she suddenly flashed upon me, gray ponies, and feather, and all. What can she be doing here? What a charming mystery!"

"Lydia, my dear," interposed Eustace somewhat gravely, "there is not the slightest mystery about the matter. The lady you speak of is on a visit with the Charltons. Mr. Charlton is the member for Seaborough, Paul. He is a very wealthy man, although not perhaps just the kind of man I should desire to see representing a borough like this in parliament at a time when dissent is growing so very strong and bold, and the House seems likely to be soon unchristianized altogether. But otherwise he is, I believe, a very respectable man, and is willing to coöperate in any good work. Of course many of us here would prefer to see the town represented by a gentleman, and a member of the Church of England. Mr. Charlton began life as a working engineer, and is now a great railway contractor."

"His name," said Paul, "is perfectly familiar to me. It is quite well known in the States. I should like to meet him very much."

"I wish I could be the means of gratifying you. But we are not very friendly; and the acquaintances he generally brings down from London are of an extremely Radical and almost (I hope I don't wrong them)—almost, I regret to say, of a free-thinking character. Mr. Charlton, I believe, intends to retire from parliament very soon; and then we hope to have Seaborough represented by some member whose opinions and position will be more in accord with the reputation this town has always maintained."

"But about Salome, Eustace?" asked Lydia, who

did not care much for the political considerations. Perhaps Paul, too, had not been a very attentive listener; perhaps he did not quite understand what his cousin had been talking about.

"I believe," Eustace replied, "that Mrs. or Madame de Luca is one of the company who have been staying with the Charltons these few days back. A gentleman named Wynter is there—we met him in town to-day—a very, very Radical member of parliament; and I have no doubt Mr. Wynter's visit has something to do with the next election."

"Wynter—Wynter," said Paul; "I knew a man of that name. I met him in Mexico, and in New Orleans, and in Paris. He was a member of parliament, I understood, and rather a great one, if I might believe his own stories, which I didn't always. He knew some Hungarians and Poles and Italians in Paris, whom I knew very well. I have no doubt it is the same man."

"I have no doubt it is. I dare say he is a very respectable man; but, of course, our political and religious opinions are very different."

"Did you speak to Salome, Eustace?" Lydia asked.

"Certainly, Lydia. Why not?"

"Salome put us all to shame to-day, Lydia," said Sarah. "She was in town hours before we got there, and was making herself most useful in getting up clothes, and food, and everything for some of the poor people; many of them are in a miserable state. She was up half the night, we heard, and she has been going about unceasingly all the day. Eustace very much admired her, and good Mrs. Charlton too."

"Especially good Mrs. Charlton, no doubt," said Lydia. "Does that good lady aspirate still?"

"Nonsense, Lydia; she talked very well and very sensibly indeed. And Salome is not the least in the world changed, as I told her to-day; and I think she one of the cleverest and best-hearted women I ever knew; and I don't believe one single word that is said against her."

"Sarah, you are the most generous of creatures! I am sure I always liked Salome very much—that is, very well; but I think, if I were *you*—"

"My dear Lydia," said Eustace, "we need not entertain our cousin with all the gossip of the neighborhood. He does not want to hear any more about Salome just now."

"Pray who *is* Salome?" asked Paul, "for I do begin to grow curious."

"I am delighted to hear it," said Lydia; "but restrain your curiosity for the present. I will tell you all about her by and by; only spare Eustace just now. Though he is a clergyman, yet you see he is not very old and venerable, and he has his feelings."

Eustace, to do him justice, did not seem as if his feelings on that particular subject were very acute. Paul might have forgotten all about the matter, but that when at dinner that day Lydia suddenly revived it by eagerly calling to her mother, "Mamma, have you heard whom we saw in town to-day? Has Eustace been telling you? We saw Salome."

"Salome? What Salome, my dear?"

"Why, mamma, did we ever know any Salome but the one? *Our* Salome, of course."

"Salome Adams? Salome who married the Italian?"

"Yes, certainly. I only saw her in the street, but Eustace and Sarah met her and spoke to her. She looks charming, and not a month older."

"What can she be doing here?"

"She is staying with the Charltons," interposed Sarah.

"And Eustace thinks she is electioneering," added Lydia. "Had we not better go to see her?"

"No, my dear, I think not. I should be glad to hear that she is happy, and glad still more to hear that she is passing a quiet useful life; but I do not much desire to see her.　If she wishes to call upon us, we are of course ready to receive her."

"Indeed I don't think she would much care to see us," said Sarah.　"She's very clever and brilliant, and I believe quite a celebrity in London.　She would find us and our ways rather dull."

There seemed the faintest dash of irony in Sarah's tone as she spoke.

Rather for the sake of talking of something which seemed to interest her, and about which she apparently loved to keep up a little mystery, than because he really felt any keen personal curiosity on the subject, Paul afterwards found an opportunity of asking Lydia who Salome was, and what was the secret which appeared to attach to her.　The story, after all, was a very trifling one.　Salome was first met by the Massies ten years before in Paris, where she was teaching in the school at which the two girls spent some time.　She was several years older than either of them.　She came home with them, and remained with them as teacher, or governess, or companion.　Eustace, being then at the very age when a youth delights to fall in love with a woman older than himself, plunged into a frantic passion for the fair Salome.　Mrs. Massie was indignant with her, although it did not quite seem that the fair Salome was in the least to blame.　Oddly enough, Mr. Massie was only angry with Eustace, who was forthwith despatched back to college, whence he had come for a long holiday.　Mr. and Mrs. Massie did not agree upon the subject, and Salome cut short the quarrel by promptly leaving the house and returning to Paris.　There she married, as the Massies learned, not long after, a young Italian gentleman of property, who was killed in some Italian battle (Lydia had not the faintest idea when, where, or how—it might have been Pharsalia, for all she knew) ; and Salome, left a widow a year after her marriage, had since been living a life of ease and enjoyment, principally in London.　Mamma did not like her at all ; and she,

Lydia, thought it was wrong of Salome to have encouraged Eustace, if she did encourage him. But Eustace had long ago ceased to think anything about her—only mamma still did not seem to like her—and that was all.

Not much. Paul had some difficulty in picturing to himself the handsome, formal, cold young clergyman under the influence of a grand passion. Still there must have been something in the matter; for nothing could well have been more constrained, uneasy, and reluctant than Mrs. Massie's manner when the few words of allusion were made to the absent Salome.

Paul made several attempts to induce his aunt to enter into conversation upon the subject of her Mexican life; but he found it very difficult indeed to draw her into any talk on the subject. He expected that she would have delightedly poured out reminiscences of places and scenes and days, which must have been strange and interesting to her, which would have been deeply interesting to him. He expected to have heard much of his mother and of his father, of whom he knew so little and remembered still less. Yet he could not induce Mrs. Massie to say more than a few words, and these, he could not help thinking, somewhat embarrassed, upon the subjects which naturally lay deeply at his heart. True, he was as yet but a stranger to his aunt, and he knew well enough that English people do not warm to the stranger at once and pour out their feelings readily to him, as so many Americans, and French, and Irish people do; so he resolved to be contented, and to wait. He felt convinced that Mrs. Massie had a kindly and feeling heart; for he often observed that her eyes turned towards him, and rested on him with an expression of tenderness and melancholy; to be withdrawn indeed with an alarmed suddenness whenever she became aware that his glance was conscious of hers. On the whole, the evening passed somewhat heavily away. There was no one at dinner except the family, and it was a relief when two or three friends from the neighborhood came in during

the evening. This the second night of his home life Paul
began involuntarily to wonder how he should pass his
time, how long he should remain in Seaborough, when he
could have some talk over family affairs, why the Massies
talked so much of purely local matters, and how soon he
could conveniently remove to London. What to do when
he got there, it was too early yet to consider; but after two
days in a calm English country residence he began to yearn
for a great city. He feared he should never be able to abide
by the crib.

CHAPTER IV.

UNCONGENIAL CONSPIRATORS.

WHILE the Massie family were quietly dining and talking one evening in the first week of Paul's stay, a little meeting took place within a few yards of their windows
—a meeting about which none of them knew anything,
about which they would hardly have cared anything if
they knew, and yet which had its influence too upon the
fortunes of some of them. When the evening had dark-
ened down, one of the small back gates which led into
Eustace's modest demesne was opened by Paul's acquaintance, Mr. Jem Halliday, who entered and made his way
in the direction of the house. He did not reach the house,
however, but turned a little to the left of it, and passed
into a side walk which conducted to a little shrubbery and
a tiny moss-house, or summer-house, or kiosk, with the
locality of which he seemed quite familiar. It was a pretty
little structure of dried and split branches, moss, shells, and
scraps of glass for windows, with a floor inlaid of pebbles
divers-colored, and some rustic seats and a central table.
It must have been no doubt a very pleasant and romantic
place in summer or in autumn; but just now, with plashy
floor and thaw-dripping eaves, it was about as cheerless a
tenement as the heir of Linn himself could have met with.

Halliday entered it with a shrug and a muttered grumble.
He should dearly have liked to light his pipe and smoke;
but one of the special horrors of the clergyman's house
was the odor of tobacco, which was associated inextricably
in Eustace's mind with drunkenness, laziness, irreligion,
and absence from church on Sundays.   Therefore Halliday
did not dare to smoke, and refreshed his mind instead with
a muttered grumble.   He had not long to wait, however;
at least, to wait in loneliness.   A light step was soon heard
on the gravel, and a girl entered the little summer-house.
She dropped to her shoulders, as she entered, the cloak
with which her head had been covered.   It was Alice the
waiting-woman, who has been casually mentioned already.
This Seaborough-house was a pattern of propriety to all
the country round.   Religion and order were the twin
guiding-stars to which its master in all honesty and good
faith directed his own course, and firmly believed that all
under his roof were directing theirs.   He believed himself
literally responsible for the morals and the happiness of
all whom the slates of Seaborough-house sheltered against
the world.   One of his great sources of regret and trial
was, that among the Seaborough population, especially of
the humble classes, there were so many who could by no
means be brought within the influence of himself or of his
two curates.   If he could have a genuine aversion to any
people on earth, it was just to such men as rough, good-
for-nothing, godless Jem Halliday.   Yet here was Jem
Halliday having a secret interview, within the precincts of
Seaborough-house itself, with his mother's maid, Alice
Crossley, daughter of honest and pious Dan Crossley the
boatman; Alice Crossley, who had been taken into the
house because of the honesty and piety of her parents and
her own exemplary behavior at Sunday-school.   Eustace
Massie liked good people.   He was not given to indulging
the doubtful, or even seeking to reclaim the bad.   Unconsciously, although not professedly, he divided humanity
into two classes—the good and the bad, or rather the reli-

gious and the irreligious. He liked to have to deal only
with the religious; and these he generally regarded as
immutable in their principles, unvarying in their good
conduct. Alice Crossley was simply an inmate of Seaborough-house, and therefore of necessity pious, truthful, and
orderly. Yet she was now having a stolen interview with
one who was not only of the irreligious and disorderly
classes, but who had evidently not long since been drinking rum, and who had at that very moment a short black
pipe in his pocket. Eustace would have been shocked at
the bare notion that anything secret and clandestine could
go on beneath his well-ordered roof. Yet here was one
little secret, at all events, which the walls of Seaborough-
house considerately refused to prate of.

Jem Halliday, then, was the "sweetheart" of Alice
Crossley, the pretty and rather dainty-looking waiting-
maid? Perhaps; but he certainly did not seem to be a
sweetheart much in favor just now, for the girl's first
words to him were sharp and unloving.

"I'm glad you've come, James Halliday," she said;
"for I'm not going to have any of this sort of thing any
more. You've brought me into trouble enough to-day
already, and I won't have any more of it—won't, I tell you.
I won't have it."

"Why, Ally, what's to do with you? What's the
matter? You take a fellow's breath away. I haven't
been drinking; no—by—by George! only one half—"

"I don't care whether you've been drinking or not;
it isn't for that; and it's nothing to me. There's your
diamond ring. Take it back at once, or I'll throw it on
the floor. I've had enough of annoyance to-day about it."

"What's annoyed you? who's annoyed you? Have
they been blowing you up for taking it? Why shouldn't
you? It's my own, girl, to give it as I like."

"How did you get it, then? Where did you get it?"

"Why, what does that matter to any one? I didn't

steal it. If any one thinks he owns it, let him come forward and say the word. Nobody can dare to say it."

"Yes, though; somebody has dared to say it."

"To who?"

"To me?"

"Somebody.? What somebody? Who's been talking about the ring to you? It can't have been—no, it can't—what right would he have?—you weren't talking to *him?*"

"Him? Who is *him?* I was talking to her, or she was talking to me."

"Who was it, Ally? tell me. Don't keep a fellow guessing that way."

"It was my mistress—Mrs. Massie. When she saw the ring with me to-day, she started, and nearly screamed out. 'Where did you get that ring?' she cried out; and really I turned red all over, as if I were a thief. I'm sure I wish I had never seen the ring. I do. believe she thought I had stolen it somewhere. She said it was hers once, and that she gave it away to a person, and that she must find out where the person was, and how it came into my hands."

"And what did you tell her?"

"Well, I told her just the whole truth. I couldn't think of anything else to say, except that I didn't tell her you gave it to me. I said that you showed it to me just to know whether it was worth anything, and that I didn't know how you had come by it; but I was sure it was honestly."

"That's a good lass! that's a regular good one."

"Now, don't, Jem—I tell you I won't; for listen: I am not sure how you came by it; and you won't tell me. But Mrs. Massie is going to send for you, and so you may make the best excuse you can for yourself. I have no more to do with the matter. Something bad will come of it, I'm sure. Mrs. Massie is in a dreadful way about it."

"Listen, Ally: did she say anything to any one else but you?"

3

"No, she didn't; and she cautioned me not to say a word about it to anybody. If she knew I was here now with you, O, what would she say! And quite right too. I have no business to be going on this way with such as you. I'll have no more of it, Jem Halliday; that I'm resolved on."

Haliday had evidently not been paying any attention to this declaration. Heavily, slowly he was trying to forge together some chain of reasoning in his deadened intellect.

"Listen, Ally," he said. "Are you sure and certain she told you to keep this quiet?"

"Yes; quite sure and certain."

"There's something about all this that I don't quite understand. There's something that it might be well for us to make out. Ally, you're a scholar; I suppose you can read *that?*"

.He fumbled in his pocket, and produced an old piece of newspaper which he carefully unfolded. From it he took a letter in an envelope; he put the piece of newspaper back into his pocket again, then took the letter between his teeth, while he pulled out a box of lucifer-matches. He tried several times to light one inside his cap; the cold wind blew it out each time. At last one blazed pretty steadily, and long enough for him to hold the letter just beneath its light. "Can you read *that?*" he asked. The girl all the time had been shivering with cold while he was trying to light his match and mumbling an oath at each successive failure. "Can you read that?"

"Of course I can."

The match went out; and he put up the box.

"What do you make of it?"

"'Paul Massie, Esquire.' It's plain enough."

"But what do you make of it? What do you think it is?"

"I suppose it's a letter for Mr. Eustace's cousin up at the house."

"I suppose so too."

"Then why don't you give it to him?"

"I have a reason. Perhaps it isn't for him, after all. Where I got the ring I got that. It came open in my hand; it did indeed; and though I'm not much of a scholar, I tried to read it. I didn't know then who it was for."

"Didn't the person that gave it to you tell you who it was for?"

"No, not exactly. The person only found it—and—and—couldn't read, and gave it to me to find out something about it. Now, will you read it over, like a good lass, and tell me what you make of it? and be sure you keep it safe. Don't let it go for your life. I think it will astonish you a bit; and if you help me out, we may follow it up; and it may do us good."

"*Us!*" The girl tossed her head contemptuously at the word; but she did not resist the temptation to get at something secret, and she took the letter, promising to read it and faithfully to give it back. He took care not to give her the envelope.

"It mayn't be for Mr. Massie at all," said Halliday; "and if it isn't, he oughtn't to get it. If it is, why it's some news for him perhaps, and maybe we can tell it to him in some better way. I can't make all out myself, for it's small writing, and I'm a bad reader."

"I think there's somebody coming," said Alice suddenly; "I must go."

There was nobody coming, as she well knew, having hearing power nearly as quick as Fine Ear's in the fairy story. But she was curious about the letter she held in her hand, and she wanted, moreover, to get away from her admirer as fast as possible. She did not, after all, insist any more upon his taking back the diamond ring.

Halliday gave vent to something like a sigh as she broke away from him in his effort to detain her. He, too, knew there was nobody coming; and he knew that she had only made a feint just to get away from him

and she knew that he knew this; and he knew that she
knew that he knew it. There was the most complete,
although tacit, understanding between them on that head.
He was well aware that she shrank from him, despised him
and his ways; that she had ceased to feel sufficient interest in him even to coquette with or torment him any
longer, as once she used to do; that she only wanted absolutely to get rid of him. Yet he clung about her, awk-
wardly, roughly, making himself more and more odious to
her. Once she had allowed him to make love to her, and
rather liked it, before she learned to give herself airs, and
to wear earrings, and to make a fine lady of herself—as he
often secretly grumbled—with a cast-off dress of Miss
Lydia's. Once she did not object to his pipe; and on one
memorable occasion, when there was some kind of merry-
making at her father's cottage, she actually condescended
to take a sip out of Halliday's glass of rum-and-water, and
grinned so prettily at the nasty taste that Jem scarcely knew
whether he was on his head or his heels with admiration.
To be sure, since that time Halliday had rather fallen into
evil ways, and Dan Crossley did not much care now to see
that awkward shadow darkening his doors. The taste for
rum-and-water, always rather marked, had strongly developed itself as regarded the rum, and diminished as regarded
the water. The taste for loafing about and doing nothing,
or at least nothing good, had been steadfastly growing;
and now people hardly knew how Halliday lived at all.
He was rapidly approaching that stage of idleness when it
seems almost inevitable that a prison must be the first halt
in the career, and a transport-ship its grand climateric.

Meanwhile Alice had been installed under the clergyman's roof, and was, in good truth, trying to make a sort
of lady of herself, and was giving herself airs, and was
very fond of fine clothes, and spoke good English, and
hated pipes, and O! would have turned almost sick at the
faintest smell of rum-and-water. Wretched Halliday knew
all this perfectly well, having a pretty keen sort of instinct

of his own, which a little of early training, and occupation, and ignorance of rum, might even have developed into intelligence. But he clung on to Alice's skirts, when he could, like grim death; and it was something like rapture to him when he saw how the first glimpse of the diamond ring made her eyes sparkle. Providence seemed to have sent that diamond ring in his way. That was something which nobody but he would have given to her! Miss Lydia might have given her a dress; Miss Sarah might make over on her the reversion of a crinoline; but there were no diamond rings given away except by poor Jem Halliday.

Now poor Jem Halliday fancied he had got hold of a mystery, and thought he discerned a small bright path to prosperity and to Alice shining through it. He had plucked the ring with little scruple off the cold finger of a dead woman (what good are rings to the dead?), and in the pocket of the dead woman's dress he had found a pocket-book with one or two old, wet, sea-stained letters. He was not going to trouble himself about these at first, until in one of the wild bright glimpses of moonlight that night he read clearly enough the name on the back of one of the letters. He had always a taste for secrets and quiet dodges of various kinds, and he thought there might be something to find out in a letter addressed to a name which he knew. Furthermore, with the instinct already mentioned, it flashed upon him that there might be decided inconvenience to him in calling too much attention to the identity of the person off whose finger he had plucked the ring which he was determined to keep. So he put the letters in his pocket. Half an hour after, he chuckled as he went up the cliff to think that he had just been talking, and even quarrelling, with the very man to whom one of the letters was addressed.

When he got home that night, or morning, to the house of his old mother,—a miserable poor woman, who washed and let pitiful lodgings to sailors, while he idled and scolded her,—he struggled to read his findings by the light of an expiring candle. He found that one paper was only an old money-account, and burned it at once. He struggled through the letter, and believed he had been providentially thrown upon the discovery of a secret. A great secret, he thought. As yet he could make nothing distinct out of it. But it obviously put him in the way of discovering something ; and he felt convinced that nobody could help him so well as Alice in discovering the whole. Therefore Alice must be taken into the secret; but she must hear nothing about the manner in which he had come by the letter. If she only knew that, and knew where he had got the ring, she would turn from him in disgust. Yet the risk was worth braving ; and he felt a hope that it gave him a last chance.

Now Alice was gone, and he stood in the little summer-house alone. He would have liked to follow her, for nature had endowed him with a stealthy wish to follow and dog people in general, and find out whether they were doing just the thing which they professed or were supposed to be doing. He did not believe that Alice really had heard somebody coming; and he was anxious to know whether she actually was returning towards the house. But he feared to be heard by her, to be detected, and then detested even more than before. So he remained where he was for a few seconds, and gave vent to the sound not wholly unlike a sigh. When the slight echo of Alice's feet could be heard no longer, he crept with stealthy step along the walk, knowing that when he reached its turning, and had the broad path before him, he could see to the house, and would be in time to ascertain by the light shining through an open door, or by the sound of the door's closing, whether Alice really had gone directly in. When he peered down the walk, however, he could see nothing—could hear nothing. Alice was not there. She could not have got into the house before he reached the corner of the walk ? Perhaps—yet it was not likely.

Could she have turned off by a side-path?—and for what? Presently he heard a sound, a step—unmistakably a step, and not the light beat of a woman's foot-fall, but the firm steady tread of a man. Halliday drew back into the darkness. Peering out, he could see that a figure approached; he could sée the glow-worm fire of a cigar. The figure turned off a side-walk. What mystery was there in that? Halliday knew the form perfectly well. It was only the cousin of the house, Paul Massie, walking alone in the grounds, and smoking the cigar which mortal being dared not puff within the doors of that well regulated mansion. Yet Halliday turned livid with suspicion, jealousy, and rage. Could it be that she had met *him*—that she had purposely met him? Could this be one of the reasons why she had tired of Jem Halliday, her old sweetheart, and tried to turn him adrift? With a pang which almost rendered him furious, he thought of the letter he had given her—the secret with which he had hoped to buy her. Was he himself sold? Had she obtained his precious finding to give it up to that man now walking a few yards from where Halliday stood? "The witch shall die—to the young Roman boy she has sold me?" Rough, vulgar, dull, bemuddled Halliday was made all in a moment of kin to the poet's Mark Antony by the one touch of nature and feeling vibrating through his heart-strings. There was not the slightest rational ground for his suspicion. He had no more reason to be jealous of Paul Massie than of the Lord Chancellor; but the furious impulse of jealousy smote him at that moment with all the rage and agony of conviction. He did not know that Massie had been but a few days in Seaborough; nor, had he known the fact, could he have remembered it or reflected on it just then. Among men of the Halliday class the impulse of jealousy is most strong and overwhelming. Respectable people somehow get over the emotion: stifle it, or hide it, or do not feel it; or, at all events, contrive not to make a row about it. When a young man of the better classes—a genteel and educated young man—shot the girl whom he regarded as faithless, not very long ago, all the world and divers of the mad doctors pronounced him, *ipso facto*, a lunatic. But in Halliday's class men shoot their fickle sweethearts, or cut the throats of their faithless wives, day after day almost unnoticed by the doctors, the writers, and the public. Every London paper tells the story daily. Across Halliday's dulled brain and embruted heart a vague, heavy, darksome thought had often brooded—the thought that if Alice utterly cast him off for somebody else, he would kill that somebody or her. He felt somehow as if he should have to do it. He thought of it now again.

But this time, at least, his suspicions found no distinct realization. He did not venture at once to follow Paul, being reluctant to make any noise. But he gradually crept to a convenient angle from which he could peer down the whole of the sidewalk. Thus, even when he could no longer see Paul, he could be quite certain that Paul was alone. Alone Paul continued to be. He paced up and down, until his cigar had nearly burnt itself out; then flung the last flaming fragment among the dark and wet bushes, and returned to the house.

Meanwhile Alice was safely in the house. She too had heard Paul's footstep, and not knowing who approached, ensconced herself behind some bushes until the way was clear, and then got easily under cover of the house, while her jealous admirer watched in vain the movements of the unconscious Massie. Alice was not long without reading the letter. She hid herself in her room, and spread the faded, stained document on her little bed, while kneeling beside it she spelled out its contents. They were vague even to her. They must have been vague indeed to Halliday. They told nothing distinctly. But they proved—proved clearly as a revelation could have done—to Alice, that somebody in Scaborough-house had a secret, a secret which the world was never to have known, a mystery which one at least would not have had exposed to keen conjecture—no, not for the house and grounds and the money, and all the silk dresses and diamond rings in the universe. But what was the mystery? That the contents of the letter did not disclose, scarcely even hinted, to any one not previously prepared by suspicion to guess. Alice thought with some complacency that her lover Halliday was wholly dependent upon her for any clue to the mystery; and she was quite resolved that he never should have even a glimpse of the clue, for the letter was to her not a first disclosure, but a confirmation. She had had her suspicions. Now she felt satisfied that she saw her way to a full comprehension of the mystery. She felt herself mistress of the situation. In good truth, she was not so, and her conjectures were utterly wrong; but she had no doubt about them as yet, and her eyes sparkled and her bosom heaved at the thought of the secret she held, and the power it might give her.

A bell rang, and she thrust the paper into her bosom and hurried away.

That night she was with Mrs. Massie in her room. Alice had once or twice thought of playing a generous part, of showing the letter to her mistress, of telling her how she had come by it, and frankly unburdening herself of all she knew, or suspected that she knew. But that night in particular Mrs. Massie was querulous, petulant, discontented—not in a mood to invite confidences, not in a temper to conciliate servants. Alice came in for a sharp word or two—perhaps for several sharp words—and she resolved to keep her secret to herself. She had been told to hold her tongue, and she determined to prove that she could do so. Once she held some silk on her wrists while Mrs. Massie unwound it, and the crumpled letter was all the while lying in her bosom; only a few folds of muslin between it and one who would gladly have grasped it, could she but have known of its existence and its whereabouts. In one of the late Eugene Sue's cheerful and healthy stories of crime and misery, there is a married lady

3*

who receives a letter which she ought not to accept, and
who places it for safety in her excellent white bosom.
There is a mother-in-law, fierce, penetrating, and relent-
less, who suspects the charmer when the charmer's husband
is all credulity and fond guilelessness. And one night, by
the domestic fireside, while the circle of family and friends
are happy, the mother-in-law asks her son's wife to hold a
little silk for her on her pretty wrists. The unsuspecting
lady complies ; and while she is thus manacled with the
skein the cruel mother-in-law suddenly thrusts her bony
hand down into that beautiful bosom, plucks out its secret
of shame, and holds it up to the horrified spectators. Why
did not some kind inspiration tell Mrs. Massie that there
lay secreted inside the dress of the demure-looking girl
before her some crumpled paper which it deeply, deeply
concerned her to have and to read? Had she but known!
had she but seized the letter !

Had she discovered the letter at that moment, it might
have saved much trouble and some grief. But it would
likewise have obviated any necessity for writing the story
of Paul Massie's visit to England.

———◆◆———

CHAPTER V.

THE MASSIES.

A FEW days passed away quietly, and not disagreeably,
with Paul ; but he did not find home so delightful a
place as he had anticipated. He had dreamed of home and
family since the boyish time when first he learned to appreciate the fact that he had neither one nor the other. In
the American college, in the New-York counting-house, in
the western log-hut and by the Mexican camp-fire, in the
mud of Balaklava and among the heights of Simla, in the
Latin Quarter and on the Pincian Hill, he had dreamed of
home. Now at last he finds something which at least

professes to be home; something which comes nearer to the nature of the sacred institution than anything he ever knew before. Is he satisfied, tranquil, delighted? Not at all. He was already beginning to feel something of the cheerless sensation which sinks upon the wretched bachelor when, returning late to his chambers after a long and weary day and evening, still consoling himself with the thought of at least a pleasant hour with book and pipe over a bright fire, he enters his room and finds his grate filled with white and desolate ashes, and, spiritless, he pronounces it too late to think of reviving the extinguished glow.

The Massies were all very kind to Paul and very friendly; but the house had no warmth in it. As the family talked to their stranger cousin the first night of his arrival, so they continued to talk, in friendly tones and on general subjects.

Paul and his family did not get on. He had had expectations of long, intimate, and loving conversations about his early life, about his father and mother, and the causes of their separation, and of his own long divorce since boyhood from the living members of his family. He heard nothing of the kind. When he opened such a course of conversation with his aunt, she at once changed the subject. He could easily see that Eustace felt no interest whatever in the matter. He did not expect that Lydia could feel any; and he had for the first few days little opportunity of conversing with Sarah. In truth, there could hardly be any common subject of interest or association binding the cousins to the cousin. Their ways were not his; their thoughts seemed to be as unlike his as their lives had been.

Eustace was a sort of model clergyman. His heart was in his work; or at least in the routine of it. His church and its decorations, its rood-screen, its flowers, its choir, its pulpit, and its schools, filled his soul and often emptied his purse. He was a strict disciplinarian; he was a wor-

shipper of the externals of religion, while not in the least
a hypocrite, but simply a man who honestly confounded
the means with the end, the outside with the inside. Eustace Massie would be called by most people a good man.
He would not have done a mean, a wrong, or a cowardly
thing for the world ; but neither would he have smoked a
pipe, nor worn a moustache, nor gone to a theatre. He
loved his church—that is, the building—with as much of
love as so very proper a heart was capable of conceiving.
He was humane and gave largely in charity, but he did
not pretend to like poor people who had frailties ; and he
sincerely believed that the only cure for all human error
was to have a pew and to attend regularly in a well-built
church of the class recognized as High. He would not
have persecuted any one for religion's sake ; but he certainly did not regard a Dissenter as a respectable person ;
and in his heart he considered infidelity of any kind as
something socially disreputable, and chiefly belonging to
Chartist tailors.

It may be an inexplicable association of ideas, but if you
spoke to Eustace Massie of anybody afflicted with doubts
on the subject of religion, the clergyman at once pictured
in his mind a sallow person, with dirty hands and a scrubby moustache. Respectability and regularity were to
him the golden rules of life. Varieties of thought and
character he considered unnecessary and dangerous,—indeed he set them down as mere mental diseases. The
problem which he understood the Church to have to solve
was to bring all men to think, act, worship, and perhaps
finally even dress alike,—each, that is to say, dressing like
his equals in station. He was not fond of literature, and
only praised Shakespeare because he accepted that dramatist as a sort of necessity to which it was proper now to
conform. Dickens he endured because of his generally
commendable moral, although he thought several of his
characters terribly vulgar ; but he supposed that certain
natures needed such entertainment, and he gently bore

with the existence of such a craving, as he would have excused children for liking Punch and Judy. Thackeray used
to puzzle him thoroughly. He could not understand how
any man of character and social position could be in earnest when he selected such people heroes and heroines, and
propounded such doctrines as lessons of life. For whatever people of intelligence might think regarding certain
social institutions and ways of existence, the Rev. Eustace
Massie always held that no doctrine ought to be preached
but that of universal content with everything. While
laboring honestly and earnestly to change for the better all
things around him, Eustace Massie preached through life
that everything was exactly what it ought to be, and had
been purposely planned and ordered by Supreme Intelligence to be precisely that and nothing else. If a new astro-
nomical discovery were made, Eustace would have lectured
to the Young Men's Association of the town for the purpose of pointing out how that precise discovery demonstrated the fitness of things, and the divine adaptation of
everything to everything else. Had the "discovery"
been next day proved to be an entire mistake, and had
some reality of a directly opposite tendency been established, the clergyman would at once have accepted the
new truth, and demonstrated how that and that alone
could harmonize with the supreme adaptation of every
thing to everything else. He was induced once to read
Mill's *Essay on Liberty,* and he merely smiled the smile
of compassion over a writer said to have great intellect
and influence, who actually wanted people to be independent in thought, and positively encouraged eccentricity.
Life to Eustace Massie was a great school of order, wherein all training was to direct itself, after one plan, to the
universal realizing of one pattern. Indeed his own chief
interest was not in life at all, but in training: not in
religion, but in the Church.

How could such a man feel any warm sympathy with a
being like Paul Massie? What was Paul's religion? No

doubt he called himself a member of the Church of England; but it is probable that he could no more have explained the difference between High Church and Low Church, or even between one form of Dissent and another, or any form of Dissent (save Mormonism) and the strictest orthodoxy, than he could have expatiated on the difference between the doctrines of Kant and the doctrines of Hegel. It was a considerable stretch of good-nature on the part of Eustace Massie not to feel an objection to a cousin who smoked; and the horror with which he regarded all laxity of religious opinion was only evaded in this instance by a charitable determination on his part to believe Paul a perfectly orthodox and even pious man despite of whatever presumptive evidence to the contrary. But this very resolve only served of itself to restrict still more the narrow circle within which the conversation and the intimacy between Paul and his cousin were necessarily circumscribed. Paul was a cosmopolitan who had no particular opinions upon anything. Eustace had a mind essentially parochial and clerical, which never recognized the possibility of a vague opinion or a second opinion upon anything.

In truth the Massie family appeared to Paul intensely egotistical. A more reflecting personage would have made allowance for their circumstances, and remembered that they could hardly be anything else. How could people who lived all their lives in one place, and had whatever exertions and occupations they undertook limited by the opportunities and interests of that one place, be anything but egotistic? The range of Eustace's parish seemed the universe of the quiet group to which he was the central sun. Paul grew very weary of the eternal talk about the church and the curates, and the curates' wives; about the schools, the bishop's visit, the confirmation-day, the Dorcas meeting, the iniquities of the town, the growing number of public-houses, the spread of Popish opinions, of Dissent, of Methodism, and of cock-fighting; the branch Missionary Society, the annual charitable bazaar, and all the rest of the interests which absorbed the attention of Seaborough-house. He could not bring his roving intellect to apply itself to these domestic questions, and he knew full well that the Massies saw his inability ; and he suspected that they rather pitied it, and bore with his lack of interest in their sacred topics as a duty which for the time they owed to kindred and the rights of hospitality. Like all men who have travelled and knocked about much, he was inclined to set rather too high a value on mere locomotion, and to regard quiet untravelled domestic ways and home-keeping youths with a feeling approaching to contempt. He liked much to talk; partly because it relieved his now-repressed energy and restless mind, and partly too because, being conscious that he could talk vivaciously, forcibly, and sometimes even brilliantly, it gave him pleasure to exercise his faculty. But he soon began to think that the Massies did not know enough about the world to care about knowing any more; and that Mrs. Massie in especial had a positive objection to any conversation which recalled even momentarily the memories of far-off days and the associations of a distant land.

Therefore Paul sometimes walked on the sea-shore alone and rather melancholy ; therefore when the young ladies would not venture out in a boat on the rough waves —now very often rough—Paul sometimes pushed off his boat alone, spread his sail even in the roughest spring weather, sat in the stern, managed the sheet, ran recklessly out to sea, was in danger, and for the time happy. He very soon made the acquaintance of divers fishermen and boatmen, and had excursions with them wherein he displayed himself so stout a seaman, with so cool a head and so strong an arm, that he won their universal admiration. Before a week he knew all their houses, and would walk in and chat with the men or their wives or their children with the ease of an old acquaintance. Alice's father he knew among the rest, and Alice's father greatly admired him ; and Alice did somehow happen more than once to come down to see the honest boatman just when Paul chanced to be in the cottage.

Paul could give advice and assistance upon almost every subject, and had strange new ways of doing everything, from the rig of a boat to the shoeing of a pony. He could climb any cliff, could steer in any sea, could knot a rope in any possible way that emergency of whatever kind could require. He always had cigars to give to everybody, and would accept a piece of smuggled cavendish with the utmost frankness. He had not hesitated to take a dripping boatman into a public-house and treat him to a glass of rum there. He had taken the dirtiest little urchins into his boat ; and more than that, there was a wild tomboy of a girl, a boatman's daughter, full fifteen years old, brown-skinned and bright-eyed, and this young person had actually sat in Paul's boat and held the sheet several times while he dropped his nets, to the pride and delight of the lassie's honest father and mother, and the scandal of one or two religious neighbors. Paul thought no harm, and suspected no one else of thinking any. But all this, although it helped to make his time pass pleasantly away, and to constitute him a very popular personage among the people about the strand, did by no means tend to render his stay very agreeable to the rector of Seaborough. Indeed, if Eustace could have allowed so unfriendly a thought to enter his well-regulated bosom, he would perhaps have wished his cousin safely established in London (whither Paul was presently bound), or in Paris, or in Vera Cruz, or in Jericho.

One day Paul had arranged with the two young ladies of the house for a ride to some neighboring ruins. Unluckily, Lydia got a headache, or a sore-throat, or something, and could not go ; and Sarah, with whom Paul would much have enjoyed the excursion, would not, or at all events did not, go. Paul rode out alone, and clearing the town, cantered along a road which mounted pleasantly over the cliffs, and commanded a delightful view of the sea, and even of the French shore. He turned to the right after awhile, attracted by the charms of a rugged, straggling green lane, which climbed over height and dipped into hollow, and so promised to lead away from the sea and the surge and the cliffs into quiet inland nature. Although the trees were leafless yet, there was a greenness and soft beauty on this landward side which irresistibly invited an explorer. Paul rode on and on in perfect solitude, the road growing narrower and more straggling. Suddenly he heard the sound of approaching horses and many voices. It was not long before he had to draw up quite to the side of the lane, his horse's feet trampling into the bed of one of those charming brooklets which are as common as wild flowers in Ireland and Scotland and Germany, and unfortunately as rare as a four-leaved shamrock in England. If he had not thus pulled up to the side, nobody could say how the party of two ladies and three gentlemen who came riding down could ever have got past ; and even as it was, the procession, in Indian file, had to pick their steps as they went past. The last of the party, as he approached, looked at Paul, and then pulling up his horse, exclaimed, " Why, it's Massie—Paul Massie ! " And Paul returned the recognition by exclaiming, " Wynter ! " And a bluff dark-bearded man of some forty-five years endeavored to rein-in a kicking and stamping horse while he grasped in friendly eagerness the hand of our hero.

" Why, Massie, who on earth ever thought of seeing *you* here? I thought you were at least three thousand miles away. How long have you been here? When did you leave New Orleans, Vera Cruz, Calcutta—where was it I saw you last? "

Paul was really glad to meet Mr. Wynter, M. P., and frankly told him so. Mr. Wynter was a gentleman who bustled about the world a good deal, delighted in supposing himself deeply concerned in the political affairs of divers foreign countries ; and was a bouncing, good-natured, exuberant personage, g ven to boasting, utterly unreliable as to personal narrative, but in the depth (easily sounded) of his character honorable, sincere, and truthful. Paul and he had often met, and had contracted rather a liking for each other, and it was a relief to Paul to be hailed by him at the present moment.

"I heard of you only the other day," said Paul; "at least, I heard your name, and I thought it must be you."

"Then why didn't you make me out? I'm staying with Charlton, the member for Seaborough, Tunnel-hall, down there where you see the wood. Capital preserve! You must know my friend Charlton. Hallo, Charlton! This is a particular friend of mine—Mr. Paul Massie, of— Well, I really don't quite know of what place—Europe, Asia, Africa, or America. He's a cosmopolitan—a citizen of the world—like myself, begad!"

Introductions were not easy in so narrow a passage; but the member for Seaborough raised his hat, and then Paul was presented to the member's wife, and then to the lady who accompanied her, in whom Paul had no difficulty about recognizing the much-talked-of Salome.

"Turn your horse round and ride with us," said Wynter.

Paul complied, and they wended down the lane again, Wynter talking for all, asking scores of questions, to which he seldom waited for answers, and pouring out voluminous extracts from his own personal experiences and adventures.

At last they came to the open road, and here their ways diverged. Mr. Charlton invited Paul to dine at Tunnel-hall that day; but Paul had to dine at home and so must decline.

"Your cousin and I are not very good friends, I believe, Mr. Massie," said the railway contractor with a frank and kindly smile, which well became his large, intelligent, and not undignified face; "at least I have heard so, for I really know of nothing which should make us anything but good neighbors."

"Except that you differ in religion and politics," interrupted Wynter. "Do you think that isn't enough, or do you hope to be better than all the rest of the world?"

"Still," continued Mr. Charlton, "I hope you and I may meet again, Mr. Massie. We are returning to town very soon; but I should be glad to see you even before we go, and I hope we shall meet in London."

The much-talked-of Salome here joined in the conversation.

"I have often heard of Mr. Massie," she said, "and indeed know him by repute already; but I hope to have the pleasure of meeting him. I live in London, Mr. Massie, and shall be happy to see you when you come to town. You are coming to London, are you not?"

"I hope to be in London in two or three weeks; indeed I am anxious to get there."

"Then I trust that we may meet there; and I shall lay all the blame on Mr. Wynter if I do not soon have the pleasure of seeing you."

Paul rode homeward. He had not seen Salome's face very distinctly, for she wore a veil; but her form was graceful and remarkable, and her voice, somewhat deeper perhaps than that of most women, was sweet and clear in its tones. There was something peculiarly agreeable to him in her frank, unconstrained, and genial manner; it impressed him, especially after the colder style which belonged to the Massie family. One better accustomed to the polite world would probably have set down Salome as a good deal too *prononcée* in tone and style; but to Paul this would have been incomprehensible, and would have mattered little, even if he had understood it. He only felt that he should have liked to ride home by the lady's side, and talk to her; that it would be pleasant to dine that day at the same table with her; and he might have acknowledged to a slight touch of genuine regret when he heard that she was to return to London next morning. Therefore he rode home perhaps rather moodily; and when he got off his horse, and entered Seaborough-house, it was with the uncomfortable sensation of one who knows himself unsuited to the circle in which he is thrown, and who begins to be conscious that in that circle there is no natural place for him.

Why, then, did Paul Massie stay? Why did he not cut short the visit. which began to be so disappointing? One reason was that he had come to stay a month at least in the first instance, and there seemed no sufficient excuse for leaving the place in any abrupt manner. He could not well tell his cousins that he wished to go away because he was growing tired of them, or because he feared they were growing tired of him. But there was another reason for his lingering about Seaborough-house. An inexplicable fascination or presentiment haunted him while he remained there. If the form of Mrs. Massie had been peculiarly charged with electric fire, to which he and he alone acted as a conductor; if there really had been some spiritualistic or mesmeric *rapport*, which drew him and her mysteriously together and isolated them from all the world beside, he could not have felt more strangely impressed by her propinquity and her presence. He scarcely ever approached her that she did not seem to start and flush. When he touched her hand, he felt that it shivered, or throbbed like that of a girl in the clasp of her lover's. When he spoke to any one else, he felt and knew that if she was in the room her eyes were fixed on him. He was, as has been stated, a firm believer in spiritualism and its influences, and he believed himself aided in his observations by mesmeric attraction and perception ; while indeed it needed no supernatural or extranatural influences to impress him with a knowledge of an obvious fact. Often and often as he stood behind Lydia at the piano, often as he stooped over Sarah to explain some Italian or Spanish phrase in the books which she loved to study, he felt, he knew that the deep melancholy eyes of Mrs. Massie were fixed on him, and he looked up and caught her glance before it could turn startled away.

When was it that he beheld an apparition which impressed him with a painful sensation never to be effaced? When was it that he first became aware, as if by the ray of a revelation from the other world, that Seaborough-house concealed some secret which must in some way, close or remote, direct or indirect, be affected by his presence?

It was a wild and wet evening, and Paul had been driven home an hour or more before dinner-time. Eustace was working in his study. Paul entered the drawing-room and found Lydia alone. She was amusing herself rather vacuously by playing odd chords and scraps of melodies and operas on the piano, and she welcomed with obvious delight the coming of some one to talk to her. She was particularly gracious and winning that evening to Paul. She played and sang for him anything and everything he pleased, and he began to grow unusually happy under the genial influence of the moment. He was not at all in love nor getting into love with his cousin; but she was a pretty, vivacious girl, who could be fond and winning when she pleased, and this day it seemed to please her to be so. Paul was joyous and warm by nature, only made a lonely man thus far by fortune and fate. He felt the influence of the hour and the presence. Before a warm-hearted man meets the one to be loved, he meets with many shadows and fair apparitions, each of which, for the moment, he welcomes as the true and chosen form. Ixion-like, men rush to embrace that which is but a cloud, and melts as they approach. The hour, the place, the circumstances, the associations often combine to throw a delightful, deceitful lustre around some face and form which thus shine upon us as the one ideal vaguely sought so long, and now found at last. As the ignorant think of the sun, so do men placed like Paul Massie often mistake for native, all-absorbing, and immortal fire that which is only the luminous atmosphere surrounding the object. It seemed to Massie as if he were sinking away into a feeling very like love towards his cousin. To be so near her was, for the time, delicious;

and he drew nearer still, and bent over her shoulder, was close to her hair, felt his hand almost involuntarily touch her waist. And it was then that, suddenly looking towards the fire-place, his eye fell upon the mirror above the chimney, and he saw the apparition.

What was the apparition ? Only a face in the mirror—a woman's face, pallid, affrighted, ghastly, with lips tremulous, and eyes which burned with the pale fire of fear and horror. The room was in dusk, and the glow on the hearth chiefly served to keep it from being in darkness. In the mirror Paul could see nothing but the face, all outline of form was lost in shadow ; the eyes gazed wildly into his, the lips parted once or twice convulsively, as if about to utter some cry, or at least to speak some startled word. Only one moment the apparition lasted. It was instantly withdrawn from the mirror ; but the eyes had met Paul's, had looked into his with unspeakable, yet distinct, expression of mingled pity, agony, and terror—nay, had returned his surprised and startled glance with one which seemed to assure him that what he saw was only too real. Paul must have started palpably ; for Lydia stopped short in her strain, and both looked towards the door. Yet there was surely nothing there to startle the weakest nerves. Only Mrs. Massie, who must have chanced to come to the threshold unheard during the music, and who now entered the room. She looked pale, perhaps ; and and when she came in she remarked what a cold dreary evening it was, and wondered that Lydia had not had the lamps lighted.

"Mamma, you quite frightened me," said Lydia. "I never heard you at the door, and you looked like a ghost as you came in."

"There are no ghosts any longer," said Mrs. Massie ; "we have got rid of ghosts."

"Paul believes in ghosts," observed Lydia. "Don't you, Paul ?"

Paul would have believed in anything just at that

moment. Mrs. Massie urged that the singing should not
be given up because she had come in; she delighted in
singing. But the charm of the moment was gone; the
room did really look very drear and ghastly, and it was a
decided relief when Lydia rang for the lamps, and there was
light enough to see everything, and commonplace talk about
nothing set in.

CHAPTER VI.

SALOME AND ALICE.

TWO or three ladies were seated in the drawing-room of
Tunnel-hall. Mr. Charlton, the host, was over his wine
with Mr. Wynter and another gentleman. Mr. Wynter
liked his wine when it was good, and when dining at Tunnel-hall had no particular anxiety to quit the table for the
pleasure of looking at prints or hearing a voice with piano
accompaniment in the drawing-room.

The ladies were not very lively. Mrs. Charlton was a
good and kind woman, who had risen with her husband
socially, but not mentally; and Salome de Luca was never
much given to the society of women, unless when they
were specially clever or distinguished, or in some way
attractive. So the group of ladies were in a fair way to
bore each other—or at least such of them as were capable
of being bored. Nothing could bore Mrs. Charlton, she
was so kindly, simple, and happy. But Salome was tired;
and did not even look forward with much pleasure to the
coming of the gentlemen. She was relieved, although
much surprised, when a servant announced that a young
woman belowstairs wished particularly to speak to her for
a few moments. "She said you would know her by the
name of Alice," added the servant in explanation.

"Alice! Of course I do," replied Salome quickly.
"One of the servants at Seaborough-house, Mrs. Charlton,
—a special favorite of mine in old days."

Mrs. Charlton gave directions for Salome's visitor to be shown into one of the rooms below. Salome presently descended. She was glad to have the opportunity of talking to an old acquaintance, though only a lady's-maid. It was a variety, at all events, from the society of the past few days ; and she could not release herself from a personal interest in Seaborough-house, which the chance meeting of that day had done something to quicken.

She found Alice in a small parlor below. The girl looked flushed and almost alarmed. Salome noted that she had grown a decidedly pretty girl. Alice made a somewhat confused curtsey, but Salome, who had not one gleam of conventionality about her, put out her hand as if to an old friend.

"Well, Alice, I am glad you have come to see me, and glad to see you looking so well and happy. How is your father—and I hope your mother is stronger than she used to be ? I remember well how she used to suffer. I would have called to see them, but I have been so occupied, and my stay is very short."

"O, ma'am, you were always so kind, and when I heard you were here I thought I could not but come to see you —and besides—"

"Sit down, Alice—you look a little frightened, I think. Nothing wrong, I hope ?"

"No, ma'am—nothing wrong. But I have come to ask your advice, if you will be good enough—I thought I might venture—"

"Indeed you might. I only hope I may be able to advise you. Come, tell me what distresses you."

"I am afraid, ma'am, I have been doing wrong." She cast her eyes on the ground. Salome started and looked fixedly at her. "I mean, that I have been meddling in matters that don't concern me."

Salome looked greatly relieved, and indeed could not help smiling.

Alice, looking up, caught a faint gleam of the smile.

There was much of a sunny warmth in it, and it encouraged her.

"Well, Alice, what have you been meddling with? I don't think you would do anything very wrong, unless you have greatly changed since old days."

"I want to ask you, ma'am, whether what I have done is wrong, and how I can put it right; or if I ought to say anything to anybody about it. Please to read that paper."

Alice took from her bosom a folded paper. It was stained, yellow, and crumpled. It smelt of tobacco, and Salome almost shuddered at the first odor of it. She looked inquiringly at the girl before her, as if to ask what the meaning of the whole transaction might be. Alice met her keen gaze entreatingly. "Do you read it, ma'am—please do," she said. "I want some one to read it besides me."

Salome's quiet eyes turned away from the girl's face to the letter. Our friend was accustomed to study faces and their expression. She read nothing silly, or frivolous, or mean in Alice's look; only alarm and anxiety.

Salome drew the lamp close to her and read the letter. It had no address; it had no signature. It might have been an extract copied from a book. It contained a statement, or rather hinted at a revelation, which might be interesting enough if it appeared in its proper place in a sensation novel, when one knew all about the person who wrote it, the person to whom it was addressed, and the people whom it concerned. Presenting itself as it did to Madame de Luca, it was absolutely devoid of interest. It could scarcely awaken greater curiosity than the proposition suggested by Mr. John Stuart Mill in his essay on Sir W. Hamilton—that Humpty-Dumpty is equal to Abracadabra.

The letter—it evidently was a letter—was in a man's handwriting; a clear firm hand, with deep decided lines; not the hand of a man of business; not the cramped hand of a scholar; not the rapid scratches and blotches of a professional literary man. It was the hand of one to whom writing did not come too easily; who was firmly in earnest about every stroke; who would not have written if he could have avoided the labor; one might say without rashness, the letter of one who meant what he wrote. This much Salome, not unused to such speculations, thought she might venture to conclude. She observed the handwriting thus keenly, partly perhaps because she failed to discover anything to arouse her interest in the contents of the document itself.

Alice watched her expression with anxious eyes.

"Well, ma'am," the girl said at last, "who do you think wrote it—what do you think it means?"

"Really, Alice, I don't know. It looks like a scrap out of some novel. But what *is* it? Where did you get it? And what on earth have you and I to do with it?"

"I got it from one whom I don't want to see any more, if I can; and where he got it only God knows."

"You don't know who wrote it?"

"I don't know—I don't know at all; I don't guess even."

Salome grew impatient.

"Then in Heaven's name, child, what do you want of it, or what do I want with it, or what does it all mean? To whom is it addressed?"

"It's addressed," said Alice, dropping her eyes and lowering her voice, "to Mr. Paul Massie."

"To Mr. Paul Massie—the gentleman now at Seaborough-house—from Mexico?"

"Yes, ma'am."

"Then why on earth did you read it, or bring it to me to read? What right have you to read anything addressed to Mr. Massie?"

"It was about that I wanted to speak to you, and to beg of you for advice. The person who found that letter means to use it to extort money from Mr. Massie, or from somebody, and I thought it would be better out of his hands; but I daren't quarrel with him, for he's violent and dreadful ; and, besides, perhaps that letter ought not to be talked about. So I thought if I could get it from him quietly—and—and—pretend to help him, it would be better; and then I meant to ask somebody's advice, and I knew no one, ma'am, but you. I thought I was doing all for the best." Tears were in Alice's eyes.

"But, Alice, this letter is meaningless to me. Perhaps it is a trumped-up affair altogether. How do you know it is meant for Mr. Paul Massie ?"

"He told me so—the person who found it—yes, he showed me the address. I remember now, he showed me the address first."

"But it has no address." .

"O yes, ma'am, it must have had an address, or an envelope, for the first thing he showed me was Mr. Paul Massie's name."

"Well, it has no address now. I think this person, whoever he was, must have been trying to deceive you, Alice, for some motive or other. It seems to me to be an absurd affair altogether ; and I don't know that anything better could be done than to throw this letter into the fire, and think no more about it."

"But, ma'am, the person who gave this paper to Halliday—to the person who gave it to me—"

"Yes—well ? "

"That person must know all about it, and must be somewhere here."

"Yes, I suppose so. But what have we to do with that ? "

Only, ma'am, that it would be no use our destroying this letter. Halliday knows what is in it, and the person who gave it to him."

"Who is Halliday ? "

"He is a young man from the village, ma'am—a sort of friend of mine—at least he was ; but he has taken to bad ways, and I don't like him, and don't want to have anything more to do with him ; and I am afraid he will be angry and desperate. I want so much to go away from this place—indeed I do. I should like so much to go to London."

"Halliday, I suppose, is a discarded sweetheart of yours."

Alice only said: "I fear he's a bad man; and I don't know how he came by this letter; but if some one does not do something to put him off it, he'll try to annoy or injure some one about it."

"But, Alice, I see nothing in the letter that need affect any one very much. Somebody, it appears, thinks he has wronged Mr. Massie—if the letter be really addressed to him, of which I don't see any proof—and tells him there is somebody in England who can set the matter right. It may be some utterly trifling affair."

"O no, ma'am, it is not."

"How do you know? You don't even know who the person in England (I suppose it means in England) is."

"Yes, ma'am, I think I do."

"Then who is it? But stay—don't tell me, if you ought not to say it. I do not want to know."

"But if you please, ma'am, I want to tell you, and to ask your advice, and I hope you will allow me. I can't bear having it on my mind."

"Well, Alice, say anything you like."

"If you please, I think the person in England who knows of the wrong, and has something to do with it, and could set it right, is Mrs. Massie."

For the first time during the whole conversation Madame de Luca at once abandoned the expression of languid interest which she had hitherto maintained. She had listened to Alice with little more than indulgence and patience. She had listened partly to oblige the girl, who seemed deeply engrossed in the conversation; partly because she had nothing in the way of interesting occupation to gain by breaking off the dialogue and going upstairs.

But the mention of Mrs. Massie's name aroused a kindling interest. She looked up eagerly.

"Why do you think Mrs. Massie has had anything to do with this affair, whatever it is?"

"Because, ma'am, I had a ring, which was given to me —lent to me, I mean—by a person,—this James Halliday; and when she saw it she nearly fainted; and then she said it was hers, and that she must have it; and then she insisted upon knowing where I got it; and, indeed, she was like one wild with alarm; and I know that that ring is the token mentioned in the letter, for I know that the person who gave Halliday the letter must have given him the ring too."

"Alice, this is a strange story—one of the strangest I ever heard; I don't understand it in the least, but I am glad you have come to me."

"Yes, but that, ma'am, is not all : there are other reasons too why I thought of Mrs. Massie."

She stopped as if for permission to speak further.

"Go on."

"When Mrs. Massie was sick, not a long time ago, Miss Sarah and I nursed her—Miss Lydia is not good for anything ; and Mrs. Massie talked strange things, and raved of Mr. Paul Massie and of her own son, Mr. Eustace, and talked of having wronged and deceived and sacrificed some one, and so went on that Miss Sarah at last would not have me to nurse her any more. No one could make anything of it; and I might have forgotten it but for this letter that Halliday brought me and the ring."

"Have you the ring?"

Alice had it carefully stowed away. She had given up wearing it. She put it into Salome's hand. It was a beautiful ring, apparently of considerable value, but old-fashioned in the setting. There was nothing very peculiar about it, indeed, except its setting. The owner of such a ring might, doubtless, identify it after a considerable lapse of time ; but a chance observer would pass it over with little notice.

"It is quite possible Mrs. Massie may have mistaken this ring for one that had belonged to her," said Madame de Luca. "But," she added, rather in pursuance of her own reflections than as if directly addressing Alice, "that does not quite explain the strangeness of the apparent connection between the allusion in the letter and her alarm on seeing the ring. I should like to speak to the man who gave you this," she said, looking at Alice.

"Shall I ask him to come to you, ma'am?"

"O no, certainly not; we must approach him in some other way. It will not be at all difficult. I think, Alice, you had better give him back his ring at once, and have nothing to do with it. Have you told Mrs. Massie where you got it?"

"O yes, ma'am; she asked at once, and I told her all the truth—"

Salome lifted her eyes, and looked quietly at the girl. The look had meaning in it.

"All the truth, that is, ma'am, about the ring, and where I got it. I did not tell her anything about the letter; but I told her it was Halliday gave me the ring, and she said she would see him; and she said, too, that she did not want it talked about. I am afraid you will think I am acting badly towards her; and indeed I was just on the point of telling her more than once all I knew, and giving her up this letter, and leaving Halliday to do his worst; but she was so sharp and harsh and strange, that I could not speak to her about it; and it would be no use; for what is to be done with Halliday?"

"Alice, the best thing you can do is at once to give back that ring to Halliday; if it is Mrs. Massie's, and she wishes to recover it, you had better leave her to deal with him. For the rest, I strongly recommend you not to have anything more to do with the whole affair. You cannot wish to injure or annoy your mistress—you are too good-hearted, I think, for that."

"But I don't mean to stay with her; I don't mean to

stay in Seaborough. I must get away out of this, ma'am —away from Halliday and the whole place ; I hate it all. Do, please, ma'am, help me to leave this horrid place. I want to go to London ; and I will run away and go there, if I can find no other way. I don't want to injure or annoy Mrs. Massie—far from it ; perhaps I could if I chose ; but I should like to be able to do a service, if it is to be done by this letter. I should like, at all events, to have a share in doing it."

"A service to whom, child ? "

"Well, ma'am, a service to any body who is wronged, you know. We should all help our neighbor if we can "

"How long does Mr. Paul Massie remain in Seaborough, Alice ? "

This question dropped as if without the slightest special significance ; yet Alice colored as she answered:

"I think not very long, ma'am; I don't think he likes being here much."

"Indeed ! And he goes from this to London ? "

"Yes, ma'am."

Alice's color was still deeper than before.

Salome remained for some time without speaking. At last she said :

"I confess, Alice, that your story has something about it which seems extraordinary. But it may be that the whole affair is of trifling importance, or can be very easily explained. You will leave this paper with me for the present—it will be quite safe in my keeping—and I will read it again, and think about it, and try to see what we ought to do with it. I am going back to town—to London, that is—almost immediately. I don't advise you, Alice, to go to London; but if you have made up your mind about it—"

"Indeed, ma'am, I have. Pray don't tell me not to. I would rather die than not go there."

"Girls think they would rather die than do or not do many things, Alice ; but they find they can conquer their feelings easily enough, if they only try. However, you seem to have determined on leaving Seaborough, and I think you are too sensible a girl—I hope you are—not to have some reason for that. If you *will* come to London, then, I may be able to assist you."

Alice's eyes flashed with delight, and she was beginning to speak, but the lady waved her interruption away, and continued :

"You cannot go there without knowing somebody, though London is not quite such a terrible place as they make it out in some of the story-books, Alice. Have you got the consent of your father and mother for your leaving this place ? "

" No, ma'am—and I don't mean to ask for it. I know my father would not give his consent ; and I know that if he didn't, I would go all the same."

Salome raised her eyebrows. "*Comme l'esprit vient aux filles*," she thought.

" So I think, ma'am, it's best not to say anything about it until I am gone ; and then I'm sure they will easily make up their minds that it's all for the best."

Salome wrote an address upon a card and gave it to Alice. There seemed nothing more to be said, and the girl rose and was taking leave of Madame de Luca in a formal and respectful manner. Rumor in Seaborough had immensely magnified the wealth, position, and splendor of the lady; the very title of Madame, so different from plain commonplace Mrs., seemed equivalent to a patent of nobility.

Salome said, as if casually, " I suppose you never remember a time when Mrs. Massie was not in Seaborough, Alice ? I mean, you do not remember when she came back from abroad ? "

" O no, ma'am, that was ever so long ago—long before I was born, I suppose. But I have heard my mother speak of it."

" Your mother, then, remembers her coming back ? "

"I think my mother remembers her going away, ma'am. She remembers her a long time." •

"Remembers her marriage probably?"

"I don't think so, ma'am—I don't think Mrs. Massie was married here; indeed I am sure she was not, for I asked my mother."

"You asked her whether Mrs. Massie was married here?"

"Yes, ma'am. I asked her whether she knew anything about Mrs. Massie's marriage—or where she was married."

"And she did not know?"

"No, ma'am." The answer was given in a tone of no little surprise, as if in astonishment that it should have been so promptly anticipated.

"You asked her that question lately?"

"Yes, ma'am."

Madame de Luca said no more, but looked quite satisfied. She had fully sounded Alice's depth—easily plumbed was it indeed, for that matter.

Then Alice went away. She tripped boldly along while she was within the precincts of Tunnel-hall; but when she had passed out through the great gate, ornamented at either side by a huge sphinx of stone, and reached the main road, she seemed to become cautious and uneasy, and often looked behind and at either side, as if fearful of being followed or watched. It was a good step to Seaborough, and Alice was out of breath before she reached it. She had to pause for awhile at the gate, in order to recover her composure, before she encountered lights, and eyes, and orders.

Salome de Luca rejoined her friends in the drawing-room. The gentlemen had made their appearance there, and Mr. Wynter was in fine talk. The prospect of a change in the representation was discussed, as Mr. Charlton only waited a convenient opportunity to get rid of parliamentary duties. Salome entered with great spirit and sense into the political conversation. She talked with the

4*

ladies too, and humored them, and threw herself heart and soul into their little ways and interests, for which ordinarily she did not profess to care a great deal. Much change had come over her since her meeting with Alice. It may have been that the revival of old associations was pleasant; or it may have been that a too active mind, always restless, was delighted with the excitement of something new and unexpected to think about. Certainly her spirits were now of the brightest.

That night she sat up late. Alone in her bedroom, she wrote some letters; of which one was addressed to a " General Lefevre, Sablonière hotel, Leicester-square, London; " and in which she expressed a great anxiety to see that person immediately on her return to town, having some questions to ask relating to Mexico and its condition some few years back, whereon she doubted not that he could enlighten her ignorance.

We, the readers and writers of fiction, who follow ladies fearlessly into their bedrooms, and look over their shoulders while they write, may be allowed to peer into their secret thoughts. Salome had studied carefully—over and over again, and word for word—the paper which Alice had left in her charge; and perhaps her reflections on it assumed something of this shape:

" This poor foolish girl has, for all her folly, lighted on something that is not a mere chimera. There *is* some secret lying hid in that quiet self-complacent family of Pharisees. Providence has delivered into my hands the chance of discovering it; I will not throw the opportunity away. I will protect this poor girl from the dangers of her own folly and vanity; and I must see what the Mexican cousin is like whom she is so very anxious to serve. Can he be like the rest? If he be, I shall little care whither for him this clue of mystery leads. Is it possible that I was really once so silly as to care, or even think I cared, for that cold and shallow creature whom I met the other day? He soon forgot me; so did they all. Perhaps they may yet have reason to remember me."

She opened the window and looked out.

"I cannot see Seaborough-house. It is quiet enough now no doubt; but a shell might reach its roof even from this—nay, even from London."

CHAPTER VII.

SARAH.

PAUL MASSIE was an unsuspecting man by nature; but he had keen powers of observation, well developed by the peculiar occupations and varieties of his life. He observed not only that there was an inexplicable strangeness in the manner of Mrs. Massie towards himself, but he soon became satisfied that the same observation was silently and habitually made by one other person in the household. This was Sarah Massie.

Sarah Massie was a very different person indeed from her pretty cousin Lydia. The latter young lady had a keen eye for dress and manners, and for little else. She was not remarkable for placidity or patience or consistency of character. She was not a magnanimous young woman. Even her attention to her mother was wholly capricious, and varied according to her mood, which varied in itself, according to a thousand things, the weather included. She would fall upon her mother's neck and fondle her; call her her dear, dear darling mamma one moment, and an hour after would be all pout and sulk, ready to complain to any one that her darling mamma did not care about her, and that every body in the house was thought more of than she. A wet day could make her utterly depressed and miserable ; a change in the sky, the visit of an acquaintance, a new bonnet, the prospect, or even the chance, of any novelty, could raise her spirits to effervescence.

No one had looked forward so eagerly as she had to the long-expected visit of Paul: no one had been so disappointed with it. At first she was charmed, and it was cousin Paul here and cousin Paul there. And she got a guitar from the music-shop, and learned a Spanish song or two, and went near to fancying herself a Mexicaine; and would have longed, only for the sake of that propriety which domineered over Seaborough, to dance Mexican dances in picturesquely short petticoats. Then she began to think Paul inattentive, careless, and uncouth. And she made no scruple of scolding him behind his back to Alice, and listening to Alice's scraps of village gossip about him in return.

The truth was that Paul had not been nearly so devoted a cavalier as she had expected. And Alice had brought some ridiculous version of the story about the fisherman's daughter, in which the brown-skinned young mermaid played the part of an audacious and designing village coquette.

Lydia's scorn and wrath flamed out at this story; and she enlivened every family conversation for two days after by sharp allusions, which only pierced the ears of the listeners, for the reason that nobody had the least idea what the allusions meant.

One thing which Eustace Massie never would sanction or permit, so far as he could prevent it, was an indulgence in even the most pardonable style of feminine gossip. Therefore Lydia had to confine her open complaints to her maid, who received and encouraged them, and obtained thereby many small presents, favors, and graces.

In fact, Miss Lydia was a discontented person. She was discontented not from any natural morbidness or malevolence, but merely because she really did not know what to do with herself. Probably she wanted to be admired, courted, and loved ; and there was no one at hand to fill up the blank, which was opening more and more every day, in her unoccupied existence. Of course there was always plenty for her to do in the way of charitable work ; and despite all her levity and heedlessness, her brother did contrive to get her to render a good deal of assistance to Dorcas institutions and pious bazaars. 'The latter indeed she liked very well, because they afforded a scope for display of dress and fascination, and for the enjoyment of delightful and harmless flirtation. But she did the Dorcas work, too, readily enough when not out of humor, and in certain ill-humored moods even she toiled at it with a positive fierceness of energy. Still the human mind, especially when it lodges in a female body, cannot be wholly satisfied by such useful, practical occupation. A pretty and lively girl of twenty may be excused if her whole heart and nature refuse to concentrate themselves upon the charitable work of making flannel petticoats and calico chemises for the poor women of the neighborhood.

Perhaps Lydia felt disappointed that Paul had not made love to her, although she would not have acknowledged such a sensation even to herself. Had she been at all of the sentimental order, she might have fed her disappointment upon the soothing, almost satisfying, belief that she was marked out by destiny to be one of the unappreciated and the misprized, whom a cold, frivolous, and heartless world understands not. Had she been of the Blanche-Amory school, she would have composed melancholy poems about Fate and Disillusions, and woman's heart and the heedless crowd. But she had not the slightest dash of sentiment about her—not the least connecting link with the sentimental, except perhaps the common tendency to be easily put out of humor. Therefore when anything went wrong with her, she only fretted and sulked : when one favorite disappointed her, she turned for consolation to another. When Paul failed to play the lover, Lydia became particularly disposed to cherish and make a confederate of her maid Alice.

Sarah Massie was quite a different sort of a person. Perhaps the position of something like dependency which she had occupied since the death of her parents had helped to cause much of the difference. Perhaps the fact that she had found her place in life, and had her future apparently all chalked out for her, gave her a firmness and serenity which she would not otherwise have had. Life seemed to promise no battle for her. It had no expectations ; bating the physical chances of mortality, it appeared to have no uncertainties. She was to be well cared for in a quiet home until the time came for making her the wife of a good husband, whom every body respected. · She was then to lead a life of steady, constant, benevolent, and religious occupation, and would probably only know of the severer troubles of the world by endeavoring to mitigate them to others. Here was surely, one might have thought, an enviable prospect. Her cousin, younger, prettier, endowed with a considerable fortune, was liable to divers struggles, chances, and calamities, from which Sarah seemed to be specially exempted. Lydia might marry some one unworthy of her ; she might make a.foolish and miserable match, or she might make no match at all. The degree of certainty, then, which seemed to attach to her career must. no doubt have tended to render Sarah calm and unexcitable. She saw the prospect all clear and regular before her, and could afford to wait calmly. The traveller journeying through romantic and delightful scenery, where glens, and rocks, and ravines, and the far purple peaks of mountains are always producing new effects and exciting new expectations, has a restless time of it : now turning here to catch a glimpse of this, now twisting suddenly the other way lest he should lose a sight of that ; straining his neck and eyes in the direction whence comes the roar of a cascade, or jumping out of his carriage to peer down into a misty valley. But he who jogs along one of the white straight French or Belgian roads, and sees the way extending level, regular, tree-bordered, and dusty, for miles and miles before him, troubles himself little about the landscape, and coolly reads his book or smokes his cigar, or buries himself in his own reflections, unexpectant, unconcerned, not to be disappointed.

Sarah Massie was in outward appearance always clear, calm—perhaps a little cold; perhaps, indeed, a little sarcastic. Perhaps to a man she seemed at first to want some of that exuberant indescribable feminine nature which, more than youth or beauty, constitutes the captivating. She did everything fixedly, but very easily. She went about her work as if all her heart were in the making of the flannel petticoats and calico chemises; but she was at the same time able to attend to many other things, which with Lydia could never have been simultaneously carried on. She read a great deal, and sometimes of books which Eustace did not much care to encourage; and perhaps she thought a great deal too. She appeared to form her own opinion for herself on most subjects, and she held to it; but as she never contradicted and never disputed, her household set her down as a yielding and easily-guided sort of person. She seemed devoted to Mrs. Massie; she never by any chance quarrelled with Lydia; she anticipated, as if she had already been his wedded wife, all the wishes of Eustace. The household could not possibly get on without her. Yet Paul Massie was not long under Seaborough roof without coming to the conclusion that this girl either had no heart at all, and that her whole nature merely expressed itself in a quiet monotonous discharge of duty, or that her heart was not given to the circumstances, the occupations, and even the people in whose midst her life was passed. He was able to observe this simply from the fact that he came into the house with the fresh perceptions of a stranger, and moreover, that of all the inmates, except herself, he alone was not wholly absorbed in his own pursuits and his own personality.

Sarah Massie was not beautiful, although the two cousins together were commonly called in the neighborhood the handsome Miss Massies. But individually she was not much of a beauty; only remarkable for clear features,

soft gray eyes, and a fine form and figure. In these days
we are not accustomed to anatomize our heroines of
romance, and to set them before the world in full description limb after limb, as authors would freely do in other
times. But it may be remarked that Sarah Massie had a fine
bust, beautiful hands, and firm ankles, set above shapely
feet, which were not too small. Is there not a world of
expression in the feet and ankles? Show me the ankle, and
I will show you the woman. A lady once remarked that
she did not like women who had an unmeaning look about
the heels. Sarah Massie would not have incurred this cen-
sure. Her ankle indicated health, clearness, energy, and
self-reliance. It is not nonsense to talk of a woman's
ankle indicating all this. There are women who show
their character in the very way in which they manage
their skirts. One woman allows her clothes to draggle
along the street and lick the dust or mud; another, if she
has but to step over the least perilous of crossings, suddenly and convulsively gathers her petticoats up to her
knees, displaying flannels and fixings not meant for the
public gaze, and then perhaps, affrighted, lets them drop at
one side, while they remain uphoisted on the other. Sarah
Massie was never negligent, and never affrighted. Her
skirts were always raised to just the proper height, and
the beholder could therefore appreciate the character expressed in her graceful walk and firm ankle.

Sarah Massie had seen little of the world. A short
visit to London once a year constituted her utmost dissipation. When at school in Paris she had lived, as has
already appeared, in the grave, genteel, and formal Faubourg Saint Germain. She had never spoken with or seen
a man like Paul Massie until the night when Paul himself
arrived at Seaborough. She had only seen and known
young or old clergyman, young Oxford collegians awaiting
holy orders, and some of the local gentry. These were all
colorless people. No strong individuality marked itself
among them. Paul Massie had a strong, distinct individ-

uality. He came out of a fresh, active-living, highly-colored, many-tinted world. He had led a life not indeed more varied and adventurous than many energetic young Americans and many Europeans of the *émigré* class have led. But Sarah Massie had never met such a man before. His talk was so vivid ; his experiences were so varied ; there was such a healthful vigor of manly life about him, that he appeared to such a woman a being possessed of far greater strength and force of character than he really owned. He was not a scholar ; but she had met many scholars, and he knew much which they did not. He was not a profound Grecian or Latinist ; he had probably forgotten the little of Greek or Latin he ever knew ; but he could speak Italian fluently, and he knew Italy and Greece from end to end. He had laughed over Don Quixote within sight of the windmills of La Mancha ; he could have explained wherein the Alhambra Court in the Crystal Palace differed in its excess of gilding from the genuine Alhambra itself. He had met most men eminent in any active pursuit abroad ; he had been shipwrecked, and had looked on stricken fields ; he had been an explorer in Central America, and a soldier in Mexico, and a prisoner in Paris. He was not a highly accomplished Goethean critic, but he could sing any German song any one pleased to ask for. He had just the education of intelligence and varied personal observation. Such men are common enough ; and a woman whose life had been brought into contact with many such might possibly have been more impressed and delighted by the polished, graceful manners of a London gentleman, or the refined scholarship of a literary student. But to Sarah Massie Paul's style of character was all new, fresh, and wonderful. To Eustace Massie Paul's idiosyncrasies were simply repelling ; to Sarah they were, it must be owned, peculiarly attractive. It was not a fortunate day for the order and regularity of Seaborough-house when Paul Massie came under its roof. It was not fortunate, but it was very natural, that, as he began to sink in the estimation of some other members of the family, he should begin to rise in the consideration of Sarah Massie. Indeed, the feelings which his coming awakened were almost the first sensation in her calm monotonous existence. It is not a happy omen for a betrothed bride when a genuine sensation is awakened for the first time in her heart by one who is not her destined husband.

It has been said that Paul Massie soon perceived a nameless something in Sarah's expression which told him that she too was aware of some peculiarity in Mrs. Massie's manner towards him. He saw how often Sarah's eye rested anxiously and almost fearfully on her adopted mother; how promptly she came to the rescue when any embarrassment arose in conversation or otherwise; how carefully she watched Mrs. Massie; how tenderly and gently she interposed between her and any troublesome duty of any kind. Was Mrs. Massie an invalid? Surely she did not appear so? A strange suspicion sometimes occurred to Paul. Did Mrs. Massie's feeble, fluttering nerves really indicate something more than mere nervousness? Was she liable to occasional attacks of mental derangement? Women not uncommonly were thus affected, and he had no reason to know that his aunt was not one of the number. But except for her fainting on the night of his arrival, and the alarming and ghastly spectacle she undoubtedly presented on the occasion of that which we have called the apparition, there was nothing in her manner sufficiently remarkable to awaken any decided suspicion. Indeed it was only towards himself that Paul thought her demeanor at all singular. Even this he might perhaps have persuaded himself was the effect of a chimerical imagination on his part, but for the fact, which he could not ignore, that he was not the only one whom the same impression seemed to haunt. He longed for the moment when his stay might fairly be cut short—longed for it, while yet in his heart a new, vague, impalpable, indefinable sensation was arising which made him wish that he could linger somewhere near the place for ever. He had thus far seen but little of Sarah Massie, save as one of the general household. She was always genial and friendly to him ; but for the first fortnight of his stay in the house they had scarcely ever had a *tête-à-tête* of ten minutes' duration. Nor did anything in the heart of either speak clearly enough to say that such opportunities must not be sought, but rather avoided.

"Where is your cousin Paul to-day?" asked Mrs. Massie one quiet afternoon, addressing Lydia. The three women of the house sat together in the drawing-room.

"Indeed I don't know, mamma," replied her daughter ; "but I daresay he's in the bay, as usual, with his pipe and his sea-nymph."

"His sea-nymph? What is his sea-nymph? Is that the name of his boat?"

"O dear, no," replied Lydia, with a smile of wondrous significance. "So mamma has never heard yet of Paul's sea-nymph! His sole companion in his boating excursions —when the weather does not allow Sarah and me—that is, does not allow ladies to go on the water. How odd! Why every one talks about them ! It's quite romantic, I think."

"Pray, Lydia," said Mrs. Massie with an unwonted sharpness of tone, "do speak rationally, and tell me what you mean, and what every one talks about. Who or what is the sea-nymph you are talking about?"

"Only some fisher girl, I believe," said Lydia, delighted at the opportunity of opening out on the subject. "A boatman's daughter, I have heard. They say she's very pretty ; I am sure I don't know, for I never saw her. But I have heard a good deal about her. She's always with him in his boat, they say."

Mrs. Massie colored, and looked inquiringly, and indeed very anxiously, at Sarah, as if to solicit some rational explanation.

"She's a little girl—indeed, quite a child," said Sarah very composedly ; "a daughter of Staples the boatman. I believe Paul has been very kind to all the family, and has taken the boy and girl in his boat. But I never heard anybody talking about it except Eustace. I believe Staples told it to Eustace as a proof of Paul's kindness. Eustace spoke of it to me." Sarah knew that Eustace's opinion was regarded as a settler in Seaborough-house.

"And what did Eustace say?"

"O, very little. He remarked to me that Paul had such a kind and warm heart."

"Then you have seen the girl, Sarah?" asked Lydia, all eagerness.

"O yes, very often; and so have you, only you probably did not notice her."

"And is she very pretty?"

"No, I think not—I really don't know—I dare say if the child were well washed and combed, and got some clean clothes on, she would look well enough."

Lydia's little bit of malicious romance seemed to fall to pieces in rather a sorry fashion.

"Who has been telling you these stories, Lydia?" asked her mother.

"Who, mamma? Why, every body."

"But tell me the name of some one of the every bodies."

"Well, there was Alice—and there was—yes, I am sure Alice told it to me, and of course if somebody did not say it, she could not have known it."

"Was there no one but Alice who spoke to you of it? You said every body told you."

"But, mamma, of course I didn't mean every body in all the world. I don't know every body even in Seaborough. I only just used the word 'every body' as we all— in fact as every body uses it. I did think that a great many people had been speaking about Paul."

"I am not at all satisfied with Alice's conduct and manners of late," said Mrs. Massie. "I must speak to her father about her."

So the matter dropped, and Lydia felt rather rebuffed,

and therefore inclined to blame "every body." But Mrs.
Massie walked a good deal along the strand for a day
or two after this, and once saw Paul's boat come in and
her nephew get ashore. This time, however, he had neither
nymph nor siren in his company; but was quite alone, and
looking rather melancholy. He did not see her, but she
looked long and anxiously after him, until tears came into
her eyes.

Was it a dream Paul Massie had that night which
made so singular and deep an impression on him? Falling
asleep, or at least into a condition approaching to sleep
after a long restlessness, it seemed to him that his room-
door softly opened, and that a timid cautious step glided
over the carpet. He lay still. He thought the form of a
woman, blanched and ghostly in the faint moonlight, stole
into the room and bent sadly over him, and kneeled beside
his bed and remained there hushed for awhile as if in
prayer. He thought he heard faint sobs and moans; and
an inarticulate, irrepressible sound broke from him, and the
figure rose up hastily, and was gone in a moment. Then,
thoroughly awakened, he started up. The room was quite
empty and silent; but as he half opened the door his quick
ears seemed to catch the rustle of a dress, and the faint
sound of a light footfall.

"Somebody in this house," thought Paul, "is surely
mad, or I myself am losing my reason. If I stay here
much longer, I shall have no reason left."

CHAPTER VIII.

THE EARLY BIRD—AND THE WORM.

NEXT morning Paul was up earlier than usual, although an early riser almost always. He could not sleep, and so got up and walked about the grounds at the back of the house, and smoked a contemplative cigar, and endeavored to think what he had best do and what could possibly be the meaning of the vague, impalpable, yet quite perceptible web of mystery which seemed to be spinning itself around him. This morning he was destined not to have any of the web brushed away, but rather a few more complicated meshes added. He had not been long engaged in smoking and thinking when a back-door of the house opened, and the figure of a woman appeared in the gray faint light of the early spring morning. The woman was shawled and had her bonnet on, and carried a carpet-bag and a small bundle. It was Alice. Paul gave her a good-humored salutation.

"You are up early, Alice," he said.

She did not reply in a word, as he expected, and then go on her way, but stopped short and addressed him :

"I did not expect to see you, Mr. Massie, or any one ; and I hope, sir, you won't say you saw me. I am going away, Mr. Massie."

Her voice became rather tremulous.

"Going away, Alice ? Where ? Are you leaving Mrs. Massie ? I hope nothing unpleasant has happened ? "

"O no, sir ; it is not that," and she tossed her head a little ; "but I have some reasons for going away, and I don't want it known ; and I'd ask you, sir, as a favor, not to say a word to any one that you saw me going—at least until I can't be brought back."

"But, Alice, this is very odd. Does not your father know?"

"My father doesn't know, and I don't want him to know. I am going away for no harm, but for some people's good, and I can't stay any longer here ; and pray don't ask me any more, sir."

"Why, Alice, I have no right to ask you anything; but I think you ought to let your mistress and your father know of what you are doing. If you are right in going, they surely would not prevent you."

"Mr. Massie—Mr. Paul—there are others who ought to go as well as me ; there are some who ought not to have come ; there are some who have enemies and don't know it. I have enemies, and I do know it ; and so I am going away."

There was an extraordinary wildness about the girl's manner as she talked thus.

Paul was utterly bewildered. He had seen the girl several times a day for weeks, and he had never thought of her but as a smart serving-woman, or as one might think of the toast-rack or the dumb-waiter. Now she too was becoming part of a mystery.

"Alice," he said at last, "I really cannot even guess at what you mean, and I ought not to try to guess it."

"Perhaps," she said, "you are not good at guessing ; perhaps you are too honorable to suspect anybody. I suppose I am not, and so I suspect and I guess ; and others do too. Mr. Paul," said she, suddenly changing her tone and manner, "do you know one Jem Halliday ? "

"Yes, surely, I know the man you mean ; I have spoken to him."

"Well, now, listen to me: he thinks he knows something about you that you would give a good deal to know. He'll want to get money out of you. He knows nothing— that is, nothing more than guess. He has got something which you ought to have; how he came by it only God and himself know. He gave it to me, and—and I haven't it. I mustn't say where it is, but I haven't it, and I have not seen him. He's a bad man, and that's one reason I'm going away; but it is not the only reason. But he knows nothing—only he may annoy you and others. So take my advice, Mr. Massie, and buy him off; give him some money —it will be no loss to you; and then you will soon be going to London, and you'll find friends there who will put you in the right way and see that you have your rights. Good-by, sir, and don't be vexed with me for speaking to you; and pray, pray don't tell any one to-day that you saw me."

She ran down the walk, passed out of a little back-gate, and left Paul as utterly confused and bewildered as a rational and sane human creature well could be.

There was a railway station at Seaborough, and Alice made for it as fast as she could. She waited until the up-train was starting, and then took a ticket for London.

The only noticeable matter about her arrival in the metropolis was that she did not seem to have the slightest doubt or difficulty about her destination. The moment she arrived at the London Bridge terminus she got a cab, gave an address, and was driven off westward. Certainly the address which she gave ended with the name of Hyde Park. So we allow her to disappear for the present, and to " drop through the tissue " of our story.

It would perhaps have been more fortunate if her chance meeting with Paul had been entirely unobserved; but it was not so. Mr. Halliday had been prowling about the place for days back, partly in the hope of meeting Paul alone, partly in the hope of getting a secret interview with Alice. He had not recovered the letter on which he built so many hopes. Alice had neither given it back to him nor told him anything about it, but steadily avoided coming near him. He began to think he was sold. He watched the house morning after morning, determined, if all else failed, to accost Paul on his own account, and try to sell what conjectures and speculations he might have as dearly as he could. Be it said that, according to his conjecture, he was about to open up the track of a secret which he held to be of great benefit to Paul, and for which he hoped to be well repaid.

But this unhappy morning he had scarcely entered the grounds when he heard voices; and he soon found a point of observation from which he could see that the talkers were Paul and Alice.

Blind wild rage almost bewildered him. He believed himself doubly betrayed and befooled. He caught no word of the conversation, which indeed had ended just as he first saw the speakers. He saw Alice go away, but no idea ever crossed his mind that she might possibly be leaving Seaborough. Had he dreamed of such a thing, her journey would have been stayed by some means. When she was gone, his impulse was to rush out and kill the man who walked so calmly within half-a-dozen yards of him. Had he a weapon—had he, above all, firearms—he might have done a murder then and there: he had all the heart to do it. But he was not a brave man: he was not a man in whom even fury supplies the place of courage. He saw no good in any frantic attack on Paul, which would probably have ended in his own discomfiture. He did not care to encounter the strength which he knew to be so formidable. It so happened that this day he had not even his knife. He kept, therefore, in his hiding-place, all the fire of hate burning in his heart. A cunning man, he believed himself foiled; a strong man, he knew his strength useless here; a man blindly and wildly steeped in love, he felt convinced that his passion had been made a scorn. Dull drops of perspiration stood upon his forehead, and he wiped them off with a wet, hot, and dirty hand. Early as it was in the morning, he had already been drinking, and up to a late hour the night before he had been drinking; and his whole faculties and senses were of late becoming bemused and stupefied with drink. Yet agony of mind now nearly soberized him. O, how

5

bitterly he felt what an abject, unfortunate, befooled wretch he was! and how in his inmost heart he cursed those who were superior to him, and who despised him!

It was well for Alice that he did not follow her. He would have been a dangerous companion just then. She was not strong, like Paul Massie. No weapon would be needed in order to enable her *ci-devant* lover to avenge himself for his wrongs on her.

Paul Massie paced slowly up and down the damp walk. His enemy lay hid within a few yards of him, and he did not know it—nay, did not know, did not suspect, that he had an enemy in the world. Alice was speeding down the road away to the railway which was to carry her to London. In the white house, whose chimneys could be seen by the two men and the fugitive girl at one moment, there were two anxious women—waking, thoughtful, fearful, and unhappy.

All these, and others too, were bound together unconsciously by the tiny imperceptible thread of one little secret. They are doomed to play at cross-purposes with that little secret through the whole course of our story. Some of them will never find it out. It would be better for others that they had never thought of it, for they will have to pay a bitter penalty for striving to track it to its meaning and its source.

One of the women we have spoken of was too restless to remain in the house just then. She had, moreover, a set purpose which she has resolved to execute. Not more than half an hour after Alice had left the demesne, this woman came out by the same back-door, and was making her way with hasty timid steps down one of the side-paths lined with trees and bushes, which, skirting the lawn, led to the gate and the road.

Meanwhile Halliday was still prowling about the place. He felt convinced that Alice must soon return, and he was resolved to wait for her. He was lounging and scowling among the trees, with his eyes fixed on the gate and his heart swelling with anger and hate, when he heard a light footstep behind him. He would have run away or hidden himself somewhere, had he not taken it for granted that the step must be that of Alice. How she could have got into the demesne again without his knowing it, he never stopped to think. He saw a woman coming along, and only when it was too late to draw back did he discover that it was not Alice. The person approaching saw him, started at first, and then hurried more eagerly towards him. Halliday now saw that it was Mrs. Massie.

She signalled to him to stop. He make an awkward attempt to touch his hat. She was out of breath, and seemed much excited.

"Halliday—Halliday!" she said, and then pausing for breath and composure; "I wanted to see you. I was going to your house. Did Alice tell you? I want to know where you got that ring? Who gave it to you? Tell me."

Halliday's first impulse, when asked any question, was always to evade or lie.

"What ring, ma'am?" he grumbled.

"The ring that you gave to Alice."

"I gev' a ring to Alice? What ring?"

"Halliday, that ring was mine; but I don't say anything against you. I don't suppose you came by it in any wrong way; I don't want to make any disturbance about it; I only want to know how you came by it. Who gave it to you? It is of the utmost importance to me to know. I should be glad to buy the ring, and I will pay you if you tell me who gave it to you."

Whatever poor and slender chance Mrs. Massie had of arriving at the truth was gone. Her own words and manner had killed it. A firm tone, a stern demand might have got something like a hint of the truth from Halliday. But the tremulous conciliatory appeal of the woman who stood before him satisfied him that she was more in his power than he in hers. He therefore coolly took time to think what he had better say.

Mrs. Massie tendered him, with white trembling fingers, a sovereign to sharpen his decision. He took it with a gruff obeisance.

"Well, ma'am," he said, slowly and hesitatingly, "I suppose I know what you mean. I don't doubt you mean the little ring I saw with Ally. But as to my giving her any ring—why, you know, if she said so, she's been telling you a lie, ma'am."

"Did you not give her that ring?"

"I, ma'am? Why bless you, ma'am, where ever could I get such a thing?"

"Good heaven, she told me you gave it to her!"

"Did she though? Well, now, whatever did she mean by that? *I* don't have diamond rings, ma'am, brought from foreign parts—I never was in foreign parts myself, ma'am."

A keen idea of combined evasion and revenge was shooting through Halliday's brain.

"Then, do you mean to say you know nothing about the ring? Are you telling me the truth? Speak the truth, for heaven's sake. Do you know nothing of the ring?"

"Nothing at all, ma'am—only that I see it on Ally's finger—and I asked her about it, and she wouldn't tell me. But I think I can guess who gave it her."

"Then who did? Tell me quickly—I must know."

"Well, ma'am, I think it was the gentleman I see her talking with here in this very place half an hour ago."

Surprise and pain spread over Mrs. Massie's face.

"Here—half an hour ago," she said, "talking with a gentleman?"

"Yes, ma'am; I saw her, but she didn't see me. Ask her, and see if she'll dare to deny of it."

"Whom was she speaking with—who gave her the ring?"

"The gentleman she was just talking with here—the gentleman who gev' her the ring—is your own nephew, Mr. Paul Massie!"

A faint cry escaped from her lips.

"He,—Paul Massie! And he gave it to her?"

"Yes, ma'am; he gev' it to her sure enough—and what he gev' it for, it's not for me to say."

"No," said Mrs. Massie, turning sharply on him, "not for you to say, nor for you to talk of. Go away—I want you no more. Be sure that you say nothing of this to any one. I will find out the whole truth of it soon enough; and if what you say is not true, depend upon it you shall suffer for it. If you are telling me lies, then I shall know that you are a robber as well. Go away."

It was well that Halliday did not want for his own sake to prolong the interview. Had it continued two minutes longer, Mrs. Massie's suddenly assumed courage must have broken down. As it was, her lips were quivering with nervous excitement, and her cheeks were ashy pale.

Halliday only grumbled out something to the effect that she might believe his word—that he was telling the whole truth, and nothing but the truth—a form of attestation he had heard in the police-court; and he then wandered away down the walk. He did not want to see Alice just now; he would have thought her premature return highly inconvenient. In his heart he felt convinced that he had done some mischief, and he delighted in the thought. He saw how his lie had striken home, and he was glad. To do the wretch justice, it must be stated that he fully and sincerely believed Paul Massie had deeply injured him. He never had but one unselfish passion in all his life, and he now felt convinced that this insolent and scornful stranger had robbed him in idleness of its object. Halliday would have ruined all Seaborough to give back even indirectly to Paul Massie one twinge of the agony which tortured his own soul.

"What I can't make out," thought Halliday, as he

lounged forth of the gate, "is about this ring business. Whose is it? Who was she that had it? What does it all mean? If Ally would have helped me to find out—ah, we might have made our fortunes out of it. But now this is what she does. One thing I know—I'll have the ring and the letter, and that before long, or I'll know why."

Mrs. Massie, for her part, walked slowly and feebly home. She muttered, as was her wont, half-sentences and scraps of broken meditation.

"At least," she said, "if this be true, then he cannot know. He could not give it away—give it to such as she, if he knew. No, no. Thank God for that! If he has given it away, he does not know."

No *éclaircissement* touching Alice's departure took place that day. Paul fully expected something of the kind, but was rather relieved when a remark, casually let fall by some one within his hearing, apprised him that the girl had asked for a holiday, and was not expected to return to the house that night. He felt extremely uncomfortable under the burden of an odd sort of secret, which appeared in nowise to belong to or even to concern him, but which yet placed him in the awkward position of a conspirator in a small deception practised on the people whose guest he was. The whole thing was small and humiliating; but he did not see how he could undertake to betray the secret of the girl's departure, which he had come to know by a purely accidental meeting.

Through the whole of that day Mrs. Massie's manner to Paul was more strange than it had ever been before. Sometimes she seemed to draw away in positive repugnance from him. Even Eustace observed this, but quietly put it down to the natural antipathy which a well-bred and delicate nature must feel towards one whose habits and ways of thought were so unlike those of calm and proper Seaborough. But there were times, too, when Paul thought his aunt seemed to approach him as if anxious for an opportunity to say something to him in private. Once or twice they were thrown together for a moment, and a prompter person than this poor lady might have spoken many a thrilling word in the ear of the young man. But though she approached him, caught his eyes, and showed by her own that she understood his wondering expression —though he could see some sentence or question forming on her lips, yet her courage seemed to melt, and the unspoken words remained all silence. Nay, there was one moment when the meditated question all but came. Paul Massie met her in the hall, and again attracted by her anxious inquiring look, he paused before the barometer which hung there, and invited her to help him in presaging as to the weather. Then she drew close to him, made an effort to speak, and, failing words, laid her hand impatiently on his finger, and tapped sharply, as if to question him of something that should have been there. This action so entirely surprised the young man and disarranged all his expectations, that he turned wild glittering eyes of amazement on her ; and her coherent purpose, if she had any, vanished.

"The ring," she said, in a faint low tone ; "I wanted to ask you about the ring—O, do not speak!"

Here somebody entered the hall, and then she was gone.

Then Paul began to regard it as certain that his aunt was simply a woman of disordered brain. For he had of late begun to think it quite possible that Mrs. Massie had to make some disclosure to him—perhaps a painful one— relating to his parents or one of them. Knowing that he had been kept purposely a stranger to his family during the late Eustace Massie's lifetime, he was not without conjecture that some explanation remained to be given to him, now a man, which might be necessary and yet painful alike to give and to receive. He had a vague impression somehow that his father had led a stormy youth, and was therefore not unprepared for some humiliating revelation. Mrs. Massie's strange demeanor this day he had readily attributed to the sensitiveness of a feeble and tender woman, who having put off to the last the disclosure of a distressing secret, still shrinks in agony from the inevitable utterance. So he had done his best by look and manner to reassure her, to bring her frankly to the disclosure, to convey to her that whatever it might be, he was ready to receive it. What, then, were his sensations when, as the supreme moment at last seemed to have come, he was accosted with words and gestures that to him were absolutely meaningless—that appeared indeed to be only the wayward ebullitions of insanity? If ever man was perplexed in the extreme, Paul Massie was. He would have longed to leave the house at once, but that the calm eyes and tranquil self-possessed demeanor of Sarah Massie reassured him, and shed on him some gleams of happiness. He felt in her presence as a child awakened from some hideous dream feels in the presence of the sunlight.

Meanwhile we must return to Mr. James Halliday. After he had left Mrs. Massie, that gentleman did not immediately return home. He lounged down to the town, and finding public-houses already open and doing a quick morning trade, he changed his sovereign and calmed his excited energies with drink. When he reached his cottage an hour or two after, he pushed roughly past his old mother, sat down in front of the fire on the chair she had quitted to welcome him, and began to light his pipe.

"Somebody's been here, James," said his mother, in a tone intended for conciliation. Poor woman! her efforts at conciliation were usually so elaborate and so obvious, that they utterly failed of their purpose, and aggravated still more the temper they were intended to soothe. "It was the same way with James's father," she always observed. She generally talked of the peculiarities of James's father with a sort of pride. James's father had often turned her out of the house in her nightgown at stark midnight, had several times admonished her with a pewter pint, and was always threatening to "do for her." Probably he would have done for her in the end, but that fate interposed in the shape of an angry and powerful publican, who once flung the drunken Halliday into the road, where he got a contusion in the head, which led to erysipelas, and so' to death. His wife always spoke of him with pity and regret, and, as we have said, usually described his little peculiarities, and her own consequent sufferings, with a kind of pride. Her son seemed to renew for her the life she had led with her husband, except that the son was perhaps the more idle and as yet the less savage of the twain. But she accepted it all quite meekly, and as one who understood that the natural condition of man was to be frequently intoxicated, and when thus affected to maltreat woman.

"Somebody's been here, James," she said again, with an elaborate affectation of gayety, and an endeavor to appear as if she felt quite sure of being thanked for her news.

James growled out that somebody might come or go, as far as he was concerned.

"O, but this is really somebody," continued the cheerful soother; "somebody you like to hear about."

"Who is it then? Don't be making a fool of yourself."

"Why, it was Ally—Ally Crossley."

James uttered a sound—half-savage growl, half-moan.

"And she's left something for you."

"Give it here then. Why the devil don't you give it here and stop your jawing?"

He had started from his seat.

"Here it is, James," said the poor woman, fumbling in her pocket for something. "I'm sure I never opened it, and don't know what it is—no indeed."

He snatched from her a little thimble-case, or something of that kind, wrapped up in brown paper. Unrolling the first covering, he came to white paper with a blot of sealing-wax to fasten it; then to tissue paper; then to the thimble-case itself; then, opening this, he saw the well-known diamond ring. Not a line, not a word accompa-

5*

nied it. He turned the case, the ring, the papers, over and over again. Not a word.

"What are you staring at?" he asked of his mother in a savage tone.

"I was not starting at anything, James; I was not looking at all." She took up a duster and began with immense energy to brush down the top of the chest of drawers, crooning with tremulous old voice a scrap of a song the while.

"Hold your noise," he said. "And look here: when did Ally give you this?"

"Well, I think it must be two hours ago; I'm sure the clock had struck six. I was just standing here when a knock came to the door; and I went out, and there, of all people in the world—"

"What did she say when she gave it to you?"

"She said, 'Mrs. Halliday,' says she, 'would you mind giving that to James? Be sure you keep it very safe,' says she, 'and give it into his own hand when—when—' I think that's all."

"When what?"

"O nothing, only just—nothing at all."

"When what? 'Give it to him,' says she, 'when—' When what did she say? Why don't you speak?"

"Well, I believe she said when he's quite sober. But she was only joking, I'm sure. 'Is there no other message, Ally?' says I. 'No, Mrs. Halliday,' says she; 'none at all.' So she went away then, and she didn't say where she was going."

He said no more on the subject, but began to smoke violently. Some vague idea possessed him that the sending back of the ring must mean something more than the final rejection of his love. *That* he knew too well had been finally rejected long ago. It meant, he dimly thought, that Alice had fairly gone over to the enemy; that she had made terms for herself out of his secret, and that he was utterly cast off. She scorned him so much, and thought him so useless, that she disdained even to keep the gewgaw which once had such value in her foolish eyes. She saw other ways opening to her, and she flung him back in contempt his one solitary bribe. But he never supposed that she was actually going away.

Well, he had his ring. There could be money got for that somehow. He felt quite sure that several guineas were to be got for that; only he must not attempt to sell it in Seaborough. There was something to fall back upon. It would help him to have his revenge upon somebody; and then, let what would befall him, he did not much care. At present he saw a prospect of some drink and some revenge. He did not want to look any farther.

One thing alone made him rather uneasy about the possession of the diamond ring. He had heard from Alice before, and he knew now for himself, that Mrs. Massie professed to recognize it, and was anxious to know how it had been got, and would probably have strict inquiries made about it. These inquiries he must absolutely forestall by getting rid of the ring somehow. Inquiries of any kind did not suit Halliday; and he had rather a special dread of any which came from Seaborough-house, where he knew that the inmates had a peculiar aversion to him. His life had not thus far been that of a criminal. Except for a pretty constant dealing in Cavendish tobacco, and a frequent assistance and participation in smuggling, he had done nothing which laid him particularly open to the perquisitions of justice. But he had so long been noted as a good-for-nothing, as an idle, dissolute, and drunken fellow, that he knew full well any chance would be eagerly availed of to rid the place of his undesired presence. He was just hovering on the verge of lawlessness and crime when the incident of the ring and the letter seemed to give him, by one sudden and bold plunge, a chance of redemption. He had made the plunge, and failed ; and he now knew that he was absolutely at odds with law, and could not halt any longer without the certainty of paying a forfeit. It was clear that he must go on; in any case it probably would have come to this. He did not indulge in any reflections about Society, or anathematize that abstraction, or endeavor to lay his sins at its door. He had not the slightest notion of Society in the Paul Clifford or Jean-Valjean sense; knowing and caring only for concrete and substantial things. But he laid his offences, his dangers, and his sufferings partly at the door of Alice Crossley, and partly at that of Paul Massie, having likewise a somewhat old and comprehensive grudge against the whole Massie family. He thought he had an old score to pay off, and he fancied that the means of paying it off would yet be in his power.

• • •

CHAPTER IX.

PAUL IS ACCUSED.

THE days followed, and resembled each other; indeed they were nearly all alike. Save that the buds and blossoms were coming out, everything looked much the same when Paul was leaving as when he came. But in Paul's heart much was different; that short time had given him more occasion for thought than he had had in his whole life before. Perhaps for the first time in his life he had made acquaintance with genuine disappointment—none the less real because its source was so vague. Within the last few weeks a great hope had been extinguished, and in its place some fierce, unknown fires were beginning to burn.

The last evening of his stay at Seaborough had come— of his present stay it was then thought; but Paul was not destined to cross the threshold of that house again.

Paul and his cousin stood in one of the rooms, the windows of which opened on the lawn.

"You will return soon, I hope?" said the clergyman;

the prospect of Paul's immediate departure reviving all his
natural kindness of disposition, and making him feel a little
remorseful that they had not been more often together.

"I must not promise," said Paul; "I am an uncertain
and good-for-nothing sort of fellow ; and I don't know yet
what I shall find to do with myself. But you have all been
so kind to me, that I shall certainly feel strongly tempted
to intrude on you once more. I shall be sorry if I cannot
see you all again before I leave England."

Poor Paul! He hesitated over the words, and felt a
choking sensation. The placid clergyman had no suspicion of the feelings which were agitating his cousin's perplexed heart. There were two great secrets establishing
themselves there—two Aaron's serpents—neither of which
could swallow up the other. One would have been enough
to disturb the best and calmest of us.

"You will not fail us at dinner," said Eustace, as Paul
made demonstrations of preparing to go somewhere. "We
must spend this last night together ; and be very happy;
and Sarah and you are to sing duets."

"I am only going down to the village," replied Paul,
in undecided tones. "I want to see some of these poor
fellows—boatmen and people—before I leave."

"Here comes one of your friends—Dan Crossley—and
in hot haste, too. Very likely he has heard of your going,
and is resolved on seeing you."

Eustace afterwards recollected that Paul looked rather
embarrassed at the sight of Crossley's sturdy figure hastening across the lawn. Indeed Paul felt ashamed and
uncomfortable because of his knowledge of Alice's extraordinary flight, and had half made up his mind to go down
to Crossley and tell him all about it.

"He looks alarmed," said Eustace. "I hope nothing
bad has happened to him.—Here, Crossley! Crossley, come
this way."

Crossley looked up, and his brown face turned to purple
and his brows knitted as he saw the cousins. Eustace flung

up the window, which opened down to the ground, and the boatman—puffing, red-faced, and wild-looking—strode into the room.

"So, you're here," he exclaimed vehemently. "I beg your pardon, sir,"—turning to Eustace, and pulling off his hat,—"but I want to know something about my daughter."

"Your daughter?" both the young men echoed.

"Yes, my daughter," fiercely replied the boatman. "You've got my daughter away from me—you—" and he made a violent gesture towards Paul. "You've taken her from me; you've carried her away—you; yes, you!"

"Man," said Paul, " are you mad, or drunk, that you talk in this way? What do I know about your daughter?"

" You know where she is now. You know where you've hidden her. You enticed the poor foolish girl away with your presents and your lies. Give me up my child; tell me where she is ; or by the Lord above us I'll have your life!"

He seized Paul furiously by the collar with both hands.

"He's mad!" said Eustace, turning pale as a ghost. "I'll call the servants;" and he made an effort to reach the bell.

" No, no," cried Paul, "don't move; don't call any one. —Crossley, let me go; don't behave like a madman. Tell me what you mean. All that I know about your daughter you shall hear in two minutes."

"I'll have my daughter, or I'll have your life!" the boatman screamed; and he grasped Paul more fiercely than before. He was strong; but luckily for himself Paul had sinews of steel. He stood quite unshaken; and at last seized the wrists of the boatman and set himself free.

"Crossley," he then said very calmly, " we must have no more of this. Mr. Massie's house is not a boatman's tap-room. If you will talk or listen quietly, you shall soon know all I know; if not, I shall have to remove you from this house at all events. Listen calmly, man, and be like a man, while I tell you all I know about your daughter.

It is not much, and I fear will hardly help you to find her, if she be really gone. I was wrong in not going to you at once and telling it."

Eustace had now quite recovered from his surprise and alarm. He had not the least taint of cowardice in him; but he was a nervous man, unused to violent scenes of any kind, and he really had thought for a moment that a mere maniac stood before him. He laid his hand now gently but firmly on Crossley's arm, and pressed him to speak out plainly and calmly. "For aught I know," added Eustace, "your daughter is now in this house, as usual."

"No, no, Mr. Massie," said the poor boatman, "she is not here; she has not been here these two days. I ask your pardon humbly, I'm sure. You're a good man, sir, and I always said it of you, and I knew your father before you. But you haven't a daughter, sir, and I have, or I had until she was enticed away from me. She was always happy here, and kind the ladies were to her. But, Mr. Massie, he's taken away my daughter; he has her hiding somewhere, and she's going away for him—away from her father and mother."

"This is madness," said Eustace. "Paul, you know nothing of his daughter—Alice, my mother's maid?"

"Will he say he didn't meet her the morning she was going away, just at day-break—there, behind this house? Will he say that to my face?"

"No," said Paul, "surely not. I did meet the girl by accident there. I had scarcely spoken a dozen words to her before. But I do not know where she was going or where she is now; and I had no more to do with her going away than you, Eustace, had."

"Mr. Massie, sir, he knows all about it. She was always coming to my cottage when he was there. They were seen meeting in the shrubbery beyond; they were seen and heard talking there the morning she disappeared. He was the last person that saw her, except one other who came and told me."

"By Heaven, Crossley," said Paul, "you are cruelly mistaken. This is the most extraordinary delusion I ever heard of. I met the girl by the merest accident early in the morning, and she told me she was going away, and begged me not to tell; and, like a fool, I promised to say nothing."

"O!" ejaculated the clergyman slowly and doubtfully. He began to be sorry now that he could not think poor Crossley an entire maniac.

"Beyond that," continued Paul, "I know nothing whatever about the girl—nothing, upon my life. Eustace, you surely don't and can't believe this poor man's mad notion?"

"Not without some very convincing reason," said the clergyman coldly and slowly, "would I believe any man guilty of such a crime—least of all a member of my own family. I am not much used to hearing accusations of this kind made, except—except in a very different class of life. But we must not shrink from the question now. You did, then, meet this girl—this poor servant—and talk to her?"

"Once, and that by chance."

"By chance. And she told you she was going away —from this house and from her parents?"

"She did tell me something of the kind, and begged me, as I had accidentally discovered her intention, not to say that I had seen her."

"And you became a party to her secret and her running away?"

"I did. Perhaps I did not attach sufficient importance to it; and I did not know that I had any right to make use of the knowledge which I had obtained by such a mere accident. Observe, I asked her nothing. What she told me she came up and volunteered, quite unexpectedly. I am very sorry I consented to have any knowledge of the matter."

"So am I," said the clergyman very slowly; "I am deeply grieved."

"Ask him, Mr. Massie, if she told him nothing else," interposed Crossley, who had been listening as eagerly as a party to a cause listens to his counsel cross-examining the principal witness against him.

"She did tell me something else," said Paul promptly. "It was that something else, perhaps, which confused me; but I cannot tell what it was, only that it had nothing to do with her own affairs; it only concerned me."

"Yet you had never conversed with her before?" the clergyman observed inquiringly.

"Never," said Paul—"never, on my honor, on my soul. I had not then, I have not now, the least notion why she spoke to me and told me—what she did."

Here, then, was some mystery. Eustace hated and despised mysteries; he regarded them as necessarily immoral or disgraceful or vulgar. He grew more and more sick of the whole affair.

"The first thing to do," he said at last, "is to ascertain whether the girl has really gone away. She may have changed her mind, and returned. My mother was always so kind to her that I cannot believe Alice would have gone away without consulting her."

"Not if it was for any good," said Crossley. "But it was not for good; it was for evil."

"Let us make some calm inquiry," said Paul. "I will go with Crossley and help him in the search, if he will allow me."

"No," replied the boatman fiercely; "I don't want your help. I know what comes of your help. I thought high of him, I did, Mr. Massie; and I often said—God forgive me!—how friendly he was to the poor, and how unlike you, sir. Yes, I did, because I thought he was honest and true: and this is the end of it."

"But, Crossley, you really are judging my cousin unfairly and harshly," Eustace said. "You have heard his positive word, and against that you have nothing to offer but the merest suspicion. I really feared at first that there was something else to be told. But if he were an utter stranger to me, I could not sanction an accusation founded on such vague guess-work and suspicion."

"Guess-work! What d'ye call guess-work? D'ye call presents guess-work? D'ye call money guess-work? D'ye call diamond rings guess-work?"

"Had she money and rings?"

"Yes, she had money lately—pounds and pounds; and she told me Mrs. Massie gave it to her; and I didn't believe it, and I was coming up to ask, when I found that she was gone. Who gave her that money? Who gave her a diamond ring?"

"Not I, I am sure," said Paul, quite composed now that the story was taking what seemed to him an extravagant and absurd turn. "I pledge you my honor, Crossley, I never gave your daughter anything whatsoever, nor talked with her for five consecutive minutes; and there never was or could be a more monstrous and ridiculous accusation brought against any human being than this against me."

"We had better make some inquiries at once," said Eustace. "My mother can perhaps tell us something which may help us. It is deeply to be regretted that there should have been any secret whatever confided or kept in such a matter. It places us all in a false position that any confidence should have been exchanged between a member of the family and this poor foolish young woman."

Paul reddened. "There was no confidence exchanged," he said fiercely. "You speak as if you half believed this story already, or wished to believe it; you religious and virtuous people are only too anxious to believe anything bad. We, the worldly and wicked, the heretics and the publicans, or whatever else you choose to call us, are not so ready to pass judgment on our neighbors."

"Nay, you do me wrong; pray believe me that you do."

"I know what you think in your secret heart. I wish

I had never come here. I will leave the house this moment."

"Much better," said Eustace coldly, "to remain until this painful matter is all cleared up. I trust you will not think of leaving under circumstances which might only seem to give some color to a charge which I most anxiously hope may prove unfounded."

"Your anxious hope," said Paul, "sounds to me very like an insult."

Eustace shook his head and waved his hands in gentle deprecation. "I do not mean it so. I should be strange indeed to my duty as a clergyman if I were guilty of any such intention."

"Will he give me back my daughter?" interposed Crossley, who was growing rather impatient of the family dialogue; "or tell me where she is? That's all I want to know from him."

"I have already told you I know nothing of your daughter; I tell you so again. I am ashamed to have to repeat it. I swear to you I know nothing of her."

"I don't believe you," cried the boatman. "It's a lie, and you know that you are lying!"

The blood rushed into Paul's dark face, until it became nearly purple. He clenched his hands spasmodically, and every limb quivered, while one foot involuntarily beat the floor. It was a heavy and terrible effort to keep down the full outburst of an impetuous nature's rage. Perhaps Paul had never before tried to control his emotions under so agonizing a temptation. He did control them, although something very like tears—tears of anger and humiliation—sparkled in his eyes.

"Crossley," he said slowly, and with difficulty, "you will regret this some day; you will find out your mistake. Just now you are mad, and I am too nearly so to argue with you."

Eustace had observed the terrible struggle for mastery which had gone on in his cousin's breast. He could not but respect the successful effort at self-control. He went over to Paul and laid his hand kindly upon his shoulder. " You have done well," he said, " to control yourself; you have acted like a Christian. This poor man is under the influence of an excitement which we cannot blame. You have done well to make allowance for his state of mind."

But Paul made no reply; he looked coldly and sternly at his cousin, and left the room without speaking a word.

" Mr. Massie," said Crossley, " he may carry it off well, and you may think I have wronged him. God knows I wish I had. But it's all true, and I have them that can prove it."

" You are an impetuous man, Crossley; and indeed you cannot be expected to reflect much at present. But I must not believe this story until I have some better proof. I must see the people who you say can prove it. Who are they ? "

" It's only one, who can prove that he saw them talking together in the shrubbery the morning the girl left."

" Yes, that my cousin admits; I mean, explains."

" Did he explain it before I charged him with it to his face ? Did he, sir ? "

" Is that all your proof ? "

" I can prove myself that she had money, and that she said Mrs. Massie gave it to her; and perhaps Mrs. Massie will say whether she did or not. I can prove that she had a diamond ring, and perhaps Mrs. Massie will say if she gave her that. I can prove that she told me when I scolded her there was others could take care of her, and keep her in London like a lady; and isn't he going to London? I can prove that he saw her last. What more proof do you want, sir ? I was in the court myself when you were on the bench, time of the murder of Betsy Marlin ; and didn't I hear the lawyer say that he that was last seen with her must account for himself and for her ? Well, your cousin was last seen with my daughter. Let him account for her."

The manner of the old man was more stern and less respectful to Eustace than at first. He thought the clergyman was disposed to take the matter far too easily. He thought—perhaps he was not quite mistaken—that Eustace's manner showed rather more concern for the peace and credit of the Massie family than for the happiness and honor of the humble Crossleys.

"Well," said Eustace, in rather a perplexed and worried tone, "we must look into the matter calmly. I will first make some inquiries: go down to the village, and I will meet you at your house in—let me see—yes, in an hour exactly."

The boatman muttered some words of half-thankfulness, and went away through the open window, as he had entered; Eustace motioned him that way. The less meeting with servants and chances of scandal the better.

Eustace Massie was, in the common acceptation of the phrase, a benevolent man. He had certainly a sincere horror of every species of vice. But the sentiment uppermost in his mind just now was not regret for a ruined girl and a despoiled father; his soul was agonized by the thought that his own family was now mixed up in an odious scandal. He hardly paused to think whether the charge against Paul might or might not be true: it was enough for him that the charge had been made. A member of his own family was to be accused by all the blabbing tongues of an idle village of having decoyed away a boatman's daughter. This abominable scandal was to become a story in the mouths of his own congregation: of the Low-Church party, who denounced his rood-screen and candlesticks as Popish abominations, and who would scarcely fail to attribute any wrong-doing by the rector's most distant relative to his own predilection for the mummeries of superstition. There was a newspaper in Seaborough which kept perpetually vexing him by the publication of letters signed "True Church," "No Popery," "John Knox," etc., etc., coarsely complaining of the ceremonials and adornments of the Rev. Eustace N. Massie's church. What would the vulgar, scurrilous, and malignant print not venture to say upon the new subject? Could he for a moment suppose that it would forbear to use so tempting a chance to the most truly unchristian purpose? O, how bitterly at that trying moment the clergyman reflected upon the Christianity of the world's practice!

Had Mr. Massie never done anything of the kind himself? Had he never labored to prove the necessary and intimate connection between heterodoxy of any kind and vice of every kind? O yes,—this was his cherished theory and pet theme; as indeed it is the cherished theory and theme of most of his class. It could be logically demonstrated. "There cannot be morality without religion—that you must all admit. Religion is my religion—that I can prove to you by chapter and verse, not to speak of the law of the land. Go to, then; if you are not of my religion you must be a wicked person." Had Eustace Massie never improved the occasion of a village scandal by demonstrating that it all began in somebody's visiting the wrong church, or neglecting to attend any church at all? Certainly: he had, in fact, always considered it his duty thus to interpret the ways of Providence; to point the moral of the divine ordinances; to act the part of the Greek chorus as between his immediate neighbors and the Powers above. There was not a mishap anywhere about the village, not a fire, a robbery, the seduction of a girl, a family quarrel, which he did not ascribe in some way to the neglect by somebody of the duties which the Rev. Eustace Massie considered exclusively religious. If you yourself did not neglect your church, then it must have been your father, or your mother, or your husband.

Eustace Massie had not, therefore, any fair ground to complain if his own measure were to be meted out to him. But therefore, of course, he did complain all the more bitterly in his heart by anticipation.

Eustace's dignity and sanctity were unspeakably humiliated by the whole affair. It was low, vulgar, scandalous. His idea of his own spiritual position was of something priestlike, sanctified, elevated above ordinary mortal concerns; something to be screened away in mysticism ; to be shrouded behind a perpetual sanctuary : to guide, instruct, and illumine, but not to be mixed directly up with any of the quarrels, wrong-doings, and vulgarities of every-day life. He had had hard work in bringing his congregation and flock even to a vague understanding of his notions on this subject. For his predecessor in the rectory was comparatively a poor man, with a whole drove of children (the living really was not a fat sinecure, but quite the other thing), and was very glad to dine now and then with a farmer, and even to smoke a pipe ; and *his* predecessor again rode with the hounds, and could sing a good song, and would have thought nothing of chucking a pretty girl under the chin. Coming after these divines, Eustace did not find it easy work to impress his parishioners with a becoming sense of the dignity and sacredness of his office. But he was at length succeeding,—having money to spend, refined and dignified manners, and a really benevolent spirit,—when now behold this shocking interruption and scandal breaking in on his labors! It used to be a hard trial upon his family feeling to know that his cousin Paul was perpetually smoking cigars and chatting familiarly with boatmen on the beach. It had cost him many a pang when on Sundays the congregation were pouring out of the church, and the three or four carriages which dignified the entrance were waiting for their owners, and he thought that those who went along the road that skirted the cliff might perhaps at that very moment observe the rector's first cousin seated on a lump of rock just above high-water mark, with a meerschaum in his mouth and a wideawake on his head. But what was all this compared to the great scandal now breaking out ? If such a man could, under any provocation, have cursed a day, Eustace Massie would have bitterly execrated the evil day which brought his heedless, rough, Bohemian relative to visit orderly and reputable Seaborough.

As he walked vaguely down the lawn, Eustace met Sarah. She was generally his counsel and right arm of support in all difficulties and emergencies. She never (like his mother) became wildly alarmed and faint; she never (like his sister) bewildered him with a torrent of questions. He at once appealed to her for advice.

"I fear," he said, "a very shocking scandal is about to be disclosed. It concerns our house; it was hidden under our very roof. A conversation has been heard, and secret meetings have taken place, between two persons, which may throw light upon something distressing and disgraceful to us all—that is, if what I have heard prove to be true; but I pray Heaven that the suspicion may be wholly unfounded and that we may be spared this calamity and shame." .

"Eustace, you terrify me. For Heaven's sake, tell me what it is!"

"I can hardly do more than hint it to you: it concerns the relationship of two persons—perhaps the fate of one. They are—one of them is my cousin,—I hardly know whether I may still call him by that name,—Paul Massie."

"Then I know who the other is," said Sarah, turning pale as death and trembling all over. "O Eustace, how did you come think of this? I never dreamed that the wildest thought of it could have found its way into any mind but my own. Let me sit down a moment."

She sat on a garden-seat near which they had been standing. Had he been less flustered himself, had he indeed been thinking less of his own share in the difficulties and scandal which he anticipated, he must have been struck by the extraordinary degree of alarm which the woman beside him—she so calm and rational in general—was now displaying.

"Then you have been suspecting something?" he asked.

"I have—something—I don't know what. I did not dare to think. What has happened—what has come to be known?"

"Something which may confirm your very worst suspicions."

"Eustace, it cannot be. You could not speak so calmly if it were. Nay, why have you spoken of it at all?"

"Calmness," said Eustace, rather flattered by the tribute to his self-command, "is part of my duty. I have a duty to do; and I must not allow my feelings, however shocked, to get the better of me."

"Why speak of it now—here—to me?"

"I speak of it to you, Sarah, because there surely ought to be nothing hidden between *us*—"

Between *us!* She almost winced at the words. Had she been hiding nothing?

"And you know there is no one else to whom I could confide it yet. The thing is not yet certain."

"O, thank Heaven!"

"I should like to make some deeper inquiry before speaking to my mother" (Sarah started and shuddered); "and I expect of you, Sarah, some calmness and presence of mind." He was somewhat put out indeed by Sarah's unexpected agitation.

"How has all this arisen?" she asked with strained composure.

"They were overheard talking—so I am assured."

"They?"

"Yes, he—and she."

Sarah shivered.

"Indeed, it is asserted that she talked of it openly—that she confessed it to Crossley."

"O, impossible, Eustace—utterly impossible! This is some wild delusion. There is either falsehood or madness about it. She never could have talked to him thus—talked, good Heaven! to Crossley—to Crossley the boatman?"

"Yes; what other Crossley do we know?"

"Eustace, I can hardly believe that I am awake. I cannot have understood you rightly. What has Crossley to do with this terrible suspicion? why is his name mentioned in connection with it?"

"What has Crossley to do with it?—with the fate of his own daughter?"

"His daughter?"

"Yes, dear; his daughter. We have spoken of no one else, Sarah. There surely is no other unhappy—no, there cannot be."

Sarah's face underwent in a moment such a change from white to red as must have convinced the dullest observer that there was something at work in her breast which the fate of the boatman's daughter had not alone excited. Eustace could not but observe her confusion and alarm. The best of Christian maidens could hardly be thus overmastered by emotion on hearing of a mere serving-woman's suspected sin.

"I am afraid you are not quite well, Sarah," Eustace said slowly and coldly. " I should not have spoken of this to you; but miserable as it is, I scarcely expected that it would have created such an agitation. Had you not better go in?"

She caught his hand and pressed it warmly : " Dear Eustace, do forgive me. I am not very well to-day, and perhaps more easily alarmed than usual. Your manner, too, frightened me a little at first. Perhaps I expected something very dreadful, and—and certain—a death, or something of the kind. I have been in a melancholy and ominous mood all day; only of course you don't heed such nonsense. Now, dear, I am much better. Pray tell me all."

"There is really nothing more to tell," he replied. " It is mere suspicion; perhaps it may turn out to be nothing in the end. I am sure I hope so. Pray go in, Sarah; it grows cold. I am going down to Seaborough. Don't wait dinner; I may not return very soon."

He was moving away.

"But, Eustace, I really know nothing of the matter as yet. You have excited my curiosity to the utmost, and now you will tell me nothing."

"Because, dear, there is nothing to tell. You said that you had had suspicions; we have now merely reason to fear that our suspicions may prove well founded. But we know—at least I know—nothing more as yet. I must see my mother at once."

"You are angry with me, Eustace, and I do not know why. Or you distrust me because I showed some foolish alarm. But do not be angry, dear—you are not used to be."

"I am not angry," said Eustace, in rather melancholy tone; "I surely have no cause to be. Good-by for a little."

He left her; his manner still cold and constrained. He did not pursue his expressed intention of going to confer with his mother, but went slowly down the lawn.

As he walked to the village his face was covered with gloom, and his heart beat with unusual quickness. He could not fail to conclude that some effect wholly unexpected had been produced upon Sarah by the story he had communicated, and he thought he guessed the meaning of her emotion only too well. There was nothing of the romantic about him; he had read few novels, and fewer poems, in his life; but still he knew that there was something in the world which people called love, and which was quite distinct from duty, or principle, or propriety, or order. With a strange and sudden pang he conjectured, as he looked on Sarah's crimsoning cheeks and quivering lips, that this eccentric and unholy influence had taken possession, and in the most inconvenient manner, of her quiet and well-ordered mind. He had always taken it for granted that she loved him, or would love him, quite as much as it is necessary for a clergyman's wife to love her husband. It had never occurred to him for a moment, until that very hour, to entertain the wildest notion of her possibly loving any one else. He never supposed that a lady of her position, and with so responsible a future before her, could be guilty of the impropriety of having excitable and uncontrollable affections. The idea of Sarah's falling in love with anybody would have seemed as extravagant as the notion of her turning Roman Catholic or taking to the stage. Yet he felt bitterly as he walked along that nothing ' but some wandering and reprehensible feeling of the kind could have awakened the agony with which she heard even a hint of the story about Paul and the boatman's daughter. Yes, it must be that she loved him—this good-looking, remarkable, dashing Paul—this eccentric, wild Bohemian —this "rowdy," Eustace perhaps might have said, had he ever known the meaning of the word. He felt miserable as he walked, humiliated and tortured. He felt as if his faith in everything was invaded. Whom could he trust —to whom could he look for sympathy, when even Sarah had turned out so different from all that he had reason to expect? How helpless he felt himself; how pitiable ; how childishly ignorant of the ways of women! He had his own purposes and designs in life—certainly none of them selfish in the word's meaner sense—and he had prepared for some interruptions and obstructions in carrying them out; but never for any inconvenient distractions of this kind. To be vexed and crossed by the women of his own household was a disturbance he should no more have expected than to find one of them supporting a rival church and putting up an opposition preacher. What now to do? How to ascertain whether his suspicions were well founded? If it should prove so, what then? Would a mild remonstrance and lecture settle the matter, or ought it to cause a breaking-off and an entire disturbance of family arrangements? Poor Eustace could not yet sufficiently arrange his ideas to come to any conclusion. He walked along, his heart oppressed by a vague sense of having been somehow terribly deceived, and having all his plans disturbed and confused, and he labored under the unusual sensation as he might under some sudden attack of physical pain, whose pangs he had never before felt, whose presence he could not explain, whose consequences he could not conjecture.

And Sarah—what were her feelings as she went back to the house?

First, then, she had not the least suspicion that Eustace suspected—what he did. She was agitated with the consciousness that she had nearly betrayed some wild secret, which indeed she herself had scarcely ventured to dream of, and which she would not of her own will whisper to any one in the world. She ascribed Eustace's anger merely to his impatience at a feminine manifestation of what must have seemed to him unreasonable alarm. She did not fear that Eustace might suspect any lurking mystery and ask for an explanation. He was not given to questioning and cross-examining. His cold, precise, and orderly temperament had much in it which a partial woman might easily think refined, dignified, and lofty. All the women of the clergyman's household were of accord in thus regarding him.

But it must be owned that Sarah felt somewhat like a guilty person. She had the knowledge that from the man she was about to marry (and he too a clergyman, which with most women is a fact of immense account) she was hiding a secret, and thus entering upon a life of reticence and evasion. Everything bordering upon that secret must hereafter be dreaded, avoided, evaded. Through their whole lives that fact would stand a wall of separation between Eustace and herself. If the secret were never discovered, it could only be preserved from discovery because of the noble confidence of a man too honorable to suspect that his wife hid anything in her bosom which he might not know.

This was bad enough; but was this really all? Was she not vaguely conscious of some other feeling—something of which she could not believe that Eustace would suspect her?

There was a step behind her at that moment. The evening was darkening down heavily and drearily, and the poplars on the lawn looked gaunt and ghastly. It may have been the chilliness of the air which made Sarah shiver; but she certainly was trembling in every limb· She could scarcely get on towards the house, and the step came rapidly behind her. She knew its sound; she had learned already to distinguish it only too well. In a moment a hand lightly touched her shoulder; and although she must have expected to be accosted in some way, yet she started as if punctured by a sharp instrument. It was a strong hand that touched her shoulder, but its touch was gentle and trepid. She did not turn round, but stopped; and a crimson hue dyed her cheeks which had never flushed there at the coming of her intended husband.

Paul stood beside her.

"I am going away to-morrow, Sarah," said the young man, "and perhaps I shall hardly see you again to-night. Good-by."

"But only for awhile," she stammered, trying to smile; "only for awhile, Paul? We shall see you very soon again?"

"Not very soon," he replied slowly and bitterly. "I am going to stay in London for some time, and then perhaps I shall return to Mexico."

"But you will come back to England?"

"Yes; I shall certainly come back some time—most certainly—if I live. Nothing but death shall keep me from coming back, some time."

He paused, seeming unable to proceed.

"England must be your home," Sarah said.

"My home? I wonder where is my home. I have never found one yet. I don't hope to find one here. No matter—I should not talk in this way. Good-by, Sarah."

He took her hand.

"You will hear—Eustace or somebody will tell you—some foolish story about me. You will not believe it, Sarah?"

"Not if it be to your disadvantage, Paul, and if you say it is not true."

"You have heard something of it already then!" he quickly observed, gathering his conviction from the expression of her face. "They were not, long in telling you of it. Don't believe it, Sarah—it's all false—there is not a word of truth in it, and it will all be set right before long; but it would grieve me to think that you believed it even now—you who have been so kind and good to me when others—others on whom I had more claim—"

The hand that held hers now grasped it so heavily that she felt pained, but she did not betray the pain.

"I do not believe it, Paul—I did not and could not believe it—and I don't think any body else will."

"I thought I might rely upon you, Sarah; although I know you for so short a time. I could wish I had never come here, but that I can always remember *you*."

Sarah turned pale. Paul fixed his keen and gleaming eyes inquiringly on her, and she trembled under the look.

"Then shall we not see you to-night again?" she asked —asking anything to distract the conversation, and calm, if possible, the growing excitement which glowed in the countenance of the young man.

"Not to-night—at least I think not," he answered. "Not for some time. I am going down to Seaborough now, and I must not keep you longer in the cold. I have said good-by twice already; but good-by again, and, don't forget me."

He kissed her on the forehead, and was gone in a moment.

What did Sarah do? Probably what any other woman would have done under the circumstances. She went to her bedroom, locked the door, and cried long and bitterly. She was a brave and good girl, but not at all of the strong-minded class; and she had her feelings.

CHAPTER X.

"LEON, WHY DID YOU COME HERE?"

WAS it a dream in which Mrs. Massie, weak and melancholy woman, lay plunged before Eustace returned to consult her? Had she only fallen asleep and had a painful dream and started up in horror, and so awakened? Awakened to find herself lying on the sofa in her darkening room, where the fading flame leaped fitfully in the chimney, and made the dimness look fantastic and ghastly —not cheery and warm? Or had she really been visited by a living being, heard the sound of a human voice, and fainted as she heard it?

She arose from the sofa, walked feebly across the room, and looked shuddering out through the window. It was a grewsome evening of a late spring, dun and cold; the cypresses looking very black, and whistling mournfully in a sad breeze. She drew the curtain hurriedly, and nervously lighted the lamp which stood upon the table, and stirred the fire. The blaze leaped up cheerily enough, and Mrs. Massie knelt upon the hearth-rug and shivered as she held her hands open before the grate. The gradual sense of renewed warmth was encouraging, and the light and heat banished all dreary aspect from the room. She began to be less afraid to question the memories which were growing clearer within her, and so endeavored at last to recall boldly and distinctly all that happened before she lost consciousness.

Well, had she heard during the evening something about Alice's singular disappearance. Lydia had been telling her of it. She had heard something too of the stories which had been founded on it; and which seemed to confirm Halliday's disclosure. This, combined with all the rest, had terribly disturbed her, and she waited impatiently for Eustace to come in and let her know the whole truth of the matter. What if Halliday's story should prove true? What if there should be a quarrel? she dreaded and hated quarrels. What if there should be strange suspicions, followed by stranger disclosures? What if anything should happen to Paul? In any case Paul was about to go away, and perhaps she might never see him again. After how many years—O, how many long weary years!—he had come at last, and they had scarcely ever spoken; and now he was going away, perhaps in anger, perhaps not to return any more! And she had no one to whom she could open her heart—no one in all the world! Cold, dreary, and repulsive the world again opened before her, full of fear and secrecy and mere renunciation. She sat shivering with chill of body and of heart, thinking over all this—and over how much more!—in the sharp spring evening. She looked in the mirror which stood over the chimney-piece, and saw a wan and wasted face, with anxious eyes looking into hers. Her mind went back to days when she was young, beautiful, and hopeful; and the time seemed hundreds of years ago. She saw other scenes than those around her; the glass became to her as a magic mirror, in which there were flickering images and visions and places which had not been seen by her boldily eyes for years, although present so often to her sleeping senses. A pang, as of terror, shot across her breast when one form and face seemed to arise out of all the rest, far more distinctly seen than any—a face browned and dark, with gleaming black eyes.

There must have been a knock at the door while she thus stood and gazed, a knock which she had not heard; for now that she did distinctly hear a tapping, it was rather impatient, as of a person who had tapped in vain before. So she hastily called "Come in!" and turned away from the glass, her mind still haunted by the presence of the face and form she had last seen there.

It was with difficulty she kept back a scream when the opened door showed her, in the fading light, what seemed

6*

the very face and form of her haunted memory ; yes, the very presence, the browned visage, the dark and glittering eyes.

Only, however, the face and form of Paul Massie.

Then it was that, after a few words had been spoken, to a purport of which she was scarcely conscious, she began to feel her strength give way, and her eyes swim and her ears throb with a strange singing sound. She must have fallen, but that strong arms bore her up and laid her gently, even with a sort of tenderness, on the sofa; then came upon her total silence and darkness, and then again gradual awakening, reviving consciousness, and light. But she scarcely knew even yet whether the whole scene had been a feverish fainting dream or a mournful reality. Once before she had felt a doubt almost similar; and that of which she had doubted proved only too real.

What had Paul Massie heard in that short and strange interview ? He had come to bid his aunt good-by—had come with feelings doubtless of no little embarrassment and anxiety. He thought, "If she be a rational woman, and has anything to say to me, she will say it now; and to her at least I can defend myself against the odious, foolish charge pressed upon me." So he was glad, although embarrassed, when opening the door he saw that Mrs. Massie was alone. He entered, doubtful how to begin his farewell; but she sprang towards him with looks of wild alarm.

"O, Leon ! " she exclaimed, "why did you come here ? Go away; for Heaven's sake go away ! You will be killed ! Go away before it is too late."

Paul Massie drew back bewildered. Was he then actually in presence of a maniac ? His look of blank dismay recalled Mrs. Massie to her senses, as a shower of cold water would awaken a dreamer.

"O, Paul ! " she said, "I beg your pardon; I think I must have been dreaming. Pray do not mind me. O, my dear, do not mind me—now that you are going away." And she flung her arms around the neck of the young man, and kissed him many times.

"Do you wish me not to go?" he asked in hesitating tone.

"O no," she said, "you must go—you must go forever. Life could not bear this; I could not bear it." She raised herself from his neck, and her eyes fell upon his hand, which held hers.

"But the ring?" she asked in a low, piercing voice; "the ring! have you it? Did you give it away? Where did you get it? Tell me—tell me."

Then it was that her words became incoherent, and she fainted. Paul Massie held her in his arms, not daring to call for help. As she recovered and looked up at him, she again called him by the name not his, which she had spoken before; then she rallied, and begged of him in a few calm words to leave her, and think nothing of her dreamings; and she kissed him tenderly and sent him away.

———◆◆———

CHAPTER XI.

SO HAB' ICH NUN DIE STADT VERLASSEN.

"So hab' ich nun die Stadt verlassen
Wo ich gelebet lange Zeit;
Ich ziehe rüstig meiner Strassen,
Es gibt mir Neimand das Geleit."

THUS does the Bursch, in one of Uhland's simplest, sweetest ballads (dear old Uhland, last of the gentle Minnesinger race), describe his lonely exodus from the home of youth and of many memories and of one love. Paul Massie knew little of Uhland; and the Bursch songs he had heard and chorussed in Leipzig and Heidelberg were of rougher strain. But he felt some sensation akin to those of the ballad as he left the place to which he had yearned so long to come. He had returned home after a

life of wandering, and now he was an outcast once more.
He was conscious of a queer, choking, sickening sensation
as he stood upon the threshold of the hotel on a beautiful
mild morning, and looked up and down the street—probably he thought for the last time—while he lighted his
cigar and prepared to depart.

He had sent his luggage on before ; it had crossed the
ferry, and been consigned to a slow heavy goods train, to
jolt along steadily for many hours over the hundred miles
or so of road, and to be shunted at stations while express
and ordinary and parliamentary trains went by. Paul was
about to walk to the ferry, the Boots of the hotel insisting
on carrying thither for him the one small portmanteau
which was to accompany him, and which had already
accompanied him over three-quarters of the globe. He
was departing very quietly, without beat of drum, without
leave-taking, or friends at the station, or pledges to return
soon, or any of the accompaniments which commonly
strive to temper the bitterness of a parting. He felt
chilled and miserable. He had been but a short time in
Seaborough ; it seemed indeed only a day or two since he
first walked down the street on which he now gazed; he
had often been longer in places of which he now retained
scarcely any recollection ; he had made friends in other
places, friends whom he valued, and had had to say good-
by to them, and had said it cheerily although sadly. Here
in Seaborough he had no friends, and yet he was leaving
the place with bitter pangs, because it seemed to him as if
in leaving it he left behind the one beautiful illusion of his
life ; because a light which had always shone upon him
before, and seemed to beckon him onwards, suddenly went
out, never to beam again. We all know what it is, after a
dreary and melancholy voyage, in which we have been
sick, cold, harassed, and miserable, to see at last the lights
of the port whither we are bound shining across the water.
It seemed to Paul as if the lights which he had all through
life dreamed of seeing had extinguished just as he came

within their range, and that his voyage must begin over again. It seemed to him as if he were shut out of the world once for all when he turned to leave the town of Seaborough.

He had always longed to find a home ; he had always pictured it as something like a heaven. He had often stood admiring upon the hearths of other men, and seen their happy household fires burn, and wondered whether he should ever have such a home. The young man brought up under the ordinary conditions of existence yearns for independence. Paul was sick of independence, that is, of the independence of the exile and the outcast. Other young men feel, even before any woman has gained possession of their hearts, vague yearnings for another kind of home than the calm and monotonous maternal circle, the yearning for wife and child. But Paul had to begin at the very beginning, and to sigh first for the home of father and mother and sister, which his childhood had never known. It may be that he was not in reality fitted to appreciate domestic life ; and it may be too that for this very reason he had longed after it with the deeper longing. At his age men can usually quit the paternal home with great composure ; most people abandon it readily and even eagerly years before his time of life ; but then they have had it, they have run their ordinary course, and at the appointed hour they go their way. Paul had felt somewhat towards the home which he expected as the childless man longs for a child : he now felt towards the home found and lost as a childless man may feel towards the one child given and taken at the same moment—just offered to life in order to be snatched by death.

He had always been perplexed by the kind of decree which during the lifetime of his uncle had seemed to shut him out from the society of his family. Then when the news of the elder Massié's death came, it seemed a matter of course that he should go home; so he was invited, and he went. He had been entertained by some friends the night before quitting New Orleans, and had talked with extravagant sentiment about going home. Had his entertainers all been Englishmen (at all events had they been Englishmen in England), they would have been much amused by the effusion of their friend; but they were Frenchmen, Germans, Spaniards, and one or two long-exiled Britons like himself, and the sentiment was accepted as favorably as it might have been on the Rhine. He could not help thinking now—now as he stood at the door of the Seaborough hotel—of the wild nonsense he had talked that parting night, and he smiled rather bitterly over the recollection. So he had had his longing, had been raised to the very height of his ambition, had found his home—and now!

He shrugged his shoulders, took two or three strong puffs of his cigar, and walked down the street, past the music-seller's where he had gone with Lydia; past the saddler's; past the Institution where he had been induced to deliver a lecture on something or other dealing with France and Mexico, for which no creature among the audience cared one straw; past the openings in the houses, through which he could see the beach below, and the boats lying on the strand, and the nets drying on the shingle, and the bare-legged children paddling in the surf; past the spot where he used to go down to the water's edge and launch his boat; past the police-station, where already a bill stared at him, offering a reward for any information which could lead to the discovery of Alice Crossley, aged 19, who had disappeared from her father's house; past the cottage of old Crossley himself. - The morning was only awakening as yet, and few faces greeted Paul as he passed along; and, indeed, he feared that of late the town had been saying little good of him, and that there would be scant friendliness in any greeting now tendered to him as he went his way.

"Sie konnten's halten nach Belieben: Von Einer aber thut mir's weh!" So says Uhland's Bursch before mentioned; Paul Massie felt bitterly something like this.   Let all others act towards him, think of him what they would, but there was one now from whom he could not part without a pang.

Yet he was not wholly swallowed up in thoughts about himself.   The disappearance of Alice, and his involuntary knowledge of it, remained always a painful presence in his mind.   He stood for a moment at Crossley's door, then went resolutely up and knocked.   Crossley himself opened the door.

"Crossley," said Paul, "you have not found her?"   It would have been superfluous to mention the girl's name.

"No," replied the boatman, rather sadly than sullenly; "I haven't; but I'm obliged to you for asking, and I'm obliged to you too for the trouble you took in looking for her last night.   I heerd something too that makes me think I did ye wrong when my blood was up, an' I'm sorry for it —an' what more can a man say?   The person that put me agen you has gone—run away, like a liar.   I don't blame you any more, and I believe it was none of your doing; but I do fancy somehow that if she'd never seen your face, she'd be at home with her mother now."

Paul made a hasty gesture, and endeavored to speak. The boatman shook his head, and motioned deprecatingly with one rough withered hand.

"No, no," he said, " you need not say anything. I don't blame you. I know it was none of your doing, but I do wish I'd never seen you."

Paul pitied the man too much to argue idly with a conviction which seemed to him the mere foolishness of grief.

"I don't blame you for what you think," he said, "although I know you are wrong. But I didn't come to talk about myself, only I want to say that I am going to London, and that I will make the strictest search for your daughter.   The first thing I will do when I get there shall be to put those on the search who can seek better than you or I could.   Rest assured that I will never give up until she is found—that I promise you. I'll write to you; and there is an address which will find me if you want to write to me."

· "Thankee," said the boatman. " I used to think that I could reckon on you for a friend, an' I think so now: an' perhaps I never would have believed anything agen you, only for some as put me up to it, and is now gone, not to have to stand to their words—some as you don't suspect maybe, and as I was an old fool to listen to."

"Never mind all that," said Paul hastily. "All will come right yet, I am sure ; and we shall find your daughter. One word, Crossley—I am almost afraid to say it, but if you would really look on me as a friend—and perhaps you may, while we are making this search, have particular want of a little money."

"No," interrupted the boatman, "not a farden. Don't offer it again; I'm sorry you offered it; your brother— your cousin I mean—he offered it too, an' I answered him sharper than I'm answering you."

"Not another word, then ; let us not speak of it any more. You will hear from me in a few days. Keep up your spirits; be sure all will come right : and good-by."

Paul held out his hand; the boatman hesitated, looked Massie full and fixedly in the eyes, and then smote his brawny palm on that which was extended to him. Paul grasped the brown and rugged hand with a gripe yet stronger than its own ; then they parted.

"Damn *me*," said the boatman, looking after Paul, "if he be'ant a fine honest fellow ! I'll take my oath I saw tears in his eyes."

A few moments and Paul sat in the stern of the lumbering ferry-boat. The sunlight fell brightly upon the white walls, the green verandas, and the glittering windows of Seaborough-house. Paul could just see the window of the room which had been his, and the balcony from which he descended the first night of his arrival. The house looked provokingly placid to the disturbed heart of the young

man. All its windows were closed. Apparently no sleep-
less figure kept watch there for him. The quiet beauty of
the whole scene had a painfully unsympathetic aspect.
Nature never did betray the heart that loved her! No,
indeed. While Pygmalion's goddess remained marble, she
greeted him always with the same placid brow and smile
of chill unchanging beauty. Him, under all moods and
passions and sufferings, she greeted thus, as she would have
greeted any body. Nature's beauty is not a little like that
of the marble goddess before her vivification. Nature is,
after all, the real stony-hearted step-mother, who changes
no lineament, veils no ray of her immortal beauty, even
though her poor human step-children writhe in torture
under her cold everlasting smile. To poor Paul Massie's
aching heart the brightness of the sun and the beauty of
the shadows on wave and lawn brought little relief:
indeed he would have gladly welcomed a driving mist, a
tossing sea, a rocky coast, a gale, and a wreck.

He had not much time to think, for the bump of the
ferry-boat on the shore soon scattered meditation. He
leaped to the little quay, a rudely built structure, which
received but rare passengers from Seaborough to the new
railway station. Involuntarily he turned round and looked
back on the Seaborough shore, the cliffs, the straggling
town, the house.

"I have had enough of sentiment," he thought in bitterness. "There is an end to *that* illusion. I have wasted
half a life looking for a home : I have come from the other
end of the world to find it, and now I am going away ; anywhere away from the home—anywhere. I have found
friends who despise me, who are ashamed to own me, and
a woman who must not love me. I must be a lonely, self-
denying outcast, ignorant even of my own identity, that I
may not disturb the happiness and shake the nerves of
those who hate me, and for whom I was a castaway from
my very birth ! Exile, loneliness, and secret shame are to
be my share. One thing at least I will do: if there be any

secret (and there must be) in all this, I will find it out.   I
will know the whole truth, even though I have to hide it
ever after as my own stigma and disgrace."

He flung the end of his burning cigar into the water,
and waved his hand as if he were tossing a half-defiant
farewell to the whole scene ; then he turned away, and in
another moment had reached the railway station.

It was thus that Paul Massie left Seaborough-house;
the house where he had looked for love and found it not ;
where love unlooked for had found him.

———◆———

CHAPTER XII.

MADAME DE LUCA AND HER FRIENDS.

IT was one of Madame de Luca's evenings.   This lady
received her friends of a general character on Tuesdays
and Fridays during a certain part of the season, and her
more intimate friends at all times and seasons convenient
to herself.

Who were the lady's friends ?

A good catechism defines our neighbors as mankind
of every description.   Salome's friends were of the same
class ; but they were perhaps for the most part those whom
an Englishman, whether he meets them near the Alhambra
in Leicester-square or that in Granada, in Simpson's or the
Hotel du Louvre, on the deck of a Chelsea boat or under
the awning of a Rhine steamer, equally and consistently
describes as foreigners.   Salome's friends were mostly foreigners, or English people who willingly take to foreign
ways and society.   Most of her friends had been at one
time or other in difficulties with the constituted authorities
of their native lands.   Many of them were refugees, against
whom sentence of banishment had been pronounced ; some

over whom a sterner edict still hung. Some there were, too, who desired to be thought objects of suspicion to their government, but for whom the said government cared no more than did Sir Richard Mayne himself. All were of decided opinions and free of thought. Most were young; and a few were wealthy. Some were princes and dukes— occasionally even princes and dukes *de facto* as well as *de jure*, having real dominions marked on the map, and living subjects. Many were artists; many were authors; a few were singers; some were English authors, journalists, and critics; some were Englishmen of wealth, who in a general way patronized revolutionary movements abroad,—for of late there has sprung up among the rich Englishmen of the upper middle class a select party who take to patronizing revolutions as they might to patronizing art or high farming. Some were American citizens seeing the world; although these latter did not take very kindly to the revolutionists, for by some utterly inscrutable law, it usually happens that the American citizen abroad delights in nothing but despotism, and is rarely known to encourage any rebellion but rebellion against constitutional government. Nearly all were men of talent, at least almost every one had a distinct, well-marked individuality. Sometimes the individuality was a crotchet, sometimes it became a craze. But there were very few nonentities. Salome despised nonentities, who in their turn, being puzzled by her, rather disliked her.

Such were in general Salome's friends. We know who Salome herself was. Not a foreigner, but an Englishwoman of energy and talent, who had fallen in love with and married (yes, the phrase is deliberate, she married him) a gallant Venetian gentleman, somewhat younger than herself, who loved her dearly, continued to love her still after she had rather cooled about him, transferred to England what property he had—and it was not inconsiderable—in order that she might be secured, and died like a hero in the campaign of 1859 against the Austrians. Every one who knew anything of the matter said that Salome behaved like a heroine during the whole of the campaign. She was at her husband's side soon after he received his death-wound, and her fair plump arms lifted the frail young Venetian's slender form into a quiet corner, where he died in peace. She finally escaped—not easily—out of the hands of the Austrians, and after living awhile in Genoa (until the authorities hinted that perhaps the climate did not quite suit her), and then removing to Paris, she returned to England, declaring that she would never marry again, and had renounced the world. Not many years had passed since her return, and she had not married, but she had certainly not renounced the world; for, although she never penetrated or cared to penetrate into the sacred circles of English fashionable life, although the *Morning Post* did not record her receptions, and her name did not figure in the list of presentations at a drawing-room, yet she played a distinguished part in her own sphere and with her own limited means, and she ruled like a queen every season over crowds of distinguished and brilliant (and some beautiful) persons, in her rooms on the north side of Hyde Park. If she did not go to fashion, *en revanche* fashion, at least in coats and trousers, not uncommonly came to her.

What did Salome look like? She was not very young. Five-and-thirty, perhaps? Ill-natured people gave her even more years. Common regard for facts would hardly allow the abatement of one year of this number. There is the less occasion to apologize or hesitate, seeing that the lady herself never had any scruples on the subject, and indeed often took a sort of pleasure in puzzling people by exaggerating her age. "When a woman like me passes forty," she would say, "she has at least the consolation of being able to choose her own company and her own ways in life." She looked about seven-and-twenty. She had eyes of beautiful lustrous gray; she had thick, not long, hair of rich light-brown; she had a sweet deep voice, which could be thrilling or merely tender, as she pleased to modulate it.

She had fine arms, well-formed hands, the whitest of shoulders, the most shapely of busts. She was a woman indeed who, although not to be called beautiful, might have fascinated most men, and had an especial charm for young men. Her attainments were brilliant: she spoke French and Italian with thoroughly un-English fluency, and with an accent which went as near perfection as British organs of sound could render. Some people said she was superficial. Perhaps she was. Some people said she was not sincere. Perhaps she was not. But she was attractive, brilliant, and generous; she liked amusement, and liked to be flattered; she was fond of remarkable people, and could welcome a poor artist, if he had anything in him, as cordially as if he were the heir to a dukedom. As her acquaintances were more often men than women, when anything evil was said of her she did not always hear of it.

This was one of Madame de Luca's fullest receptions. Her rooms were filled with men and some women, and every now and then the rattling hansom brought some addition to the company—generally somebody who flung away the end of a cigar just as he reached the door. There were French, Italians, Spaniards, Americans, English. Men were there who had played parts in many a great political game, and dared all and staked heavily, and lost, and were now swallowed up in the obscurity of a London life. There were some who had flashed out upon the world in a streak of momentary light, and then, ere a man had time to say, "Behold!" the jaws of darkness did devour them up. Names were announced in that drawing-room which once used to be shouted in *vivats* from the shores of the Bay of Biscay to those of the Adriatic. Statesmen were there, now retired from business, and writing for journals, or maybe teaching languages; soldiers who had gone to the very edge of splendid victory and immortal renown and just failed, and came back to set up military schools in Paris or London. Some were there whose light has since gone peacefully out for ever, and some whose fire has since flashed up again, and signalled nations the way to freedom before the astonished eyes of an admiring world. This gray-bearded man was a hero to the last generation. He will presently die in a lodging in Leicester-square, and there will be three lines of an obituary in the London papers, reminding the world that thirty years ago he did this or that, and he will be forgotten the day after to-morrow. This other had the destinies of a nation in his hand ten years ago, but he let them slip through his fingers, and has gone mooning about the world ever since, imploring of anybody, everybody, to find them out, and pick them up, and give them back to him again. That small, infantile-looking person is one whose impassioned and thrilling eloquence used to set in a flame the hearts of bloused and bearded thousands during that great crisis of the other day, which history now records in a chapter of a few pages. He has genius and heart; he is nothing now; he may be something yet again, as he was before. He who converses with him is the monomaniac of the Revolution, the man of the high, thoughtful, brooding intellect, the earnest conscience, the one solitary purpose; the theorist doomed to everlasting plot and plan and frustration. Behind them is a soldier and a patriot; a man all bravery and gentleness, on whose neck the axe will fall before long, and whose name will be execrated or despised as that of a ferocious villain or a maniac. There is another whom few care about now, but whose praises will be sung by every voice, whose portrait will be worn on every breast before many years. Then there are the men of mere crotchets—this one with his mania about Russia, and that one his craze about Austria, and this other his chimera about universal revolution—and the few who will afterwards apostatize and become respectable men, and fill loyal posts at good salaries; and there are some too who have not troubled themselves about politics at all, but have merely written books, painted pictures, sung or composed operatic songs, explored distant rivers and deserts, dashed off end-

less columns of vivacious nightly criticism, or perhaps
merely dreamed and smoked through life,—thus far intend-
ing to do something, but never quite ascertaining what it
was to be, or making up their minds to set about doing it.
There were some English members of parliament too,—
those who had brought on, or were about to bring on,
motions concerning the Polish, the Hungarian, the Italian,
the Schleswig-Holstein, the Patagonian, the Nova-Zemblan,
the Saharan question.   All these were mixed up very
pleasantly; and the rooms were crowded, brilliant, and
resounding with music and unceasing vivacious talk in
many languages.

Madame de Luca talked to everyone, and almost
always about the subject which especially interested him
or her.   It is not likely that she really understood all the
difficult questions of which she sometimes talked ; but she
certainly seemed as if she did.   Who could be as wise as
Thurlow looked ?   Who could be as sympathetic as Salome
de Luca seemed to be ?   Everyone was at ease in her
presence, and there all were equals.   Of course, to say that
Madame de Luca had no favorites would be to say that
Madame de Luca was no woman —and she was every inch
a woman.

This night, in particular, she appeared as if something
were wanting to her enjoyment; she turned her large
deep eyes often towards the door, and looked away disappointed.   At last she turned determinedly away, and
buried herself in conversation with the author of the newest
sensation drama.

A new-comer entered the room and made his way, exchanging a word with almost everybody as he passed, up
to where the lady of the house was seated.   He was carelessly dressed.   Madame de Luca's only rule with regard
to her evenings was the rigid exclusion of all rule.   You
might come in a shooting-jacket if you liked, or in knicker-
bockers, or in a court dress, if you had been to the Speaker's dinner; or in any sort of costume you pleased.   The

new-comer, then, was not singular in being carelessly dressed, nor in having a dark sallow face, nor in having black eyes and a black moustache. The only peculiarity which for us distinguishes him from the roomful of people is, that we have met him before; for it is Paul Massie.

He stood behind the hostess's chair before she was aware of his presence. She happened to glance at the mirror opposite, around which the wax-lights burned, and she saw his face reflected there. She gave an exclamation of delight, and stood up.

"So you have come at last," she said, holding out her hand. "I really thought you would never come. Sit here and tell me what you have been doing, and why you are so late."

The author of the sensation drama politely gave way, and found companionship somewhere else.

Paul Massie had been some months in London, and had been leading a life of apparent idleness. The means which he possessed were such as might enable an economical bachelor to make a decent appearance in London life, and Paul was determined to be very economic. He soon, however, came within the range of Madame de Luca's influence. She liked him, and told everyone so. Most people indeed were drawn towards him. They liked his frank unaffected manners, his vigorous untrained intelligence, and the unstudied vividness of his conversation. He knew something of every plan and every subject. If he had read little, he had seen a great deal. At Seaborough Paul Massie seemed to pass for a rough Huron, and was only tolerated. Here in London, by some odd process, he came to be thought a man of great natural ability, force of character, and promise. Madame de Luca lost no opportunity of praising him, and predicting great things for him.

"Why don't you have a foreign secretary who knows something?" she asked of a distinguished member of parliament. "Your foreign secretary was never anywhere, and knows nothing. His French, I have heard, is dreadful ; and the Italian attachés make fun of his attempts to say one or two words of their language. You should have Mr. Massie ; he has been everywhere, and knows everything."

There is no manner of acquirement which makes a greater impression than intimate knowledge of foreign countries and fluency in talking half-a-dozen languages. Paul Massie was a most unskilled politician ; and yet politicians talked much to him. Even the member of parliament we have mentioned, although much amused at the idea of thus creating a foreign secretary by a sort of competitive examination in geography and languages, made Paul's acquaintance, pronounced him a remarkable man, and expressed his belief that our friend would get on in the House, if he could only overcome his semi-Yankee accent. To Englishmen everything American is Yankee ; or was, at all events, until the Secession war corrected the error. Thus Paul soon made many acquaintances, and even some friends. He had come to London to find out a secret, and to prepare for a final departure from England. The secret was certainly not yet discovered ; and the departure was now scarcely thought of. What of the economy of living ? Paul's means were not large, and his prospects were hazy. He ought to have been living very prudently, and accordingly he was not.

But the secret unfound was not unremembered. It pressed upon his heart day and night. He liked company all the more because it sometimes banished this ghost ; although when he entered a drawing-room he felt like an impostor. Other thoughts and scruples, too, kept him down. What with anxiety, doubt, and late hours ; what with vexation and with pleasure, he was looking thinner now than when he arrived at Seaborough. Often he asked himself why he stayed in England ; why he desired to penetrate any further the mystery which hung over him ; why he did not go to America, or India, or anywhere, and take up an active life and lose himself in it. But he still kept

7

vaguely on, living a life of idleness and pleasure in London; and now he began rather to like it. The atmosphere of Capua was telling fast upon him.

Did he ever think of Sarah? Many times; but at first he strove to banish the thought. To what avail thinking of her? Doubt, if not shame, seemed to hang about him; and the removal of either from his life might but overwhelm somebody else. In any case, Sarah's fate was fixed. Therefore he strove not to think too much of her at first; and perhaps took to society the more eagerly, that he might forget her. The deeper he plunged into society, the less right he seemed to have to any memory of her whom he had seen too early and too late. Meanwhile London life is pleasant, and Paul has still friends; and Madame de Luca is a fascinating woman, who makes little scruple of conveying her predilections through her eyes. Therefore Paul's unhappiness sometimes seemed not very unlike delight. He certainly was not quite broken-hearted; only at times perplexed in the extreme.

Salome and her guest talked awhile apart. Meanwhile such conversation as this went on through the room:

"Don't believe a word of it," said Mr. Wynter, M.P., in his full jovial voice, which seemed, as you heard it, exactly to suit with his burly person. "I put it to Palmerston myself this way: you support Austria in Venetia and Turkey in the Herzegovina; what's the result? You're playing into the hands of Russia. What's Couza? An agent of Russia. I know the man who pays him his salary."

"What's his name, Wynter?" asked a journalist, who had not the most unlimited faith in the revelations of the honorable member.

"Do you think I mean to tell you? Do I want to see it in print in a leading article to-morrow morning?"

"But, my dear sir, you don't comprehend what Austria is," small Dr. Fleiss, a waif of the Vienna insurrection, urged upon a somewhat sceptical listener, whom he endeavored to hold by his glittering eye. "You do not comprehend dese Hapsburgs. Dey know everyting dat goes on all over de globe. Spies every place; yes, in dis very room. My wort on it."

"My dear Fleiss, if one were to believe all he hears, he might fancy that our friend yonder" (glancing towards a distinguished Hungarian refugee) "is a spy of the Hapsburgs."

"How do you know dat he is not? I do not like him. I have no fait in him. What was his proclamation at Pest? Who wrote it? Whence came it?"

"You see," said Mr. Grove Grant, M. P., a rising man, profound on foreign politics, somewhat pragmatic, and rather dull as a speaker, "I put it in three ways. First, as a question of secession; next, as a question of local and popular right; thirdly, as a question of *haute politique*. Now, on all these grounds, I contend that Denmark has no case. I deny that she has any title whatever to Schleswig. In 1524—"

"Its artistic value may not be very great," observed Mr. Heywood Ford, a young dramatist; "but I do say, that just as an acting piece it deserved better treatment. I know all about the matter. I know that Fanny Trumper had made up her mind from the very first that it shouldn't go. She declared at the first rehearsal that she couldn't see herself in the part, and Bobster is afraid to quarrel with her, so he took it out of the bill. I am satisfied it would have made a run, if it only got fair play."

"No, I can put faith in nothing where France is now," slowly spoke a grave man, with a sweet sad smile. "I love France; but now she is France bewitched—France under a spell. I grant you the abilities of the man of December. The Bonapartes never want for talent. But I cannot believe in those whose vernacular is perjury." He spoke in French, with an Italian accent.

"But he is sincere in his pledge to the principle of nationalities," earnestly urged a tall dashing soldier of fortune, an Italianized Hungarian, half-political intriguer, half-military adventurer. "It is not his fault if England suspects him and thwarts him, and whispers in the ear of Austria. England is the stop-gap—the obstruction. Palmerston rules England, and Lady Palmerston rules *him*."

"Who's coming in for Seaborough, Wynter?" asked a member of parliament of his brother senator.

"Don't know, I'm sure. Somebody with more money than brains, I should think."

"Somebody with more brains than money, *I* should think. Men with money are getting sick of parliament. What does it do for them?"

"Men with brains ought to be getting sick of parliament," struck in a pale, youngish man, with long hair, and an unmistakable aspect of Radical Dissenter about him. "Men with brains and hearts ought to be sick of it. It is empty, frivolous, good-for-nothing—a mere talking club."

"Staines is tired of parliament since they counted him out on the Circassian question," laughed jovial Wynter, who never was counted out, because his parliamentary eloquence never carried him beyond a question to the Foreign Secretary.

"Here is General Lefevre," Salome suddenly said, breaking off the conversation which she had just been carrying on with Paul under four eyes. "I wish you to see him particularly, as he knows Mexico, and is deeply interested in it—and I think in you as well."

General Lefevre was a white-haired old Frenchman, subdued and rather melancholy of voice, but energetic of gesture. He carried perpetually on his mind the wrongs of at least two generations of Frenchmen; and it seemed to have been his perpetual misfortune to have to lend his courage and his considerable talents to some government or people at odds with French rulers. He became a voluntary exile when Charles the Tenth was king; he returned jubilant after the Three Days of July, to retire in disgust before a twelvemouth; he hailed Lamartine and Ledru

Rollin in 1848, and intrigued for Cavaignac soon after, and exulted over the return of the Napoleonic Empire, and plotting immediately against said Empire narrowly escaped Cayenne. He had been in Mexico several times, and in Poland and in Hungary, and always quarrelled with the leaders of a revolution when things looked most prosperous, and so quitted the field in anger. He was a brave, honorable, punctilious French gentleman, much given to snuff-taking and political eccentricities.

Salome captured General Lefevre.

"This is Mr. Massie, general," she said, "and I wish you to know him, if indeed you have not already met him, as you seemed to believe."

"Much honored to be presented to you, Mr. Massie," said the general, who spoke English admirably. "No, I have not had the honor of meeting Mr. Massie before. I have met in Mexico Captain Paul Massie, but it is twenty years since we last met. We were friends very intimate, and I esteemed him much. Indeed we bore arms together. You are perhaps, a relative?"

"It must have been my father," said Paul. "He too was Paul Massie. Unfortunately I do not remember him; he died almost immediately after I was born."

"Ah, then, it is not he. The Captain Massie of whom I speak lives as yet; at least he did live some five or six years ago, for I had news of him, not direct; and I think I should have heard if he had died, unless very lately. Besides, he was not like you—not in the least; he was fair-haired and bright-skinned—indeed a true Englishman; while you, Mr. Massie, pardon—you look not like a son of Albion."

"Strange, though, the coincidence of name," said Paul. "Was it at Vera Cruz you met the Captain Massie of whom you speak, general?"

"At Vera Cruz, yes; but also at the capital, and at Matamoras and Puebla, and many other places. We travelled some time together. He told me he was married; but not of any child."

Salome suddenly struck in and changed the conversation. Not that she felt no interest in it; on the contrary, she had followed every word of it. Gradually other talkers came up, and she drew herself away from Lefevre and Paul. These latter conversed long upon subjects connected with the French campaign in Mexico, and the foundation of the new Empire.

The rooms were beginning to thin, when Salome found an opportunity of exchanging a quiet word with General Lefevre.

"I must exact a pledge from you, general," she said. "No plottings, mind, in which my impressionable young friend is to be engaged. I know your powers of persuasion and your genius for enterprise; and my friend is cast in your own mould. But I don't want him to throw himself away in any enterprises anywhere. *Vive* Maximilian or *à bas* Maximilian, or anything or anybody else you like; but I make it a special request that you will plan no enterprise with Paul Massie."

"Madame, rest assured of me. Your wish should be a law to me, even were I preparing any enterprise. Alas, I am not. My days of enterprise are gone. He is a brave and gallant young man, and I am glad to know him. But that is all."

"I feel much interested, general, in the few words you spoke about his namesake—about the other Paul Massie. You would, perhaps, gratify my curiosity a little—some day when you have time?"

"Any day, my dear madame—any hour you please. Now, if you will—it is not much to tell."

"No, not now, thank you very much. But you will visit me some day—perhaps to-morrow?"

"To-morrow, with my whole heart. It will give me the extremest pleasure to be permitted."

"To-morrow then and many thanks. I shall be at home, and alone, all the afternoon."

She smiled her sweetest smile upon the general, who bowed after a fashion that savored more of the Faubourg St. Germain than of republican manners.

"May I see you to-morrow?" said Paul Massie a few minutes after, as he took leave of his hostess. He spoke in a soft deep tone—not meant for many ears.

"No, not to-morrow," she replied, in tones equally attuned. "To-morrow I must give to business—to a sort of business; and I cannot waste friendly hours by mixing them up with details and dulness. Nay, don't look disappointed—the worst of the loss is mine. Good-night."

"Come with me, Massie," said Wynter. "My cab is at the door. We will call at the House, if you don't mind; and then—"

"House is up, Wynter," observed a legislator, who was lighting a cigar as he stood on the door-step preparing to depart. "It's been up this hour back."

"All the better," said Wynter. "Then we'll go to the club at once."

Paul rather listlessly entered Wynter's cab, and the pair drove away. Wynter talked, and Paul smoked.

It was late when Massie reached his own lodgings, in one of the streets running off Piccadilly. He was weary and rather out of spirits. He had been drinking wine pretty freely all the night: it had flushed his cheeks a little, but sent no excitement to heart or head. In the house where he lodged, people rarely came home early; and there was a common understanding that he who on entering found but one candle on the hall-table, should consider himself as last in, and lock the door accordingly. In the house there lived, besides Paul, two members of parliament for country boroughs, one man about town, one gorgeously-dressed Jewish gentleman, who was interested in races, and the dramatic critic of a morning paper, who wrote original comedies from the French. The members of parliament came home generally as soon as the House got up, the time whereof varied from half-past eight to half-past three. The Jewish gentleman's hours were unknown to anybody. This time Paul Massie was last of all.

He lighted his gas, sat down in an easy chair, and tried to think.

"What is to be the end of all this?" vaguely ran the current of his thoughts. "Am I to waste away here until I become a beggar as well as an outcast? England is likely to prove my destruction. I have lost all happiness, and now excitement gives me no pleasure, scarcely any relief. I am rusting away. I am in debt and difficulty. I am living fast and hard. I am not one step nearer than ever to the discovery of my secret—my grand secret. Curse on the day when a thought of it ever crossed my mind! I might have been happy if I had never come here, and never filled my thoughts with such folly. Home and relatives! This is my home"—and he glanced bitterly round the dull room—"these are the kindly reminders from my relatives!"

There was a little pile of letters lying on the table—"Paul Massie, Esq.," on each of them. "Paul Massie, Esq.," he thought, "ought to have friends enough, if letters received were testimonials of friendship. Here is a pretty crop for one day."

He shuffled the letters through his hands like a pack of cards. The purport of nearly all of them could be read on their envelopes. The wine-merchant, the livery-stable-keeper, the hotel-keeper, the tobacconist, the tailor, the bootmaker, the jeweller,—these and all the rest of the friendly little appeals familiar to the youth of London. It must be owned, however, that Paul Massie in debt to a tailor was something new. But in debt to a jeweller! Who wore the jewels?

Lying on the table, not mixed with the rest, was a pretty pink envelope, addressed in a woman's handwriting. The letter it had contained was now in Paul's pocket. He had received it that morning. It held a dainty little scroll from Salome. It was only a note asking why he had not come last night—would he come to-night, etc., etc. As

Paul's eyes fell upon the little envelope, his face, to use an
Americanism, "kind of" quivered. "She is not a relative,"
he thought, "and therefore she is kind to me. I wonder,
if she knew how near I am to being utterly hard up, would
she cease to trouble herself about me? No, by Heaven"
(it may be that he even swore a deeper oath), "I don't
think she would!"

In truth, Paul Massie seemed almost hopelessly swallowed by Capua. He had fallen at once, when he entered
London, into a kind of life which admirably suited people
who had plenty of money, or people who not having it
could live without extravagance. It suited Wynter, who
had means almost unlimited, and who could not get into
what is called good society, and therefore was in point of
wealth a British Triton among the home and foreign min-
nows with whom he loved to associate. It also suited
General Lefevre, whose source of income lay chiefly in
teaching languages, and occasionally translating for newspapers, and writing articles, and indeed romances, for foreign journals published in London, which paid about four
francs a page for first-class contributions. But it did not
suit Paul Massie, who could live with the poor on next to
nothing, but when mingling with the rich was fain to spend
as they did. He had lived, as we have already heard, in
Bohemia, the genuine and only Bohemia of Mürger and the
Latin Quarter (all gone long since, destroyed by time and
change, and common sense, and the Empire, and Baron
Haussman); and he had dined for twelve sous and been
happy like his neighbors. But then he had no money, and
none of those around him had any; and Mürger once
christened a student "The Capitalist," because he had
been seen to change a louis d'or; and through all that
student's shifts and struggles thenceforward he remained,
as it were, crowned with the splendid title acquired on the
one bright day. But now in London Paul had some money
—just enough to make a thoughtless man try to spend
three times as much; and those with whom he consorted

7*

were not poor, or if they were, had no pride in their poverty. Poverty was not the badge of that Bohemian tribe which Massie found himself almost unconsciously joining in London. Country houses, opera-boxes, and seats in the House of Commons, were the pleasant possessions of some at least of that joyous band. Paul Massie, who had lived in New York and in San Francisco, found that, despite their reputation, these were not the places on earth where money might most easily be spent. Therefore he was sinking into debt and approaching difficulty. But though a generous, thriftless, often thoughtless man, he hated debts, duns, and all the meannesses they bring; and his mind began to be filled with pain and shame as he saw such enemies thickening and darkening round him. He resolved that he would not endure it longer, at least not much longer.

"I will give up this kind of life," he said ; and he smote his hand upon the table. "I will leave London. I will see *her*, and tell her so to-morrow. To-morrow? No. I am not to see her to-morrow. Well, then, the day after to-morrow."

"I will do the deed to-day," means something ; "I will do it to-morrow," may perchance come to something ; but what of the purpose which has to be postponed until the day after to-morrow?

CHAPTER XIII.

MORE OF MADAME DE LUCA'S FRIENDS.

"GENERAL LEFEVRE, madame," said Salome's maid. "Show the general in."

Salome had been sitting alone, writing letters. She sat at a stout substantial writing-desk of heavy walnut; not like the kind of pretty toy on which ladies love to scribble tiny perfumed notes. She was writing rapidly but equably; making the most of her time, but not at all in a hurry: punctuating regularly, underlining nothing; writing, indeed, except for the feminine character, more in the style of a secretary than as a woman usually writes. She sat in a handsome ground-floor room, the one large window of which looked on a garden not much exceeding in size the mainsail of a yacht, but exquisitely kept, glowing with many flowers, and gleaming with the sparkling spray of a tiny fountain. The room was elegantly furnished, but not with any appearance of costliness. It had a few pictures, most of them the gift of the artists themselves; and it had a marble Venus, nearly life-size, emerging from a shell. Over the chimney-piece hung a sword. Its blade was stained in many places; its edge was dinted. It had stricken at Solferino and San Martino. It was the sword of the dead husband—of the Venetian youth who had loved Salome so well, who had lifted her from poverty, endowed her with his heart and his fortune, and died in time to become idealized in her memory. She had not loved him with her whole soul while he lived; but his early death transfigured him in her remembrance, and he became as a hero and a saint.

General Lefevre came in, and was cordially received. We may pass over the introductory portions of the conversation, and come to that which chiefly interested Salome.

"I felt very anxious, my dear general," she said, "to learn from you a little more about the Captain Massie whose name you mentioned last night. I have a deep interest in knowing something about him, and, if possible, his family. Mr. Paul Massie, whom you met last night, is the nephew of a lady with whom I once lived on terms of intimacy; and I believe—I am confident I heard that her husband had a missing relative—a cousin, or something—who was supposed to have gone to Mexico or South America. My impression was rather that South America was the place, but I may have been mistaken. I should be so delighted if I could become the means of discovering his whereabouts."

"My dear madame, all I know is totally at your service. It was twenty years ago I knew Captain Paul Massie. He followed for a time the fortunes of Santa Anna—so did I. He was drawn perhaps to that daring personage, as I was, by certain elective affinities—is not that the phrase?—of character. We stood by Santa Anna until—in 1846, was it not?—the flag of the stars and stripes floated in the capital where now, I shame to say as a Frenchman, the tricolor of France is flying. When things were coming to that, it was *sauve qui peut*. I got back to Europe—my friend said he would lose himself in the American backwoods. I do not know if he then did; but I know he got safe away. Never have I seen him since."

"But his character, his habits, his family, his early life?" Salome was a little impatient of the purely historical part of the narrative, although it was a vigorous condensation, as coming from General Lefevre.

"His character? He was brave, and, to me, friendly and loyal."

"Yes, no doubt; but—"

"I believe he had had a stormy youth. We interchanged no particular confidences, but so much I could learn. We talked not much of our past. Soldiers of fortune and exiles, madame, love not always to revive the past. But I did assuredly understand that he had had a stormy youth, and that he was somewhat of an outcast—not political—no, no; your happy England has not political exiles—but social."

"Did he ever speak of his family?"

"Lightly—scornfully—with cynicism, I think. No doubt he had his faults of youth, and his parents, his family, were strict, and could not make allowance. It is the common story, madame. I preferred no inquiries. Allusions he sometimes made, but particulars he gave not many; or, if he did, I do not remember."

"But you said he told you he was married?"

"Yes; that I can recall quite with certainty. But I think he had left his wife, or she had left him. He spoke of her with bitterness. Indeed, he spoke of the sex with much of scorn and anger. Pardon; I may have wronged a lady whom I had never the honor to see. But I assumed that his marriage had been unfortunate, and perhaps his wife had been—had been—that is, not wise." The old Frenchman gave a Frederick-Lemaitre sort of shrug to his shoulders.

"You never heard him talk of a child—of a son?"

"Assuredly never."

"Yet people who have children from whom they are separated generally do talk of them."

"Truly yes. I doubt not I talked to my friend Massie often then of my brave son who is since dead. He never spoke to me of any child."

"You heard from him not long since, general, I think you said?"

"Of him, rather than from him. At least the person who came to me professed to come spontaneously, and not from him."

"With a request on his behalf?"

"Madame, you divine with your usual rapidity. Yes, a request, which I grieve to say I was not able to concede."

"In short, it was a request for money?"

"It was indeed an application for some small loan, for a passage to Europe. *Parbleu*, it was what your people call coming to the house of the goat to seek for wool; I was looking out anxiously for the means of a passage to Europe myself."

"Was it in Mexico, then, that you received this application?"

"No, in New Orleans."

"And he was then there?"

"Doubtless he was there, although the personage who came to me did not say so."

"The gentleman who came to you was a friend of his?"

"The—yes, the personage who came to me professed to be of his intimate friends."

Salome understood at a glance the meaning of the general's slight embarrassment when he referred to this mysterious messenger. She said quietly,

"In fact, general, the messenger was a woman?"

The general smiled. "The same quickness as ever," he said. "Yes, the emissary was of the fair sex."

"Another request now. Can you find out for me with certainty—with complete, undoubted certainty—whether this man is living now, and where? Or, if he is dead, where he died—and when, and how? Something, in short, distinct and definite about him?"

"I think so. Yes, surely, I may venture to promise that. Unless he had some motive for withdrawing himself from the face of civilization, I can discover something of his fate."

"Within what time?"

"Within, say, six months from this, you shall know all that I can learn."

"Six months!—a long time."

"Pardon, the ocean rolls between; and both Mexico and the States are now alike perturbed."

"It is true, general; but you know what is woman's

impatience. Six months then; we can wait. Yet another question. Do you know the handwriting of this Captain Massie?"

"I did know it; but many years have passed since I saw anything written by his hand; nearly twenty years. If his character of writing had not much changed, I could assuredly recognize it; but much depends—"

"Do you think *that* was written by him?"

Salome had been searching in her desk while the careful Frenchman was endeavoring to define his capacity as an expert in handwriting. She found there a paper carefully made up in a package tied and sealed. The paper which she took out was soiled and creased. She folded it so as to present to the general only a few of its lines, and she looked on with eyes of keen anxiety.

He adjusted carefully his double eye-glass, and inspected the document with precision.

"I feel convinced that that is his handwriting. Its general character—its soul, you comprehend—is exactly that which I remember in the letters of my friend. Something of change there undoubtedly is; but the tone, the character is his."

Salome drew a quick breath. Her eyes lighted with triumph.

"I thank you very much, general. Your information will, I trust, prove most valuable, and I am greatly indebted to you for it." (The general made vivacious gestures of earnest deprecation.) "I need not ask you to regard this conversation of ours and its subject as entirely a secret?"

"Madame, you may rely with absolute confidence that the interest you have been gracious enough to show in the history of my former friend shall never be made the theme of one sole remark."

"Thank you again. It is not indeed for any purpose of my own that I wish the matter to be kept a secret. But for the sake of his family I could wish to discover something of one long lost; and I would not excite hopes which may only prove illusions. And now tell me your latest political news. How are the chances of empire in Mexico?"

After the general had left, there came what might have been for Salome an interval of quiet and repose. She always kept an hour clear—from two to three—for the business of the toilet, she said. But she did not often trouble her waiting-maid during that interval; she generally read or wrote. She was absolutely never under the care of Madame Rachel. Her waiting-woman acknowledged that her mistress had literally no secrets of make-up.

"She bears her years well," said this young person to the cook on one occasion. "She don't need to make-up at all. I do declare—only it would be very improper, of course—she might dress before a whole room full of company, and they couldn't find out a pin's-worth false about her. Look at her hair. Isn't it wonderful? I do assure you she never curls it. I've known her to dress for a ball in ten minutes, and reading letters half the time."

Therefore Madame de Luca did not set about dressing herself after her visitors had gone. She rang her bell, and her waiting-woman came.

"Did the man who has been looking for the place come?"

"Yes, ma'am, he's below now."

"Send him up."

Presently there was introduced into the room, of which Madame de Luca was not the least attractive ornament, a shabbily-dressed, hulking, shambling, not ill-looking young man. He had been in that room before, and if awkward now, was not so because of any embarrassment caused by the richness of any of the objects around him. He looked carelessly at the elegant furniture, the beautiful curtains, the flower-vases, the marble Venus in her shell, and turned his hat round and round. Then he made an awkward sort of shambling bow, and looked not in the least abashed at the lady. There was something unpleasant about his look. Indeed his glance was never very fascinating, but there was something peculiarly disagreeable about it as he looked at Madame de Luca. She was perfectly composed, and did not appear to care in the least about his looks or demeanor.

"This is the man, ma'am," said the maid.

"O, this is the man; very well.—You say you can keep a garden?"

Surely this was only spoken for the benefit of the retiring woman. Anybody less like a lady's gardener could not easily have been seen. The maid was gone.

"I must say," said Madame de Luca, "that if you call yourself a gardener, you ought to try to look more like one. To me you seem more like a ticket-of-leave man."

"It wasn't I," grumbled the man, "who said I was a gardener. It was you—your—" he stammered, uncertain whether he ought not to say "your ladyship," and at the same time, perhaps, reluctant to yield too much to politeness.

"O, it was I who converted you into a gardener, was it? A great mistake on my part. I hadn't looked at you very clearly. Well, now that I look at you again, I am afraid you will never do for the gardener's place. Besides, I have heard that the lady has engaged some one else. No, I can do nothing for you. I think you had better go back to the country."

Her uncouth visitor gasped at this, and looked as if perfectly bewildered.

"Don't you understand me?" she said. "You had really better go back; London is not the place for you."

"Well," he growled, "if this doesn't beat all! What's the humor of this? I don't want to be a gardener, and I never did. I don't want to go back to the country—and —and—"

"And in fact you can't go back," she quietly remarked.

"Maybe I can't," he said, "and maybe there's others that can't go back any more than I. Anyhow, I won't go back."

"Well," replied the lady, with the utmost composure,

"I do not, of course, pretend to regulate your movements; you are quite as free of London as I am. I only advise you. London does not seem to me the place for you. But you can go or stay, as you like; only I do not think it would be well for you to waste your time by coming here any more. You are not fit for the duties you offered to discharge. Good morning."

She put her hand upon the bell-handle.

The man looked, and even murmured, as if a terrible oath would greatly relieve him. But the immovable composure of the lady was too much for him.

"Am I to go this way?" he gruffly asked.

"This way, or any way you please. I do not require to detain you any longer."

"And what's this for? What's the meaning of all this? What am I to be turned away for? Am I to starve? Haven't I done all I said I would?"

"You have done nothing for me that I know of, except to hang about my steps and look like a burglar."

He interjected a sort of grunt—it might be anger, it might be mere deprecation.

"You said you could tell me a grand secret about a gentleman in whom I have some interest—a secret which it would serve him to know—and you can tell me nothing at all."

"Nothing!" he grumbled. "Do you call that nothing, ma'am? Haven't I told you about the letter? Haven't I told you how I came by it? Haven't I told you what I suspected? Haven't I told you that I could find the whole thing out for you, or for him, if he liked?"

"Yes," said Madame de Luca; "but you never told me who gave you all this information. You told me you found it all out yourself. Now I happen to know that you did not. *I* know who told you the whole story; and that you know no more about the matter yourself than I do. Therefore if you can find out nothing better than this, your story is no use to me, or to anybody else. I think the whole tale is some trumped-up invention. Where is the girl who made up all this tale? Where is Alice Crossley?"

"I don't know," he said in sullen tone.

"So I thought."

"I've tried to find her out on my own account, and can't."

"Is there such a person at all? or have you only invented her?"

"Ask *him* if there isn't; ask *him* if he didn't know her? Perhaps he can tell you where she is now."

"If he could, we should hardly want your services. That will do; you can go now. Come back to me this day week. Stay—let me see; this is Wednesday. No; come back here next Tuesday, if you have anything to tell me; and if not, don't trouble yourself to come back any more. Here, you may take that in the meantime, and keep yourself sober if you can."

She took out a tiny purse, and put some money on the table. He took it up, clawing it into a shaking hand, and looking anything but grateful.

Then Madame de Luca moved as if to ring the bell. Apparently recollecting something suddenly, she checked herself, and said, "O, stay; I had almost forgotten. You say you have a ring that was given you by the person who gave you the letter. Where is the ring?"

"The ring, ma'am? Yes; I have the ring, or I had it awhile ago; but—"

"But you have not got it now? I quite expected as much. You talked of having a letter. I ask you for it, and it appears you have not got it. You tell me of a ring; I ask you where that is, and I receive the same answer— you have not got it."

She shrugged her shoulders, and again turned towards the bell.

"But listen, ma'am. I always told you Ally Crossley had the letter. I gave it to her, like a fool as I was, and now I can't find her. I've sought for her high and low—"

"Yes, yes; you said all that before."

"But I have the ring. I'm—I'm blessed if I haven't—"

"Why, you said just now you had not."

"Well, ma'am; but let me explain. I can get it. I can put my hand upon it. I only lent it. I got money on it. You see I was knocking about London without a friend or a home, and I must starve if I didn't get money somehow, so I pawned the ring. Look here, ma'am."

He had been fumbling in his pocket, and he now drew out a dirty scrap of paper, which he unfolded, and which showed some lines of print, with names, dates, and other words written in.

"What is that filthy scrap of paper?" asked the lady, eyeing it with very unfavorable glance.

He scowled. "It's a pawn-ticket, ma'am—a ticket for the ring. If you take that to the place an' pay the money marked down there, they'll hand you the ring."

"O, if I go to the place and pay the money, they'll hand me the ring, will they? It must be a nice place, I should think? Do the police know anything about it?"

Madame s'amuse. Salome was rather enjoying the embarrassment and suppressed anger of her visitor.

"And that's a pawn-ticket, you tell me? What a dirty-looking thing!"

There was a time when Salome, then a little girl prematurely sharpened by the world, knew something of pawn-tickets. Nor would she have shrunk from owning the fact now, but it suited her to treat her present visitor with ostentatious contempt. She was keen-eyed enough to see that his was one of those natures which can only be kept in check by those who show that they despise them. Doubtless, too, she rather enjoyed the little excitement of the encounter.

"Well," she said, after a moment's pause, "this trinket can be of no earthly use to you. You don't, I suppose, intend to wear it? You know best yourself how you came by it; and perhaps you don't want to explain that little matter to the police. You are in need of money. If you sell me this thing, I will give you some money—not much, mind—for it. If not, you can go."

He was only too glad of the offer.

"One word," he said, "is as good as twenty; take it for a fiver. That won't break you; and I won't take no less."

She opened her purse, and took out a bank-note.

"No, no," he said, "not paper; gold's the thing for me."

She went to her desk and took out five sovereigns, which she laid on the table. He clutched them. She allowed the dirty pawn-ticket to remain where he had laid it.

"Now," he growled, "that's done for. The ring's gone. Once I meant not to sell it, but to give it—to her."

Salome looked up at him with, for the first time, a sort of pitying interest.

"To the girl Alice?" she asked.

"Yes, ma'am; I was fond of her, and she made a fool of me, and laughed at me, and cast me off; and now I'm growing to be a devil. But it don't matter; and you don't care about such nonsense."

"Half the world," said she, "plays at cross-purposes in the same way. Why should you expect to escape? But I am sorry for you, in good truth. Forget her, if you can."

"I can't," he said; "but if I only find her, I'll take care that if I don't have her nobody else shall. Thankee, ma'am; I am obliged to you for being civil."

There was a singularly sinister expression about his face as he spoke of Alice. Salome showed no more inclination to amuse herself with him. She rose from her seat to mark decisively that the interview was over. She rang the bell, and her disagreeable visitor was shown out. The lady immediately opened all the windows, and scattered the contents of a scent-bottle over the room.

The visitor shambled down the steps and out into the

street. He shambled in an edgewise sort of fashion along
Connaught-place and past the Marble Arch and the Edge-
ware-road, and down Oxford-street. He was, as has been
already mentioned, a young man—some eight-and-twenty
perhaps—tall, strongly built, not ill-looking, but very unpleasant of aspect, with light eyebrows, and sandy hair
short behind and leaving the broad thick back of his neck
disagreeably displayed. He had rounded shoulders, long
swinging arms, and the often-mentioned shambling gait.
There was an expression which might be either habitual
sullenness or habitual sottishness about his face. He was
not a sailor, he was not a stable-man, he was not a regular
London ticket-of-leave man, he was not a costermonger.
He seemed a blending of some of the external peculiarities
of each and all. He rolled in his gait a little, like a sailor ;
the back of his head suggested ticket-of-leave ; his arms and
shoulders reminded of the stable ; his ankle-jacks were
peculiarly costermongerish. Taken altogether, he was the
sort of man who is generally found lounging about the
door of a gin-palace, a betting-house, or a police-office.
Perhaps it is hardly necessary to say that his name was
James Halliday, and that he came from Seaborough. He
shambled down Oxford-street, glancing into the open bars
of many public-houses as he passed. Whenever he met a
policeman, the guardian of society invariably turned right
round, and looked keenly after our Seaborough friend. In
more than one instance the policeman followed him some
little distance down the street. But while Halliday was
shouldering his way among a little crowd of ladies, or
peeping over somebody's shoulder into a shop-window, the
policeman never troubled himself to watch his movements.
Whatever unflattering suspicions official misconstruction
might attach to this young man from the country, he was
evidently deemed incapable of picking a pocket. Those
brawny, knuckly hands were obviously guiltless of any
fumbling among the silken skirts of the fair sex.

Halliday had in his hand when he left Madame de

Luca's several pieces of gold. He sniffed at them rather contemptuously. Then, with the memory of his sea-side ways on him, he untied the knot of his neckerchief and made them carefully up in it, except for one small gold coin, which he carried sometimes in his hand and sometimes in his mouth, until he reached a public-house. There he changed it ; had a pretty long draught of Scotch whiskey, very mildly diluted with water, and went on. Midway down Oxford-street, he stepped aside and had another draught. Then he began to talk and grumble to himself.

" What the devil good's these few shiners to me ? " was the burden of his complaint. " That —— woman was only making a fool of me. I ought to have got more out of her. If I could only find that girl, I'd make her pay for all this —I'd make her pay. If she's above ground, I'll get hold of her some time ; and then if she doesn't come with me and share with me, and help me to get paid for all this, and keep me comfortable—I'll be hanged for her, that's all."

He did not deliver himself of all these sentiments, as they have been here put forth, in the fashion of a confidential speech addressed to himself. He jerked them out in broken incoherent fragments of sentences,—sometimes between the teeth, which held now a shilling, and now a black short pipe ; he sometimes turned them over with the quid which he chewed, or spat them out on the pavement with the tobacco-juice. He grumbled them out into the whiskey-noggin which he raised to his moist shining lips at many a public-house counter ; he mumbled them as he rolled up the tobacco in the hollow of his hand to make a fresh pipeful ; he edged them out sideways as he lighted his pipe ; he delivered them word by word as he counted over, sixpence by sixpence and penny by penny, the change he received. As he looked over people's shoulders into picture-shops, they heard him disagreeably muttering something, and presently got away from his immediate vicinity. He did not exchange any civilities with the landlords of the many public-houses he visited, nor chaff with fat land-ladies, nor call any of the barmaids " Polly," and attempt to chuck them under the chin. He stopped everywhere, and on any pretext. He looked on at a Punch performance for a few minutes, and seemed highly to relish Punch's treatment of his wife, and to enjoy the subsequent hanging process. He looked into a phrenologist's window, and stared with deep interest, and with a sort of sympathizing approbation, at the plaster heads of various worthies, such as Greenacre, Rush, and Manning. Seeing a group of persons at another shop-front, he elbowed his way in; but observing that the attraction was only a Parian Greek Slave, or Venus, or something of the kind, he turned away with a contemptuous shrug, and grumbled words about it being " only a woman." In this slow and desultory way he got somehow down the whole length of Oxford-street. Arrived at Holborn, he shambled up a street to the right, and then took a turn to the left.. He reached a public-house, whose very panes of glass seemed somehow to suggest incipient burglary and systematic dog-fighting. Evidently he was known here. He entered with a sort of grumbling demi-salutation to the woman behind the counter, and one or two nods and growls to some of a little group who were drinking in the bar. Then he made his way into a kind of a tap-room, flung himself on a seat, stretched out his head and arms over a little table that stood close beside, grunted again, and presently fell fast asleep.

CHAPTER XIV.

THE HEART OF HIS MYSTERY.

THERE is a story told, somewhere or other, of a man who was persecuted by the affection of a goose, which persisted in following him wherever he went, making him ridiculous in the eyes of his friends and occasionally even tripping him up on the public way by its misplaced and awkward demonstrations of regard. The story went on to say that the persecuted man, driven to fury, attempted at last to kill his inconvenient admirer, probably with the view of eating him likewise; but the effort failed; the goose survived, and by renewed and increased exhibitions of love so completely conquered the regard of its idol, that the man at last consented to be followed and adored by the tender-hearted bird to the close of its days. Something of the same kind is told of one who had a seal for his worshipper; and, indeed, La Fontaine has a *nouvelle* which may be said to rest on quite a similar foundation, except that the patient and long misprized worshipper is a woman, and not a goose or a *phoca*. In these stories, however, and the many others which doubtless point the same moral, the ungracious hero is always fully aware of the homage he excites, it is ostentatiously and painfully pressed upon his attention, he cannot possibly evade it, and he must make up his mind either to repulse it as roughly as St. Kevin flings off the young woman in the Irish legend, or accept it graciously and make the best of it. Perhaps it was fortunate for Paul Massie that if he was followed during one passage of his life by an admiration equally full and futile, he at least did not know anything about its source, even when it most impeded and embarrassed him. Certainly he was not wholly without hints that some good-natured personage was kindly watching over his fortunes, and taking an interest in him. Sometimes, on returning to his lodgings at night, he found little anonymous letters awaiting him ; now conveying a warning of some rather undefined danger, now urging him not to neglect the recovery of "his rights," and more than once asking him pertinently if he really knew who he was. At first these missives did actually interest our hero. He was puzzled by them almost as much as Antipholus of Syracuse when he found citizens of Ephesus, whom he had never seen before, lavishing chains of gold and other such gifts upon him. Perhaps for a short time he even fancied that the hints and warnings came from his new friend Salome ; for they were obviously in a woman's hand, and of woman's concoction, as indeed three-fourths of the anonymous letters forwarded through the British Post-office generally are. No man who has the slightest claim whatever to be considered a public character, no man who ever wrote a book, or delivered a speech, or figured in some remarkable case in a court of law, or edited a newspaper, but has received sheaves of such documents. No such person of course is surprised, at least after the first letter or two ; he accepts the fact that there really are persons upon earth who have so active an interest in other people's affairs as to sit down, unsolicited, and even unrecognized, and address to them long letters of commendation, or appeal, or remonstrance, or denunciation, to which, in the nature of things, no answer is expected. But Paul Massie was not before the public in any way, and was only known at all to a very few people, comparatively speaking, in England. It is not wonderful, therefore, if he was a little surprised at first that anybody should take the trouble to write letters to him which bore no signature, and were not to be answered ; and perhaps it was natural enough that, seeing they undoubtedly came from a woman, he should at first associate them with the only woman in London who appeared to take any interest in him. But he very soon gave up the idea. There could be no earthly motive for

Salome's taking such a roundabout and mysterious way of communicating with one whom she was in the habit of meeting face to face several times a week; and when once or twice he ventured upon a slight hint or leading question tending towards the authorship of the letters, he was met by such an expression of obviously genuine unconsciousness that he abandoned the notion altogether, and felt a little ashamed of having even half entertained it.

Paul was not much of a scholar or a literary man; nor had he been in the habit of reading the *London Journal.* The style, therefore, of the letters did not convey to him any suggestion as to the education and class of the writer. Perhaps he thought them at first rather fine than otherwise.

For example, one letter would run thus :

"Time is passing away, and you still take no heed of the advice of one who can serve you, and is resolved that you shall not be wronged. You have rights, and you do not claim them; you have friends, and you do not know them; you have enemies, and you do not avoid them. Find out who you are; you have but to ask, and the truth will all appear. I am near you when you least suppose it. We have met, and you know me not."

Or again:

"Last night we met. You saw me, but knew not. I would have warned you of danger, but could not. Do not seek to know me. When the hour comes, I will appear."

And much more of the same sort, which at last Paul grew to regard with slender interest, seeing that nothing came of it. The one consideration, however, connected with this nonsense, which did really give him any concern was, that it was quite evident somebody was, or believed herself to be, in possession of some knowledge about him and his family which could not be made known without disturbance or scandal of some kind.

Now it has already been shown that Paul was long convinced of the existence of some uncomfortable secret connected with his own relationship to the Seaborough family. But he shrank instinctively from investigating it. His strong manly common sense, untinctured by unhealthy elements of any kind, rejected at once the notion which his anonymous correspondent was evidently trying to force upon him, that some sort of wrong was being done him with regard to the property of his family. The idea of a fraud of any kind being carried on by such people as the Massies, in regard to an inheritance the whole adjustment of which could be ascertained by half an hour's visit to Doctors' Commons, seemed too absurd to be entertained by him. Indeed, the conventionally romantic and worn-out nature of any such mystery and conspiracy would of itself have made Paul reject it as utterly unsuited to real and practical life. But he did not doubt that there was some painful story or other mixed up with the family history in relation to his father and his own early years. Many slight indications and circumstances had of late led him to believe that his father, whom he had since boyhood supposed to be dead, must have been living up to a very recent period at least. That fact alone prepared him to accept the conclusion, that there was something strange and painful to be learned which he should probably one day have to hear, and of which, meantime, he shrank sensitively from anticipating or hastening the disclosure. It may be imagined, therefore, how little he relished the consciousness that somebody, at whose identity he did not guess, and over whose movements he could have no possible control, was claiming a knowledge of the family history which he did not possess, and arrogating a right to the direction of his affairs. It was a vexation all the more because he could not well confide it to any one.

Sometimes these letters were dropped into the box at his door. He found them as he came in at night ; or just as he was about to go out in the evening, the servant brought him one which had that instant been put in. So he had the comfort of knowing that if he had but been going out, or even looking out of the window at the right moment, he might at least have seen the bearer of these confidential appeals and remonstrances. But he never hit upon the appropriate moment. And much to his relief, after a time the letters became fewer and fewer.

Once, in talking with Madame de Luca, the conversation turned in some way upon anonymous letters.

"Do you ever receive such things?" he asked.

"O yes; very often. Generally abusive; sometimes grateful and affectionate. I suppose everybody does, more or less. I cannot imagine who the people are who write them; but there evidently are persons who have feelings which cannot be relieved unless they write an anonymous letter to somebody, announcing that they adore or detest him or her. One of my friends, who is a successful author, tells me he commonly receives whole packages of closely-written manuscript, containing elaborate criticisms of his works."

"But anonymous letters about people's private affairs must be still more unpleasant."

"Have you been receiving any?"

The promptness and directness of the question made Paul smile.

"Yes, I have been a good deal favored of late by the attentions of a correspondent who insists upon knowing more about me than I do about myself. But it does not matter; it's all nonsense and rubbish, and I dare say she will soon get tired."

"She? It is a woman, then. But, indeed, I need hardly have asked such a question. Men do not usually take such an interest in each other as to write letters which can be avoided."

"Yes. I think, indeed I have no doubt, my correspondent is a woman."

So the matter dropped, Paul not caring to carry it any further, and, indeed, having almost unconsciously put the opening question which led it thus far.   Salome showed no further curiosity, but felt a little, nevertheless.

The day when James Halliday visited her was not long after this short conversation.   When her visitor had departed, and while he was yet shuffling and shambling his way down Oxford-street, Salome went out of the room into a little corridor, and stopping at the foot of a staircase, called "Alice."

She called twice, not very loudly perhaps, and got no answer.   Then she went up the stairs, opened a door on the next flight, and looked into a pretty little room.   A girl was there, seated at a table, bent over it and writing. She started when Salome entered, and seemed as if about to huddle away what she had been doing.   Salome's keen gray eyes beamed brightly, and an irrepressible smile— half pitying, wholly good-humored—rippled over her face.

"I don't want to disturb you, Alice.   I see you have been writing.   To your father and mother, I hope?"

"Well, no, ma'am, not exactly; not to-day, that is. But I mean to write to them at once."

"Yes, we must not leave them in any doubt about you. Of course my letter would satisfy them that you were well and safe; but they will like to hear from yourself, and they will not be angry with you any more.   But I wanted to tell you now that I have just seen your old friend, James Haliday."

Alice started in genuine fear, and grew quite white.

"Why, you foolish girl, you are quite afraid of that man ! Why do you fear him?   What claim has he upon you?"

"None indeed; none at all.   But I am so much afraid of him.   He is very desperate and cruel, and he thinks I have not acted fairly by him ; and indeed, indeed, madame, I know he will do some harm to me, or to somebody; I know he will.   I have dreamed of it, and I have had it foreshown to me when awake, and I know it will happen some time."

"He cannot do any harm to you, Alice, as long as you

remain here; and I hope the somebody who you think is in danger can take care of himself. But although I don't think Halliday quite so terrible a person as you do, yet I do think that while he remains in London you had better not go out much, unless with somebody. He spoke of you harshly just now. You need not go out alone, Alice; especially at night. If you want to have letters posted, they can be sent with mine. That is the better way, is it not ?"

Alice grew red and hot. An eye less bright than Salome's could have read her embarrassment as if written in the largest print.

"That letter you have been writing now, is it for the post ? I shall be sending some letters just now, and it can go with them."

"No, ma'am, thank you very much ; it's not for the post ; in fact it's not exactly a letter."

Alice was uncomfortable, and Salome did not want to increase her discomfort. So she changed the subject at once.

"I don't well know what we had better do with your friend Halliday. I don't want quite to quarrel with him— just yet, at least. Indeed, I cannot help pitying the unfortunate creature."

Alice tossed her head slightly and slightingly with regard to Halliday, as if to deprecate the idea of a lady's pity being wasted on so good-for-nothing an object. Alice had quite forgotten, or wanted quite to forget, the time when she condescended to sip his rum and water. *Cet âge est sans pitié*—in women at least. To Alice at present her quondam lover was simply detestable and dreadful.

"Yes; I pity him rather," continued Salome, who had no fear of his ever paying attention to her, and therefore could afford to be compassionate and magnanimous. "I wish anything could be done for him—that he could be got to keep at some decent and honest employment; but I suppose that's past praying for."

"O yes, madame; there's nothing he could do or would do. For years back he has not done a stroke of honest work, or work of any kind, in fact. I wish he would go to America, or New South Wales, or the gold-diggings, or somewhere of that kind. Perhaps he would, if somebody would pay his passage."

"I would pay his passage readily enough to America, at all events, for the sake of getting rid of him."

"It would be money well laid out, ma'am. Depend upon it, Jem Halliday will do some harm if he isn't got out of the way before long."

"Well, Alice, I am not so much afraid of him as you are. I don't know that his wolf-like anger and hatred of the whole human race does not rather please me. At all events, it interests me. While he was talking to me to-day, I thought several times he was exactly like a wolf in expression. Do you know what a wehr-wolf is, Alice?"

"O yes, ma'am." Alice brightened up with the delight of displaying her accomplishments. "I read all about it in a story. It's a man who has the power of transforming himself into a wolf, and then rushing wild about the forest, and tearing people to pieces, and drinking their blood. It's a dreadful story."

"Well, I thought your friend Halliday looked just one of the sort of men who might have put the notion of a wehr-wolf into people's heads; but I don't know that I liked him much the less for it. Society does somehow seem to make a set against some persons, and hunt them out into the forest; and some of the hunted people become sheep or hares, and some become wolves or wehr-wolves. I like the wolves best."

"Halliday is one of the wolves, indeed. I do so wish he were away, far out of this—somewhere from which he never could return."

"I will think it over, Alice, and see what can be done. If he is willing to go to America, there will probably be no difficulty. When I have made up my mind on the matter, I will send for him."

" Send for him !—here, ma'am ? "

" Yes, here ; why not ? I am not afraid."

" No, ma'am—madame. I wish you were a little more so, for he is dangerous."

" In any case, Alice, I don't see how the danger threatens me ; and it cannot threaten *you*, if you simply take a little care, and don't go out alone for the present, especially at night ; with letters, for instance."

These last words were spoken with the slightest possible emphasis. Still there was emphasis enough to make Alice color and tremble, and bend over what she had been writing, as if she must at any risk guard it against being looked at. Not otherwise, perhaps, looked and felt Diana's nymph—what was her name?—when sternly ordered to bathe under the keen eyes of her suspicious mistress, and only too conscious of the revelation which obedience must make, and disobedience could not avert. But Alice's secret was not quite so serious, and Alice's mistress was not quite so stern.

Salome pressed the matter no further. She knew all she wanted to know.

" Little fool ! " so, as she returned to her own room, ran the current of her criticism,—" little fool and little traitress ! All this she would do and has done without my knowledge, and, perhaps she flatters herself in her heart, to my disadvantage. These miserable poor girls have not a particle of gratitude about them ; at least, where women are concerned. Poor little creature ! I dare say she would go near to laying down her life for me, too ; but where this nonsensical notion of hers is concerned she would sacrifice me, or deceive me, or betray me, if it were in her power, without a grain of compunction. I wonder if, under the same circumstances, I should be found ready to do the same. Perhaps so. Little unfortunate ! I don't like her

8*

any the less for her childish self-conceit and her folly.
Heaven help us all ! We are all fools alike."

Nothing amused and delighted Salome more than to
observe and moralize over the weaknesses and idiosyncrasies of her own sex. She criticised them and was
amused by them, even in herself. She had a fine contempt, pity, and affection for women, or perhaps rather
for womanhood. She scourged it with her tongue ; and
always, where questions arose between it and its idol, worshipper, and immemorial enemy, man, Salome pronounced
dead against the offender or complainant in petticoats.
But her heart was, nevertheless, all full of pity, and yearned
towards her own sex ; and where women could be helped
and served by her, she never failed to help and serve
them. So she scolded at poor little Alice in her mind, and
pitied her in her heart ; saw her weaknesses and even her
diminutive treacheries, and, scorning them, felt compassion for the harmless traitress.

Indeed, Alice deserved some pity. Her life was a miserable, scared, foolish, ambitious, self-conceited, unself-
reliant sort of existence. She was in painful terror of her
discarded lover, to whom she was conscious of not having
acted very honestly. She was occasionally tormented by
remorse for the equivocal part she had played towards
the Massie family, who had been so good to her. She
dreaded to see her own family, whose simple honest truthfulness and scorn of deceit always humbled and accused
her. She was now beginning to discover that her conduct,
even towards her latest benefactress, was far from irre-
proachable. And all this for what ? For an object which
began to seem more and more utterly hopeless day after
day—an object which she would now scarcely have had
the courage to acknowledge, even to herself.

Salome's parting words filled her with fear. She knew
that something had been discovered, or was in the way to
being discovered, which might compromise her in the eyes
of one who had so generously befriended her ; and plung-

ing, like all small-minded and feeble people, at the merely material consequences of the false step at once, she forthwith pictured herself as turned from Salome's house, and wandering, hungry and homeless, in the London streets, with Halliday, vengeful and murderous, lying in wait for her at some dark corner. So Alice found relief in tears and in bitter regrets that she had ever left Seaborough.

Meanwhile Salome congratulated herself that she had probably put a stop to Alice's letter-writing, for a time at least.

Several days after, when talking with Paul Massie "under four eyes" and yet in a crowd, she suddenly reverted to the subject which they had passingly talked of before.

"I suppose you don't receive any more anonymous letters just now?" she said.

"No," he answered, a little surprised at the correctness of her conjecture; "I have not had any these several days. But how did you guess that they had ceased to come?"

"Nay, you really don't expect me to tell you how I come to know things? Did you notice what Lord Palmerston said the other night, when he was asked where he got some piece of information or other? He said, 'If I told where I got my information, I should very soon have no information at all.' Take that as my answer too."

"But was it information, or was it only a guess? I am really anxious to know that much."

"It was not exactly information, and yet it was not only a guess."

"Then you do know something about the matter?"

"Well, I have divined something, but it is not to be told; and if I did tell it, it would only spoil whatever of romantic interest may be in the affair. So ask me no more. Be sure *I* did not write the letters, and had nothing to do with them. I don't deal in the anonymous."

So Paul had to be contented; and indeed the subject was one from which he was perhaps only too willing to escape on any conditions.

Salome thought a good deal over the advantages of getting finally rid of James Halliday by sending him off to America, and came to the conclusion that nothing better could be done with him. But Halliday did not come in her way for many days, and she had lost any clue to his lair. In fact, he had money, and he was busily engaged in spending it after his own fashion ; and while that occupation lasted there was not much chance about his troubling himself with anything else.

Salome, who really did feel towards him the odd sort of half-interest she had described, was bent on finding out some honest way of living for him, which should be open to him the moment he reached the other shore of the Atlantic, and which should give him a chance of redemption. Had she seen him within a few days after her conversation with Alice, this might even then have been done. He might have accepted her offer; he might even have been touched by her generosity ; he might—who shall say ? —have been conducted by her hand to a path of honest and creditable industry. But Halliday did not suspect her of any kindly or charitable feeling towards him. It was not his way to suppose that anybody entertained such sentiments towards even a neighbor ; and he had too long had practical evidence that most people regarded him as a mere nuisance to expect compassion or toleration from a stranger. He certainly did not mean to let Madame de Luca off without some time or other exacting more money from her ; but just for the present he had enough, and was not inclined to consider the future.

The London season, meanwhile, was touching to its highest noon. Soon the sun of fashion would begin to descend towards the verge of the horizon ; the roses of the season, having put forth their fullest leaves, would begin to wither. Rotten-row was crowded every day; the rival opera-houses were straining their utmost to bring matters to a triumphant close ; the flowers in the Temple-gardens were in the full glory of their bloom ; the debates in the House of Commons were beginning to languish and drag, the business of the Budget having been finally cleared off; and political friends and even political enemies were arranging for pleasanter meetings at each other's country-seats and shooting-boxes during the recess. Paul Massie had had several invitations for the autumn,—to shoot in Scotland, to fish in Norway, to cruise in the Mediterranean or round the Devon coast; to chase the wild-boar in continental forests. He had become very popular among many sets; his name was put up for this and that club; meanwhile he was a frequently-introduced visitor at many clubs. Nor were the invitations he received at all confined to autumnal shootings or pleasure-makings. He might, if he liked, have become a member of secret conspiracies directed against almost every throne in Europe, and against the one bran-new throne in America which was offensive to democracy. By Salome's advice, however, he kept from anything stronger than a platonic connection with democratic conspiracy. General Lefevre, too, born conspirator as he was, obeyed implicitly the injunctions which his patroness had given him, and did his best to keep Paul safe. So our hero's coöperation with the cause of continental revolution was confined principally to visiting the lobby of the House of Commons along with a deputation representing this or that oppressed people or outraged nationality, and cramming some one of the half-dozen or so of members who are always ready to raise a debate on such questions.

Naturally Paul saw a good many Mexican exiles, and made their cause his own, and pushed them and pleaded for them with all his energy and ability. At this time the French government had it all its own way in Mexico, and was banishing suspected Juarists with full-handed vigor. They, the suspected Juarists, were literally streaming out of the country, most to find refuge in the United States, but not an inconsiderable number to England. Men who had lived and intrigued there for thirty years unharmed, who had taken part one way or the other in every revolution and revolutionary effort since the first appearance of Santa Anna, and who had yet contrived to remain in the country through all changes and convulsions, were now being ferreted out by the eagle eye of Marshal Forey or General Bazaine, and hunted out of Mexico, to intrigue against the new government with infinitely more effect abroad. An enemy perfectly harmless in the next street to Maximilian's palace became dangerous the moment he landed in Havana or in London, and a most formidable foe if he established himself in New York.

Paul Massie saw and mingled with all, or nearly all, of the exiles who found their way to London. Some of them had known him personally in Mexico; some of them remembered his father's name; to not a few his purse, scantily furnished as it was, he freely opened.

Lefevre of course did not neglect, while talking with each new arrival from the distracted land of the Montezumas, to make inquiry into the subject which Madame de Luca had intrusted to his confidence. For the most part the inquiries were fruitless. Paul Massie the elder had disappeared from Mexico for many a year, and people there did not usually concern themselves much to follow the fortunes of a comrade who had vanished from their midst. But an incident did occur which gave General Lefevre some food for perplexing cogitation.

He found an old friend and companion-in-arms among the refugees; a Spaniard who had sided with the cause of Mexican independence; a man who had seen many vicissitudes, and dared much, and lost and suffered much too, and upon whose character and demeanor a deep, calm, melancholy gravity had been stamped and burnt by fate. To this man Lefevre talked, at the earliest opportunity, of Paul Massie. They spoke in French; they were conversing in one of the hotels near Leicester-square, then a sort of head-quarters for Mexicans at odds with fortune and the government of France.

"You have not seen Massie yet?" Lefevre began.

"Massie? No. What is he, that Massie?"

"Pául Massie. He fought under Zaragoza, and, I believe, well. I thought you had perhaps known him *là-bas*." And Lefevre pointed over his shoulder in the direction of the Mexican Republic.

"No. You do not surely mean Paul Massie the Englishman of Santa Anna's day? They told me he was dead."

"Not him, but his son."

"Indeed! No, I have not met him."

"But you will be glad to meet him. Is it not so?"

"No, not glad."·

"What have you against him?"

"Nothing, surely nothing. He is of your friends, my old comrade—that is enough to speak him an honorable and brave gentleman. But his name is not of agreeable sound to me. I knew his father, and I have a painful memory attached to him."

"Is it a secret?"

"But, no—not at all. He killed one of my closest friends."

"Massie killed him?—in a duel?"

"Yes."

"But duels, you know, we all fought in those days. *Mon Dieu!* you were sharp with the sword yourself in those times, *mon vieux*."

"It is true: and I believe Massie fought the poor youth—he was very young, and I fear heedless—quite fairly. But Massie forced the fight on him: and it was done alone, at night, in the darkness."

"No witnesses?"

"Only the stars and the trees—and *le bon Dieu*."

"Then how do you know that it was Massie's act?"

"My poor young friend was found dead in the woods near Massie's home. For a time it was to me a mystery. I thought but of clericals or brigands. But Massie came to me himself—himself, do you understand?—and told me it was his deed; and told me he forced my friend to fight; that he was resolved to kill him, and did kill him."

"Did he tell you the cause of the quarrel?"

"No; he declared that nothing on earth should induce him. I demanded to avenge my friend then and there. He refused; he vowed by his word of honor that his provocation was such as must justify him even to me did I know it. I refused to listen; I forced him to fight. He was a marvel with the sword, and he disarmed me, and then flung away his own weapon. It is but just to say that he behaved like a brave man. But I could not endure to see him any more, and we never met again. Therefore I do not wish to see his son."

" And you never heard what the cause of quarrel was?"

"No; I may have suspected something, but it was only guesswork. My friend was young, handsome, loving, reckless; reckless of himself, and perhaps of others. Massie was wild and reckless too; fiercer and sterner nature, scarcely then emerging from the storms of a very stormy youth. I heard that after the tragedy Massie left his home, and never returned there."

A friendly hand was here extended to Lefevre, who looked up, seemed a little confused, but pressed the hand warmly, and the new-comer passed on to another part of the room. Lefevre's companion had not looked up. A moment's silence followed; then Lefevre spoke.

"I am sorry, after what you have said, to keep up painful memories; but that is Paul Massie the younger who has just entered the room."

" Where is he?"

"There; in that corner." Lefevre motioned to the place.

His friend turned his eyes thither, and something almost like a flush passed over his sallow face. He gazed long in silence, like one bewildered. At last he said,

" Are you sure you are not being imposed upon? Are you sure this is not some strange mistake or delusion or cheat? Does that young man call himself Paul Massie's son?"

" Assuredly he does."

" And you are convinced he is not an impostor ? "

" *Mon Dieu*, if I am convinced ! Without doubt I am. Madame de Luca knows him ; M. Wynter, deputy of parliament, knows him. He has lived but now in the house of his cousin, who is a man of fortune and a divine of the Church. And for me, I have seen letters from poor General Zaragoza to him ; and I know that he was brought to Paris from Puebla a prisoner, and released by the exertions of his family. My own identity is not to me an affair of more absolute and positive assurance."

" Then a veil is lifted from my eyes and I know something of the past, and I blame no longer the elder Paul Massie. Pass for the rest : I was mistaken ; I was confused ; my question was a foolish one. Let us speak of it no more."

Lefevre did not press the subject, nor did he manifest any curiosity. Whatever he may have felt, however he may have wondered at his friend's words and demeanor, or mentally racked himself afterwards to put a meaning to them, he asked no question and betrayed no emotion. Nor when his friend, having apparently abandoned his original determination, expressed a wish to speak to Paul Massie, and did converse a few minutes with him, eyeing him keenly and sadly the while, did Lefevre make any remarks. The old Frenchman had been intrusted with so many secrets in his lifetime, that he had come to regard social life as all made up of secrets ; and he had in general little curiosity to penetrate into any recesses where he was not invited or permitted to enter. Besides, in this instance he had a deliberate reason for desiring to be told nothing. His commission from Salome was to ascertain something of the fate of the elder Massie ; and on that point his present companion could in no way assist him. Confidence on other chapters of the Massie family history might place him in the dilemma of having either to conceal from Salome or to divulge to her unpleasant news. He preferred to avoid the alternative ; he shrugged his shoulders, and asked no questions.

Lefevre's friend did not long remain in England, where the chances of Mexican revolution and counter-revolution found little help, or even encouragement. He went to New York, and worked not ineffectually the long arm of the lever there which was meant to hoist Emperor Maximilian from his throne. Before he left, he had one or two interviews with Paul Massie, who was not a little impressed, and indeed puzzled, by the strange and sad, but evidently deep and genuine, interest which one of whom he knew so little appeared to take in him.

" You knew my father ? " Paul said to him the last day they met.

The other seemed disturbed by the question, and a few embarrassed seconds passed before he could reply calmly.

" Yes, I knew him—long ago, very long ago." And he instantly spoke of something else.

" Strange ! " thought Massie; " my father's name imposes silence on all who knew him. There is something painful which I shall yet have to learn. I ought to know it ; I ought to insist on hearing the full truth from those who could tell it to me; but I am a coward just now, and I shrink from the discovery."

CHAPTER XV.

SALOME ADAMS.

THAT was rather a heavy day when (some years before the opening of this) Salome Adams left Seaborough-house never to cross its threshold again. The passionate friendship which had been formed in Paris, and under the influence of which Lydia Massie found life insupportable without her dear, darling Salome, and Mrs. Massie hoped to find a new and firm arm to lean on and a new head to council—all that dream, obeying which Salome had come

from the Faubourg St. Germain to the English seacoast
village, had faded drearily away.

Salome was out upon the world again—a world which
it soothed her to regard as peculiarly unsuited to her, and
incapable of comprehending her. There had been, perhaps,
no actual quarrel between her and her patrons; but her
stay in the house had simply become unbearable to all
parties, herself included, and she went away voluntarily, so
far as words go, but feeling exactly as if she had been
driven out.

Ladies, especially when they have vowed eternal friendship, soon grow tired of each other; and perhaps in no
case could the friendship of Lydia have long retained its
early warmth for her darling Salome. But there was
something else operating to produce the estrangement.
Salome had a fatal facility in the attracting of all members
of the male sex, from old gentlemen to small boys; and
she exercised her powers with a boldness and perseverance
which might have been innocent unconsciousness, if you
chose to regard it in one light, or unscrupulous audacity,
if you thought fit to look at it in another. Mrs. Massie
took the latter course; her son took the former. What
was worse still, Mr. Massie senior was of his son's way of
thinking, and blamed his wife and openly petted Salome,
who allowed herself to be petted very complacently.
Who was in the wrong? Perhaps everybody; perhaps
nobody. Salome Adams was at this time only a thoughtless, goodnatured, well-meaning, sentimental young woman, conscious of her powers of fascination, and a little
unscrupulous but not in the least evil-minded in her use of
them. She might have acted much more prudently; and
she was not even at this time, be it observed, *very* young;
but then let it likewise be remarked that her mother was a
Frenchwoman and her father an Irishman, and both had
left poor Salome at a very early age to teach her way
through *pensions* and existence. It pleased Salome to
regard her dead father as a sort of Irish brigade hero—a

Thomond or a Beau Dillon—and her mother as a saint. But the Irish gentleman was only exiled by the civil laws of the Saxon—he preferring not to pay any debts ; and he died a victim rather to fast living than to foreign rule. The mother was a weak and harmless little woman, who married under age, and in spite of the laws of her country ; was nevertheless forgiven, and soon spent all her *dot* upon the husband she adored. He was very fond of her, when he had time, and was not engaged in training horses, playing billiards, writing for French sporting journals (which had just begun to exist), or drinking cognac.

Salome wept over her parents' memory annually ; and while near the spot always took care on the proper days to lay a fresh *immortelle* upon their grave. She cherished in her bosom a deep conviction that their fate much resembled that of Abelard and Heloise, whose tomb she loved to gaze upon.

She was, then, thrown upon life too young. Her sole relative was a priest of a Paris church, who was of Irish extraction, and of kindred with her father, and who kindly procured her engagements to teach and be taught at *pensions* kept for the instruction of English *demoiselles*. It was thus that she met the Massie girls and their mother, that she vowed an eternal friendship with Lydia (much younger than herself), and was formally invited by Mrs. Massie to make Seaborough her home.

In bitter spirit, then, did she leave Seaborough. The servants were sorry for her going: she was always genial and friendly to them, and gave little trouble. Many of the village people were deeply grieved to lose her. Dan Crossley and his wife were among her devoted friends; and Alice, then recently installed as Mrs. Massie's maid, shed plenteous tears. Sarah Massie sympathized with Salome for many reasons ; they were both orphans, and in some sort dependents. But there was little of congeniality in their natures, and Sarah, of course, was much the younger.

Salome went away regarding Mrs. Massie as her especial enemy.

Her life was hard enough for some time, but she was never without lovers. The best of them in every sense was the young Venetian exile (his father was killed in 1848, a devoted follower of Daniel Manin), and him she married. In company of him and of his friends she unlearned quickly enough the politics and the ways of the Faubourg St. Germain, and was drawn under the shadow of the Palais Royal. She began to develop a fine genius for political intrigue, and her receptions in Paris were always full of interest for the Prefect of Police. She flung her old life wholly behind her and became luxurious, brilliant, and distinguished all at once. The poor little grub had changed into a gaudy butterfly. The 1st of January, 1859, came, and brought with it the imperial trumpet-call which aroused the nations. Our Salome too went to the wars, and rendered gallant assistance to the sick and wounded. Among the latter was her generous husband, and he died, as has already been mentioned, in her arms.

Then Salome thought for awhile that the gates of the tomb had closed over her and severed her from the living. She thought to pass her life away a lone watcher by her husband's grave. But she was still young and full of fiery energy, and, although she did not then know it, of deep unsatisfied love. So she rose from her prostration by the grave, and went back to the living. She was soon absorbed in political intrigue again. Such occupation seemed a sort of duty—a legacy left by her husband. She had no children.

After 1859 came the imperial desire for peace, and the wish to conciliate established powers. Paris became an inconvenient place of residence for persons occupied like Salome ; and so the widow transferred herself to London.

In the whirl and brilliant excitement of her married life, and in the pain of her widowhood, she had nearly forgotten the Massies. While she was a poor and struggling teacher, she remembered them bitterly enough, and, with all a woman's unreasoning anger, seemed to regard Mrs. Massie as the cause of her loneliness and trials. In the light of prosperity, these feelings faded out; and it was only a pressing invitation to pay a visit to the Charltons near Seaborough which renewed to Salome the memory of what she called her wrongs. She could not resist the temptation to look upon the old scenes again. It takes a vast amount of philosophy not to acknowledge a desire to make a display and create a brilliant impression in a place where one has been poor and humble, and perhaps despised. Salome had left Seaborough in lowly style—almost like a menial dismissed from her place. When she left it, she carried all her little property with her in a small portmanteau and a slender purse. She was returning to be the distinguished guest of the new potentate of the place; with a romantic and mysterious sort of reputation preceding her, with a foreign name, with money, and with style. She drove her hostess's ponies and rode her hostess's horses through the town with the air of one quite used to such possessions. She visited many of her old friends; and being really most generous and kind-hearted, she gave substantial proofs of her regard to those who were poor. The wreck which was mentioned in our opening chapters gave her a brilliant opportunity for displaying in the most impressive light her energies, her talents, and her benevolence. She delighted every one, and herself more than any. She met the Reverend Eustace Massie and patronized him kindly, and wondered in her heart whether she ever could have been for one moment inclined to feel any warmer interest in him. After all this, however, the visit to Seaborough might have grown very dull, but that, to give Salome's mind a new occupation, she suddenly had her attention aroused to the existence of Paul Massie.

In the first instance, Salome felt curious to know what sort of being the Paul Massie might be whose name she well remembered having heard in old days from the lips

of Lydia, and about whom she had once or twice asked
Mrs. Massie some question, without receiving any satisfactory answer. Then she was quickened into peculiar interest by the news that Paul had been in the Mexican war,
and had been a prisoner in Paris; for the anti-Bonapartean
sentiments, banished for a moment by the Lombardy campaign, but revived by, Villafranca, burned strongly in
Salome's breast. Then she met Paul himself, and was
taken with a personal interest in him. It must be owned
that from that moment she endeavored to captivate him,
if she could. Nothing could be a more delightful mode of
vexing the Massies and of pleasing herself. Providence
seemed to have delivered into her hands this delicious
opportunity of revenge.

Providence, or some other power, did more to encourage this fatal notion of revenge than Salome had anticipated; for it sent Alice Crossley, full of embarrassment
and resentment, to consult her about the perplexities and
temptations which had just then arisen. Salome had
always been Alice's friend, and the girl hailed her presence
in Seaborough as the most fortunate coincidence. From
Alice, Salome heard, as we know, in five minutes enough to
convince her that there was some secret or other in the
Massie family which concerned the newly returned cousin.
It took her little trouble to obtain through Alice and
through Halliday the custody of such evidences, other
than oral, as the situation could offer. Salome determined
that, as far as possible, the secret should be wholly in her
own keeping: a weapon with which to smite, or a treasure
with which to reward. She did not see her way to the
meaning of the mystery. All the obvious theories of
solution she tried and found absurdly wanting; she invented divers fantastic solutions, and had to reject them
with equal contempt. Still there was one grand fact clear
and indisputable. A secret of some kind attached to the
Massie family, and especially hung around Paul. Salome
would have loved the little mystery at any time, for its

own romantic and exciting charms. It was now inestima-
bly precious to her. Of course she ought not to have condescended to cabal with a maid-servant, and to read a
document never meant for her eyes, and not obtained
through any creditable channel. Obviously all this was
very improper. A man of honor would never have done
it; and although women are not much affected by what we
call honor, let us hope there are many women who would
have yielded to no temptation of curiosity, spite, or any
other impulse which offered gratification by such a course.
We are not defending what Salome did; we are only stat-
ing what she did. We are not contending that this was
what she ought to have done; we only say that this was
exactly what she did.

Salome returned to London in the highest animation.
We know that Alice Crossley soon went to London likewise. We know that Paul Massie became a visitor, then
a frequent, finally a constant visitor, at Salome's house.
Her interest in him deepened. She was charmed by his
simplicity, his frankness, his vigorous natural ability, his
fresh, unsophisticated, manly ways. "Don't you admire
Mr. Massie very much?" she once said to one of her few
female friends. "*I* do; I cannot quite tell you why, but
he seems to me different from most other men I know. He
seems to me at once a boy and a man. Indeed, I suppose
that is the charm of perfect manhood—and I think he has
it." And Salome involuntarily sighed and her friend
looked knowing, and smiled.

For awhile Salome felt more anxious to conceal from
Paul than from any one else the existence of the secret
which she suspected. Perhaps if it was to prove "something to his advantage," she wished to have all the merit
of the discovery for herself, and to reserve it for a grand
final moment. Perhaps she feared that his generosity and
his manly frankness would scorn all concealment, and bring
about an *éclaircissement* by precipitate measures. It is
certain that she did not yet admit into her confidence the

man most deeply interested in her speculations, and always uppermost in her thoughts.

One result of the acquaintance had been as unexpected as uncontrollable. It threatened perhaps at some moment to baffle all her calculations. Salome had made up her mind to fascinate the Mexican *ingénu*. She had assumed that this would be an easy task. She was a perfect mistress of the weapons of fascination, and the *ingénu* was but an overgrown child. But we have all heard how the best of fencers has sometimes been utterly baffled by the absolute ignorance of an opponent. Was it so in this instance? Paul was obviously and avowedly the most attached friend to Madame de Luca. But was their nothing more than friendship denoted by his manner? Salome looked with her whole soul into his open heart, and seemed disappointed. What of herself? She had lived, one might say, many lives. She had been loved many times. She thought she herself had loved more than once. She had suffered and struggled ; married, and been widowed, and mourned ; and after a perturbed and much-varied life, found herself—no longer youthful—the victim for the first time of a sensation which in this instance she had not sought. For "she grew acquainted with her heart, and searched what stirred it so. Alas, she found it love."

9

CHAPTER XVI.

THE MASSIES IN TOWN.

THE Massies of Seaborough were in town; that is, Eustace and Lydia and Sarah.   Mrs. Massie never left Seaborough; but the rest of the family always paid a visit to town in the season.   This time there were special promptings.   Whatever may have been the reason, the serenity of Seaborough-house seemed to have been quite broken up by Paul Massie's ill-omened visit.   Nor did his sudden departure tend to make matters any better.   Eustace feared that he himself had acted ungenerously,—how he hardly knew; and little skilled as he was in observing the ways of those around him, he could not help thinking he had somewhat fallen in the eyes of his mother and of Sarah.   Thus, at least, he construed the increased nervousness and agitation of the one, the constraint and coldness of the other.   So the place became unhappy to him, and he longed for a little change.   Lydia openly and incessantly grumbled at the dulness of everything and everybody, and demanded variety and London.   So they came to town, and went solemnly to work at amusing themselves.

Eustace always did the same things when in town in the season.   He made the usual and proper round of visits; went to see the Academy's Exhibition, dined with a bishop, took his feminine companions to a flower-show, and one or two evening parties of a mild kind in a good quarter of the West-end.   Lydia and Sarah went, in company of some more secular friends, to the Italian Opera; which Eustace did not discourage, because the Queen patronized the Opera, and therefore it must, of course, be a proper sort of place.   He himself went to one or two religious meetings, and heard a debate in the House of Lords.   For the Commons he did not so much care; he thought it rather noisy, irreverent, and radical. He had not been there since his county member, young Evelyn St. Vane, made his maiden speech,—a very fine piece of eloquence indeed, Eustace thought, which unfortunately the next morning's papers disposed of in six lines. During this present visit to London, however, Eustace had a little personal concern with the affairs of the House of Commons, for the actual representative of the important borough of Seaborough itself, Mr. Charlton, the dissenting railway contractor, was notoriously about to accept the Chiltern Hundreds, in consequence of a large contract he had made with the government of Russia ; and Eustace and all his friends were very anxious that some one of genteeler birth and Church connections should be found to represent the place in parliament. This, however, is anticipating.

Perhaps there could be found on earth no sight more dear to the heart of the pretty Lydia Massie than Rotten-row. She thirsted to be there. So as General and Mrs. Trenton (London friends of the Massies) always went there, Lydia found a seat in their carriage. Sarah did not usually much care to go ; but one particular day, being pressed to accompany her friends, and Eustace being otherwise occupied, she went.

Of course she enjoyed the sight when there. Man or woman must be very philosophic, or cynical, or stupid, who does not enjoy that wonderful scene, that kaleidoscope of faces and dresses, that ever-changing panorama of carriages and silks, fine horses and fine women. Lydia was in serene delight, and felt as if Heaven itself could offer no higher reward to the good than a Rotten-row stretching out to all eternity, and from which there was no going home. The Trentons knew a great many people—ladies who bowed so gracefully, handsome dashing officers with thick moustaches, who bent to Mrs. Trenton and looked so fixedly at Lydia.

Mrs. Trenton had a thirst herself for acquaintances and salutes. Therefore when, just as they had left the Park and were reëntering Piccadilly, she suddenly saw some one approach, who looked very fixedly indeed at Lydia, and had already raised his hat, she cried out, "Lydia, there is some one bowing to you."

Lydia and Mrs. Trenton sat together in the principal seat; Sarah and one of the young Trentons faced them.

A gentleman it was who came riding upon a stylish-looking black horse, and beside a pretty low carriage, in which two ladies sat, one of whom held the reins. The gentleman was dark-eyed and dark-moustached, but his face flushed as he saw Lydia,—flushed and burned for a moment.

"O," exclaimed Lydia, "Sarah, it's cousin Paul!"

Cousin Paul bowed a familiar farewell to the two ladies near whom he had been riding, and rode up to the carriage where the Massies sat. He flushed again on seeing Sarah.

The greeting was certainly warm, but somewhat embarrassed. Sarah's hand trembled in that of the young man; and yet perhaps his strong fingers quivered more palpably still.

Mrs. Trenton was most friendly, and pressed Mr. Paul to dine with the cousins at her house that evening. Paul had unfortunately another engagement; but he would do himself the pleasure of calling next day, if that would be convenient.

Yes; to-morrow they would certainly be all at home in the early part of the day; and the general would be delighted.

Paul rode away, and Sarah fell into the deepest silence. The whole scene floated and swam before her eyes.

"You don't know who the ladies were your cousin was speaking to, dear?" asked Mrs. Trenton.

Lydia had not noticed either of them.

"One of them," said the elder lady, "was very handsome."

Indeed! Lydia had not observed.

Sarah said nothing; but she knew one of the ladies, who was very handsome.

"Foreign looking, I thought," said Mrs. Trenton.
"Odd-looking, at all events."

"I think my cousin's acquainances are mostly foreign," said Lydia, adopting a tone slightly scornful. "He has been so much abroad."

"A handsome young man," said Mrs. Trenton, "but wants manner. London will improve him—in manner, that is. I don't know that it does much to improve young men in any other way." Then followed one or two appro-. priate and exemplary anecdotes.

At dinner that evening there were only the Trentons and Massies and the general's nephew, a captain of cavalry and man about town; a good-natured, harmless, and not too irregular young man, who came to dinner just now at what he considered a slow house, because he had been rather struck by Lydia's bright eyes and attractive ways.

Of course, during dinner the meeting with Paul Massie was talked of. Eustace did not care to hear much on the subject, but could not decently stop it up.

"Why, don't mean to say," asked Captain Trenton, suddenly breaking into the conversation, "that Paul Massie's your cousin? How odd the name never struck me before! Wouldn't now, if you hadn't called him Paul."

"Do you know the gentleman, George?" asked his aunt.

"Know him? I should think I do. It must be the same; there can't be two Paul Massies. Dark man, black moustache, American accent?"

Of course that was he.

"O yes, I know him very well. He often comes to our club with Grigsby and Morton. A very good fellow too, they say. I am very glad he is your cousin," said the young officer, bowing expressly to Miss Lydia. "I'll be sure to come here to-morrow to meet him. He's rich, I suppose? Lives rather fast, I hear."

"I should be sorry to hear that," said Eustace rather gravely, "for my cousin is not rich.

"O, pray, Mr. Massie, don't take it on my word, for I only repeat what I have a vague recollection of hearing somebody say somewhere. I dare say it isn't true at all."

"I dare say none of you live fast in London, George," said the general jocosely.

"Some of us haven't the chance, uncle, and can't help ourselves. I dare say we all would, if we could."

"O, for shame!" articulated Lydia in tones of dulcet reproach.

"There were two ladies with Mr. Massie," said Mrs. Trenton. "One of them I thought handsome and odd-looking. I wonder who she is—I think I have seen her face before."

"I haven't the least doubt it's Madame de Luca," said the nephew. "Massie is always with her. Some people say—but really it's no use minding what fellows say."

"But what do they say?" asked Eustace earnestly. "We know that lady, or did know her very well."

"O, nothing—only that perhaps Massie would marry her. She's a handsome woman, and rich, I believe, and a widow; and she certainly appears to have taken a great fancy to him."

"A foreigner?" said Mrs. Trenton, with a shade of contempt and wonder in her voice.

"No, an Englishwoman; but her husband was an Italian, or Venetian, or something. They say she fought in a battle, or a siege, or a something of the kind. Précis of the Foreign Office says he saw her somewhere—Milan, I believe—in '59, with pistols at her belt, and dressed like a *vivandière*,—short skirts and trousers, and that sort of thing."

"Really, Mr. Massie," observed Mrs. Trenton, "I think the sooner you get your cousin back into the country again the better."

The general laughed. How should the young ladies like a new cousin dressed like Jenny Lind in the *Figlia del Reggimento*, he asked. "I think it rather a becoming costume myself."

"O, nonsense, general?" observed his wife. "I don't mind what George has been saying—it's all his club gossip."

Eustace had been growing so manifestly uneasy, that this last remark was made with the good-natured hope of soothing his trouble. Sarah had not spoken a word all the time. When the ladies had left the room, the clergyman talked a good deal more on the same subject with the young soldier, and extracted not much—indeed there really was nothing of any consequence to be said—but enough to make him wish that the respectable and religious Massie family had no cousin in London.

Yet Paul kept his appointment, and went next day to the house of Mrs. Trenton, Cumberland-street, Hyde-park. It must be owned too that he dressed with unwonted care in order to get there. He was received in very friendly fashion by Mrs. Trenton, and had the pleasure of "assisting" at a lively conversation between Captain Trenton and his cousin Lydia. That bright-eyed young lady received Paul with great good-humor and courtesy when he presented himself, and presently dropped him out of notice altogether. The Rev. Eustace Massie had left an apologetic message, expressing his regret that sudden and important business compelled him to go into town; and Sarah was unfortunately rather unwell, and could not be seen. Mrs. Trenton, with whom Paul's conversation was principally carried on, did not ask him to dinner or press him to return. He received from her the most gracious farewell. Lydia rose as he was going, and held out her hand, talking all the time to Captain Trenton. There was no mistaking all this. Paul Massie was "cut." His cousins would have no more to do with him. He left the house with the feelings of one who is conscious of having obtruded himself where he is no longer welcome, and having been turned from the door. It was with a bursting heart that he mounted his horse and rode into Hyde-park. He was almost choking with humiliation and anger. He felt that his passion must be glowing through his cheeks and eyes. He was an untutored, almost an uncouth man—born with an ardent impetuous nature, unused to endure calmly anything but climate and hard life. Here, in London, drifting vaguely about, he felt like a child; scorned and rejected by those on whom he had relied, he felt all a child's fever of disappointment and passion.

He rode up and down under the trees, plucked a few leaves from stooping branches and bit them, lighted a cigar and smoked it with vehement fierce puffs. Perhaps he was turning over in his mind furious incoherent·plans of vengeance. Perhaps if one of the poodles following their mistresses in the Park had taken to pursuing Paul's movements—had accompanied him to his lodgings, and there grown bigger and bigger, at last changing into Mephistopheles, and offering a contract for his soul, Paul, like Faust, might, on certain conditions, have cried "*Topp!*" and closed with the bargain. But no such tempter appeared. The vagaries of Paul's exercise, however, brought him soon in front of the street running at right angles to the railing of the Park, where Madame de Luca lived. After a moment or two of doubt, he crossed, dismounted, and knocked at the door. The lady of the house was at home to him.

"You left us very abruptly last evening," she said, "and broke your appointment too. Never returned, never went near the theatre; we lost the overture, and half the first act, by waiting for you and you did not come after all. Have I not a right to scold you now? I took another escort, and was quite determined, if you came, to make you jealous; but you didn't come; and I don't think you would have been very jealous in any case."

"Indeed," said Paul, "I am quite ashamed. The truth is that I was not altogether well; and I forgot that I had a very particular appointment, and—"

"My dear friend," and she smiled significantly, "one of the few things you really cannot do is to make an excuse or invent a story. Don't place yourself at such a disadvantage. If you want to make an excuse to any one else, always tell me and I will invent a tale for you ; only even then I don't think you could deliver it in such a way as to make people believe you. Don't I know very well why you did not present yourself last night? And I am so good that I pardon you. So take it for granted that I know all, and come and tell me something about your pretty cousins."

Paul grew red, and almost started.

"Ah, so I really have touched you! I thought so. Which of the two—the lively laughing one, or the graver and paler? I think, if I were a man, I should be for sentiment; but you used not to be sentimental. Come, confess all."

"Indeed I have nothing to confess," said Paul, "except—except that I am in a bad humor."

"Then I must try to win you into a good one. Bid me discourse; I will enchant thine ear. Seriously, you do look vexed and distressed. What is the matter? Tell me and I may set everything right. Have you had a quarrel with one of the pretty cousins? Or has the reverend brother been lecturing you about the good-for-nothing life you have been leading in London? Shall I go as an ambassadress on your behalf? Or shall I have a certificate of good conduct drawn up for you, and signed by all Bohemia?"

"No," said Paul, "I fear no one can help me; I cannot even help myself. I fear I have been making a fool of myself, Madame de Luca, and you would have good reason to laugh at me, if you knew but half."

"If you have only been making a fool of yourself, you have been merely imitating the wisest of men, especially if the folly has been about a woman. Be consoled upon that point. But tell me what particular freak of folly you have been committing—there are so many ways of being foolish : and I don't know whether I ought to pity you just yet, for there are so many ways of being foolish which are very, very pleasant."

"Mine are not pleasant," said Paul rather bitterly.

As yet Madame de Luca had spoken to him somewhat coldly, or else in a tone which was not without its sarcastic sharpness. She now turned her eyes, which before she had kept averted, fixedly on the young man, and she saw that pain, genuine pain of some kind, was written on every line of his face. The expression of her countenance, the tone of her voice, changed in a moment.

"You are really disturbed," she said gently. "I did not know it, or I would not thus have trifled with you, I fear there is something more in this than the anger of the pretty cousin. For all you men say about us, I doubt whether we are so necessary to your happiness as to cause you very much pain. Tell me what vexed you—see, I have dropped my teasing mood."

She touched his hand kindly.

"I cannot indeed—I wish I could. It would relieve me to tell you; but you do not, you cannot know."

"What if I know much more than you think?" she said very quietly, and slowly fixing her eyes full upon him.

He started, and a sudden thrill passed visibly over him. "You!" he stammered; "can it be? No—you can't know. Impossible."

"I know many things about many people. I know some things about some which they hardly know themselves; perhaps you are one of those. I have asked you to give me your confidence. How if you could tell me nothing I do not know, but I could tell you much which you long to hear?"

Paul started to his feet. "O, Madame de Luca!" he exclaimed, "if you can really tell me anything—if you know anything which would relieve me from the torture of doubt I have so long felt, give me some hint, I beseech you. I received hints before, but they only tormented and maddened me. *They* did not come from you. Tell me something, and I will—"

"Will what?" she said, looking calmly at him.

"Will thank you from my very heart—will be grateful to you for my life."

"So many people have been grateful to me for their lives," she said, "that I shall scarcely know you from all the rest. But it does not matter. All I know you shall know—only not all at once—and you must not ask any questions about my source of knowledge. Now, then, what do you wish to ask?"

Paul still hesitated. He hardly knew how to begin. Suppose, after all, they were speaking of different things? Suppose that on which he really sought knowledge he should only be betraying in vain by a question.

"Come," she said, "I understand your silence. I might be offended by it, and leave you to pursue your own course unaided. But I am not easily offended, and I desire to help you. You are afraid that I really know nothing, and that you may only betray yourself by asking a question. I can easily convince you that I am not now talking in woman's true style of things that I don't understand. Stay a moment."

She went to a table which stood in a corner, opened a beautifully inlaid *bijou* of a writing-desk, and sought for something.

Paul had taken a flower out of a glass vase, and was assiduously plucking it to pieces. Madame de Luca glanced at him and smiled. "Loves you, or loves you not?" she asked; "which is it?"

He looked up amazed, not in the least understanding the question.

"I thought you were working Margaret's charm," she said. "But perhaps you do not need any such spell. No matter. You will not speak out until you understand what knowledge I have of your affairs. Cast a glance over that letter."

She put into his hand a stained and creased piece of

paper, faded and yellowing. It was covered with writing in a clear bold hand.

"Stay," she said ; "one word before you read it. Do you know the writing ?"

"No, I think not. I don't think I ever saw it before."

"Read it, please."

He read it. It appeared to carry with it no particular meaning, for Paul glanced up at her inquiringly more than once ; and receiving no explanation, looked perplexedly at the letter.

"I have read it," he said ; "but really I can make nothing of it. To whom is it addressed ?"

"Suppose it were addressed to yourself ; would it then be more intelligible ? "

"Suppose it were ; but then—"

"It is, or it was, addressed to you. It was meant for you."

"Who wrote it ? "

"Nay, that I must not tell; just now, at least. Assume it to be addressed to yourself, and read it over again ; and then say if you think it of no interest."

With a flushed cheek the young man read the letter. Why did he keep one hand above his eyes as he read, so as to hide the expression of his face from Salome's earnest gaze, as she stood near him ?

When he had read it through, he looked up and said, "I don't understand it still; I don't, indeed. But I will not pretend to say that things have not occurred which convinced me that some family secret of a disagreeable nature is hanging over me. That I have long thought. I will not say that I have not even had conjectures—although only the wildest—as to its possible nature. Madame de Luca, I have never seen or known my father; and yet of late I have come to think that he is not dead, as I was told; and if he be living, and that letter is addressed to me, it comes from him. But what it means I cannot guess."

"I conjecture that the writer of that letter is dead. But you shall know; and perhaps before long."

"Was it sent to me through you?"

"Assuredly not. How can you ask me such a question? If it had been sent to me for you, do you think I would have delayed in giving it to its rightful owner? It has simply fallen into my hands, and I have only just received the information which confirms my conjecture that it was meant for you."

"How did it come into your hands?" he asked, in slow and unsteady accents.

"That is my secret. That I know all about your affairs does not entitle you to know all about mine. No, no. I am the great wonder; I am the woman who keeps a secret. Perhaps I am a spiritualist, and have messages from the other world through tables; perhaps I am at the head of the secret police. But I think I can serve you, if you will be guided by me, and will promise to do what I order, and to ask no questions. You believe I am your friend, Paul Massie, do you not?"

The young man impetuously seized her hand and kissed it. I do believe she blushed.

- "Friend!" he said, "you have been my only friend here. You have been to me more than—"

"More than a mother!" she exclaimed laughing, and drawing away her hand. "Yes, that is what you were just going to say. More than a mother! You might have finished the sentence. I should not have been at all offended, and we could have concerted our arrangements with all the more propriety. If I were the age of one of the fair cousins, then indeed there might be danger in our conferences. But we who have free souls, it touches us not."

Nevertheless, the lady glanced at one of the mirrors, which indeed reflected a fine face and full form; eyes that might have moved many a young heart, and hair in whose meshes many an affection might have been caught. But she looked at Paul, and he was poring over the document, spelling out its every word. She smiled perhaps rather bitterly.

"Do you really know the meaning of this?" he asked.

"Perhaps I know it; perhaps I only guess it. But be sure that where so much has been discovered, the rest will be made clear."

"But I doubt, I much doubt, whether I should inquire any farther. Perhaps I may only learn that which I have no right to know, and should be the better for not knowing. Something tells me that I ought to tear up this old sea-stained rag and think, or try to think, no more of its pretended secrets."

"Perhaps so; but let me see the letter again."

He handed it to her. She calmly took it and relocked it in her desk. Paul looked surprised.

"My good Paul," she said, "do you really think I would have taken all the trouble to obtain this knowledge of your history in-order that you might perform a feat of romantic generosity and give up the pursuit? That letter I keep for quite a different purpose. It may be of infinite importance. Don't you see that somebody besides yourself or me has been all along looking over the cards? Don't you think it will be important to know who that person is?"

"I have received," said Paul slowly, "one or two strange hints."

"Yes, and so have I. You see the mysterious agent has chosen to mix me up in your affairs. I have not obtruded. Now that I am in the business, I am not to be got out—no, not even by you; although I can very well see, my poor Paul, that you don't relish the prospect of a woman's interference in your affairs. But you are not able to manage them for yourself,—that is clear enough; and I am an old and practised intriguer, who have had to do with more complicated and dangerous transactions than this. And I take an interest in you, Paul, which I cannot help, and I like you well, and I will try, as you have said, to be even more than a mother to you. Now good-by for the present. Ask me no questions, for I shall answer none; impose no pledge, for I shall promise nothing. I will see you to-night, if you like. Good-by."

She extended her hand. He took it, and looked with embarrassed air and in silence into her face.

"You look," said she, "as if you were in doubt whether you ought not to kiss me. Foolish boy! never have any doubt on such a point; especially where you only mean gratitude, and are thinking of a mother."

He did kiss her on the forehead, and went away without speaking. He mounted his horse, and rode rapidly away. She looked out of the window; he did not turn in his saddle. He was gone in a moment.

"He will ride where he thinks they will be," she murmured. "I know it. What matter? Men in love have no spirit; nor women either."

Madame de Luca sighed, and looked as if she were not quite so contented and resigned as her words gave out. But she had visitors soon. Not often was she left alone after noon had set in; and she was presently rapid, vivacious, and joyous in her conversation.

————◆◆◆————

CHAPTER XVII.

MR. WYNTER, M. P.

MR. WYNTER, M. P., was one of the happiest of men. He had all he wanted in life. At least, if he had not in his actual possession every object of his ambition, he imagined he had it, and was satisfied. If Fortune denied him anything, he took it for himself in imagination. Many, however, of his gifts of fortune were goodly, solid reality. He had plenty of money. His father had been in business, and left him a fortune. He himself continued in business until he made another fortune; and then he deliberately

and wisely gave up money-making, and betook himself to
the task of being happy.   He did not marry, for his notion
of happiness by no means consisted in domesticity ; and if
any man could have been born purposely for old bachelor-
hood, Mr. Wynter was that man.   He liked club life, club
society, incessant motion, change, and bustle ; and he liked
to fancy himself a statesman.   These enjoyments seemed
to him hardly compatible with married life.   Perhaps the
fond delusion which he cherished could least easily be
made consistent with the silken bands of matrimony.   For
it would have been hardly possible to get a wife so foolish,
or so sublimely wise and superhumanly forbearing, as to
refrain from endeavoring some time or other to open Mr.
Wynter's eyes to the reality of his position as a statesman.
Mr. Wynter was indeed in parliament, and meant always
to continue there.   By never-failing subscriptions to local
charities, by generous dinner-giving (at the club and in the
House), and by his genial and genuine *bonhomie* and kindliness of heart, he had made the support of his constituents
certain.   But his parliamentary displays were entirely
limited to the putting of an occasional question to the foreign secretary touching the attitude of England in relation
to the affairs of this or that oppressed nationality, or the
treatment of some political refugee.   Among the members
of the House, in the dining-room, the tea-room, and the
smoking-room, Mr. Wynter was a general favorite.   Those
who did not care about him personally, liked to draw him
out and chaff him.   Good-natured members lent themselves
to his harmless fussiness and innocent self-inflation ; and
the Premier himself had many a time, out of pure kindness
of heart, and a genial twinkle of his knowing eye, drawn
his friend Wynter into a specially conspicuous corner of
the lobby, and there gravely and ostentatiously plunged
into deep converse and council with him on the weightiest
questions of foreign politics.   There were indeed, some few
grave and reverend seniors in the House, and some few
dull and grand young prigs, who, taking everything *au*

sérieux, declined to humor or even to acknowledge Wynter. But that happy individual never observed their demeanor towards him. He was too good-natured to expect offence, and not sharp enough to notice it, unless in its very broadest expression.

Foreign politics were Mr. Wynter's hobby. Some people may think such a study rather difficult; but they only show their innocence when they acknowledge the thought. Rising young member of parliament, or ambitious old personage entering the House late in life, let foreign politics be your pursuit. Difficult, weary, perplexing, and unproductive is the study of home affairs. Every one about you knows as much of Church questions and land questions and legal questions as you are likely ever to know ; and there are sure to be people always at hand who have a dreadfully intimate and practical knowledge of them which will horribly confound you in your hour of fancied triumph. But who knows or cares anything about Montenegro and Servia, and the Herzegovina and Uruguay and the Annamite Empire? Suppose you make a speech, the result of vast labor and daring cram, on the Law of Settlement or the Bank Charter, and some one from a back bench, who knows all about it, and has had it forced upon his practical attention for years, gets up and demolishes all your facts, the unhappy result is that the House generally understands quite enough of the question to see that he is right and you are wrong; that he is a sensible man, and you are an ass ; and you are written down an ass accordingly. But suppose you talk nonsense about the condition and internal politics of Roumania, and that some member, superfluously blessed with a complete knowledge of the question, springs to his feet to confute you, who is to know which is right and which is wrong? Your facts seem just as good as his facts ; your conclusions sound quite as plausible as his conclusions, and your parliamentary reputation is secure. Besides, all home questions are complicated ; but all foreign questions are to British eyes perfectly simple. If you are a Liberal, you are always on the side of the people, the oppressed nationality. If you are a Conservative, you are against the revolutionists. There is the whole secret. Your ground is marked out for you, and nobody concerns himself to catechise you as to the soundness of your reasons for taking your stand there. Mr. Wynter had chosen his ground and his action. He took his stand on foreign politics, and he acted for the Nationalities. So he obtained a sort of reputation as a man conversant with continental affairs. Politicians from abroad always had letters of introduction to him; and there were even some far-off foreign journals (in Servia or Wallachia perhaps) by which Mr. Wynter was treated as a great British statesman, who was only kept out of office by the English aristocracy because of his friendship for the oppressed—a sort of Ormuzd to the ministerial Ahriman.

Mr. Wynter walked into the library of the House one evening, and met his friend Mr. Charlton.

"Well, Charlton, so you really are giving up Seaborough?"

"Yes, I am indeed. I could not attend to the business any longer; and I don't know that I would, if I could. I have not your taste for this sort of life, Wynter; I see nothing come of it. Progress moves too slowly here for me."

"Progress?"

"Well, yes—I came in as a Reformer, and where is Reform? The papers are all talking of a Conservative reaction; I am too old to wait until the Conservative reaction runs its time out. I came in, hoping to help in giving the last kick to Church-rates—and Church-rates are on their feet again. I know this cannot last; but neither can I; and I prefer my own work."

Mr. Wynter never looked at things in such a light. He only concerned himself about the rights of freemen abroad. An annual vote against Church-rates, and for the Ballot, satisfied his conscience as regarded projects of domestic reform.

“Who suceeds you, Charlton ?”

“Don’t know at all. The Tories are putting up a local man, an eldest son, with good family influence. But we could return our man, if we had a good one.”

“Of course you don’t resign until somebody is found.”

“Certainly not; I would wait another twelve months rather. You don’t know of anybody ?”

“N—no,” said Mr. Wynter slowly, and as if carefully meditating. “That is, not just at this moment. I dare say I could find some one though. I’ll think the matter over.”

“Do. Once or twice it occurred to me that perhaps your friend Massie would like to try his chance.”

“By Jove, and so he would.”

“Yes ; he’s a clever energetic fellow, and his family is well known down there.”

“You are quite right. Indeed I thought of the matter myself before, but I had not a good opportunity of talking the thing over with him.”

“Talk it over with him then as soon as you can. I suppose he has money ?”

“O yes, plenty of money,” said Wynter, off-hand ; knowing just as much of Paul’s finances as he did of Hegel’s philosophy.

“Because if he had not a great deal to spare, and proved a suitable candidate, I don’t know that there would be any great difficulty about the expenses. The fact is, that cost what it will, a Tory shan’t come in for Seaborough. I wish Massie would come and see me.”

“So he shall, when I’ve talked the matter over with him.”

“Yes, of course, when you’ve talked the matter over with him,” said Mr. Charlton, with a faint smile. “Goodnight—I’m going home.”

Mr. Wynter was charmed with the idea, which had never presented itself to him before. He liked Paul Massie much, and would have gladly had him for a colleague in the House. Indeed, Wynter would have liked all his friends to be in parliament, if only that they might be able to see and appreciate his position there. He was not in the least exclusive or jealous. Had he been King Candaules, he would have found it quite natural to invite Gyges to a full inspection of his treasures of domestic beauty.

"It's the very thing for Massie," thought Wynter. "If he has not the money, I dare say the family have; and if they won't give it, no doubt it will be found somehow. There's no time to be lost; I'll go and talk to *her* at once about it."

To her? *Cherchez la femme!* One might have thought Paul Massie himself was the proper person to be consulted. Mr. Wynter knew better. Before he had spoken a word to Paul on the subject, Wynter wrote a note to Mr. Charlton, telling him the affair was all right, and that he might apply for the Chiltern Hundreds as soon as he pleased. For Wynter had gone straightway to Salome, and talked to her of the propriety of getting Paul into parliament. Salome rejoiced at the suggestion. In the first place, she wished that Paul should be prominent and distinguished, and, in true woman's style, took it for granted that his entering parliament was the great step on the way to his being at least foreign minister. Then she delighted in the excitement which a contest promised, he being the candidate. Finally, she found it imperatively necessary to do something which would absorb Paul's attention for at least six months. He was constantly talking of going away, and endeavoring to resume an active career across the Atlantic. Salome had determined that he should not go just yet, but she was often puzzled about the means of keeping him in England. To get him into parliament would be to give him a new career, and Salome resolved that the thing should be done. She never doubted for a moment of her own powers of persuasion.

Meanwhile where was Paul? He was haunting Hyde-park; he was riding in Rotten-row; he was leaning dismally against the railings of the Drive; he was looking wistfully up and down Piccadilly; he was smoking listlessly, and anon allowing his cigar to go out, and then lighting it again, and then flinging it half-smoked away. He was idling about town with particular friends whom he had met for the first time the week before last or the day before yesterday; he was looking at pictures in the studios of jolly, bearded young artists; he was trying horses for less skilled acquaintances; he was playing billiards, drinking champagne or bitter beer; he was running in debt; he was growing daily more and more idle, listless, sick of existence, and unhappy. He longed to see Sarah Massie, and he knew no good could come of it, and he went persistently wherever there seemed the remotest likehood of his meeting her; and he was always unsuccessful. He even found himself pacing backward and forward in the street where the Trentons lived, and he fancied that every servant at a door must know what he was hanging about for; and he felt ashamed, and went away vowing he would never go there again, and went next day accordingly. It was a bad thing for Salome that she had broken ground with him even in jest upon the dangerous theme of his affection for his cousin. It was a bad thing for her peace of mind that she had invited his confidence, and talked of herself as one who might be regarded in the light of a mother. Poor Paul took all this *au pied de la lettre,* and did not hesitate occasionally to pour his confidence into her bosom. Salome thrilled and quivered and turned pale under the ordeal; and poor Paul did not suspect the pain he caused her. He believed everybody, and he really thought for no short time that Salome's expressions of maternal regard were only the simple truth. He sickened of his listless, hopeless life, and she sickened at the frank acknowledgments which he sometimes made to her. Her very appearance seemed to tell that something was wrong; her manner grew more careless and capricious and impulsive; she laughed more loudly; she wrote less; she sat more often alone and silent and sad.

So the prospect of a new excitement to him was a great relief to her. Anything to pass over the next few months. She hoped to do him a great service: to make some grand, vague discovery. No doubt she hoped too to separate him utterly from his uncongenial relations. Therefore she expounded to him the parliamentary project as a splendid scheme, absolutely essential to his prospects and his name. He accepted the proposal just as he would have agreed to a distraction which presented itself in the shape of an exploring expedition or a yachting trip. Moreover, he was by no means as indifferent to political questions as a young Englishman of his age and temperament generally is. Paul had been reared in America, where every man is a politician; and had lived a good deal in countries where every man who is not an avowed politician is a conspirator. Therefore, if he knew but little of the precise bearings of political parties in England, he had no inconsiderable aptitude for politics in general, and his extensive practical information might well serve him in better stead in the House of Commons than a high-class University education. So he agreed to contest the seat recommended to him. He was ashamed to tell Salome the condition of his finances; but this difficulty was removed by a preliminary assurance that the contest should cost him nothing. The patriotic electors of Seaborough could not think of allowing their representative to pay for the privilege of entering parliament on their behalf. Mr. Wynter had, therefore, been commissioned to arrange for all that part of the business. So indeed he had. A cheque from Salome had conveniently enabled Seaborough patriotism to dispense with any pressing demands upon the purse of its candidate.

Salome's friends rallied round (we may appropriately adopt electioneering phraseology) the new candidate. Many of them seriously regarded him as a person likely to be of service to their views, if in parliament, because of

his acquaintance with foreign affairs and his democratic
opinions. There was a sort of vague plan just then floating or drifting about certain circles, for getting into parliament a few representatives of the continental school of
democracy. Observe that the continental school is composed of very different personages from the British school
of democrats. The latter follow Bright and Cobden
(*eheu!* did follow Cobden, one should say—may England
long preserve his glorious memory !), and strive for universal peace. The former swear by Mazzini or Herzen or
Victor Hugo, hate the Emperor of the French, and place
their first hopes in universal war. Paul belonged naturally to the Mazzini, Herzen, and Hugo school ; but his
politics were, of course, rather a feeling than a science.
Perhaps not a few of those who now most eagerly urged
him forward did so because they saw that his political feelings were deep, and that his political science was shallow.
An energetic man who can drive others, and at the same
time can himself be easily led, is a model politician in the
eyes of well-governed political coteries.

The retiring member for Seaborough, Mr. Charlton,
gave Paul his earnest aid and full interest, partly because
he liked him, partly because he detested High Church, and
partly because himself and his wife had generally been
snubbed by the old-established families of Seaborough.
Some of Salome's friends were delighted at the candidature
solely for the amusement of the thing, and would have
thrown their souls into the contest, if they had the slightest means of being able to render any service thereby. As
for Salome herself, she would have been only too happy if
her life had been cast in the more exciting days when she
might have worn her candidate's colors, driven about in a
coach-and-six to canvass for him, and bribed (not with
fond shekels of the tested gold) the more gallant of the
independent electors, like the famous Duchess.

CHAPTER XVIII.

THE WEHR-WOLF.

" I AM to see the wehr-wolf to-day, Alice," said Madame
de Luca one morning to her attendant or *protégée*.
" You had better go to your room now, unless you would
like to have an interview with your old friend, and to
renew your acquaintance."

" I, ma'am?   O, no.   I should be quite afraid."

" Well, I hope we shall soon be rid of him.   He's going
to America."

" O, how glad I am ! "

" Yes, I have promised to pay his passage, and give
him a trifle to start with.   My own advice to him would
be to enlist at once in the Federal army; or in the other
if his natural instincts should conduct him there ; and get
honestly and decently shot.   I don't think anything better
could possibly happen to him."

" No, indeed, ma'am."

Alice did not much care what army he joined, or what
he did, provided he put himself securely out of the way by
any operation.

" Yes, he is coming here to-day.   I saw him by the
merest chance yesterday lounging about near the betting-
place in Hyde-park, under the tree.   He was looking wilder
and more out of sorts than ever.   I pitied the unfortunate
wretch; and I went up and spoke to him.   He seemed quite
amazed that anybody should take the slightest interest in
his movements, or in his existence, poor creature; and I do
believe he thought I must have some sinister motive in offering to do anything for him.   I told him if he would go to
America his passage-money could be provided for him; and,
after a few moments' parley, he accepted the offer.   Not
gratefully though, or graciously, but as a much-injured

man consents to accept an instalment of his rights. So he is coming here; will be here soon, in fact; or ought to be, if he keeps his word."

Salome was soon left alone to wait for her visitor.

It was strange, or at least would have been strange in any one else, the interest she took in the wehr-wolf, as she chose to call him. She pitied the wretch, and was touched by the kind of instinctive ferocity with which he seemed to regard the human race as his natural enemies. This peculiarity would assuredly have repelled and disgusted almost all other persons; but it had an odd sort of attraction for her. She always averred that she liked anything that was real; and this pleasant attribute of Halliday's was at least a reality. There was not much of personal affectation about him, although he could lie and cheat when it suited his purpose. To all ordinary eyes he was a low, drunken, ferocious ruffian; but Salome, who generally preferred the more romantic aspect of things, transfigured him into a wehr-wolf, whom a sense of wrong had driven to sorcery and the forest. There was something interesting in trying to reclaim him; it was like endeavoring to tame a wolf. It roused her faculties; and she liked it. But let us not deny that mere kindliness of heart and pity had much to do with the interest she felt in Halliday.

Her visitor came true to time. His money was out, and he would probably have paid her a visit very soon in any case. He was looking worse and worse. The man was fast fading, and the wolf becoming more and more conspicuous. His walk even had now something stealthy and wolf-like about it; and his eyes, reddened by drink, had that distrustful restlessness which the animal-tamer despairs to remove. When he entered the room, Salome sat at her desk, and did not at first look up or speak; she was curious to find out how he would open the conversation.

Halliday stood silent a moment or two, and turned his old cap about in his hands. Then he made some guttural sound, which he probably intended as a delicate hint that

10

he was waiting. This producing no effect, he spoke at last.

"Well, ma'am, you see—I've come, you know, as you told me."

"Yes, I see," said Salome, looking up and laying down her pen; "and I am sorry to see that you have been going on badly."

"What's it matter how I've been going on? I'll not be any the better for talking of it."

"No, I dare say not. I don't suppose anything I could say would do you any good."

"It wouldn't!" exclaimed Halliday, with a positive fierceness of sudden energy; "it wouldn't, ma'am, do me any good in the world; and where a word from you wouldn't serve me, a day's preaching out of the pulpit from nobody else wouldn't do me any good. I'm past all that. You're just about the only one in the world that I'd do anything for; and why? Just because you're about the only one in the world that ever offered to do anything for me. But you can't do me any good; you nor nobody else. I'm in the way here, and you'd like to get rid of me; and you're quite right. Very well. I'll go. I can't do anything by staying here; and I'm ready to go. To America, or anywhere else; it's all the same to me. I suppose there's drink in America, and tobacco; and I don't care much about anything else—now."

"No; but once you did care about something else."

"What signifies? What's the use of talking of *that?*"

"Because I think there may be some good in you yet, Halliday; and I don't like to give you up as quite beyond hope. You did care for something besides drink and tobacco once; and not so long ago. I think you do still."

"No, I don't. If you mean Ally Crossley—"

"Yes, I mean her."

"Then I don't care about her; what you call care about her. I'd like to see her—I'd like some one told me she was in this house."

Salome was almost betrayed into a start, and an expression of alarm.

"Why do you wish to see her?"

"Because if once I see her, I'd never let her go again. I'd drag her with me, or I'd kill her. She's ruined me, and made a fool of me, and laughed at me; and I'd make her come with me, ay, and make her as bad as myself, just to punish her and have my revenge. Yes, I would; or I'd kill her."

"Why," said Salome, "you poor fellow, you are madly in love with her still. I am really sorry for you; but I don't believe you are half as bad as you give yourself out to be, and I am glad to find you have so much of feeling left in you which has nothing to do with whiskey and tobacco. Pluck up some courage, man, and begin a new life. Go out to America; and I will take care to put you in the way of getting employment there; and you will soon make your way. You are too young not to be able to get rid of your drinking habits."

Halliday shook his head.

"I don't know now," he said. "My father died drunk; and so, I've heard him say many a time, did his father. I think if things had gone differently, I might have got over it perhaps, and pulled out all right; but now everybody is against me, and I don't care. But I'm obliged to you, ma'am, and I don't want to trouble you. You offer to send me out to America?"

"Yes, to New York; and from that on to the West. I don't yet quite know to what place; but you are not to stay in New York, not a day. It shall be arranged so that somebody will meet you in New York, and pay your fare on to some other place, where employment will be ready for you."

"Will you give me the price of my passage in the ship?"

"No, not a penny of it. You know very well what would come of it if I did."

Halliday smiled grimly.

"You're right," he said. "But what am I to do, then?"

"You are to come here again in two or three days—say three days—and you shall then be told what ship you are to go in, and what you are to do. You will have to leave from Liverpool, I fear; but we must arrange to have your safety looked after on the way from the train to the docks—a perilous journey, I hear. And for the meantime, I must give you a little money; but it shall be very little—just enough to keep you without drinking. I must trust to you, Halliday, not to spend it in drink. May I trust you so far? Will you promise me? Come, now, I am doing something for you; will you promise me this?"

Halliday hesitated, moved uneasily from one foot to the other, and twisted his cap many times.

"I think," continued Salome, "I see a great chance for you, if only we can manage to transfer you to some fresh western town of America, with an interval of sobriety between. But to do any good you must begin well. Now, promise me that you will not spend in drink what I am going to give you."

"Well," said Halliday, after a little more hesitation and shuffling, "I'll promise. Yes, I'll promise. And what's more, I'll do my best to keep my word."

"Come, that's right; and I will trust you. Here." She gave him a small sum of money—only a few shillings indeed.

"You will come back," she repeated, "in three days; and then I will tell you what has been done for you, and where you are to go. We shall make something of you yet. And America is a broad place, Halliday, where people do not know a great deal about the gossip of Seaborough; and it will be your own fault if any one learns that you were foolish in England. There are pretty girls there too, I am told; and I dare say you will contrive some day to forget all the past, and find a good wife, and make her a good husband. Now, good-morning."

Halliday lingered a moment.

“Well?” said Salome, looking inquiringly at him.

“I don’t know,” he said slowly, and evidently trying to follow out the thread of some idea in his puzzled brain. “You are very good to me—very. I can’t well make it out. There isn’t any dodge in all this, is there, ma’am?”

“Any dodge? In what?”

“It isn’t anything, you know, just to get me out of the way? It isn’t anything that Ally Crossley is mixed up in? It isn’t because I threatened about her, is it, ma’am?”

The shrewdness of the suspicion a little surprised Salome. The instinctive and rooted distrust of all human kindness was something to think over and to study. Salome had to own to herself that in this instance the distrust was not altogether unfounded.

“There is no dodge, Halliday, as you call it, unless a. dodge to try to do you good. It is quite true that your threats did make me a little anxious to get you out of the way; but that consideration alone would never induce me to take any trouble about sending you to America. I should rather have you handed over to the police, who would take good care that you did no harm to any one—even to yourself. No; I really want to save you, if I can; and if you act like a man, I at least will always be your friend, and will hope to hear that you do well, and are happy.”

“Thankee, ma’am. I believe all you say; and I hope, once I’m off, that you’ll never hear of me again. That’s about the best wish I could give. Good-by, ma’am. Would you mind just—just shaking hands with me?”

Salome put out her hand without hesitation, and it was held for a moment in the hot dirty fingers of Jem Halliday. Then her visitor was gone—to return in three days.

“I think I have brought the wehr-wolf back to his old shape of man, for the hour, at least,” thought Salome. “Perhaps—who knows?—I may succeed in restoring him altogether at last. It would be something to accomplish. It would brighten one’s life a little if one could feel sure of having done so much. Poor wretch! It will be a good thing for Alice when he is fairly out of the country; for I do think the girl is not perhaps altogether so foolish in her dread of him. He looked wonderfully dangerous when he spoke of her. Well, after three days she may breathe freely, and my experiment in human reclamation begins."

Alice knew when her discarded lover was leaving Salome. She heard his heavy tread upon the stairs. She became possessed with a sudden and unconquerable curiosity to have a look, a safe look, only one, at him. So she ran to the window of her room, drew aside cautiously one corner of the blind, and peeped out. She heard the hall-door close behind him, and saw him shamble into the street. He crossed the road to the other footpath, and then, turning back, looked up at the house.

Alice dropped the curtain in haste, and did not venture to peep out again for several seconds. When she did cautiously and timorously look from the window, there was no one visible anywhere in the sunny little street, except a page who held the heads of a pair of ponies attached to a basket-carriage. Halliday was gone, then; must have gone straight away, and could not have seen her. What a lucky escape! Who could ever have thought of his crossing the road at once, and looking up? So odd; but just like him; his prying eyes were always where no one expected to meet them. This time, however, it didn't matter; Jem hadn't seen her. Indeed, he could hardly have recognized her up so high. Still it was an escape; and Alice laughed with satisfaction, although her little heart palpitated still pretty smartly with the fright she got when Halliday looked up.

A few moments afterwards, she heard from Madame de Luca that Halliday had pledged himself to go to America, and she began to breathe freely once again.

Had she, however, seen a little more of Halliday; had she been able to note the expression which came over him when he looked back at the house,—she would have had less cause for satisfaction. He gave only one glance back.

She only peeped for two seconds from the window; yet he saw enough in the time. He had eyes like a cat or a lynx; and he saw Alice, and knew her, and took in, or thought he took in, the whole of the situation in a moment. He felt as if he had had a sun-stroke. Something seemed to to have pierced his brain, and to keep throbbing in his head. The pavement and the houses danced before him, and he put his hands out as one who has to clutch something to save himself from falling. Yet he had wit enough, and self-control enough, to suppress in a moment any outward demonstration of surprise and anger; and though in the first flash of his fury he had some wild notion of rushing back, dashing at the door, and forcing his way to Alice, he saw in an instant that such a mad proceeding could only end in his utter discomfiture. So he held his way down the street just as if nothing had happened; and before Alice ventured to look out again, the place, as has been said, was clear of his presence.

But his heart was full, and his brain was maddened. He now saw in Salome's kindness only what he would have called "a plant." He had been deceived, " done," from first to last, and by "a pack of women." How many a day and night had he turned himself into a human ferret to find out Alice Crossley! And she was there all the time! Why, Madame de Luca had scolded him for not finding out something about the girl, had coolly asked him whether there was really such a person in existence! And she was upstairs in the same house while they were talking! This was why he was to be sent out of the way, anywhere and anyhow; this was why they wanted to ship him off to America! They had been laughing at him all the time; they were laughing at him now. Perhaps some of them would laugh another way before all was done.

Probably that was a crisis, a turning-point in Halliday's existence, when Alice looked so unluckily out of her window. He was actually on the verge of believing in human sincerity and kindness. A little more, and he might have known what it was to have hope. Now faith and hope were suddenly blown out of his nature, and for ever. The wehr-wolf loses his old power of returning to his original shape. He howls and ravens in the forest, to be a man no more.

— ◆ —

CHAPTER XIX.

PERPLEXED IN THE EXTREME.

THERE were few men of his class and character in London more uncomfortable than the Rev. Eustace Massie. Everything seemed of late to have gone wrong with him, more especially during the few weeks of his present stay in London. There could be no doubt that three-fourths, five-sixths of his vexations were to be traced to the unlucky propinquity of his cousin Paul. As Fitzjames, in Scott's poem, is pursued everywhere by some association of the Douglas, so poor Eustace could not turn to right or left without being encountered by something which disagreeably reminded him of Paul Massie. It made his situation more uncomfortable that he had no confidant. When he thought of speaking on the subject to Sarah, a keen twinge, agonizing as a dart of neuralgia, passed through him. To talk of it to Lydia would have been a pure waste of time and breath. He heard everywhere of Paul's fast life, of his odd manners, of his queer companions, of his one especial friend, the lady with the Italian name, of his expenditure and of his debts. All this did not come to him in the way of slander. Good-natured people sometimes spoke to him of his cousin in words of praise, called Paul a fine fellow, and asked Eustace to bring him to their houses. Ladies sometimes put direct questions to Lydia that amused or confused her, and much annoyed Eustace. But this was not all. Nay, all this, vexing enough in its way, was nothing to some other new and mysterious sources of vexation.

Letters from Eustace's man of business at Seaborough began utterly to perplex him. They talked about queer rumors afloat in the town, odd inquiries being made, mysterious ransackings of old parish books and records, singular visitations of persons whom the man of business thought he knew to be connected with the office of a London attorney. These odd persons had been to Crossley the boatman, and to Crossley's wife. It was given out too that Crossley's mind was quite at rest about the safety of his daughter Alice ; and that she was somewhere in a good place in London ; and in a vague way the man of business, suspicious no doubt, connected her disappearance with the subsequent setting on foot of queer inquiries all about the town. What the precise nature of the inquiries was, he did not say ; but from the tone of his letter it might be inferred that he presumed that they ought in some way to be of interest to Eustace Massie.

Eustace could make nothing of all this ; but he had been stopped in the Strand one day by a half-drunken, dissolute ne'er-do-well from Seaborough, whose name he remembered to be Halliday, who asked him for money, and on getting a shilling or two out of charity and shame, offered for a five-pound note to put the clergyman up to something that would open his eyes, and put him in a way to prepare for squalls. To this metaphorical warning the clergyman would have paid little attention ; but Halliday endeavored to make his meaning clearer by intimating in a thick whisper that Eustace's cousin and "her" were plotting against Eustace, and trying to do him a bad turn, and that he, Halliday, knew what it all meant, and could open their eyes. Whereupon Eustace indignantly declined to have his eyes opened, and turned scornfully away from his fellow-townsman. whom he set down as mad, either by

10*

providential or spirituous deprivation of senses. And now Eustace remembered clearly enough that he had heard this dissolute creature described as thé discarded lover of Alice Crossley; and idiotic as his talk appeared to be, he could not help connecting it in some inexplicable way with the perplexing hints he had just been receiving from Seaborough.

Vexations come in battalions. It has been said that part of Eustace's business in town was to assist in finding a candidate for Seaborough. A fit and proper person had been found. The eldest son of a peer—a young man of the most strictly orthodox character, brought up in the best school, who used to make the prettiest speeches on the platforms of various Church societies; a Conservative of mild propensities; on the whole, the very nonpareil of candidates—had kindly consented to stand for Seaborough. Eustace exulted, in his decorous way. There would be, could be, he felt sure, no opposition. Eustace hated a contested election, with its riot, its coarsenesss, its vulgarity, its bribery, and its drink. Some of the London papers already spoke of the affair as settled—a quiet walk over. The local paper on Eustace's side congratulated the electors of the borough on the prospect of Seaborough's at last assuming its proper place in the councils of the nation. The opposite party kept very quiet; gave absolutely no sign. Eustace himself, sitting under the gallery of the House of Commons, had heard a gentleman, who rose up from one of the ministerial seats, mumble something in which the word "Seaborough" occurred; and it was explained to him that this meant moving for the writ. So the affair was apparently all right, and there were only three or four days to run.

The very next day Eustace was passing down St. James's-street, when he was hailed rather impetuously from the steps of a club. The hail came from the lips of one for whom Eustace had a high respect—the senior member for his county, who had been a prime mover in discovering the fitting candidate to rescue Seaborough from its degrading position in the councils of the nation. Eustace had to shade his eyes from the early morning sun of London (half-past twelve P. M.), as it fell glowing on the pavement. Thus he recognized the utterer of the vehement call.

"Hallo, Massie," said the senator, "this is a devilish queer business about Seaborough! Very glad I met you. What does it all mean?"

"What is it, Sir John? I have not heard of anything particular."

"Not heard of anything? On your honor, Massie, don't you know anything about it?"

"Really, Sir John, I don't even know what you are alluding to—and I think my word will be enough without any other pledge. What's the matter?"

"Well, Massie, I'm glad to hear what you say. I couldn't believe that you had anything to do with it—I couldn't believe it, sir; and so I have been telling Stokes and Freshman."

"Do, pray, tell me what you are speaking of?"

"Why, man, we're going to be opposed in Seaborough after all, and by somebody who they tell me is a cousin of yours,—some Mr. Paul Massie."

"Good heavens!—what is the meaning of this? Are you sure? Paul Massie! It can't be serious; it must be a joke, Sir John; this is sheer stuff and nonsense."

"Stuff and nonsense it may be, but I can tell you it's devilish serious stuff and nonsense. It's all over the clubs to-day, and little Tellers of the Reform told me just now that he met Brand this morning, and Brand told him the thing was quite serious, and Mr. Peter—Paul—what's his name?—Massie was to have the Government support. I saw the address. Supports ministers powerfully on the foreign policy—pitches strong into Tories—talks ever so much about local interests, and making Seaborough a port, or a dockyard, or an island, or I don't know what—and insists upon having the place represented by a member of a family always identified with its progress. That's the whole dodge, in fact. Foreign policy, local interests, no strangers,—these are the points to touch up the rabble. I hear that Massie started last night for Seaborough, and that old Charlton went down to introduce him. It's very vexing."

"Vexing, Sir John! It is indeed vexing to me; and I have only too much reason to fear that it is done chiefly to vex and insult me. It is a heavy insult, and one which I did not deserve. But it is not the only one I have received from the same quarter."

"If I were you, I should make a point of running down at once, else you'll find half your voters pledged against you, under the impression that they are voting for you— thinking that they are supporting your candidate when they are supporting your cousin. I bet anything the fellow will tell them so. A fellow capable of such a trick as that is capable of anything. I'm going down at once; come with me."

"It's a very painful position for me," murmured poor Eustace; "but I ought not to shrink."

"Certainly not—certainly not. Don't you see the awkward position it places you in with our men, having a fellow of your own name—a member of your own family— opposing the candidate you yourself invited to come forward? Would you think of seeing him, and having some sort of explanation?"

"Seeing him!—seeing whom?"

"Why, your cousin—this Massie; perhaps you could persuade him to retire, and not make a fool of himself."

"No, I'll never see him. I'll never make any appeal to him. I wish I had never seen his face."

Do you know anything about his means? Where does he get the money? People tell me that he lives fast; but they say that there's some woman with plenty of cash—"

"Sir John, I really know nothing of my cousin's ways

or means. I have certainly no reason to suspect him of any-thing dishonorable, or of living upon anybody's money but his own. He may wish to vex and grieve me; but he belongs to a family which does nothing disgraceful."

After all, blood is thicker than water; and a cousin is the son of one's father's or mother's sister or brother; and Eustace Massie was not a bad sort of a Christian for a clergyman, and he did not like the tone in which his friend spoke of his misguided relative.

Even while these two were talking came up several who knew them both—among the rest little Captain Trenton; and some congratulated Eustace in good faith upon his cousin's candidature; and some who understood the state of affairs rather better, sympathized with his unpleasant position. But no one seemed to have any doubt about the genuineness of the candidature. Everybody had seen somebody else who told him something which led him to believe that the new candidate and his friends were really doing their very best to win.

Eustace drove frantically home in a hansom, left a very hasty note for his womankind, who were out somewhere, and caught the next train for Seaborough. We shall not attempt any analysis and exposition of the feelings of that clergyman as he sat in the railway train and tried to read the paper.

When he reached Seaborough, he found the contest already raging. Happily for the peace of the neighborhood, it had not long to rage. Both sides were haranguing incessantly; the speaking was on both sides very vehement, and, for the most part, untrained. There were some great foreign questions stirring even the minds of villagers at the time, which gave Paul and Paul's supporters an immense advantage. All the Dissenters and Democrats, of whatever kind, rallied around him. Men came down from London —men with names which had reached even Seaborough— and delivered harangues full of epigram and splendid sentiment in his behalf. All the wrongs ever done to peoples

by despots, from Macedonia's madman to the Swede, were
flung tauntingly in the faces of Paul Massie's opponents.
The misdeeds of every Government, from that of the Tuiler-
ies to that of St. Petersburg, were made a bill of indictment against the Tory candidate. You might have thought
that Seaborough had a special mission to chastise tyrants ;
that the aristocratic candidate was the nominee of every
reigning autocrat and the secret agent of every dethroned
despot; and that the universal brotherhood and solidarity
of nations all the world over had chosen out Paul Massie
for their prime spokesman and representative.

On the other side, be sure that hyperbole did not lack.
The friends of aristocracy painted a ghastly picture of the
results which must follow, as the night the day, if in
evil hour Paul Massie should be returned for Seaborough,
The throne overturned ; the crown flung into a ditch, like
the diadem in Uhland's pretty poem, or hung on a hedge
like the regal coronal of Bosworth ; the Church profaned
and destroyed; the laws of property and marriage abolished;
the English language prohibited ; British beer cruelly taxed
to favor sour and rancid foreign mixtures ; Communism,
Socialism, Chartism, Red Republicanism, Yankeeism, Italian Revolutionism ; flat burglary and flat blasphemy ram-
pant everywhere : these were a few, and indeed only a few,
of the hideous consequences which must follow if poor Paul
Massie should be returned for Seaborough. The crisis was,
in short, a death-grapple between the British Constitution
and Paul Massie : the hour had come to end the reign of
the Church of England or of Paul Massie. Two stars keep
not their motion in one sphere; nor could one England
brook the double rule of the wisdom of our ancestors and
Paul Massie. The moment was supreme : the destiny of
Britain was in the hands of the Seaborough electors. Elect
Paul Massie, and the British Lion would have roared its
last, and the battle and the breeze would never more be
braved by the Union Jack.

It was sore for Eustace Massie to have to bear opposition to the candidate of his choice. He had himself assured the young nobleman that the affair would certainly be a walk over. Eustace liked influence, and the repute of possessing influence; nor did he, a Christian minister, hate the sons of peers. He felt as if his personal credit and honor were assailed the moment his candidate was opposed. Clergymen are generally as impatient and illogical politicians as women. Eustace felt that any opposition was hard to bear. But it was harder still that the candidate of his choice should be opposed by one who bore his own name, and on whom Eustace had quite made up his mind that he had showered unmerited kindnesses.

Yes; that was a heavy dispensation. But there came something far harder still; for the British Lion was left to howl in vain; the Union Jack was furled and flung in the dust; the son of the great British peer, the orthodox scion of England's proud nobility, the member and the ornament of so many religious societies, the chosen candidate of Eustace Massie, was defeated! Leicester-square had triumphed over Belgravia; Runnymede was left nowhere by Bohemia! The close of the poll came amid storm and stress; and the returning officer, serene amid a rain of eggs and brickbats, proclaimed Paul Massie, Esq., duly elected to serve in parliament for Seaborough.

As Eustace Massie walked home on the evening of this final day, he had to pass through many excited groups, and had been favored by some cheering and not a little hissing. He was determined to show that he could bear any obloquy and misconstruction, even where the scandal of a family quarrel was concerned, in the discharge of his duty. Therefore he took fortune's buffets and rewards with equal favor outwardly; but he did feel a pang when, passing one of the public-houses, he saw a huge painted caricature hung out, purporting to represent himself, Eustace Massie, in the act of selling the borough to the aristocratic candidate's father; himself, Eustace Massie, on his knees receiving a

huge bag of money from that nobleman—a peer on whom
he had never once set eyes in all his existence.

But something took place the night before the polling
which must be told in another chapter.

CHAPTER XX.

SEABOROUGH REVISITED.

IN compiling the natural history of ghosts there appears
to be one peculiarity of those uncomfortable creatures
upon which all poets, romancists, and philosophers, from
Virgil and Dante to Defoe and Mrs. Crowe, seem to be
quite agreed—that is, their habit of hanging perpetually,
and for no apparent purpose whatever, round the places or
the ruins of the places in which they once lived and loved
and hated and were happy and suffered. Your ghost is
no adventurer or explorer: he clings like a cat to the old
hearth, though its fire may have been extinguished for
generations; he wanders about the old home, even after
successive races of men and strange guests have been sheltered beneath its roof-tree. Therein the ghost, after all,
only gives the clearer proofs of his earthly origin, or shows
perhaps how truly a subjective creature he is whom we
have evolved out of the depths of our moral consciousness;
for there is no foolishness more common to living humanity
than the tendency still to linger and hang about places
between which and ourselves Fate has interposed her
wand of inexorable separation, and with which we know
that we have no longer anything to do. The murderer in
all the old stories comes back for no practical purpose
whatever to the scene of his crime, and of course gets captured there for his pains; and the discarded lover clings

about the place which once was full of hope and brightness to him, but which can never shine for him again ; and indeed sentiment of one sort or other thus sometimes sways the most practical of us, and renders of no account the calculations of the knowing, who always assume that men will only act as their substantial interest directs them. No ghost ever took a moonlit walk around a ruin to less practical purpose than Paul Massie had in his mind when, the night immediately before his polling-day, he set out alone to haunt the precincts of Seaborough-house and the shore which lay beneath its windows.

He had thrown himself into the business of the election contest with quite a feverish energy, and had canvassed and made speeches and discussed plans of action with all the zeal of the most devoted politician thirsting for a parliamentary position to serve his country or to satisfy his wife. He worked all the harder, perhaps, because of a vague dread that if he were to leave off for the moment, he might become suddenly disgusted with the whole affair, and inclined at any risk to back out of it. But the night before the polling he became seized with an unconquerable desire to escape for a few moments from the excited atmosphere of electioneering, and to breathe a purer air. So he contrived to accomplish a strategic movement which enabled him to free himself from his friends and backers and agents at the head-quarters in Seaborough and at Mr. Charlton's house, and, once clear of pursuit, he directed his steps towards his cousin's residence.

He had no business there. Nobody wanted him. He had not known before reaching the scene of the election how directly and completely his position in the contest placed him in opposition to his cousin. An hour in the town showed him this unpleasant fact. Eustace Massie, who would gladly, at almost any personal sacrifice, have avoided anything like a family scandal, conceived himself bound in honor and conscience not to draw back from the prominent position which he had pledged himself to take in the support of the noble candidate of his choice. The affair, therefore, began to assume quite a Polynices and Eteocles appearance—a sort of family fight, in which the closest relatives were marshalled upon opposite sides, prepared to cut each other's throats. A set of supporters, too, rallied to Paul, of whom he was himself much ashamed, and who threw into the struggle a vehemence of personal hostility quite superfluous to the actual issue, and indeed made it indisputably evident that they supported Paul Massie only because they hated Eustace Massie. These were the Low-Church men and the most uncompromising of the No-Popery Dissenters. In the eyes of these stern sectarians poor Eustace, who hated Popery as sincerely as the most virtuous Protestant ought to do, and who was as firmly convinced that poverty and Romanism go together as Exeter-hall itself could desire—poor Eustace was regarded as not one whit less odious than Cardinal Wiseman or Judas Iscariot. Therefore, had Paul Massie been the Rev. Dr. M'Neile or Father Gavazzi, his No-Popery supporters could not more aggressively have insisted on the fact that he came to put down Romanism, altars, candlesticks, auricular confession, and ritualistic practices. They placarded the town with oracular announcements in big print, to the effect that " The Rev. E. N. Massie is a Papist in disguise ; " or proclamations of "No candlesticks ! " which publications, though they might seem to the superficial mind widely removed from the questions at issue in the contest, yet were supposed to have a tremendous effect in working up the slumbering Protestantism of the constituency, and directing its mighty energies into the true channel.

All this, of course, Eustace supposed to be directed, or at least encouraged, by Paul Massie, who had nothing whatever to do with it, and indeed had nearly forfeited all chance of his election more than once by the angry emphasis with which he repudiated and condemned it.

Paul well knew that these incidents of the contest must

contribute heavily to make his name odious in Seaborough-house. He would not for anything have had to meet his cousin Eustace alone and face to face; he would have dreaded equally, but for different reasons, a meeting with Mrs. Massie. He knew well enough that Sarah and Lydia were still in London; yet his feet bore him in the direction of Seaborough-house.

He walked along the strand, on which the moon shone softly and sadly. The sweet air of the summer flowers rested even on the sea, and the lazy waves hardly throbbed upon the still glowing shingle. He soon reached that part of the shore which ran beneath his cousin's demesne, and was only divided from it by the little wall he scrambled over the first night of his visit to England. He could see the roof and chimneys of the house, and he could not resist the temptation to draw a little nearer; to cross the wall and lose himself for a moment among the trees and the walks. The house, as he approached it, seemed all dark, as if no life whatever were stirring there; and indeed it seemed to repel him as most of its inmates had done. He came to just the spot where he had parted from Sarah—where he might almost say that he last saw her, for he could hardly call the momentary glimpse of her in London a meeting. He was not a sentimental man, but he remained fixed to that spot for some time: he clung to it as one clings to a cherished grave. He stooped, gathered some leaves from the spot, and laid them carefully in his pocket-book, among electioneering accounts, and heads of speeches, and names of pledged supporters, and other such rubbish.

A sound startled him while he was thus engaged. It was the sound of a footstep, and nothing could well have seemed to him a more untoward event just then than to be seen by anybody while he was thus secretly as it were within the precincts of Eustace Massie's demesne. He grew hot with vexation. It was too late, however, to retreat or to escape observation; the footstep, which was that of a woman, came nearer and nearer. Paul drew

back and leaned against the tree near which he had been
standing. In a moment the figure of Mrs. Massie entered
the walk.

Evening had by this time given place to night, and, but
for the moon, darkness would have concealed our friend
from anyone passing hastily along the walk, for the tree
under which Paul stood was some yards away and many
shrubs grew between. Paul still hoped that he might
escape unobserved. Mrs. Massie was walking slowly
along, her eyes fixed on the ground, and Paul could hear
distinctly that she was speaking or murmuring to herself,
as she passed. She wore no bonnet or cloak, but had a
dark shawl thrown, mantilla-fashion—perhaps a memory
of the old ways of the Mexican life—over her head, and falling down her shoulders. The paleness of her face showed
all the whiter from the frame of black in which it thus was
set. Her figure looked wonderfully youthful ; despite of
the dream-like vacillation which seemed to characterize all
her movements, she might have passed in the eyes of anyone who stood where Massie was then standing for a girl
of twenty. She passed on without seeing him, and Paul
began to breathe a little more freely. The walk was
almost circular, and, after fringing the grass on which he
stood, curved away in the direction of the house ; therefore, when she passed him, he hoped she would follow the
path, and that he might then be able to retreat altogether.
But he was mistaken. After she had gone a few steps he
knew that she stopped, and then he heard her slowly returning. Still it was not beyond hope that she might
again fail to see him. She came on ; she was walking
very slowly. As she approached the tree, she turned her
face in that direction, and the moon fell full upon it.
There are legends of mysterious beings who assume the
form of young and lovely women, and beguile men, but
whose real nature is revealed at a flash to him who has the
fortune to see their faces under the earliest beams of a new
moon. Then the purple light of youth fades from the

cheeks, and the flesh withers and looks shrivelled, and the
eyes are sunken and gleam with a baleful fire, and the
whole illusion melts under the exorcising ray. So it
might have seemed in one sense with poor Mrs. Massie.
The figure, the step, the shape of the head, the contour of
the face, the fair locks that escaped from under the shawl
—all these spoke of freshness and youth. But the face on
which the moonlight now fell with so disenchanting a
lustre looked withered and worn and hopeless and old.
Paul thought he had never seen an expression of sorrow
and pain and fear so completely congealed upon a human
face as that which was stamped in livid colors upon the
features now turned towards him. Absorbed and almost
fascinated by the sight, he forgot for the moment his own
position. At first he was unseen. The eyes which were
turned towards him seemed to have no sight for any
earthly object around. They looked into the past, or into
the future. But as she was turning her face away, and the
shadow was again about to fall on it, Paul made some
involuntary movement of his arm, and disturbed a branch
of the tree. The sound reached Mrs. Massie's ears; she
stopped, looked towards the spot where Paul was standing, and saw him. She looked wildly at him. He remained perfectly motionless an instant under the embarrassment of the situation. Her lips opened, and she
seemed as if she were about to scream, but she suppressed
any sound more penetrating than a long, deep, agonized
moan. A moment yet she looked at him, then, still moaning and shivering from head to foot, she fell upon her
knees on the ground, and pressed her hands over her eyes,
as one whose only present thought is to shut out some
sight too fearful for human nerves to bear.

Paul had expected some manifestation of surprise or
displeasure, but assuredly nothing like this. The very
strangeness of it served at once to rally his composure
and self-control, as a sudden shock sometimes recalls to

firmness the trembling nerves.   He sprang to Mrs. Massie's side, and lifted her from the ground.

"Dear Mrs. Massie, dear aunt," he said, "I have alarmed you dreadfully, and I do not know how to apologize.   I ought not to be here; but pray do not be alarmed.   It is only I—your very unlucky nephew, Paul Massie, of whom I hope you do not think too hardly."

She pushed him sharply, angrily, from her, and said, in tones that quivered partly with fear and partly with vexation :

"You have no right to come here, and—and frighten me.   I cannot bear it.   This is not the first time.   You torture me.   Why—why have you come here?   Why did you stand that way—here, at night—when all is lonely and ghastly, and look so, and terrify me?"

"Indeed I had no notion of doing anything of the kind. I never expected to see you; and I came in merely by chance.   I am sure I don't know why, but because in passing the place something seemed to draw me in.   But I know well I ought not to be here, and I will go, and not return any more.   Pardon me for having alarmed you; and good-night."

He was half offended, and yet ashamed to show any feeling of bitterness when talking with one of whose full sanity he felt no small doubt.   He did not turn immediately to go; he hoped she would say some kindly word, or at least some word which might reassure him as to her mental condition.

"I wish you had not come," she went on.   "O, how much I wish you had not come!"

This was too much.   He raised his hat, bowed coldly, and was turning to leave the place, when she caught him by the arm :

"Paul, Paul," she said, "you must not go—not now, not this way.   Don't mind—O, my dear, don't mind what I was saying.   Indeed I hardly knew myself what it was.   My nerves are wretched, and I have been much alone all the day,

and I am easily frightened; and I scarcely know now what
I thought when first I saw you. Perhaps I took you for a
ghost. Some people believe there are ghosts, don't they?
But I am glad, very glad, to see you; and it was kind of you
to come. It was very kind; only you shouldn't frighten
timid people late at night. Come, give me your arm."

She talked now with a forced vivacity not pleasant to
listen to. When she took his arm, Paul could feel that she
was still shivering all over.

"You will come in," she continued. "Eustace is not at
home; that is, he is in the town, in Seaborough, busy
about this unfortunate election. But he would be very
glad to see you if he were here, and perhaps he may be
back soon. Come in."

"No, aunt, I cannot go in; and you must not ask me.
I did not come to see you, or anyone here; I must tell you
that. And I cannot enter Eustace's house. We are not
friends; why, I do not know; but he, I suppose, thinks very
badly of me, and thinks me his enemy, which Heaven knows
I am not, nor anybody else's."

"I do not know," Mrs. Massie said hesitatingly, "why
Eustace and you should have quarrelled. It was my dearest wish that you should have been friends, and lived like
—like cousins; as cousins ought to live. It was my earnest
wish that you should come to this country; but I don't
believe our dearest wishes ever are fulfilled in life. Mine
have all gone wrong. Why have you and Eustace
quarrelled?"

"In truth we have not quarrelled. But I think he never
liked me; and he was too ready to believe anything bad of
me, or at least to put the worst construction upon everything."

"But why have you opposed him in this unfortunate
election? Why make a public scandal here for the sake of
thwarting him?"

"Indeed you do me wrong, as well as he does, by suspecting me of having done anything for the sake of thwarting

him. I never knew, or had the least reason to suppose, that he had any interest in the matter—any real and personal interest, that is—one way or the other, until after I had pledged myself to stand, and put myself and my friends prominently before the public. Half-a-dozen friendly words' from him, or from anyone on his behalf, would have settled the whole matter. Had he come to me, or written, or sent to me, and frankly explained his position, the thing could not have occurred. But I never knew that Lord—I forget his name—was Eustace's candidate, until Eustace rushed down here and flung himself into the ranks of the opposite party. He made the scandal—not I. What could I do? I was pledged to my friends. I could not throw them over."

"Is it true that Salome Adams is one of your friends?"

"Yes. Salome Adams—Madame de Luca—is one of my friends, one of my best and kindest and most valued friends."

"Is she your friend because she is our enemy?"

"My dear aunt, these are mere dreams and delusions. She is no more your enemy than I am. Why should she be? I don't believe she is or could be the enemy of any human being. Certainly she has been kind to me—as no one else has."

He spoke these latter words with slow and deep emphasis. Mrs. Massie appeared not to notice it.

"Do you mean to marry her?"

The abruptness of the question startled him, and somewhat embarrassed him too. He had rather a dark complexion for blushes, and yet it is not unlikely that he blushed. But he answered in as careless a manner as he could assume:

"Madame de Luca is only a friend, and is quite unlikely ever to be anything more, so far as I am concerned. I am not in a position to marry anybody; and I am sure Madame de Luca never bestowed a thought on the subject."

"Paul Massie, I don't like Salome de Luca; I fear and dislike her both; and she has little friendly feeling to me. But if you loved her, I had rather hear that you married

her than that you were married to a queen on a throne.
Do anything—commit any folly; but never, never marry
unless for pure love alone. Kill yourself, rather than
marry anyone to whom you do not give your whole heart—
or who does not give her whole, whole heart to you. All
other marriages are curses. There are those who know it
—who have the knowledge written on their hearts in fire—
ay and on their lives in blood."

Her manner was so wild and earnest—so unreasonably,
unnaturally earnest as it seemed to Paul, that all his doubts
about her reason began to return. She clutched his arm
with all her force as she was speaking. They were now
slowly pacing up and down along the walk where Paul had
first seen her.

He was anxious to turn the conversation into any other
channel, and so said with an assumed lightness of manner :

"Well, aunt, I am not a marrying man just yet, nor likely
to be soon. It would be hard indeed to find anyone to
marry me; and I really don't mean to marry for money at
any time. But I am much grieved about this confounded
election business. It never ought to have come to this; it
never would if I had been frankly, or indeed fairly, dealt
with. I am very glad that you give me an opportunity of
explaining myself on the subject, and showing that whatever unpleasantness may have arisen, I am not to blame
for it."

Mrs. Massie's mind was not deeply fixed upon the subject
of the election. She only answered vaguely, "I am glad of
it—I am sure of it ; and I think Eustace will be glad of it
too. He is very good and just, Eustace is—he would not
wrong anyone : and then he is firm and strong. You must
see him, and this must all be settled."

"I am anxious for a reconciliation as much as anyone
can be. I do not know why we should be anything but
friends. But there is something strange which I cannot understand. Aunt, can you tell me anything about
my father ?"

11

Mrs. Massie's fingers grasped his arm more tightly and feverishly than before.

" About your father ? "

" Yes.   You knew him, did you not ? "

" I knew him ?   O, yes, I knew him."

" In Mexico ? "

·" Yes, in Mexico.   But I never saw him since you were born,—I believe he died soon after,—I do not know.   How cold it is ! "

It was a very warm night ; the atmosphere still glowed with the embers of the fiery heat which had burnt on the landscape and on the sea all the day.

" Had we not better come in ? " Mrs. Massie continued ; " I begin to feel it quite chilly.   I do not often walk here so late ; but this evening the house was so dull, with the girls in London and Eustace not at home, that I thought it would brighten me to walk here a little ? so I came, and I saw you."

" No, aunt, I must not go into the house, and cannot; but I will not keep you here any longer.   Only, I may not see you soon again ; and I know there is some painful secret about my father which ought to be told to me.   I know there is.   People are even now guessing at it and hinting at it—people whose very names I do not know ; and I am in utter ignorance of it.   What *is* it ?   If there's anything to be told, you must know it.   Better I learned it from your lips than from those of a stranger.   Tell me—I beg of you, tell me."

" I can tell you nothing," she replied after a pause, during which she had more than once, it appeared, begun to speak and stopped, or tried to speak and failed.   " I can tell you nothing : your mother and father "—another pause —" were not happy, I believe—and were separated at last."

" But that is not all.   Is there nothing more ? "

" What else could there be ? "

" Is my father dead ?—can I not know even that for certain ? "

"He is dead." The words were faint—indeed almost inaudible.

"I see that my questions torture you; but, good heaven! how can I avoid asking them? Useless my cross-examining and distracting you,—I do not even know what to ask. If there is anything which I ought to know, do, I pray you, tell me of it. No matter how painful it may be, let me hear it, let me know the worst at once. I feel that your motive is kindly and good, and that you only wish to save me from pain; but, believe me, the pain of knowing it—be it what it will—is slight compared to the torment of guessing. I beseech you to be frank and tell me all."

There was no answer: Paul bent down to look in Mrs. Massie's face. A strange conflict of cruel emotions was working there. Neither spoke for a moment.

"Once more, aunt, and I will trouble you no more. Is there nothing—is there really nothing which you have to tell me?"

"O, Paul, Paul!" she said, and she broke into bitter tears, "why have you asked me? Why have you come here—why did I bring you here? I strove with all my power to avoid this; but it has come on me at last."

Paul braced his nerves and feelings for the painful disclosure of some kind which he now expected to hear. Mrs. Massie drew her arm from his, stopped, and fixed her eyes upon the ground, while she interlaced with feverish restlessness her quivering fingers. Was she making up her mind—was he about to know all?

Perhaps so. Another moment, and all might have been told. But the gravel of one of the walks crashed at that moment under a quick footstep. Mrs. Massie heard it and started. Her whole expression changed.

"No," she said, in faint and broken tones, "there is nothing to be told; I know nothing, nothing at all. Hush! here is Eustace."

And Eustace that moment entered the walk, and looked

amazed indeed when he saw his mother in such company.
He raised his hat with a cold and distant courtesy.

"Have you long returned?" asked his mother, asking
any question to break the embarrassing silence.

"Only this moment," he said; "and I came to find
you, surprised that you should be out of doors so
late."

"It is late," she replied; "I was going in.   But do you
not see your cousin Paul?"

"Yes, O yes; certainly.   I hardly expected the pleasure
of a visit.   I am surprised, under the circumstances—"

Paul was embarrassed at first; but rather because of the
embarrassment of Mrs. Massie than on his own account.
He was not conscious of any cause to be ashamed, and
he scorned conventional hypocrisies and meannesses of
any kind.

"I did not come to see you, Eustace," he said, "or
indeed anybody.   I wandered in here out of a mere impulse,
and I met your mother.   I am very glad I did; for it gives
us all the chance of an explanation which may remove mis-
understandings.   I am sure you have misunderstood me; I
dare say I have misunderstood you.   Let us talk the matter
over, and be friends.   It can all be settled even now; at least
so far as this absurd election affair is concerned."

Paul was quite making up his mind that, no matter what
might be said, he would not carry on a contest which placed
him in direct antagonism to his only relatives.   Let some
one else be found—Wynter could easily find some one even
now, at the last moment—to take his place, and fight the
battle of liberty unfettered by the thought that his blood
relations were in the opposite ranks.

But Eustace answered very coldly.   "I don't know that
there is any misunderstanding, or anything to explain.   I
am doing what I feel to be my duty; I assume, of course—
indeed, I do not doubt, that you are acting upon a similar
conviction.   I regret that we should be opposed; but I am
not aware of any course which could now avoid the neces-

sity. All that could now be said ought to have been thought of and said before."

For in truth Eustace did not want reconciliation, and moreover did not believe it possible. Eustace conceived that between Paul and himself there lay a far wider gulf than any election compromise could bridge over. He was a good man—a terribly good man was Eustace; and he did not see how he or his could possibly associate with any but good men. He had—the truth must be spoken—got it firmly into his head that Paul Massie was not a good man. He felt convinced that Paul seldom, if ever, went to church; he had no doubt that he gambled, and heard the chimes at midnight, and consorted, if not with a wild prince, at least with many a Poins; and he did not like the stories he had heard about his friendship for Madame de Luca. Paul's appearance in the electioneering contest he only regarded as a natural and consistent proceeding on the part of one who had no fixed principles, and from whom, therefore, nothing was to be expected. He had no very angry feeling towards his cousin; but he regarded it as simply impossible that he could associate with him. And so his words and his manner very plainly showed.

So Paul felt his overtures of reconciliation thrust back upon him, and his cheek grew hot while his heart grew cold.

Another woman than Mrs. Massie—a woman with some glow and force of character—might nevertheless have brought these two natures together then and there. She might, with the warmth of love and womanly confidence, have forced Eustace to thaw, and thus brought the waters of human affection gushing forth. But she was incapable even of such an effort. She looked from one to the other with an expression of fearful and almost abject misery. Indeed, she seemed positively afraid of Eustace. He was not by any means a strong man—had little real vigor of character; but he had just that amount of egotism and superficial firmness of manner which, when they are combined with any fair degree of high principle, and more especially when they are sustained by any appearance of religious inspiration, commonly impress women with the idea of a heaven-sent strength and dignity. Mrs. Massie quite accepted her son as a spiritual and moral ruler sent to guide and govern the weak, though himself too strong to have any share or sympathy in human weakness.

Eustace was firmly convinced that he was doing right when he thus positively repelled Paul Massie, and bade him to stand off. Mrs. Massie's heart was pierced, indeed ; but it had been pierced many times, and often bleeding had not yet bled to death. She bowed to the decree of religion and justice, and morally abandoned Paul Massie.

He made but a brief and hasty adieu. Mrs. Massie took his hand, and, after a furtive frightened side-glance, pressed it to her lips. He drew it away quickly, almost sharply. There was a secrecy about her manner which offended him. She was evidently afraid to acknowledge one gleam of affection for him before her son ; she pressed his hand as a timid girl might demonstrate her affection to her lover while the watchful eyes of a stern mother were on them. Nay, worse than that ; as a faithless wife might strive to convey some acknowledgment of an unlawful confidence in the presence of her husband.

Paul left the place in bitterness of spirit. He felt ashamed of himself more than ever he had been before. Had he been spurned from Eustace's door, he could not have been steeped in a deeper sense of degradation than that which penetrated him as he left the place. He went directly to the committee-rooms of his party in the town, and they worked there long and late that night. Then they returned —Paul, that is, and some half a dozen or more of his principal supporters—to Mr. Charlton's, where they were waited for by a tolerably large gathering of sympathizers. The dawn of a summer morning was shining on them when they broke up and went to their bedrooms, after many wild speeches had been delivered and pledges of success interchanged. Paul did his very utmost to put his supporters in good heart. He was now resolved that no effort of his and no feeling of his should be spared to defeat the candidate of the opposition. This was not truly a very magnanimous resolution, when we consider the cause which lent it special earnestness. But Paul was not in a humor for magnanimity just then. He was determined to succeed, and full of confidence. To adopt his own phrase, he was " bound to win."

But before he reached Seaborough, after leaving his cousin's demesne, an incident befell him, which, were he in a cooler mood, might have left something puzzling behind.

Walking towards the town, chewing the cud of very bitter fancy, he saw approaching him the tall stooping figure of Dan Crossley the boatman. Paul would rather not have met him just at that moment. He was not in a temper, perhaps, for friendly greetings of any kind. But moreover the sight of Crossley filled him with a sort of penitent feeling. When he was leaving Seaborough for London, it will be remembered how earnestly he promised Crossley to devote himself to the discovery of Alice, for whose secret and successful disappearance he could not help holding himself accountable in a sort of indirect way. Now he did not indeed fail in his promise. He did set inquiries going ; but he very soon heard that the girl had "turned up" somewhere, and was safe, and that her people were satisfied. Since then he had not troubled himself to make any definite inquiries as to Alice's whereabouts ; and, indeed, once he was relieved of any doubt as to her safety, very soon forgot all about her. Therefore the sight of her father made him feel a little ashamed and compunctious. There was nothing, indeed, with which he could be reproached. There was nothing he ought to have done and did not do. In fact, as it turned out, there was no occasion for any effort of his. But his own conscience reproached him for the rapid fading away of his interest in the poor boatman and his family. And he would now have avoided a meeting with Crossley, if escape were decently possible.

It was impossible, however. Crossley came up, pulled at his cap with homely courtesy, and warmly greeted Paul. The latter held out his hand and shook the boatman's brown fingers.

"Glad to see ye, Mr. Paul—proud to see you, sir. I hear your chances are very good, sir. You shall have my vote, never fear. And when you get into parliament-house, I hope ye'll often come to see us down here."

"Thank you, thank you, Crossley. I am glad to find I have so many friends here. I hope you are well, Crossley. You look strong and stout, I am glad to see. And your wife?"

"Thankee, sir, pretty well, though the times are not very good."

" And your daughter—she too, I hope, is well ? "

" Yes, Mr. Paul; I hear she's very well. Much obliged to you for the trouble you took to find out the foolish girl. There never was any harm in her ; only nonsensical notions sometimes, I'm afraid."

"She does not live with you, now ? "

" O no, sir. She has a place in London, you know, and doesn't want to come back. I dare say it's all right; but I'd rather she came back and remained here under my eyes and her mother's eyes."

Paul's mind was abstracted. He hardly heard Crossley's words ; and the boatman kept on for a few moments in the same strain unheeded. At last he appealed to Paul's attention by a direct question.

"Pray, Mr. Paul, did you ever happen to meet that fellow called Halliday—Jem Halliday, you remember—in London ? "

" No, Crossley, I never saw him there."

" Nor heerd of him ? "

" No, indeed. Is he in London ? "

" So I'm told, sir. He left here immediately after poor Ally went. He's a great liar, sir ; God forgive him, and me too for believing his lies like an old fool. He told me horrible lies about Ally, and all that. Mr. Paul, I hope you mayn't meet him. He's an enemy of yours."

"Why, Crossley, I have never done him any harm, except some few angry words that I once spoke to him."

"Yes, but he has got something into his drunken good-for-nothing head; and he's a bad man; he's sure to come to something bad in the end. Give him a wide berth, Mr. Massie."

"Well, Crossley, if ever I see him I shall give him as wide a berth as possible. But I cannot imagine what cause he can have to be my enemy; and I don't see what possible harm he can do me. I am much obliged to you, and I hope I shall see you again before I return to London."

Paul again held out his hand, and was going on towards the town. The boatman hesitated, and at last said:

"I'm told there is to be a lawsuit, Mr. Paul. I'm sorry for it. Fam'ly quarrels are always bad things; and once your in a court of law, there's no saying what mayn't be brought up. But if it is to be, sir, them that know anything must only speak the truth. We know, my wife and I, very little. We were never much given to minding other people's affairs; but of course, whatever we are asked, we must answer, without fear, favor, or affection. Good-night, sir; I'm keeping you waiting with my talk. Somebody must win, sir, and I can't help hoping it will be you."

Paul Massie went on his way, not indeed understanding very distinctly what the boatman was talking about, but assuming that it bore reference to the election, and the possibility of a petition following it,—a thing which both sides were already beginning to anticipate,—and the hunting-up of evidence to support a case of bribery and intimidation. Therefore the words made no impression on him, and he felt relieved when he had got rid of the boatman, and could follow his own road and the train of his own thoughts alone. Not long, however, was this latter luxury allowed to him. As he approached the suburbs of Sea-

11*

borough, the sparks of the unwonted political excitement already began to shower thick and fast about him. He was promptly recognized by little knots of people at corners, and cheered ; and the knots began before long to form into an attendant crowd, and follow him with hurrahs. Then other little knots began to groan for him and his supporters, and to cheer for the other candidate; and little skirmishes took place here and there, and Paul's friends, being much the more numerous and obstreperous, were not very patient of opposition, and Paul had more than once to exert the utmost of his muscular strength to rescue some too demonstrative champion of his enemy from popular vengeance. So he was the centre of a mob when he reached his committee-rooms, and then he had to mount to the window and deliver a speech. Decidedly, wherever else he might be out of favor, Paul was the pet candidate of the Seaborough populace.

━━━━━◆◆◆━━━━━

CHAPTER XXI.

THE FIRST BLOOD DRAWN.

MADAME DE LUCA had gone to the Opera. The election was still an incomplete event, and Paul Massie was not in town. About nine o'clock the door of Madame de Luca's house opened, and a person came out, who looked cautiously and timidly up and down the street before venturing farther. This was a young woman neatly and smartly dressed, as one might see even in the comparative darkness. She might perhaps have passed at a hasty glance for Madame de Luca's waiting-maid, but if looked at with any attention, would be observed to have something in her movements not at all corresponding with the way of that Gallicized and peculiar style of person. Having looked up and down the street, she went forward and passed into the main thoroughfare. She had seen nobody, but somebody had been watching her. The somebody was a man who had been skulking in the depths of a dark portico just opposite. He followed her, still keeping in the dark, at a considerable distance behind. Once they were both in the main road it was easy for him to keep her movements in his eye, without being noticed by her among so many hurrying passengers. She kept on for some distance, and then turned into a quiet street. Her follower only glanced down the street, as if in passing, then turned back and glanced again. He saw her standing at a door which he knew well. He could see by her gesture that she had dropped a letter into the box. Perhaps he did not count upon her immediately coming away, for he had not made any effort to conceal himself, when the girl turned back and came down the street towards him. He made two strides to meet her, and stood on the pavement just before her. She gave utterance to an ejaculation of surprise and alarm which was almost a scream.

"Hallo," said the man, "so we've found you out at last, and so you ain't drowned at all, nor dead at all, only living in grand London lodgings all the time, and paying visits to your swell friends! And ain't he at home, after your walk? So Mr. Paul Massie ain't in, ain't he? Maybe you'd better wait for him."

"Let me pass," said the girl; "don't attempt to stop me."

"Am I stopping you? How grand we are! We won't speak to old friends that have been waiting so long on the lookout for us! We must cut our old sweethearts, must we, because we have got grand gentlemen and ladies now? We must leave our old fathers and mothers too! This'll be a fine story for Dan Crossley to-morrow, to hear that his daughter is walking London streets of nights."

"Dan Crossley's affairs and my affairs are nothing to

you, I should think," said the girl, recovering, or affecting to recover, her courage, and tossing her head; "Dan Crossley and Dan Crossley's daughter are free to do as they like, I should think. I told you often enough, Jem Halliday, that I would have nothing to do with you and nothing to say to you, and I tell you the same now again once for all. I'm my own mistress, and I'll do as I please."

"No, you ain't," said Halliday with an ugly leer. "I don't know whose mistress you are, but I've watched for you long enough, and now I've found you I'll take you home to your father."

"Don't dare to touch me," cried the girl; "if you do, I'll call the police."

"Do, and I'll show them the bill offering a reward for finding of you; I've got it here. Ain't you Alice Crossley? and haven't I got your height here, and the color of your hair and your eyes, and isn't your description all right? Except your clothes—perhaps they weren't quite so fine when you ran away; but I suppose you can explain to your father how you came by them."

"I must go," she said, endeavoring to pass him.

"Not a bit of it;" and he seized her by the wrist. "Do you think I am going to leave you to Mr. Paul Massie? Do you think I'm not going to have my revenge on you for the way you treated me? I was good enough for you once, until you saw him."

"You were good enough for me until you made a drunkard and a low vulgar fellow of yourself. I wasn't going to put up with a person like you. Nor Dan Crossley, as you call him, wouldn't let me, even if I would. And Dan Crossley won't thank you for this."

There was tremor in the girl's voice as she talked this way, although she strove to speak in an easy and scornful tone.

"Whether Dan Crossley would thank me or no, I'll act the part of a friend by him, and I won't leave his daughter to walk London streets. I've watched you now long enough. Don't I know that your grand lady would turn you out of doors if she knew you were running out the moment she turned her back, to pay visits to her own sweetheart? A nice lot you've got into! If I told the lady·of this, where would you be to-morrow? Yes, I've had my eyes on you when you didn't think it. I've seen you from across the way and through the blinds in the lady's bedroom, and ·fitting on her bracelets and things, and fancying you looked a fine lady yourself. O, I found you out, when you thought I didn't see you! And the lady herself, she thinks she has me under her thumb. But I'll let her see she hasn't; and now come away."

"Let me go," she said; "you shall not drag me with you. I must go."

"Listen, Ally," he said in a growling tone. "Sooner than let you go, I'll cut your throat here with my own hands, if I gev' myself up to the police a moment after. I wouldn't think twice about it. I've been waiting and watching and half starving here about London, until I'm like a mad dog; and I'll have my revenge—you sha'n't stay here for him."

"I've never seen him; he doesn't know I'm here."

"Gammon. Tell that to the marines. We have had enough of talk here now; come along with me; we'll talk on the way."

"Jem," said Alice, "if you only want money, I'll give you a little. I'm sorry you lost your time here looking for me. It was very kind of you."

He burst into a rude loud laugh, which made people passing along the great thoroughfare from which this lonely street emerged looked round surprised.

"Gammon again, Ally. I'm up to all that now. Where's your money? Show it to me."

She took out a small purse. He snatched it from her hand, and chuckled. "Not much," said he. "Do you spend all you get? Anyhow, 'twill pay for us in the train home."

The girl shuddered. There were tears in her eyes. She looked vainly up and down the street. A policeman tramped past the corner. She thought for an instant of calling him; but her voice choked in her throat. An appeal to a policeman would have been discovery all the same.

"Come along," said Halliday; "I know a place where we'll be safe—and quite proper—O yes, quite proper—until the time for the train. And we'll have a cab to the station—such swells! And we'll send a note to your ladyship to tell her that she needn't trouble about you any more. Ain't I happy that I've got you at last! Crying too! Cry away; it doesn't soften me. I'm very glad to see you crying. I suppose you're crying because you can't come knocking any more at Mr. Paul Massie's doors of an evening, and leaving such a fine place as London too! Come along; perhaps you'd like to take my arm."

The girl started, and made a frantic effort to run away. Halliday caught her in his strong gripe.

"No, you don't," he growled. "Try that again, and I'll take you off your feet and carry you. I tell you again, Ally, it's no use. If I can't take you away alive, I'll take you away dead, and that's all about it."

He was dragging her away. She scarcely dared to struggle, and yet looked wildly round for help or chance. She still would not cry aloud. Anything rather than exposure. Suddenly a hansom cab rattled round the corner. A man was in it smoking a cigar. There were portmanteaus on the roof. The light of the lamp flashed full in the face of the passenger as the cab drove into the street. It was Paul Massie's face. Scarcely knowing what she did, the bewildered girl shrieked out:

"O, Mr. Massie, Mr. Massie! save me, save me!"

Halliday swore a savage oath, and tried to drag her away, putting one hand over her mouth and nostrils; but he was too late. Paul had heard the cry, and not knowing what it meant, leaped from the cab. Just as he rushed

up he saw something glitter, and heard a wild scream
of terror or pain. Halliday flung the girl to the ground,
and was gone. Paul's first thought was for the woman.
He raised her from the pavement. She was bleeding
in the neck, and senseless. Of course he knew the face of
Alice Crossley.

"Here," he called to the cabman. "Don't let us have
a crowd. Let us get the poor girl out of this. Drive
to ——," and he mentioned the address of Madame de Luca.
It was the only place he knew where he could venture
to carry her.

Only one or two people had gathered round ; and their
impression was that a woman had fallen in a fit, and that a
medical man was carrying her to a hospital. By the time
the customary policeman had at last come up, the cab was
half a street off. Paul sat in the cab and held the wounded
girl in his arms, with his handkerchief to her neck. He
could feel that her heart was beating stoutly, and he
did not believe that the wound was serious.

A few moments brought them to Madame de Luca's
door. In that irregular establishment nobody wondered at
anything. Paul deposited his poor burden with Mademoiselle Clotilde, who broke into a thousand little shrieks
at first, but presently subsided, and pledged herself to
have everything done that was needful. Then Paul drove
off himself to the nearest surgeon, and despatched him
to look after Alice. Finally, having ascertained that the
wound was only a sharp stab which would not prove serious, he thought the best thing he could do would be to
drive off and announce to Madame de Luca at the Opera
that he had taken the liberty of converting her house into
a hospital.

Had he thought nothing of the assassin, or attempted
assassin, all this time? At first, very little. Before he
had raised the girl from the ground the man was gone ;
and the sight of her face, the discovery of her identity, the
sight of her streaming blood, the imperative necessity of

doing something at once for her, drove everything else out of his mind. Now that cooler reason was beginning to return, he repented that he had not contrived by some means, by the help of somebody, to secure the man. As he drove to the theatre, he tortured his mind with vain cogitation as to the identity of the man, why he had attempted the deed, and why poor Alice came to be in that place, and with such a man at all. He never thought of Halliday.

In the excitement of all this, Paul quite forgot his recent electioneering triumph. Perhaps it was as well that he forgot it. Already he was beginning to feel painful doubts whether he had acted well in seeking such a triumph under such circumstances ; already a sense of shame and self-reproach had begun to possess him..

He soon found Salome's box. *Traviata* was the opera; and the consumptive frail one was beginning to fade away to Verdi's music, when Paul distracted the attention of his friend and her companions by entering the box.

She, Madame de Luca, welcomed him glowing cheek and sparkling eyes. Her small gloved hand pressed his with the softest, warmest, most thrilling pressure.

"Welcome to the honorable member for Seaborough," she said aloud. "Welcome, Paul," she added in a lower tone.

Her friends likewise gave their congratulations. These were a Hungarian refugee and his wife, a distinguished theatrical critic, and our acquaintance Mr. Wynter.

"How delighted I am that you have come !" she said. "We wanted you so much to-night. The prima donna is coming to sup with me after this, and we should all have missed you sadly. Besides, there is a Spanish gentleman coming, and, except you, we have no one to talk to him; so I am very glad you have come for this reason." But she looked, and modulated her voice when speaking, as if these were not the sole reasons. "And now," she added, "don't tell me anything about the election until all this is over."

“But I really have something to tell you—not about the election—which may startle you.”

“Indeed! Startle me! What can it be?”

“I have just been to your house.”

“Yes,—well? Did you see—” She looked a little uneasy.

“I only saw Clotilde. But I took the liberty of converting her into a hospital-nurse, and leaving her a patient.”

“Good heavens! what do you mean?”

“I found a wounded girl in the street and brought her to your house. You will forgive me, I know; particularly when you know who it is.”

“Well, who—who?”

“Why, poor Alice Crossley, who, as you know, has been missing so long, and whom I unexpectedly lighted on this night in the most extraordinary fashion.”

This conversation had been carried on so far in a sort of whisper, Paul occupying a seat behind the lady, and leaning over her shoulder.

“Pray let me collect my senses and understand all this. —Mr. Levison, will you kindly exchange seats with me?” She seated herself close to Paul. “Now then let me hear all this. Do I hear that you found Alice Crossley wounded in the street, and brought her to my house?”

“Yes, that is my tale.”

“Alice Crossley in the street and wounded! In what street?”

“In the street where I live. Just as I drove up I heard a scream, leaped out, and saw her.”

“In your street! Who wounded her?”

“That I don’t know. Like an idiot as I was, I allowed the fellow to escape.”

“A man—of course a man?”

“Yes, a man; I saw him run away.”

“Is she badly wounded?”

“Not badly, I think. I brought a surgeon to see her.”

“O, I’ll attend to her myself; I’m a better surgeon

than half of them. But this is the most extraordinary story I ever heard."

"Is it not? I cannot understand it. No doubt she will be able to tell who the man is."

"Will be able! Then she has told nothing yet?"

"Nothing. She was quite senseless when I brought her to your house."

"Who took her up stairs?"

"I did myself."

"And she was quite unconscious? Did she not speak at all?"

"Not a word."

Madame de Luca seemed somewhat relieved.

"Well," she said, "this is one of the strangest adventures I have heard for a long time. Paul Massie, you have a positive genius for adventure. I only wish you would make me the heroine of some scrap of romance. And you say that Alice did not, after all, recognize her deliverer?"

"Poor girl, I was not her deliverer ; I only wish I had been ; I came too late. If I have a genius for adventures, it also seems to me that I have a genius for coming in at the wrong period of every adventure."

"Then you must not take part in any adventure of mine. But this was indeed a singular occurrence. What could have brought the girl there?"

"And who could the man have been?"

"O, on that point I have very little doubt. I know the man."

"You know the man! By what extraordinary guess can you know him?"

"How often must I tell you that I know everything, O you of little faith?"

"Yet you seem not to know why this poor girl came to be stabbed just in my street."

"I don't know; but that too I promise you I will very soon find out. Now let us just hear the last of this, for I delight in this music. Verdi may be very noisy and vulgar, but I like him. Don't you? But I needn't ask you, who do not know Mozárt from Wallace, or Beethoven from Balfe."

"Nay, you might go a little farther, and say that I don't know Handel from the great musician who composes for Christy's Minstrels; for in good truth I don't."

"Yet you have the face to praise my singing, and I have the folly to be pleased and flattered by your praise."

"I praise your singing because it delights me; because I like to listen to it. What I say I feel. Believe me, I never paid a compliment in my life; I am too dull, and don't know how."

"Well, I believe you don't pay insincere compliments, and therefore I will still allow myself to enjoy your praise, even though it be not critical. I would sing to you to-night, if we had not musical guests. Now do let us listen, and then we will see to our poor little patient."

It was soon over, but not soon enough for Paul, who cared little for the opera, and was moreover far too bewildered and excited to care much for any musical performance under such circumstances. Having but just returned from the confusing triumph of an election contest, into which he had plunged himself Heaven knows why, and in which he had succeeded Heaven knows how; having his brain perturbed by doubts whether, after all, defeat would not have been a far better result; and further tortured by miserable uncertainties and sickening conjectures about his future and his past, it was rather too much to have the additional surprise and bewilderment of finding the girl whom months ago he had vainly sought lying in her blood near his own door. His head ached; he was tired, sleepy, hungry no doubt; and the music sounded but faintly in his ears, like something heard from a far distance. Perhaps he was actually fading away into sleep. Certainly the lights and sounds seemed to change; and he was again upon the beach at Scaborough, and he thought he saw the face of Sarah Massie gazing upon his, and heard her voice whisper into his ear. She touched his hand with a gentle touch; and he looked up—and it was the soft white hand of Salome which pressed his, and her voice which whispered in his ear. But as his eye wandered suddenly and vaguely around, he saw—or felt sure he saw —in an opposite box the face of Sarah Massie turned on him. He saw her eyes; he felt sure he saw her eyes, and that they met his. Only for a moment: all the people were leaving their seats now, and in the box where he had seen or fancied he saw that face, nothing could now be discerned but the retreating backs of some ladies whom one or two gentlemen were shawling as they went. Yet the fancy was strong upon him, and he would have stolen from his companions if he might. He felt almost as if he were captured when Madame de Luca said to him :

"You are quite tired out, my poor Paul; quite weary and sleepy; and I dare say you have had no dinner. It is cruel of us to have kept you here for this stuff; Verdi is dreadful stuff, after all. Come, give me your arm, and let us get to the carriage and away."

Paul hardly spoke a word on the way; Mr. Wynter and Mr. Levison did all the talking. Salome's beautiful eyes were fixed on our hero with an anxious interest, which ought to have bewitched any man, even though half asleep, if he were not wholly engrossed in his own doubts and difficulties.

Arrived at Salome's, they supped rather vivaciously. Paul brightened up immensely under the influence of supper and champagne, of which latter he drank some vast and stupendous draughts. The lady of the house quietly visited her patient in the first instance, and reported the wound not at all dangerous. Few words, however, were exchanged between her and Paul on this subject. There was indeed no opportunity. Mr. Wynter told all his various adventures in all the great political struggles over the world, in every one of which he had been the prime mover. Other men have seen everything, know everything, are authorities upon everything. But Mr. Wynter went far beyond these. He had himself personally done, or at the least initiated, everything. All the monarchs, statesmen, heroes, and revolutionists in Europe and the two Americas, to say nothing of Algeria, Georgia, and Afghanistan, were but his pupils or his puppets ; and they all knew and acknowledged the fact to Mr. Wynter. There was not one of them who had not said over and over again, " My dear Wynter, I am quite aware that you have done all this, and that without *you*," etc., etc.

Mr. Levison, the critic, had a pretty wit of his own, and drew Mr. Wynter out delightfully, slightly contradicting him every now and then upon some point of detail, just to put him on his mettle. Afterwards Mr. Wynter took Paul aside to give him a little instruction in the proper way of beginning and conducting his parliamentary career, and to explain to him the art of obtaining and retaining the ear of the House, and how ultimately, if he thought fit, to secure a seat on the Treasury bench—an honor which Mr. Wynter indicated had been again and again offered to him, and declined for reasons which he considerately remarked need not influence his younger and less conspicuous friend. It would obviously weaken Mr. Wynter's influence with various imperial, royal, and republican cabinets and parties, if he were to become an official organ of the British Government. But there was, of course, no such reason for Paul's turning his back on promotion; and Mr. Wynter kindly promised not only to keep an eye upon him, but even to give a hint to the Premier himself on the subject.

It was at last time to go away, and Paul was terribly sleepy. Mr. Wynter reminded him that their roads lay together for some distance. Adieux were made, and Salome spoke a few quiet words to Paul about her patient's condition. She promised to explain the whole matter to him very soon, and meanwhile begged him to speak to no one on the subject. All this she said in Italian, which she felt quite sure was safe from Mr. Wynter's comprehension, despite that gentleman's intimate acquaintance with every European language and people.

Then Paul and Wynter walked home together, and smoked their cigars as they went through the silent streets, where only the rare rattle of a cab and the rarer tramp of a policeman's boots now told of life. Mr. Wynter explained to Paul as they walked along how he had enabled the allies to take Sebastopol by the use of secret maps and plans which he had received from a Russian officer whom he once helped to escape from Siberia.

Paul smoked, and did not listen to a word.

As they were parting, the senior M. P. rather abruptly said, "By the way, what do you mean to do with our friend yonder?" He jerked his fat and bearded countenance somewhere towards the west.

"What friend?"

"Why, of course, our friend the Countess, the Duchess —O, confound it, I mean Madame—yes, Madame de Luca. She's a fine woman—splendidly preserved; her make-up is capital; and I know she's got plenty of money. I happen to know it, sir! I knew her husband. I was close by when he was killed by a round-shot at Novara. The Duke of Savoy—that's King Vic now—was near. 'Wynter,' said he, 'I'm glad you're at hand. Poor De Luca is down; you'll see to him.' So I did, of course. I took him out of the row. I know the Marchioness well; she's safe, as far as money goes, and she's devilish fond of you. In fact, I put the question to her myself, and she told me so. She's older than you; she was born in June '28; but there's nothing in that. Give me the word whenever you like, and I'll make it all right."

Paul's impulse was to throw his glove in the face of his friend; then to turn upon his heel disgusted, and walk away in the middle of the harangue. But he controlled himself somehow, and Mr. Wynter would never have perceived the anger and disgust which he was creating unless the most emphatic of overt acts had manifested them. So he took Paul's silence for gratitude and modesty, pressed his hand affectionately, and walked away.

So, then, it was settled that Paul was to marry Madame de Luca. Of course he gave no heed—at least, he attached no belief to the babble of the self-conceited and talkative creature who had just left him. He was not foolish enough to believe that Madame de Luca had ever spoken confidentially to Mr. Wynter on that or any other conceivable subject. Wynter was not a bad fellow, and only cared to represent himself as a person of importance; otherwise he might, with just as much show of reason, have described himself as the lady's favored lover. Still, even babble like that shows too well how the wind of gossip blows. Therefore Paul saw that it was set down by some of his friends, that he was the accepted suitor of a woman to whom he had never spoken one word of love. This was not pleasant, in one sense at least. He could not but feel deeply grateful for the warm kindness he had received from a woman to whom he could make no return; nay, he could not but feel a thrill of gratified pride—of something like delight—when he saw the expression which burned in her eyes as she sometimes gazed on him. But did he love her? Could he contemplate with full satisfaction—even with content or resignation—a life wholly spent with her? Was this exactly what he had wished for—dreamed of? She was a beautiful, a clever, a brilliant, and a sincere woman; she was much better than what some people call a good woman—the mere dull, plodding, soulless mistress of a household. But was she the woman of his youth and of his dreams? Nay, was she even the woman of reality and life whom he had met face to face and felt that he could love? Paul Massie was not given to mere sighing, but he almost sighed.

He was drifting—had been drifting blindly and helplessly since he came to London. He seemed to have lost or abdicated all control over his own existence and his own

movements.   He had drifted into open enmity with his
cousins; had drifted into relations with Madame de Luca
which seemed to bode still closer ties; he did not see his
way out, or backward or forward, or in any direction.
He was a poor man, and he had been living like a rich
man ; he had no future clear before him, and he had been
playing the part of one for whom splendid prospects
opened.   What next?   A failure of some kind must come ;
some *fiasco*, some humiliation, or some feeble compromise with fate, which might be worse than aught else.
Still he could only drift.   In all save physical strength
and courage, and a certain capacity for personal endurance and enterprise, Paul Massie was a weak, gentle, easily-
moulded man.   In London he felt himself becoming daily
more and more like a child.   He swore mentally at himself
for an imbecile and an idiot.   Many times a day he had
lately been vowing that he would steer some clear and
decided course; and still he only drifted.   He felt that he
could not be happy with Madame de Luca, and yet he felt
quite unable to do without her.   He could scarcely call
himself fascinated; he was rather controlled and guided.
She waved her fan, and he obeyed as though it were a
wand ; he ceased to be his own master when within ear-
shot of the rustle of her petticoat.

CHAPTER XXII.

SARAH KNOWS HERSELF.

"DID you see him?"

Lydia spoke in an angry half-whisper to Sarah Massie. They were alone, in one of Mrs. Trenton's rooms, after their return from the Opera.

"Did you see him, Sarah?"

"See whom?" most women would probably have replied, although knowing perfectly well to whom the question referred.

But Sarah answered directly, and rather sadly, "Yes, I saw him."

"And her?"

"Yes, and her."

"Wasn't it shocking?"

Sarah could not help smiling at the fervor of the question.

"I did not think there was anything particularly dreadful about it."

"Not dreadful? Not to see him there openly?"

"Well, no. I do not see that there was anything very alarming about it. I was not surprised to see him in her box. But I was rather surprised to see him in town at all. I thought he was still in Seaborough."

"Didn't he look dreadful—worn-out, and pale, and that?"

"Yes, he looked very tired."

"Tired? Dissipated, I thought. Tell me your company! I wonder who were those horrid people with him —with her I mean."

"One I thought was Mr. Wynter—a very good sort of man, I believe; the others appeared to be foreigners."

"I hate that woman. So do you, if you would only speak out."

"Indeed, Lydia, I do not hate her at all. I always used to like her, you know. She is very clever, and I always thought her sincere and kind-hearted."

"Mamma detests her, I know."

Sarah said nothing. She was not always guided by mamma's dislikings.

"Then, Sarah, do you mean to say that you were glad to see a cousin of ours, who has been behaving so ungratefully and shamefully towards Eustace and all of us, exhibiting himself in that sort of way in the theatre, as if he had done nothing in the world?"

"No, I was not glad to see him there;" and Sarah undoubtedly sighed. "And I wish he had not crossed Eustace's purposes in Seaborough."

"I wish he had never come to England at all."

"So do I—sometimes."

Lydia had been looking in the glass. She turned suddenly and sharply round.

"Sarah, you never like to hear a word said against Paul Massie. I wonder why you are so partial to him?"

"I like Paul Massie very much. I never saw anything in him that was not kind, and good, and true. I think he ought not to have opposed and thwarted Eustace; but then I don't think Eustace acted quite generously towards him.

"O, then, you think Eustace was all in the wrong perhaps, and Mr. Paul Massie all in the right?"

"There was not much of wrong or right in the matter. I think Eustace is rather prejudiced against his cousin, and does not do him justice, and I am sorry for it—very sorry."

"Do you know, Sarah, I have sometimes thought it would not take much to make you in love with Paul Massie?"

Sarah grew very red; but she controlled herself, and answered very composedly: "I am not so much given to sudden likings and dislikings as you are, Lydia. I do not love people without some cause, or dislike and distrust them without having reason for it."

"But neither does Eustace. Come now, you may say what you like of me—and, for that matter, of mamma too —but you know very well that Eustace does not form hasty likings or dislikings. You know he is very particular never to say anything against anyone, unless he has good ground for it; and you know that he does not like Paul Massie of late. He wishes from his heart he had never left Mexico, Eustace does; and perhaps he may have better reason to wish it before all is done."

Sarah was in no humor to argue the point. Lydia could not carry on the discussion alone; but she fired a Parthian shot in retreating.

"Good-night, Sarah," she said, kissing her cousin with manner of blended pity and affection—"Poor Eustace!" And she sighed elaborately, and was gone.

The Seaborough election had kept the two young women in town much longer than was originally intended. Eustace did not choose to take them home to a place where such an election contest was going forward. The stay was very agreeable to Lydia, for Captain Trenton's attentions to her, fully favored as they were by that young gentleman's relatives, appeared destined to lead to a decisive result in her life. And Sarah liked being in town much better now than before the dawn of the Seaborough contest. She liked it for a reason which, while present in full force to her consciousness every moment of the day, she did not as yet dare to acknowledge even in the secrecy of self-communion. She liked to be in London now because Eustace Massie, her intended husband, was not there.

To this it had come. But this condition of feeling might have passed away. Had Sarah Massie not gone to the Opera that night, she might have married Eustace at the appointed time, and been a good and faithful wife to him, devoted to his interests and his personal comfort, properly affectionate in manner, and on the whole perhaps not actually, at least not actively, unhappy. She and Lydia were to return to Seaborough in a day or two; indeed they were pressed to go to the Opera because that was to be almost their last night in town. Had she not gone to the Opera, she would probably have left London without seeing Paul; she would perhaps never have seen him again in life; her existence in Seaborough would have flowed once more in its old, passionless, monotonous channel. She would have glided into the quiet pool of married life with Eustace. She would have attended to his schools, and looked after his poor, and helped to dress his church, and reared his children, and entered into all his pursuits, and would perhaps have scarcely known—certainly would never have confessed to herself—that she had got into a wrong groove; that her life was not what it ought to be— that a breath, and only one, of love had fanned her for a moment and then gone by her for ever.

This might have been. But truly says Carlyle, that the Might Have Beens are mostly a vanity.

It was decreed in some mysterious place of decision that Sarah should not be allowed thus to follow the path of routine prescribed for her. She did not want to go to the Opera that night, and probably would not have gone, but that Lydia pouted and sulked, and said she could not go without her; and Sarah at last consented to go.

Of course she had not been there long when she saw Salome. This in itself was rather a painful sight, although Sarah tried to persuade herself that she felt no emotion whatever. For during the progress of the unlucky election, Sarah had many times heard through Captain Trenton and others that the opposition was all Salome's doing; that Paul Massie was her devoted slave, and that he was destined to be her equally devoted husband. What was this to Sarah, herself engaged to be married? Nothing, of course nothing; and so she said to herself many times —except that, in a cousinly way, she would perhaps have liked Paul not to marry a widow, and one of so pronounced a style; perhaps she would have liked him to marry a woman with a little more of freshness and less of

the world's enamel and patchouli about her. That was all,
of course. Had Paul only found the sort of woman who
seemed suited to him, Sarah would have been delighted—
yes, delighted at the prospect of his happiness. So delighted, that when she thought of such a thing her eyes
involuntarily filled with tears, which somehow did not seem
like drops of joy.

She averted her gaze from Salome's box, and fixedly
looked at the stage. But a woman's eyes will wander.
Hers involuntarily glanced back as the night wore on, and
she saw that Paul Massie was sitting beside Salome. The
glance that revealed him to Sarah revealed also her own
heart. Her inmost soul stood mirrored and bare before
her. No self-deception could hide or deaden the force of
the keen, cruel pang of grief and passion and jealousy which
shot through her. Nature surprised had betrayed herself,
and Sarah knew that she loved Paul Massie.

With the shock and the revelation there arose simultaneously, equally clear and strong, born of the same
agony of self-detection, one fixed determination. She determined that she would never, never marry Eustace Massie.
Whatever might happen, that she would not do. The
woman who thus throbbing with passion and jealousy at
the sight of one man could deliberately marry another
would be a traitress and a criminal in soul. Sarah left the
theatre in agony of heart, but free.

Agony is not always unhappiness. Your most profound metaphysician or psychologist would perhaps be
sometimes puzzled to analyze his own emotions under
certain given conditions of excitement, and tell whether
they consist most of the elements of pleasure or the
elements of pain. Certainly there are some natures,
quiet, perhaps a little slow, but deep, which always feel
relieved and brightened—relieved of the burden of
their ordinary selves, as it were, and brightened as
by the lifting of some common-day curtain—when an
event occurs which thrills them with excitement, though

it be little better than that of despair. Sarah Massie had
a nature somewhat of this mould. The emotions of her
soul had hitherto slumbered a stagnant pool; now for the
first time the storm-breath of passion swept over them, and
tossed them into waves ; and the change was the development of a new power—the consciousness of a new existence ; nay, perhaps the first true consciousness of existence
itself. Now for the first time she knew that she was a
woman, and not a dumb-waiter, sewing-machine, cooking-
stove, or other such useful and steadfast piece of domestic
mechanism. The instinctive truthfulness and worth of her
nature told her when she made this discovery she must
never, never be the wife of the man who was not the
source of the revelation.

So she went home, much tormented indeed, but not
absolutely, drearily unhappy. Life did not look rosy.
Sarah Massie was poor. The miserable little annual sum
which she could call her own would scarcely, with whatever
economy, enable her to dispense with some occupation for
the earning of money, even if she were the sort of person
who could possibly remain idle; and she knew not where to
turn for the means of living. It was certain that she must
cease to be an inmate of Seaborough-house. It was equally
certain that she would be considered - ungrateful and
unworthy by those who had sheltered her there since her
infancy. She must bear no doubt the plainings of Mrs.
Massie, the angry and scornful reproaches of Lydia, the sad,
solemn, unreproving grief of Eustace. She must even submit to the prospect of having the secret of her resolution
guessed at and talked over, and perhaps made an open
reproach to her. She must go away, out into the wide
world, which she had hitherto only read of, or peeped at as
through the bars of a cage; and she must live alone until the
time when she might die alone. Even so : she would go ;
and gloomy as the prospect was, it did not yet make her
quite unhappy ; it was at least to be something—to have an
individuality, a human nature, to be a woman with a living

heart. Poor human egotists, we all comfort ourselves in moments of stress by discovering the special guidance and inspiration of Heaven in our little difficulties ; and it now seemed to Sarah Massie as if through the ceiling of the great theatre where the huge chandelier hung, and beneath which *Traviata* was crooning her consumptive death-plaints, a distinct ray of providential inspiration had flashed down upon the box in which she sat, and lighted up for her the course of duty.

She resolved to act, and had no fear. She bore with Lydia's hints and sighings quite calmly, and of course never breathed a word of her fixed determination. That she resolved should be told first to him whom it most concerned, frankly and face to face; then she would take leave of Mrs. Massie, and make to her just such revelation of sentiment as would suffice to explain her conduct, if not in such eyes to justify it. And then she would go away from Seaborough—to Belgium, she vaguely thought—and return no more.

CHAPTER XXIII.

" BROKEN."

SALOME DE LUCA had, as we have seen, many friends, among the male sex at least. Is it humanly possible that a woman can have many such friends without having some lovers ? Perhaps there are instances in which this may be possible ; for Nature, among her other exploits, has certainly accomplished the making of some women whom no male creature ever can associate with womanhood; and these may be good and sweet, and even tender and loving, and have any number of male friends, not one of whom is ever likely to degenerate or become exalted into the character of a lover. But Salome was not one of these, and she was therefore an exceedingly difficult sort of person to keep on terms of friendship with. She had had since her widowhood many lovers and many pressing offers of marriage. But she resolutely, good-humoredly, declined them all; and at last those who came within her circle began to make up their minds to the fact that she really did not intend to marry, and that they must be content with friendship or nothing. The appearance on the scene of Paul Massie, however, disturbed this calm conviction. He was so much with her, she was so markedly partial to him, that people could or would see only one end to the business, and many of Salome's rejected suitors became angry, and regarded themselves as injured and outraged beings. Perhaps some women might have consoled them by the assurance that, if Salome really felt any deep and genuine emotion towards Paul, she never would have allowed herself to exhibit an open preference for him. Judging by their own ways, which are doubtless the ways of women generally, they would have been quite right. But Salome had none of the small arts of her sex, and what she really was, for good or otherwise, that she showed herself—that and nothing else.

It may be that for a long time she did not fully see her own love face to face; know it and call it by its name. It may be that she even yet occasionally tried to persuade herself that she felt only a warm friendship for Paul Massie. But some of those who watched and studied her most keenly had long given up all doubt. One of these was our old friend Lefevre; another of course was Wynter, who indeed took the thing quite for granted, and spoke of it everywhere as settled. So it got talked about very commonly in the circle which Paul Massie frequented, and even in circles where he was not known; and though he knew nothing about the matter himself, yet his friends and neighbors were acquainted with its whole progress, purpose, and details. Therefore it is not surprising that, on the very

first night of his return to England, after several months'
absence in Italy, wild Charley Millton should hear that
Salome de Luca was about to be married to a man named
Paul Massie, who had turned up somehow while Millton
was roving about Lombardy, and Florence, and the Two
Sicilies—now the kingdom of Italy.

Who was wild Charley Millton? His career is easily
told. Alfred de Musset, in one of his splenetic moods, called
Italy a Messalina, and described her as hot with the kisses
of many lovers. If anything of the kind is to be said of her,
we might surely compare her more fairly to that famous
bride of the King of Garbe, whom La Fontaine sings, and
whose mishap it was to have to submit in turn to so many
rough wooers before she was fortunate enough at last to
find her way to her rightful husband and master. But
Italy—Messalina or not—has surely had a marvellous
power of attracting lovers to her ; and not kings and con-
querors merely, but humble, passionate, devoted lovers
from far-off lands, who held it their highest happiness to
labor and brave danger unrewarded, even unrecognized, in
her cause, and who would have longed to die in her service.
Our England, with all its smooth good sense and practical
selfishness, has furnished more enthusiasts to that fascinating cause than any other land in the world after Italy herself. One of the noblest maladies, the most splendid mad-
nesses of any age, has been this Italian fever, which has
seized the cold Englishman of our generation, and dragged
him from his college and his counting-house, from his east-
end shop and his west-end drawing-room, and sent him to
risk his life for Italy. Some years before 1860, the mania,
if less common than in the time of Garibaldi's great success,
burned where it struck with a yet fiercer intensity. One
of its victims was Charley Millton, the son of a man who
had made a fortune in business, which fortune Millton had
well-nigh spent in striving to serve Italy. He had labored,
and intrigued, and flung away thousands, and risked over
and over again his gallant life in the old days when the

12*

white-coats were in Milan ; he had exulted over Solferino, and been dashed to the ground by Villafranca; he had been a Garibaldian volunteer at the Volturno ; he had been profoundly disappointed by the annexation of Naples to Piedmont. For Charley was of the Mazzini school, and dreamed impassioned dreams of a republic, and he hated the statesmanship of Cavour with all the hatred of generous fanaticism ; and he had only just now been engaged in a long course of fruitless intrigue against the supremacy of that northern monarchical province of Piedmont, and that House of Savoy which he had helped, in his wild, humble way, to raise to the place of pride.

Salome's late husband was one of Charley's dearest friends; and while that husband lived Charley never allowed mortal to know, never acknowledged even to himself, how tenderly and passionately he, De Luca's friend, loved De Luca's wife. But when De Luca had been some time dead, then he spoke, poured out his whole heart and its secret, pleaded with all the fervor of his passionate nature, and was tenderly, lovingly, resolutely rejected. He was given firmly to understand that his pleading was hopeless; and he took his rejection like a man and a gentleman, and went away. He gave himself and his fortune up more than ever to what he believed the cause of Italy, and lent his aid to organize movements here in Venetia against the Austrian, there in Rome against the French and the Pope ; and again, we grieve to confess, in Naples and in Tuscany against Piedmontese preëminence and the House of Savoy. Some few years ago there was—most of our readers have perhaps forgotten it—a poor little futile insurrection, or armed demonstration, in Friuli against the Austrian. It ended in the loss of a few brave lives, and nothing more ; it was over so soon that Venetia hardly throbbed in recognition of it. Charley Millton bore a part in this attempt, and escaping the Austrian now arrived in London.

Salome received a few lines of a note from him next

morning, in which he announced that he meant to pay her a visit that day, and hoped she could spare him half an hour of quiet conversation.

She would rather not have seen him. Memories centred around him which she did not care to revive, and which perhaps she feared that he might attempt to revive all too fervently. Besides, she had of late begun to lose her zest for political and foreign intrigue. Not often are politics anything but a distraction for a woman, unless indeed when the cause to which she devotes herself is personified to her in the form of the man she loves. Salome was growing listless and sad of late. It was becoming more and more difficult to rouse her to a genuine interest in the old subjects and the old way. She often leaned upon her desk with paper spread before her, and wrote or read nothing ; only looked into vacancy, and was steeped in thought. She did not wish to see Charley Millton. His presence would be a reproach to her in a double sense, even if he should have left his foolish passion wholly behind him.

One only compensating reflection there was. She did not want to see Paul Massie either that day—at least to see him alone. This was the day after Jem Halliday's attempt ; and she could not meet Paul *tête-à-tête* without having an explanation forced upon her, which she had yet hardly made up her mind how to give. Her plan for the reclamation of the wehr-wolf she acknowledged to herself had wholly failed ; but she did not quite see whether even now it would be wise or well to abandon the wehr-wolf to his pursuers, have him torn from his lair in the forest, and given over to open human vengeance. In plain words, she did not exactly desire that Halliday should be discovered just then, until she at least should begin to see her way out of the complication of embarrassment and small secrecies in which she had been entangling herself ; and she feared that if Paul were once made certain as to the identity of Alice's assailant, it would be difficult indeed to induce him to delay or compromise with the obvious duty of putting criminal law upon Halliday's track. For this one reason, then, she welcomed any visitor, even wild Charley Millton.

The latter came strictly punctual to the hour he had appointed. Salome and he had not met for more than a year; and he was considerably changed.

In Gustave Doré's illustrations to Balzac's witty, scandalous *Contes drôlatiques* is a sketch of a brave and ruined cavalier, the hero of a story the name of which this writer has forgotten. But to identify the picture for any reader who cares to look at it, perhaps it is enough to say that the story is of a lady whose lover is about to be decoyed into an ambush and slain on her account, and who endeavors in her despair to save his life by a cruel stratagem. There is a poor broken cavalier who long has adored her in silence and at a distance, and him she resolves to decoy by looks of feigned encouragement to follow her, and thus to lead him into the trap that he may be mistaken for her lover, and so slain. Now Doré has drawn the face of the devoted and unsuspecting victim; and the drawing is a masterpiece. It is a gaunt, long, noble face, with deep dark eyes and lank falling hair; a face all bravery and unselfishness and consuming passion, and profound disappointment which has yet too much of manhood left in it to acknowledge despair. That face may be studied for hours as a very picture-history of ruined nobleness and wasted passion and dignity that nothing can subdue. Such a face and expression exactly had wild Charley Millton when he stood waiting for Salome. Such a face—although he was no cavalier, no hero of romance, but only the son of a London business man, who had flung away his father's property on mad political ventures, and had reached the age of forty to know himself in politics and in passion a disappointed man.

Salome welcomed her former lover with a genuine warmth. Her cheek colored deeply as he touched her hand. He might have kissed her doubtless unreproved;

but he did not. In Balzac's story the lady actually offers a kiss to the betrayed cavalier when she has confessed that he is brought to his death ; and he refuses it. He does not want to have life made sweet lest he should become less willing to die for her pleasure.

They talked for awhile of the state of Italy, and the failure of the attempt in which he had just been engaged.

"How happy that you escaped!" said Salome.

"Yes, in one sense," he replied. "I should not have liked to die in so miserable and hopeless an affair. I should like another try at it yet. Good heavens! we cannot *always* fail; and yet it looks horribly like it sometimes. If nothing better can be done, then I shall be sorry I was not killed even there. I begin to despair sometimes, and to think there is nothing but failure in store for Italy. Do you know that I get so sick of the everlasting hopes and everlasting disappointments, that I sometimes wish I had never known where to find Italy on the map? I sometimes begin to think we are all idiots for our pains. Do you never think so? But you, I understand, have begun to draw out of all this sort of thing of late. Is that true?"

"No; that is not perhaps exactly true. But of course I have little opportunity here of knowing what is going on; and time, perhaps, makes us all less sanguine and more cautious. If I were like you, and could actually bear a hand, perhaps I should still be as foolish as you, Charley, and should be found risking my life for nothing. But what can a woman do?"

She spoke in a tone of embarrassment, for she knew well by his looks what he was coming to.

"But you have given up politics altogether, or you are going to do so—I mean, of course, Italian politics? I heard so at least."

"I am in no way changed," she answered coldly.

He rose and stood on the hearth-rug. His eyes sought a place just over the chimney-piece.

"So you keep De Luca's sword there still?" he said.

"How well I remember it! Indeed I ought to recollect it. I am glad you have not taken it down—yet."

Still Salome was resolved to avert as long as she possibly could—altogether, if that should be in her power—the explanation which she felt that Milton was endeavoring to compel her to make.

"It is not so long there," she quietly remarked, "that either of us could fail to recollect it; 1859 is not so very far gone by."

"O, then, you do remember the date?" he said, turning sharply on her. "I really thought you had forgotten all about it. Yes, it was in 1859 that sword was left to you; and it is now—let me see; what year is this? I get confused in my dates. And you keep De Luca's sword still! How long is it to remain there?"

Impossible to bear this any longer.

"I don't know what you mean, Charley Millton," said Salome, in a voice of undisguised anger; "I cannot believe that you have come here to insult me. Why should my husband's sword not remain there?"

"Ah, you should know—not I. Is it not true what I have heard even already? Can you venture to deny it?"

"Deny what? I do not mean to quarrel with you, or to be angry; but you try my good-nature a little too much. What am I not to deny?"

"You know well what I mean, Madame de Luca; but I will make my meaning clear beyond all doubt. I asked you why you still keep your husband's sword as a relic, when you have already resolved to fill his place?"

"This is positive insult," said Salome; "but I am quite resolved not to be offended. You shall not make me quarrel with you, Charley Millton; but neither shall you suppose that you have the slightest authority over me, or right to question me. Nobody has. Let us speak of something else, or let us not speak together any more."

"It is true, then," he said sadly. "I was your husband's closest friend, and I could not hear of it without being sorry. It is soon—very soon."

His tone of sadness vexed and offended Salome even more than his tone of anger had done.

"Soon!" she said—"soon! And you tell me so? How long has this tenderness for the memory of my husband and your friend grown up? It is a full year, I think, and more since here in this very room you begged me to fill his place. Where was your sensitive regard for his memory then, when you entreated his widow to take you for her husband? For shame, Charles Millton! You make me ashamed of myself when I bring up recollections like these; but you force me to it. I never before thought there was any selfishness in you; now I see that there is, and that you are much like all the rest—selfish, yes, and mean."

"Call me anything you please. Selfish I am and always was where *you* are concerned, and mean too, or I should not now be here arguing hopelessly with you. Yes, you are right : I did think little of poor De Luca's memory when I thought there was any chance or hope for myself. But, let it be selfishness or not, I cannot bear the thought of your marrying some one else—a stranger—Heaven knows who he is. Where does he come from ? What has he done ? What sort of man is he that is thought fit to succeed De Luca, when—"

· "When somebody else more worthy is not thought fit," Salome interposed with a bitter smile. An ungenerous retort, but she was vexed out of her generosity.

He waved his hand, as if he put away all irrelevant remark, personal taunt or otherwise.

"You told me yourself," he said,—"you assured me here in this room, *that* time, that you never would marry. You pledged yourself to that, did you not?"

"I did not, because I never condescended to make any pledge or promise to you or to anybody on such a subject. I told you I never meant to marry again, and I told you truly. How do you know that if you had come with the manner of an old and valued friend, and put the same question to me to-day, I should not have given the same answer?"

A gleam of brighter light flashed for a moment across Millton's face; but the expression of hers served in some way to deny the meaning which her words might have implied. The brighter light soon went out.

"No, your very look tells me the whole truth, even if you would conceal it."

"Conceal it! I have nothing to conceal. People conceal when they have done something wrong, or are afraid of somebody. I have done nothing wrong, and there is nobody of whom I have need to be afraid. Come, Charley Millton, we are old friends; let us not quarrel: why should we? All that you have been talking of and scolding me for is mere nonsense—I don't mind being good-natured and telling you that much—mere nonsense and talk. It is nothing but gossip; and you used not to be in the habit of paying attention to such stuff."

"But you are about to be married?"

"You will, then, go on as if you were really determined to vex me? Must you have the whole truth out? Another woman would die before she confessed it; but I am not proud, and I cannot continue to be angry with you. Well then, perhaps this full confession will satisfy you: no man has ever asked me to marry him since you yourself were silly enough to do so. Come now, will that satisfy you?"

He shook his head.

"The day before I asked you to marry me, I too had not done so; but you had seen to the depths of my heart months before. No, Salome; I would rather hear the worst at once. You are in love. All your friends talk of it, and you are certain to marry."

"If you choose to listen to the stories of people whom you call my friends, I cannot answer for what you may hear; but there was a time, I think, when you would not so have listened. And if that were true which you say, it would not still be a shame. I should not expect that it would change Charles Millton from my friend into my enemy."

"I am too selfish, as you have rightly said, to bear the thought; I know it. I have loved you, Salome, long and deeply, as you know. I did hope that you might have loved me in return, and you would not."

"Don't say would not."

"Well then, let me say could not. Does that make it any better? You tried hard then, let me say, and you could not —*could* not love me; hated me, I suppose. I could have borne even that—yes, so selfish am I—so long as I saw your love given to no one else. I am not generous enough not to hate the man, whoever he is, who has stepped in between you and me. You might have loved me in the end but for him."

"Charley, it pains me more than I could say to hear you speak so strangely and so unkindly. Have you no feeling for me when you talk thus? Do you not care what pain you are giving me? We are not young enough, either of us, to talk in this wild and foolish way. We are not boy and girl any longer, and we must have some sense and self-control. Are we not friends?"

"No; I can never be a friend of yours; never. Between us there could be no such thing as friendship."

"At least we are not enemies? You could not be my enemy."

"Your enemy perhaps, rather than your friend."

"I don't believe it, and I don't fear you in the least. Why, I know you better than you do yourself, and I know you to be as chivalrous as a Paladin, as Roland of Roncesvalles himself. If I were to be married next week, I should expect you to fight meantime by the side of my intended husband, and stand between him and the enemy's sword or bullet for my sake. But let us talk no more of this folly. We have not met for a year. Can we find noth-

ing better to talk about than idle gossip or romantic nonsense?"

Some of Salome's words, spoken with a too palpable effort
at gayety, sent Millton's mind wandering in another track.
His eyes were again fixed upon the sword which hung above
the chimney-piece. He stretched out his arm and took the
weapon down, and poised it in his brown sinewy hand, on
which the glowing veins stood out.

"I *have* fought by your husband's side," he said, " and
I often endeavored to shield him from blade and bullet,
though I loved you madly all the while, and fancied perhaps
sometimes, like an idiot that I was, that he alone—his life
—stood between you and me. For I saw into your heart,
Salome, and I knew you did not love him, no, not with your
whole soul."

" O Charley, for shame! You must not and shall not
talk in this way. I will not listen to it ; I have borne with
too much."

"Forgive me this once," he said in an impatient tone;
"I shall not be here again to offend you. Let us say no
more of that. I stood by your husband's side, but not that
last day. I wish I had been there. I wish to God I had
been cut down with him! But I helped to bury him, and
it was I who took this sword from his hand, and I brought
it to you as his last bequest. I did ; did I not?"

" Yes, it is quite true."

Salome's tears were flowing fast; but she strove to
humor her wild lover, of whose sanity horrible suspicions
were growing up in her mind.

"That sword you had from me ; is it not true?"

" Quite true, indeed."

"Then, as I gave it to you, I take it away from you
again. It shall pass into no other man's hand; it shall
ornament no woman's hearth who has ceased to be De
Luca's wife."

Before she could even guess ·what he was about to
do, not to speak of the possibility of her preventing the

action, he had shattered the weapon into fragments across his knee, breaking it again and again with a fierce energy until the floor was strewn with twenty gleaming splinters of steel. In the vehemence of his action he had cut his hand, and the blood trickled to the carpet.

"See," he said, "there's blood! An evil omen for a coming marriage!"

Salome's courage and endurance wholly gave way before such a display as this. She was grieved, offended, humiliated, frightened all at once, and the whole conversation had been a terrible strain upon her nerves. She sank on the sofa, covered her face with her hands, and burst into a passion of tears. Her weakness, however, proved her strength in this instance, for it recalled wild Charley Millton to himself. He knelt on the ground beside her; he seized her hand and kissed it; he begged pardon of her in tones of the deepest sincerity and sorrow over and over again. He denounced himself as a brute and a coward; he vowed he would not leave the room until she had promised to forgive him; and he pledged himself never to intrude upon her presence again. For awhile Salome really could not rally; the whole scene had been far too much for her to bear. At last, seeing the imperative necessity of bringing the painful interview to a close, she sat up, smiled as well as she could through her tears, and declared that she forgave him.

"Then," he said, "I have no more to ask, and I will stay no longer. It is like yourself, your old self, to forgive me; for you were always kind and generous, and loving too—except to me."

"Yes, loving to you too, Charley,—always loving to you,—though not as you would have had me to be. If I were not loving to you, how could I now forgive you for your extraordinary conduct, your strange violence to-day? But we must not often meet—for a time at least. We shall be wiser and calmer as years go on; and some time or other you may be able to call me your friend."

"May I not return?"　He stood disconsolate—a strong man made craven by love.

"When you can feel you are my friend," she replied, gently but decisively.

"Then good-by, Salome," was all he said; "good-by for ever."

She made no effort to detain him, but only held out her hand.　He touched it lightly to his lips as he bent over it, and left the room without a word.

Salome did not look after him.　She remained sitting on the sofa just as he had left her, except that, with her chin resting upon her hands, she looked fixedly upon the fragments of the broken sword and the blood-stains, which were distinctly visible upon the bright carpet.　She gazed long in silence, until at last a deep involuntary sigh seemed to break the chain of thought, and to arouse her from her reverie.

"Poor Charley," she murmured; "poor wild loving fellow!　How deeply he loved me!　Ah, I shall never be loved so again, never; and I might perhaps have loved him in time; but now it cannot be.　Ah, I might have thought more of him if he had thonght less of me!　If he only knew all, he would pity me, not blame me.　Like himself, I am made a clinging coward, and throw myself at the feet of the conqueror who cares nothing."

Her eyes again fell on the carpet.　She gathered up the fragments of the sword.

"Yes, there is blood,' she said; "and it is a bad omen—as he told me."

CHAPTER XXIV.

THE WEHR-WOLF IN THE FOREST.

LET us follow for a few hours the steps of the wretched man whose attempt at murder had so signally failed ; let us see what became of James Halliday.

There was no pursuit of course; and he had hardly turned the corner of the street when he became satisfied of that fact. But just now it brought him little comfort—indeed he cared nothing about it. He had attempted to kill Alice, and he had failed. He knew perfectly well that he had failed. He knew too that he had left her in the arms of the one man whom, on her account, he hated more than any other man on earth. To her he was henceforth but the assassin from whom Paul Massie had rescued her. His miserable failure had brought about the crown of his enemy's triumph. In a few days, let him hide where he would, he must be hunted down like a rat and dragged into daylight. And then !

Yet it was not this last thought that troubled him most. The thirst for revenge had for the moment transformed him, as the passion for glory or for country, or the love of a woman, sometimes transfigures other selfish beings ; and he was for the hour no longer selfish. He hardly bestowed a thought upon his own safety. He thought only of redeeming his failure by another attempt to end in success. This hope, nay this firm implacable resolution, sustained him, and made freedom and life still something of an object to him.

He did not wander far from the scene of his attempt. He lounged slowly and listlessly along Oxford-street, and sometimes stopped and looked in at shops, as if he was deeply absorbed in considering the value and the prices of the objects exposed for sale. Not many shops indeed were then open ; and it was somewhat odd to see this great hulking fellow, with a listless straw in his mouth, gazing for several moments together upon a white horse of plaster or a flaring red bottle in a chemist's shop. Perhaps some observant persons as they passed set him down for a raw country youth fresh come to Lunnun town, and were amused at the rustic innocence of his curiosity. When anyone stopped and looked in at the same shop—and nobody ever did look at anything in London without attracting somebody else to stop and look in likewise— Halliday at once became recalled to himself, and moved on. At last he straggled to one of the gates of Hyde-park, and lounged in.

Was he mentally vowing vengeance? Not at all. He was vowing nothing, mentally or in any other way. When a man leaves his business in the evening and mounts his omnibus—or one ought to say perhaps, in deference to the finer tone of modern literature, steps into his carriage —to go home, he does not keep mentally vowing all the way that he will eat his dinner. When a man is madly in love with a girl, he does not mentally vow that he will try to keep on loving her. When a man learns that he has been elected to parliament, he does not mentally vow that he will walk down some evening to Westminster and take his seat. A vow of any kind suggests the possibility of the person who vows taking some other course than that to which he pledges himself; and Halliday's mind just now had no room for the reception of any other possibility but the one. His life now was only to have revenge. He had no other object ; that done, let what would follow.

He strolled about the park for awhile. It was too early yet for the nightly camp-life of scoundrelism to have begun its bivouac there, and Halliday found or fell upon a lonely place where he could walk up and down or lie on the ground, and, in his wild incoherent way, review the situation. Presently he left the park again, and made his way into the street where Madame de Luca lived. He walked up and down, and took the bearings of the rooms

and the windows very carefully. There was a light in the
window, which he knew to be Alice's. The rest of the
house was dark. He went round to the back. A little
lane ran down between the row of houses in which Salome
lived and that which stood *dos-à-dos* with it. Each house
had a small garden and a little back-door, the latter of
course opening into the lane or avenue. Halliday well
knew that the room into which he had been admitted when
he was received by Salome opened upon the tiny garden;
and he knew too that that window was rarely closed. He
lightly touched the back-door, as if in passing, and found
that it was locked or barred. But the garden-wall was
not the height of even a medium-sized man. Standing on
his toes, Halliday could look quite over it now, and could
distinctly see the little fountain which he had noticed as
it sparkled and leaped in the sunlight each day that he
stood in Salome's room. What was to hinder him from
climbing over that wall some night,—late of course, very
late,—and then ? Of course Alice had been brought there.
Of course; but he must make himself absolutely sure and
certain of this. Easy to do that. A sharp lookout to-morrow would soon settle that question. To-night he could
attempt nothing ; people would be on their guard. Perhaps Alice would have to be removed to the hospital or
somewhere else, and another blundering attempt on his
part would spoil all. No ; he must wait. He was becoming more cool and collected, for he began to see his way.

He would not return that night—perhaps not any more
—to his old quarters. They were far off—down somewhere in the regions lying off Holborn ; and if any search
were made for him, some track might be found to guide the
pursuers there. Besides it was too far ; he must keep
fixedly on the ground where he had to play his part.
And he owed money to the people down Holborn way, and
they would perhaps be little inclined to run any risks on
his account. No ; he had often heard that men and
women and children found good and gratuitous lodgings

in Hyde-park : he would take up his quarters there too.
It would not be worth his while going far out of the way
—now.

There was a public-house at the farther extremity of
the little avenue in which he was now skulking. He went
in there, and spent three-quarters of an hour in drinking as
much spirit as he could afford to pay for. It cannot be
said that it gave him courage—he did not want for courage now—but it brightened up his faculties and steadied
his nerves. As he passed up the lane again, a policeman,
who came tramping down, looked at him rather suspi-
ciously. But policemen generally did this, and Halliday
did not mind. He was used to it now, and did not believe
anything would come of it. As he passed in front of Salome's house, it was all lighted up, and he could hear many
voices—and men's voices too—in animated talk. How
lucky he had not made any foolish attempt ! But he
knew better than that. Not such a fool ! Halliday almost
chuckled. He felt quite bright and happy. You see his
mind was made up.

The park-gates were now closed ; but Halliday soon
found an easy place to climb over. It is easier for robbers
or murderers to hold meetings there than for Mr. Beales's
friends of the Reform League. So Halliday had no occasion to break down any railings. He got in, and at first
felt almost elate, and began to whistle. He lay down
under a tree, and thought he could hardly be better off.

This was while the influence of the whiskey lasted, and
while the night was fine. But the strength of the one gradually faded, and the beauty of the other suddenly disappeared. A sharp wind began to blow the dust about
Halliday's ears and eyes and hair, and presently rain descended. His tree was a tolerably good shelter, and
wretched creatures speedily found their way there and
swarmed around him. He hoped it would soon get fine
again ; but it did not get fine. It began to rain harder
and harder; at last became a drenching down-pour.

Some of those who were near Halliday got up and ran from the rain, as if out of the mere instinct of running rather than because they hoped to find any better shelter elsewhere. They were new and raw to the business as yet, and had evidently been until very lately accustomed to expect shelter of some kind when rain came on. The experienced had chosen their places from the beginning, and knowing they could get nothing by changing their ground remained where they were. Some of them grumbled and some of them blasphemed, and one or two women gathered their clothes more tightly about them and giggled; and some took it as a matter of course, and did not seem to care whether it rained or left off. Halliday made no move. He had nowhere else to go; and to have got up and left the spot would moreover have involved the disturbing of some of his neighbors, and an almost inevitable interchange of talk, and he was in no humor for talk just then. The rain plashed down upon his wreched clothes, and he hated to feel it streaming on him—he had always a keen objection to physical discomfort; and he associated in his mind this other suffering with the beings who, he firmly believed, had already wreaked so many wrongs on him. He was lying there under that rain that he might be the better able to keep watch upon his enemies; and was not this misery therefore another count in the indictment against them, another item in the long catalogue of his grievances? Why, if there could have been required any possible motive to prick the sides of his revengeful intent, the rain which now streamed down upon his homeless form would have supplied it.

He lay still and tried to sleep. He did at last fall into a dull doze; but the moment his faculties began to lose themselves in dreams, he must have begun also to rave and talk rather loudly, for one of his near neighbors gave him a friendly drive in the ribs with his elbow, and said: "I say, mate, can't you manage somehow to hold your noise? Can't you let any fellow sleep but yourself?" And Halliday leaped up wildly at the thrust, and began fumbling in his pocket, and clutching around him ; and some of his companions burst into laughter at the sight, and mastering the meaning of the demonstration at once chaffed him for his fear of the bobbies. He tried to exchange a little gruff banter with his pleasant companions; but he was never much of a wit, and his country accent supplying a fresh theme for mirth to his assailant, Halliday speedily withdrew from the game and tried to go to sleep again.

"Vot have you been doing, mate?" inquired his friend again, giving him a second dig in the ribs just as he prepared himself to undertake another doze.

"What d'ye mean?" Halliday fiercely demanded, sitting up, amid the titters of some of the women encamped near him.

"Vy, you're like a man a expecs to be took alive or dead, and is going to fight it out. Something vorse than burglary, I should say. Vere's your ticket-of-leave? I'm a perliceman in disguise, I am."

New laughter followed this sally. Halliday jumped to his feet, shuffled his way among the forms, some of them sleeping around him, and made for some quieter resting-place. Curses from those he had disturbed and yells of laughter from others pursued him as he went.

He trudged through plashing grass, trampled with reckless hoofs over flower-beds, and strode across railings, going he knew not whither. It streamed with rain; and yet even on the open turf, almost everywhere he went, he could see through the darkness some figure huddled or stretched on the ground. The park was dotted all over with crouching forms. If the dead could have risen from their graves in some populous churchyard, each one to brood, like the ghosts of the heroes in Ossian, over the spot of earth which lately received his bones, the cemetery could hardly have been more thickly sown with shapes of humanity or looked more drear and ghastly than Hyde-park was that wild and dismal summer night when Halliday tried to sleep there.

He sat down. at last, tired of purposeless tramping, near a cluster of shrubs, and after awhile closed his eyes. He was soon disturbed by a thick breathing near him, and looking up saw a miserable old woman, apparently a mere heap of rags, had squatted on the ground at his side. She was looking at him with curious gaze when he opened his eyes, and half-sleepy and much confused as he was, he positively thought at first it was his poor old mother, and he grunted fiercely, and tried to turn on the other side, as he used to do long ago, at the opening of his drunken career, when on ·awaking in the morning he heard his mother groaning and lamenting over him, and endeavored to close his ears to her feeble plaints.

"Faith, ye're in the right of it to go to sleep, if yez can," said the woman, in a tight South-Munster brogue; "on'y I'm afeerd yez have bad dhrames by your groanin'. It's a terrible night, agra, isn't it? I'd like a penn'orth o' coffee to warm me. Will you stand a penn'orth? A dhrop o' whiskey 'ud be more in your way, I'm thinking. Wouldn't it, alanna?"

Halliday growled something unintelligible, and began to move farther off.

"O, ye're not in the humor for company, maybe? Bedad, an' ye're right enough there. Ye seems to me just the sort o' chap that's maybe been cuttin' somebody's throat. I don't like the looks of yez. Ye won't stand the coffee? Maybe ye'd do the other thing—lave it alone. Good-night, and pleasant dhrames and better humor to yez."

He saw no more of her, for he kept his eyes resolutely shut for some time, and when he opened them again she was gone. But he never once fell asleep without presently waking up to find somebody or several people near him who were not there when he closed his eyes. A hideous restlessness seemed to take possession of many of the campers in that region. What with his fatigue and the perpetual pres-

sure on his mind, the whole thing began at last to change
into a sort of phantasmagoria, which he only looked at now
and then with a languid and vacuous curiosity, but in which
he saw no meaning or coherence. Strange figures were
always near him and always changing—that was all.

The rain never ceased. All through that dreary night,
the dark hours of which seemed so many and which yet
must have been so few, the torrent streamed down thick
and merciless. Halliday was conscious of no longing for
morning or definite desire of any kind. His mind had sunk
into that sodden state which accepts everything as it comes,
and cannot rouse itself to wonder, or hope, or wish of any
sort. He bore the rain and the night and the discomfort
now as a snail might have done; and had scarcely faculties
enough left in activity to be sure whether life was or was
not all a perpetual lying on soaking grass under heavy rain,
with strange people always coming to crouch beside one.
At last he fell fast asleep, and the curtain of life was down
for the time.

When he awoke, it was gray morning, and the rain at
last had nearly ceased. Over in the east might be seen a sort
of livid attempt at brightness, which foretold the struggle
of the sun to make his way through the one cloud which
covered the whole sky. Halliday rubbed his eyes and sat
up. Near him on the grass sat a young woman who was
endeavoring to squeeze the rain out of her shawl and skirts,
and to put herself into something like order for the approach
of day. Halliday was still half asleep, and perhaps not much
better than half insane. The face and figure of a young
woman produced a wild effect upon him. He cried out
" Ally ! " in a fierce savage tone, and seized the girl by the
shoulder.

She slipped out of her shawl in a moment, and leaped to
her feet.

" My name isn't Ally," she said; " and you'd much better
let me alone. Who are you and what are you about, that

you catch hold of people in that sort of way? Are you drunk? Take care you don't get locked up."

She was not in the least afraid, and she took up her shawl, and began to shake it out before putting it on.

Halliday had his eyes and his senses open now. "I didn't mean anything, I'm sure," he said; "and I beg pardon if I gev' offence. I was asleep I suppose, and I thought you were—"

"Your wife, I dare say," said the girl with a shrill laugh, "or your sweetheart—and very pretty notion of a good-morning you seem to have too. I shouldn't like to be your sweetheart, I know, if you go to choke her the moment you see her. Perhaps she's been throwing you over, and you're a jealous fellow. Well, if I see her, I'll tell her to look out, for I'm sure her life isn't safe when you're near. Good-morning. Pleasant night, wasn't it? I never was so wet in my life. Have you anywhere to go to? I haven't; but I've had enough of this for one night."

He made no answer of any kind, and she went away, after paying some compliment to his pleasant manners and cheerful disposition.

Halliday was shivering all over when he rose from the grass. He stamped up and down for awhile to get a little warmth; but he knew that nothing could restore him to anything like his usual condition save the fire-water which had long been his only cordial. He had still some of Alice's money left. His one set purpose had given him a self-control which in life before he had never been able to exercise; and he had taken resolute care the previous evening not to have more drink than the fair share which he had allotted to himself as one evening's allowance. Determined not to leave himself unprovided for the coming day or two, he had put aside all temptation, and husbanded his resources as firmly as a provident commander in a siege, or captain of a becalmed and dismasted vessel, measures out the proportion for each day's sustenance.

So Halliday's first feeling was one of satisfaction that he was not without something to enable him to begin the morning, and to weather through the day until the night came on again.

With the morning too returned all the clearness and firmness of his purpose. Gray and drear lay the park around him now, and the spectres of the night were everywhere preparing for a flitting. Like obscene birds, they seemed unable to endure the face of day. It wanted hours yet to the time when the park-gates were to be opened and the day-side of nature was to reign, with its traffic, its noise, and its brightness. The creatures who had lodged gratuitously within the precincts of the crown demesne might have lodged there undisturbed for a good time yet. No policeman threatened to invade them; no summons to "move on" vexed them; no park-keeper troubled his head about them. But they were all gathering their rags around their limbs, and preparing to do their only homage to the god of day by disappearing from his presence. It seemed as if they could not bear to encounter the sight of each other with the light of morning, such as it was, upon their faces. Even the beauties at a ball, indeed, do not, after their night of pleasure, bear very well to meet each other's eyes, and to look in the face of the cold morning, as they stand upon the steps in the dawn, and await impatiently the carriage which is to hide their faded cheeks, hollow eyes, lank curls, and collapsed garments. Some of the wretched creatures in the park, now wringing the rain from their draggled clothes and trying to put back their soppy hair under their shapeless bonnets, were animated, doubtless, by feelings very much akin to those of their silken-clad sisters on the steps of the houses in Connaught-place, and Park-lane, and Hyde-park-gardens, not far away.

Halliday too prepared to go, but did not trouble himself about the appearance of his hair or the condition of his clothes. Nor did he care for the fact that he had no place to go to.. Beyond a sentiment of physical satisfaction that the night of rain was done, the approach of morning and the abandonment of his sleeping-place brought to him no particular emotion of any kind. "He was not all un-happy," says Tennyson of Enoch Arden; "his resolve sustained him." A bad resolve has sometimes as much of a sustaining power as a good one. His resolve sustained Halliday through hunger and cold and wet and homeless-ness. He felt himself true unto death. But he had learned a little lesson too during the broken sleep of the night. He had learned that something of his purpose must have been expressing itself in his face. Not one who addressed a word to him, even in the mid-darkness of that hideous night, but hinted, or broadly declared, that his counte-nance and his manners bespoke some fierce and felon reso-lution. Now Halliday knew that he must not meet the day, and the ordinary life of the streets, with that purpose stamped upon him. Therefore he must keep out of peo-ple's observation when he could; and when he could not accomplish this, he must at least endeavor to look like an ordinary human creature. So he resolved to go at once to some small public-house or coffee-shop and get himself dried and washed, and put a smooth expression on his face, and not drink too much. He told over his money: It was very little; but, carefully managed, it would carry him through that day and the next. It might easily be two days before he could do anything, and therefore he must be very cautious in the meantime. The wolf's rage would not be so formidable but for the wolf's cunning and patience and steady stealthy step.

The day began to brighten as he left the park; and even the sweet scents of the flowers, which the rain of the night had drenched and beaten down, were beginning to be a delicious influence to the senses of many an early milliner and workman going to the morning's toil. Halli-day hastily crossed the road, and buried himself in a public-house and a glass of raw spirits.

CHAPTER XXV.

TROUBLES CROWD ON EUSTACE.

THE perplexity of Eustace Massie did not disappear with the turmoil of the election contest; it did not even diminish. Nay, in some respects, it absolutely increased. He had some consultations with his man of business touching the hints which he had received from the latter about mysterious inquiries going forward in the town; and he could receive no satisfactory explanation. Indeed, the man of business had none to give. The inquiry, whatever it was, was conducted with the utmost secrecy and skill. All that he could say was, that he felt sure it had some sort of relation to the Massie family and the Massie property. In the most vague and delicate way possible he hinted at a conjecture he had formed, begging at the same time to guard against being supposed to have any ground whatever for such surmise, or even for the notion that anybody entertained such surmise—any ground, that is, beyond the mere conjecture of one who, finding that a mysterious and secret inquiry is going on, and that money is actually being spent on it, is compelled to set about conjecturing some sane motive for it. Now, the man of business could only think of one possibility which had any aspect whatever of sanity behind it. What was this? Eustace firmly pressed for an explanation. Well, Mr. Massie's grandfather was a little wild in his day. He brought home his wife from abroad, and she did not seem a person of very high station. Suppose—he only said suppose—some foolish busybodies took it into their heads that the pair never were legally married at all? There were Massies in existence to whom the proof of such a thing might bring benefit.

Eustace scouted the idea. He was a good deal shocked

at first, but soon recovered. A man may easily manage to discuss with tolerable calmness a question concerning the virtue of his grandmother, who died long years before he saw the light. Besides, it at once occurred to him—and he wondered it had not occurred to a business man before—that whatever the result of such an inquiry, it could not in the least degree benefit Paul Massie. It seemed to be beyond doubt that whatever inquiries were afloat were made on behalf of Paul Massie. What possible object could he have in endeavoring to prove that his own father was an illegitimate child?

The man of business looked embarrassed ; and, indeed, even reddened a little. He changed the subject quickly, remarking that it was quite a sudden conjecture of his, and one which had obviously nothing in it.

But there was something about his manner, his hesitating speech, his averted eye, which struck Eustace, and presently caused his cheek to flush with a deep flame of crimson. Eustace made no further allusion to the subject, and somewhat suddenly took his leave.

For the conjecture really formed by the man of business was not the chimerical and utterly unmeaning speculation which even Eustace Massie could dismiss without hesitation. He had merely made the suggestion because he thought it might delicately serve to convey to Eustace a hint of the true nature of his conjecture, which he shrank from conveying in plainer form of speech.

Mr. Freestun, the man of business, well remembered the wild youth of Eustace's father. He remembered the suddenness of his supposed marriage, and his Mexican journey ; and he had had opportunities of seeing the terms on which, for many years before his death, he lived with the mother of his children. What if his legal marriage with her had been a late and a reluctant one? He was just the sort of man who had virtue enough not to cast away a woman who had been to him as a wife—not virtue enough to accept his duty without compunction and complaint.

What if some people were thereby led to suppose that the marriage was an act of reparation? Mr. Freestun did not believe this; and knowing all the circumstances of Mr. Massie's death, and the disposition of his property, did not see how it could legally affect the existing condition of things, even if it were true. But he could easily understand how the next heirs to the property might suppose they could secure a vast advantage for themselves by the proof of such a thing. Besides, a discovery of that kind could be most effectively used as a means of extorting money. Mr. Freestun thought this a very likely object. In his eyes Paul Massie was a mere adventurer, of whom anything might be believed. Mr. Freestun vaguely regarded him as a sort of cross between the traditional Polish Count who runs off with school-girls and writes begging-letters, and the Yankee swindler who hawks hickory hams and wooden nutmegs.

On his way home Eustace encountered Dan Crossley the boatman. He had been much amazed to find that during the contest Crossley was one of the most demonstrative supporters of Paul Massie. When the clergyman remembered what he had seen one day, as these two men stood face to face, he marvelled to find Crossley doing henchman for his cousin. Such a course seemed full of ingratitude to the Seaborough family, who had been always so kind to the Crossleys. But Eustace was just now more surprised at the inconsistency than angered by the ingratitude.

Crossley saluted Mr. Massie respectfully enough, but not very cordially; perhaps with the air of one who was not quite certain whether a salute from him would not be resented as a piece of impertinence.

Mr. Massie stopped.

"So I hear you have found your daughter, Crossley?" he said.

"Yes, Mr. Massie; I've heerd from her, that is."

"I hope she is well placed; and with your full approval?"

"Yes, sir; she's well enough. I'm not badly pleased

that she's out of here. She's in the care of a good
lady."

"Why did she go away in that strange and sudden
manner? And why did you not tell us when she was
found?"

"Well, Mr. Massie, to own the truth, it was a sort of a
secret—not mine, sir ; for I don't have any secrets, an' I
don't like 'em ; but another person's ; an' my wife thought
we oughtn't to say anything about it. Then there was
the affair · of the election ; an' I thought perhaps you
wouldn't take it quite friendly of me that I went with your
cousin. I went with him, sir, partly because I wronged
him before, and partly because I like him better than
t'other candidate."

"You have quite a right, Crossley, to vote for whom
you please. If your conscience told you to vote as you
did, I could not find fault with you. I am glad you have
found your daughter, and that you are satisfied with her
position. Good-morning."

Eustace was moving coldly away. Despite his own
declaration, he still thought in his heart that he had a
good right to blame Crossley. It is very hard to get it
thoroughly into the mind of a certain class that a poor
man really ought to have a political conscience, and to
obey it, independently of his local superiors.

Crossley saw the coldness of Mr. Massie's manner.

"I'm afeerd, Mr. Massie," he began, in a low, awkward,
hesitating tone, "that you think I'm against you, and giving evidence against you. But you mustn't believe it, sir,
for I haven't."

"What do you mean by giving evidence against me?"
asked Eustace sharply.

"Answering questions, sir, that was put to me,—to me
an' my wife,—about what we remember here—about old
times and Mr. Massie your father—an'—an' all that. A
man couldn't help answering, sir, as he knew—and right
is right, an' I don't want to help one side or the other, but

only to let the right be done—an' I'm sure, Mr. Massie, that's all you ever want or wish for yourself."

"Crossley," said Massie, "what you are talking of is utterly without meaning for me. I do not try—I do not want—to know what it means, or if it means anything. Neither you nor any other being in the world can injure me by telling the truth about anything. I have no secrets to hide; and until within the last week or two I did not know that I had any concealed enemies to guard against. Not another word; I won't hear any more on the subject."

Abruptly he walked away, and left Crossley perplexed and half-ashamed.

"Doesn't he really know anything?" the boatman asked of himself. "And have I been saying something I oughtn't to say that offends him?"

But if Crossley was bewildered, Eustace Massie was far more so. Some mysterious investigation then was going forward, some scrutiny into the past history of his family! The very notion of such a thing made his cheek flame with anger. He would not allow his mind to dwell for a moment upon the horrible suggestion conveyed by Mr. Freestun's manner. The remotest gleam of such a thought was an insult and outrage to the sacred memory of the dead, and the yet more sacred reputation of the living.

"Are such things allowed?" thought Eustace, as he chafed and fretted on his homeward walk. "Is there any law in this country? Have we no protection against the base artifices of enemies? Are the private histories of the oldest and the most unsullied families not to be sacred from prying investigations which can have no real object but to insult, and from the whispered calumny, deliberately and knowingly concocted for evil purposes? Why are there laws to protect society from robbers, and none to save religious people of social position from the outrage of such infamous speculations?"

He reached his home at last, and made for his study.

There he sat down, leant his head upon his hand, and tried to think.

Was he really going to alarm and vex himself about the ignorant gossip of a village boatman? Was he to attach any importance to the coarse and vulgar insults which were got up in connection with a contested election, and only in the hope of somehow influencing its result? Why, there would be nothing surprising if there had been a charge of robbery or infidelity, or even atheism, got up against him or any member of his family at such a moment. Sensible men, accustomed to politics, never, he had heard, pay the slightest attention to such things. They take them as a matter of course, as the common and characteristic incidents of an election contest, just like the banners and the beer-drinking. Had he not himself been charged with selling the borough to the noble father of the defeated candidate? Eustace positively tried to smile the smile of pity and scorn. This was what people got by mixing. up in such squabbles. After all, a clergyman should have nothing to do with political wranglings. Henceforward— !

And yet—and yet? What bodings had he had of late which made Crossley's words seems not unexpected? What had Mr. Freestun written to him and spoken to him? What did drunken Halliday tell him in the Strand —of people plotting against him? Why, had not even Lydia heard something vaguely to the same effect? In Heaven's name, what did it all mean? Had Eustace been a guilty and conscious schemer, instead of a pure and honorable man, he could not have felt more keenly thrilled through than he now was by the bare suspicion that somebody was plotting something, he knew not what, for his humiliation. He did not care to conjecture what the plan might be. He scorned even to admit the idea of there being any possible foundation for reproach against his house. No thought even for a moment intruded itself upon his mind of the scheme, whatever it might prove, being other than a base plot to disturb or intimidate him.   Yet he literally shuddered at the prospect of any such plot being put into practical operation, although it must end in its own discomfiture and defeat.   It would at the very best be a family quarrel, an exposure, and a public scandal.   In a well-regulated household—especially that of a clergy-man—there should be no exposures and family disputes. Such things were nearly as disgraceful to those in the right as to those in the wrong.   Eustace sighed as he contemplated the prospect opening before him.

Only one person in the world, so far as he knew, could give him the slightest information which might guide him to understand even what his persecutors meant.   That person, of course, was his mother.   If there were anything whatever in the nature of a mystery, or a supposed mystery, anywhere lying half hidden among the family traditions, she must know of it.   She was about the last person he would have willingly consulted in any ordinary case on any such subject, but in this instance he had no choice. He could not help remembering with what painfully evident reluctance his mother had always approached any subject bearing on Paul Massie's birth and parentage ; and he felt that any inquiry he now might make must be productive of uneasiness.   He did not feel quite sure that he might not have to encounter a scene.   But he relieved himself with a sigh, made up his mind for the encounter, and went to seek his mother.

Mrs. Massie was alone.   The girls had not yet returned from London.   She was seated in an arm-chair, and had been reading; the chair drawn to the window, where the warmth of the evening sun might be fully enjoyed.   Mrs. Massie loved warmth and the sun.   Eustace thought she was looking out upon the pleasant lawn ; but as he came nearer, he saw that she was asleep.   He could hardly avoid being struck by the singularly youthful appearance which she still preserved.   Her fair thick clusters of hair, her delicate complexion, the youthful outline of her face and figure, produced quite an illusory effect upon the eye. At a little distance you saw a fair and graceful young woman sleeping, and smiling in her sleep. Only when you approached quite near did you begin to see that the skin was slightly loosening and wrinkling; that there were hollows under the eyes; that the hands were thin and withering; that there was an ominous transparency in the flesh. But the hair had not one shade or streak of gray, though the smiling expression changed on a near approach to one of feebleness and sadness.

Eustace had a great affection and a sort of protecting sentiment towards his mother, as nearly approaching to tenderness as such a nature might feel. He would not on any account have disturbed her, and was therefore about to steal softly away. But she was the lightest of sleepers, and she awakened in an instant.

"Dear Eustace, I did not know you had come in. I was reading a novel—a very dull one—and I fell asleep. I am glad you have come in. You look perplexed. What is the matter?"

"The fact is, I *am* perplexed. I don't want to annoy you about these matters; but really I want to ask you to enlighten me a little about a very puzzling and rather unpleasant affair."

"What is it, Eustace? Tell me quickly, please."

"Well, it is about—in fact, it is about my cousin, Paul Massie."

She turned deadly pale. All the youthful expression had faded away from her face. Her very figure seemed to shrink and cower. She was quite an elderly woman now. She drew back into her chair, away from the questioner, and placed across her lips and chin the hand which had just been laid so tenderly on his.

"What about Paul Massie?"

"Indeed, mother, I hardly know what I want to ask. But there is idle talk everywhere of some claim he, or somebody on his behalf, means to set up against us; there are odd inquiries being carried on in Seaborough—Dan Crossley the boatman is mixed up in it; or if not he, at least his daughter is—that unfortunate and ungrateful Alice; and I can make nothing of the whole affair, except that it is unspeakably vexatious and offensive. What *do* these people mean?"

"I do not know. How should I?" Words spoken with compressed lips, and in a low hollow voice, without cadence or body in it; words sounding as if they came through some tube or passage, and were spoken in another room.

"No," said Eustace perplexedly; "of course you do not know. But do you know anything at all about Paul Massie which might lead to the supposition that he could think or fancy he has any unfulfilled claim of any sort against my father or me?"

"Does he fancy he has any claim?"

"Why, mother dear, I have said already that I really don't know what he fancies. But if he does not fancy something of this sort, I cannot understand for the life of me what he and his friends mean. Is there anything about him and us which I do not know? Is there any secret of any kind? If there is, it ought at least to be told to me."

"Eustace, I do not believe Paul Massie ever did or ever will urge any claim against you—against us. He could not. He cannot."

"But is there any claim, mother? Is there?"

"He had no claim on your father. He has none on you, except the claim of blood."

She still spoke in her cold, low, almost toneless way. She continued: "Your father dealt with him generously, magnanimously. Much more so than I—than he—could have asked or hoped for. If any claims of any kind are being raised, be sure it is not Paul Massie who raises them."

"But, mother, somebody is moving secretly in the matter, and it must be on his behalf. Tell me something more about him and about my father. I know my father would not see him. Tell me why."

"I cannot tell you ; how should I know? Pray do not ask me any more about it."

"There is, then, some family secret?" said Eustace fretfully ; and rising from his chair, he paced the room. "There is some mystery or other; some scandal which somebody is bent on ferreting out, if indeed he does not know it to the full already! And I have been kept in ignorance of it—am not suffered to know anything about it now. Crossley the boatman, and the serving-girl his daughter, may gossip and speculate over it, and make money out of it ; and I am left in darkness. Mother, if you knew of this, and did not tell me, you have not used me well."

"Eustace, Eustace, do not reproach me!"

"I cannot help reproaching you. What is to come of all this? What *is* it? In the name of Heaven, tell me what it is all about?"

She drew herself together as if collecting what of firmness there was in her weak and sensitive frame, and looking calmly at her son, she answered:

"Eustace, I can tell you nothing now. Some time you may perhaps know whatever poor secret remains to be known, whatever miserable memorial of days with which you have had happily no concern has been preserved a secret by me. Then you will wish you had not known it. But believe me that for the present it cannot concern you. I can arrange for that. I am going to London."

"Going to London! You?"

"Why not?" she asked with a pallid and a ghastly smile. "Am I too old to make a pleasure-trip? London must be a good deal changed since I last saw it."

"I will go with you if you really want to go."

"No, Eustace, I would much rather go alone."

"You will at least take a servant, or wait until Sarah comes back, and let her go with you?"

"No, I want to go alone. I want no one with me. Am I child, Eustace, that you think I cannot be trusted to go alone on a journey to London?"

"No, no; but I only thought, as you are not in the habit—"

"Pray don't tease yourself and me by raising foolish objections. It is convenient that I should go alone for a day or two, and I hope I am mistress of my own movements." She spoke with a sort of petulant feebleness painful to observe.

"Surely, dear mother, no one thinks of preventing you from doing as you please. I was only anxious for your comfort. And I own I am a little surprised and confused by the discovery that there really are secrets of some kind connected with our family which have been kept purposely from my knowledge." He rose and was leaving the room. His mother called to him in a faint voice; he returned and came towards her rather coldly.

"Eustace, my dear son, do not be angry with me if I am a little petulant. I am much tried, and have long been so. You cannot understand it, dear. Forgive me for my manner—ah, if that were all!"

She kissed him tenderly and sadly. The poor clergyman left the room like one who walks in a dream. Life was to him now only one great enigma. Order was nowhere. Ill-regulated feeling and inscrutable mystery seemed to rule over all. The little world which he believed he had constructed around him, to move according to his own wise laws, had suddenly begun to whirl with the most eccentric movements, and threatened to become chaos once again.

It was with a thrill of joy that he welcomed that evening the return of Sarah and Lydia. The one might give him sympathy and even counsel; the other at least would help to make the place look like itself again.

He had to go into the village after dinner. Sarah asked him when he would return, and by what way; she said she would go to meet him. He was glad of it, and he resolved to take her into his confidence, in the hope that the light of her quick intelligence might guide him out of his perplexities.

He loitered on the way home that he might have the greater distance left to walk in her company. He had hardly ever done anything before with so much of design in it. His uneasiness and his need of sympathy were converting him into something almost like a lover.

He turned slowly round a corner, and he saw Sarah Massie approaching. His sober heart did not indeed beat with the wild and half-painful ecstasy which thrills the breast of passionate and ill-regulated youth at the sight of the one only and chosen being. Such passion his calm and steady temperament little knew ; but he was glad, very glad, and his heart softened, and the world seemed less lonely and less perplexing.

"I am so glad you came, Sarah—Sarah dear," he said in a burst of unwonted demonstrativeness; "I wanted very much to speak to you alone." He got out the last word with a sort of effort; it seemed like the confession of a kind of impropriety.

She looked up to him with a startled expression. She paused, hesitated, then summoned courage.

"Eustace, I wanted very, very much to speak to you alone. I have something to say that deeply concerns—us. I ought to have said it before now."

She faltered. He came to a stand on the road and looked into her face. Little read as he was in the language of woman's eyes, he knew what was coming.

"Eustace, we can never be married—never."

It was all out now ; the die was cast.

He made one or two efforts to speak collectedly. " Why so ? " was all he could articulate.

Sarah had gathered courage and calmness now.

" Because, dear Eustace—dear brother, I ought not to

marry you. I love you, but not in that way ; and, and—I don't think you love me as I would have myself loved."

"But why," he stammered, pale and pulseless,—"why did you think of all this now?"

"I have thought of it a long time, but not clearly, and I could not decide ; and I feared to pain you and aunt."

You and aunt ! The very coupling of the names in such a manner, as if the revelation concerned the one quite as much as the other, showed painfully how little Sarah counted on the element of love having any share in the transaction.

"No," said Eustace slowly, and speaking with teeth firmly set, "it was not that which prevented you; and I don't believe you have thought of this for a long time. You never thought of it until last February ; you never thought of it until you saw Paul Massie."

"O, Eustace ! " - She turned on him her eyes full of reproach. "For shame ; be generous."

"Generous! Who has any right to expect generosity of me ? Is it he ? What has he brought but misery into this house? Since he came, nothing is as it was. You, you, Sarah, are casting me off for him. You know it—you dare not deny it. You would if you could. Deny it now if you can."

He would have given much to hear a denial from her, even though it were extorted by anger. Her face grew crimson as he looked searchingly at her, and laid his cold fingers on her wrist.

"I do not deny it," she said, with a thrill of indignation in her tones, "though it is unmanly of you to press me to it. I do not deny it. I might never have known how little we were suited for each other had I not seen him. I am not ashamed to acknowledge it, although you might well be ashamed of forcing the acknowledgment from me. But listen ; and as you know so much, know all. I do love Paul Massie ; but he and I never exchanged one word or look of love in all our lives, and never shall. Hear the whole.

He cares as little for me as I do for—" and she was going to speak a cruel word, but happily checked her tongue, and only said, " as I do for the merest stranger who passes us on this road."

Yes, she was at the moment on the point of saying bitterly : " He cares as little for me as I do for you." Women are cruel in their love, and are specially pitiless to the egotists who would fain have assumed sovereignty over them without taking thought to win the allegiance of their hearts' affections. Eustace would have found it hard to believe even then how bitter and hostile were the sentiments towards him which now inflamed the heart of that once patient and docile creature whom he thought to have moulded in all things to his will.

But he too had his transfiguration. Passion burned in his heart at last. He broke out into an uncontrollable storm of anger.

"I hate him ! " he exclaimed. " I hate that heartless, abandoned, ungrateful, scheming villain ! Why did he come here to torture and destroy us all ? We were happy until he came with his brutality ; and now with his plots and schemes he has made us miserable. You would have loved me—yes, you would !—but for him ; and now you cast me off for him who has not even the heart to see your love and to be grateful. He is sunk in debt and dissipation, and he tries to redeem himself by low tricking and lying and swindling ; and you—you love him, and you fling me away for him—me, though I have loved you and clung to you since you were a little girl. For him, for him—for such a wretch."

" Shame, Eustace, Shame ! You do him a cruel wrong, and you do yourself a worse wrong to talk in that way, and to believe the mean calumnious stories which were told to set you against him. You speak like a madman."

" What wonder if I did ? Is there not enough to set me mad ? Do you not know that he is plotting against me, against my mother ? Do you not know the vile lies that he and his associates are trumping up? No, you do not know them; for if you did, even you would turn from him in disgust."

Sarah looked aghast at him. What did he mean? What could he have heard or guessed? For him, he misinterpreted the look of alarm in her face, and thought he caught from it a wild gleam of hope for himself.

"Yes," he said eagerly, "if you only knew, you would abhor the thought of him. Listen, Sarah, and I will tell you—all."

Poor Eustace! He saw before him a woman in love; and he was simple enough to fancy that all he had to do was to prove her lover unworthy, and she would forthwith renounce him; nay, more than renounce—forget him.

Sarah stopped him.

"It would be useless, Eustace," she said with a faint smile. "Even if I could believe all you might have to tell, and see it all with your eyes, it would make no difference in our position. I had rather not hear anything against him. I had rather not believe him bad. Were he noble and generous, as I think or thought him; or mean and wicked, as you believe him,—he and I can never be anything to each other; and you and I can never be more than we now are."

"No, no," he exclaimed; "do not say so. You will think more of this; you will think of it again. I will wait —I can be patient. You will not always remain under this fatal influence. You will forget one who, believe me, does not deserve a thought from you, and you will turn to me who always loved you and appreciated you. Give me time —give yourself time; will you not?"

"Eustace, I beseech of you to spare me. It is in vain— all in vain. I never, never can feel otherwise than as I feel at this moment."

"And you leave me lonely and miserable—here, with no one to understand me, to care for me?"

"I leave you, indeed. Heaven knows I leave you to be lonely and miserable myself. I go from this place, which was always my home—go, I do not know where; to live alone, work alone, and in the end to die alone."

"But why, why do so? Why thus cut yourself off from us? Is my mother not as a mother to you? You have told me frankly what you feel to—to *him*. Well, I will bear with that, and will trust to your heart changing in time and coming round to me. You cannot and would not marry him."

She made an impatient gesture.

"Then why not marry me? I do not ask your love— at least not at the first. I will wait for it, and work for it, and deserve it—and perhaps it will come at last. Do, do, Sarah. I ask, I beg of you; do think of this, and remain with us—with me."

"O, Eustace, Eustace!" she said, with streaming eyes, "you do not know what love is at all, or you would never talk in such a way. Do not ask me to commit so great a sin. I can never marry you. Were I to consent for a moment to such a thing, your own hand ought to be the first to fling me away. Let us be friends; we can never be anything else to each other."

His passion raved a little longer. She had never supposed him capable of so deep an emotion. Perhaps she liked him the better for it; perhaps she never in her years of close and constant association with him had gone so near to loving him as in this moment when she cast him off for ever. But her resolution was unchangeable. He calmed himself at last, and quitted her side in cold and sullen silence. Indeed he knew not whither he went. The firm earth seemed to tremble under his feet. Nay, the whole of his microcosm, once so orderly and fast, was shattered into pieces, and he was falling, falling into unknown depths, where strange lights and wild darknesses alternate swallowed him and bewildered his whole sense.

CHAPTER XXVI.

THE FOUNTAIN UNSEALED.

SARAH had perhaps even a greater repugnance to the necessary and inevitable scene of farewell with Mrs. Massie than to that which had just been accomplished with poor Eustace. Her aunt had always been kind and loving to her, and indeed had literally treated her as if she were a daughter. Left, as Sarah had been, from her very infancy in a condition somewhat approaching to that of dependence, she had never been allowed to feel for a moment any of the humiliations that even under the most favorable auspices almost invariably attach themselves to such a position. The late Mr. Massie was very fond of her, and had so high an opinion of her intelligence and of her superiority to women in general, whom he had come to distrust, that he talked with her and confided to her more than to any other member of the family. Mrs. Massie never showed the slightest jealousy because of this preference, but indeed, on the contrary, seemed to regard her husband's high opinion of Sarah only as another reason to justify her own regard and esteem for the girl. It was hard, therefore, to have to break up the domestic plans of a family to whom she owed so much. It was hard to announce that she who was bound by so many ties of gratitude to that home was the first and the only one to destroy voluntarily its whole future. It is a peculiarly hard thing too to have to tell a mother that you do not and cannot love her son. Mothers generally have their minds made up that an angel from heaven ought to feel honored by the preference of their sons. But Sarah had to do all this, and to do it quickly; and it was with a beating heart that she prepared for the ordeal.

Moreover she had long ceased to esteem her aunt. She had heard and seen and guessed enough to know that Mrs.

Massie must in her early life have been guilty at least of some fatal weakness, the shadow of which still hung over her existence. She had seen with pity her aunt's miserable mental struggles, and she knew that some sad secret was weighing on the worn woman's heart, and that her life was a long concealment. Perhaps Sarah might have learned all, had she sought to arrive at the knowledge. But she endeavored, on the contrary, to shut her mind against even conjecture. Something there had been which she could not fail to hear, and which must make a deep and painful impression; and this was quite enough to make Sarah feel her position in the household a trying one. It was not always possible for her, do what she would, to keep from interpreting many of Mrs. Massie's subsequent acts, and some of the incidents which otherwise would have been utter puzzles, by the light of the strange half-revelation that the delirium of fever once allowed to escape from the lips of her aunt. Therefore Sarah felt almost like a spy in that household, and would, in any case, had Eustace's engagement never been made and broken, have longed for a purer air, and some time or other sought it. But the very consciousness of what she knew only made her parting with Mrs. Massie more trying. Suppose her aunt should suspect that the cause of her leaving was something not directly connected with Eustace? Suppose she should question her? Suppose, still worse, that she should confide in her, and implore help and counsel? Sarah knew too well how completely Mrs. Massie had been accustomed to lean on her, and how utterly incapable she was of walking alone in the world. She dreaded a wild and wailing appeal; the appeal of the affrighted child about to be left alone in the darkness—of the weakly traveller who has fallen in the desert, and whose last companion prepares to abandon him.

There was no help for it, however. Sarah walked slowly home, in order to gain time to calm her nerves and dry her eyes. She was thinking far more now of the parting scene she had to go through than of that she had got over. She was by that very consciousness, however, beginning to learn more and more clearly how little hold Eustace had ever had upon her heart; and the knowledge helped to strengthen her and to justify her determination.

Was it not natural that coming to the tree beneath which she had stood when she parted from Paul, Sarah should rest a moment there? She ventured now to think of him. Her late interview with Eustace had not merely set her free, but had quite broken down any poor attempt at shutting Paul out from her mind, which before she might have endeavored to maintain. Eustace had openly and vehemently accused her of loving Paul, and in the heat of the moment she had actually confessed to him—to Eustace—there in the open day, with her own lips, what she had never before dared to acknowledge to her own heart under the protecting shadow of night and silence. Here then, on the spot where she parted from him, it was a compensation and a luxury to be able to think that she loved Paul. She almost revelled in the thought. She had never known one gleam of the higher joys and capabilities of life until she came to know and own that she loved him. What though *he* must never know it, it was something to make life worth bearing that she need no longer shrink from feeling, and in her heart acknowledging, her love.

Perhaps she might have been beguiled into remaining long on that spot, and thus postponing her unpleasant, unavoidable duty. But she presently heard voices, and she started from the place as hastily and confusedly as if anybody finding her there could possibly have divined the secret attraction which made these few square yard of greensward so dear to her. Continuing her walk towards the house, she came nearer to the voices, and at last into the presence of Mrs. Massie and Lydia.

Lydia began : " O Sarah, do you know—mamma is going to London to-morrow ? "

Sarah was really surprised. A snail making up his mind to be off with the swallows could hardly seem a more

unlikely project to any of the Massie family than that of
"mamma" undertaking a journey. But Sarah caught at
the idea with alacrity. If she might go with her ! It would
be so much easier to explain all when once outside the
precincts of Seaborough.

"Yes, and she won't let me go with her ! Did you ever
hear of such a thing ? And I should so like to go back."

"I cannot take you, Lydia," said her mother. "You
will soon, I suppose, see enough of London. You might
surely remain here for the rest of the time with Eustace
and Sarah."

Lydia slightly reddened at the allusion conveyed in Mrs.
Massie's words about the probability of her future residence
in London; but she said nothing.

Sarah had not the nerve to ask composedly what Mrs.
Massie was going to London for. She felt that it must be
a serious object which could draw her aunt from the shelter
of her home. But she caught at the chance which seemed
to open for her own escape. "May I go with you, aunt?"
Once away from Seaborough, once in London, the rest
would be comparatively easy.

"No, Sarah, my dear. I don't want anybody. It is not
a very dreadful undertaking."

"Only, mamma," broke in Lydia, "you never go anywhere alone, and I don't understand why you should do so
now. I really think if you won't take me, you had much
better take Sarah."

"I think Sarah had much better remain—and you too—
to keep Eustace company. He has been much troubled and
vexed of late ; and he ought not to be left now without companionship here, in this lonely place." Mrs. Massie positively shuddered as she spoke of the lonely place.

Sarah felt that she could not much longer put off her
explanation. Perhaps too Lydia's presence, embarrassing
as it was, might be a protection against yet deeper embarrassment. So she took her courage in two hands, to adopt
the French phrase.

"But, aunt, I think I had better go with you. I am going to London to-morrow."

"You, Sarah, going to London?"

"Yes, aunt, I am going."

Lydia opened wide round eyes, and holding her mother's arm brought all the party to a stand-still. They had fallen back, strangely enough, to the spot just in front of the well-known tree, and the sight of the place gave Sarah new courage. She could go through it all now.

"Only just returned from London, Sarah, and going back again at once! Does Eustace know that you are going?"

"I think he does."

"Think he does!" interjected Lydia with expressive emphasis.

"Does he know what you are going for?"

"I think he does, aunt. At least he will easily guess it."

"O—mysteries!" said Lydia, shrugging her shoulders.

"And what on earth are you going for, child? It is not a secret, I hope."

"O, no, aunt; but I think Eustace can tell you—"

"You have not quarrelled?"

"No, we have not quarrelled; but it is better I should go away; I must go indeed."

"O, yes, I am sure you have been quarrelling. What nonsense! I thought you both had more sense. But you will soon settle it. Can I help to make a reconciliation?"

"I think not, mamma," interposed Lydia in a low tone. Her intelligence was quicker in this affair than was usual with her, and she saw at a glance that Eustace and Sarah were parted.

Her mother did not notice the interruption.

"Come, Sarah," she said rather impatiently, "tell me all about this. I don't like mysteries."

What a relief to Sarah were these few words! Mrs. Massie, then, never knew that any expressions of hers had betrayed to Sarah her own involvement in a lifelong mystery. Had she suspected anything of the kind, she never would have ventured to make such a declaration.

"Why are you going to London; and how long do you mean to stay?"

"Not long in London, aunt."

"And when are you coming back here?"

"Never, never." Sarah's eyes filled with tears, and her voice broke down.

"Never coming back here! O, my dear, this is impossible; this is utter folly. Why, what has Eustace said or done?"

"Dear mamma," Lydia broke in, "you quite surprise me. Can you not see it all? Sarah has made up her mind not to marry Eustace; and she has told him so, and told him she does not care about him any more. I saw this long ago."

Sarah felt grateful to Lydia for cutting the whole matter short and setting the truth nakedly out, although there was little of tenderness or generosity in Lydia's way of doing it. But it was all out now, and the worst was over.

Mrs. Massie turned very pale.

"This is not true, Sarah," she said. "This surely cannot be true, my dear."

"It is true, aunt; it is true indeed, every word! O, forgive me, and beg of Eustace to forgive, and try to make him forget me. I would not have told it to you here or now if I could. If I might have gone with you to London, I could have told you the whole; and then—"

"And then you would not have had to tell it before me, I suppose?" said Lydia. "But, my dear Sarah, you told me no news. *I* saw it long ago. I think too you need not want to keep it a secret from me any more than from mamma. We have always been like sisters—people thought we were sisters often—and I did not think there could be any secrets between us; I did not expect it of you, Sarah."

And Lydia plunged her face in her pocket-handkerchief. Her tears were always ready to flow.

"Indeed, Lydia, I did not mean to keep any secret from you; and I was only going to say that, if I could have gone to London with aunt, I might have broken it to her gently, and then it would not have come so strangely upon her. But it is true, aunt, and there is no help for it. O, how much it grieves me that I should appear ungrateful to you and to Eustace, and to all who have been so kind and loving to me since I was a little child! But I have thought of it long; and I cannot help it. Aunt, I can never, never marry Eustace. I should be doing him the cruellest wrong if I did."

"You do not love him?"

"Not as he ought to be loved. O, not as somebody far more worthy of him than I will love him some day —for indeed he deserves to be loved. But I could not; I feel, I know, I never could; and so I must leave you all and go away."

"Poor Eustace!" sighed Lydia.

"Poor Eustace!" echoed Mrs. Massie in tones of far deeper sadness. "Does he know of this, Sarah?"

"He does, aunt."

"And bears it."

Sarah could make no answer.

"How unhappy we all are!" Mrs. Massie went on. "Nothing goes well with us! How miserable I shall be here for the rest of my life when Lydia is gone and you are gone! Every one leaves me. I do not know what has befallen us lately—"

"*I* know," Lydia interposed,—"I know what has made us all miserable, and put us out in every way. We were all very happy always—except, of course, when poor papa died, and that—until last February. I know what happened then; and the house has never been the same since, and nobody has been the same. O, I saw it long ago."

Of course everybody understood this allusion, but it passed without remark. Neither Mrs. Massie nor Sarah felt inclined to accept the challenge. Poor Paul Massie! he had no evil intentions to anyone, and yet here and there disappointed people were laying on his head the murder of some cherished hope.

"If your mind is made up in this matter, Sarah," said Mrs. Massie, after awhile, "there is no use in our endeavoring to reason with you. But I do not see why you should leave us, my dear. I do not know how I can live without you. Surely you may remain with me. Soon I shall be alone here, if you do not remain. Lydia, I suppose, will be married almost immediately to Captain Trenton" (the coming of this event has not, we believe, been formally announced before) ; "and Eustace will probably travel somewhere, and I shall be all alone if you leave me. There cannot be any occasion for your rushing out of the house and flinging us all away. I am sorry you cannot marry Eustace, my dear ; and it is a heavy disappointment to us all, after all these years ; but I do not the less love you ; and you have always been a daughter to me. You will not leave me, Sarah —not yet at least—not just yet, my dear ? "

She leaned on Sarah's arm, and looked piteously into the girl's flushed face.

"I am sure, Sarah, you need not go," Lydia added. "I don't see the slightest necessity for it ; and what on earth you can want in London, I cannot imagine."

"I am not going to stay in London, Lydia. I mean to go to Belgium."

"But I don't see why you should not stay with poor mamma. I don't see why she should be left alone. But she sha'n't be left alone. I'll stay with you, mamma. I don't care for anybody, or what anybody wants or says, if I may not stay with you. Yes ; I'll stay, since Sarah won't."

Lydia's self-sacrifice was cheap, for she knew perfectly well there was no chance of her magnanimous offer being accepted.

"My dear, you know you cannot stay ; and I would not have you to stay. The circumstances are quite different. I ask Sarah to stay with me because I see no reason for her going away. I do not know of any tie which is stronger to her than that between her and me—since she will not marry Eustace."

"O, very well, mamma. Of course, if you don't want me, and only care about Sarah, I have nothing more to say. I hope there is somebody in the world who does care about me, and who wants me." And Lydia wept afresh. She was determined to be the martyr of the situation.

"At all events, Sarah, you will wait until I come back. This much you must do. I shall not be long : and then we can speak more fully and more calmly about what you have told me. Now it has come with a shock upon us all, and we cannot collect our senses at once, and look quietly at it. We must not part in this hurried way, my dear : and you will wait—only a day or two—before you make up your mind to anything."

Sarah had no reason for refusing to promise this much, painful as the prospect of the coming day or two might be. She did promise; and Mrs. Massie thanked her with a tenderness which was sad to observe.

They walked home, and said not another word on the subject. Lydia kept in front, still choosing to be offended at something, and really much vexed with Sarah for two things ; first, for having the impertinence not to be glad to marry her (Lydia's) brother; and next for having, even during an hour or two, caused a sensation in which she (Lydia) had no part.

That evening dragged wearily through. Eustace did not return until late at night, and was seen by neither Sarah nor Lydia. The three women were very silent and dull. Sarah left the drawing-room early and went to her own room.

She sat up some time writing letters, chiefly to one or two school-friends in Belgium, who had often invited her to pay them a visit, and with whom she now intended to pass a few weeks while arranging for her future course of life. It was late when she put aside her paper and began to undress.

A low slight tap was heard at the door. She threw a dressing-gown over her shoulders, and opened the door to Mrs. Massie.

"I wanted to speak to you, Sarah dear," said the latter, "and not before Lydia, who is very foolish, though good-hearted. So I remained up, that we might be alone for a few minutes. I suppose your mind is quite made up about your future course—about Eustace?"

"It is quite made up, aunt, quite; nothing on earth could induce me—"

"My dear, do not be afraid that I would try to alter your resolution. Heaven knows how dearly I love Eustace, and how I lament over anything that disturbs his happiness. But if I had known before that you did not love him, I would myself have bade you never to marry him. I have seen what comes of marriages where the wife has not given up her whole heart to her husband. Yes, I have; and though you are not like weak and vain and thoughtless women, yet you had better be dead than married, if you do not love your husband with all the love you have."

"You relieve me much, aunt, when you speak to me in this way. My own conscience and heart told me I was doing right; but something seemed to reproach me too, and to whisper that I was acting ungratefully to you all. Now you give me new courage to do what is right. It is very, very kind and generous of you."

And Sarah took her aunt's hand and pressed it—a slight demonstration of affection, but one which, poor as it was, Sarah had not made towards her for more than a year.

"I don't mean to talk yet of your future plans, my dear; we will leave that until I come back from London; but I feel there is something else I ought to ask you. Lydia is often very foolish, but she said something to-day which startled me. Sarah, may I have your full confidence? Will you speak to me as if I were your mother?'

Involuntarily Sarah drew away her hand. Mrs. Massie's face flushed.

14*

"I have not offended you, my dear!"

"O no, aunt; how could I feel offended by your kindness?" Sarah had already repented of the sudden impulse which made her withdraw her hand, and she again pressed her aunt's thin and delicate fingers. Mrs. Massie had no suspicion of the nature of the thought which had flashed through Sarah's breast. She assumed that the girl only shrank with a girl's natural modesty from revealing a heart-secret. But that was not the cause.

"I do not want to press you to tell me anything, Sarah, which you think you ought to keep to yourself. But you heard what Lydia said to-day; at least, you knew what she meant. She talked of having known this some time why you would not marry Eustace. Is it true, dear? You may tell me."

"Yes, aunt, I knew what Lydia meant. And Eustace himself—he too spoke of it to-day; and he spoke harshly, and I am afraid that I answered him rather bitterly, and so we parted in anger. Yes, it is true."

Sarah stood up and leaned against the window, turning her face away for a moment. Then she looked round again and said in a firm voice :

"I do not want to hide it from you It is true, quite true. I never knew whether I loved Eustace or not until the time she spoke of to-day—until Paul Massie came here. Then, after awhile, I found that I did not feel towards Eustace as I ought to do if I could be his wife."

"But why, then, not speak before?"

"Aunt, I do not know, except that I was not sure. It may look strange and bad; but indeed I was not sure. No, not until the other night, and then I saw him in the theatre; and I knew it all, and I made up my mind."

There was something of positive pride in tone of her voice.

Mrs. Massie smiled sadly. She admired and pitied and envied the girl. Envied her above all. To love, and not to be ashamed ! To see the right path, and have the nerve to follow it, even though it led through pain ! Ah, these were triumphs this poor woman had never had, and she looked back to a crisis in her own life, and thought with grief and shame of the contrast. She sighed deeply.

"Ah," she said, in a low voice full of tenderness, "you have disappointed us sadly, and you do not even give us the relief of being able to blame you ! No, Sarah, you have done right, and I can only love you the more, and be the more sorry when you are gone, and I am left alone. I will not try to keep you, my dear. What sort of counsellor for such as you would be a creature like me? But I wish I had known of this before. I might have done something. One word more, my dear, and then I will keep you from your rest no longer. Does *he* know of this? "

" He—Eustace ? "

" No ; Paul."

Sarah bent her head, and said, in a faint low voice,

" O no, nothing."

" Does he—do you think—pray don't be angry if I ask it—does Paul Massie love you ? "

Sarah burst into tears.

" O, I don't know, I don't know ; and I don't want to know. It is enough for me that I love him, and always shall until I die—yes, and after death too, if our souls can love. But I never want to see him again ; I never want him to see me. He will be happy, and I will not come in his way. I will live alone and far off, and I will think of him."

The rod had touched the rock indeed, and the living waters were flowing. This had always seemed the calmest, coldest, wisest of girls, this passionate creature; who now buried herself sobbing among the cushions of the sofa she had been sitting on, and thus, in hysterical accents relieved her heart of its burden by pouring out the assurances of its love.

Mrs. Massie's own tears flowed, partly from mere sympathy, but partly because she fully believed that Paul's destiny was otherwise cast, and that Sarah's love was doomed to be wasted.

"Unhappiness pursues us all," she said. "You have at least some consolations which others cannot hope for; you can look into your own heart and not feel remorse or shame. Good-night, dear; you are better now alone. And I can only love you and envy you."

Mrs. Massie stooped over the poor girl, and kissed her shoulder, which was bare. She kissed her in a tearful and humble sort of way, as if conscious of inferiority and unworthiness, and acknowledging the consciousness by the very action. The Bayadere in the great lyric might thus have approached the pile whereon lay the assumed form of her immortal lover. A Magdalen might thus lay some poor flower-wreath in a shrine dedicated to the Virgin.

Descending the stairs to reach her own room, Mrs. Massie passed the door of Eustace's chamber, and heard him pacing up and down. She paused for a moment and listened. He must have known she was there, for he opened the door at once and came out. He was looking strange and worn; and Mrs. Massie noticed that his dress was disordered and soiled, as if, in his grief and anger, he had flung himself somewhere on the ground. That must indeed have been emotion which drove the lover of order and propriety to any such demonstration.

"Mother, you have heard it all?" he said.

"Yes, Eustace, I have heard it; I know all."

"But you will speak to her? you will reason with her? you will entreat her to change her mind?"

"No, Eustace, my dear son, I cannot; I cannot indeed. She sees what is right; she follows where her conscience guides her, and it is not for us to try to lead her away. No; I have seen much wrong in life, and done wrong too, for want of that sense of right which she has; and even for you I would not say one word to weaken it. No; God forbid. I am not so wholly weak and bad."

He took no heed of her last words, but drew back into his room and shut the door.

CHAPTER XXVII.

SALOME KNOWS ALL.

SALOME sat in her room, at her desk, alone. She had a packet of correspondence before her, and she was trying to interest herself in the contents of the letters. Some of them were from Italy, and (as we who have the privilege of reading over her shoulder may know) were filled with the hopes and plans and wild chimeras of the party of action.

Something was about to be done immediately in Venice: Garibaldi had all but promised his assent; this or that member of the Italian cabinet had been understood mysteriously to intimate that if the thing were not done quite too openly and roughly, the government would contrive not to see more than might be convenient. On such hints and hopes lives always that undespairing, unresting, unrewarded party of action; on such air it feeds, promise-crammed. Salome glanced at some of the letters, and tried to fix her attention on them. But her thoughts soon wandered away, and the paper presently was allowed to fall from her hand and lie unnoticed on the table.

"I used to take an interest in this sort of thing once," she said half aloud. "It is not so long ago. And now—"

She leaned her forehead on her hands, pushing back the hair which shaded her temples.

"I can't answer these letters to-day," she murmured. "I am in no humor for writing, or for politics, or for anything. I don't wonder that so many women poison or drown themselves, or try the effects of charcoal. I am sick of life."

She pushed away the letters with her hand, as one puts away some object suggestive of special weariness and pain, and she remained with her forehead held between her hands, still thinking or dreaming.

A light knock at the door did not appear to rouse her from her dream.　The knock was repeated.　Salome heard it, but did not look round.

"Come in, Clotilde," she said.

"It is not Clotilde," a voice replied; "it is George."

"Then come in, George," said Salome, still in a half-inattentive tone.

George came in, crossed the room, gently encircled with arms Salome's neck, and kissed her twice on the cheek.　There was nothing very shocking in the transaction.　George wore petticoats, and was only a pretty, black-eyed, crisp-haired, slender girl.

"George has not seen you this long time," said the latter, "and he grows jealous.　You might have come to him, or sent for him.　And I have been so vexed and grieved and worried in ever so many ways, that I came to get courage and counsel from you."

Salome looked up and smiled.　"Well, my dear, I am truly glad to see you.　I ought to have looked after you; but I was much occupied."

"Much occupied!　Nay, I think you were not quite well.　You look very pale and thin—and sad too.　Something is wrong with you.　How I wish I had come before!　Pray, pray tell me what made you ill and sad."

The girl sat on the carpet at Salome's feet, and laid her hand upon her knee, looking up into her face with a wistful, childish expression of anxious affection.

"No, my dear, I was not ill—not in the least, and not sad; that is, not particularly, not for any special cause.　But you said you were vexed and grieved yourself.　Come, tell me of your troubles."

"O, mine are nothing—mere nonsense.　I have been just a little cut-up in one or two of the papers—ill-naturedly, I think—called masculine and hoydenish, and I believe indelicate, and I don't know what else, because I can't play women's parts.　And I cried a little over all this the other day.　For the people read this in the papers, and they form a dreadful opinion of me. And I have no friend but you; and O, how I wish I were really a man!"

Miss Georgina Renville (her real name was Renn) was the daughter of a very, very small *littérateur*, who was once rather in the amateur revolutionary line, and whom Salome had befriended. Dying, he left Georgina alone; and Georgina would be nothing but an actress. Salome, through her dramatic-author friends, had no trouble in getting the girl an engagement. Georgina soon displayed a wonderful talent for the playing of all vivacious vaudeville, or farce, or burletta parts which required the wearing of doublet and hose. She was the Prince of the Fairy Islands, the Midshipman, the Little Pickle, the Pet of the Petticoats, the Fortunio—anything which was boyish and smart and saucy. She looked the parts she assumed to piquant theatric perfection; that is, she never was so exuberantly feminine as to render her costume ridiculous; and yet in her best disguise, and with her most swaggering gait, she always retained the grace and charm of womanhood. Honestly, her great grief in life was, that she could not help being a woman; her chief delight, to be even dressed like a man. Those who only saw her on the stage never by any chance saw her in feminine garb. She was a true, affectionate, simple-minded girl, thoroughly modest in spite of her familiarity with pantaloons, and in spite of the occasionally sharp remarks of some critic in a fit of virtuous indignation. Salome was always fond of her, and glad to see her, although George knew no more of foreign politics or revolutionary secrets than a robin-redbreast.

So much for George's past. We shall perhaps take up her story one day on its own account, and for its own sake. Now she comes in by chance, merely an incidental and unimportant figure.

"Now these are all my troubles. Not much, you will say; but I wish I could tell you how these papers vex me, when they don't praise me. I was in bed the other day when a paper came, addressed to me, and with such ill-natured remarks about me, that I assure you I cried over it, and could hardly bring myself to get up even to rehearsal. I shall never get over such folly. I don't think any of us ever does. Haven't I seen our greatest stars over and over again bursting with rage because somebody in a paper found fault with them? You don't know what it is to do your very best, and study hard, and look your best, and dress your best, and then to be cut up after all; and your bread depending on it, to say nothing of your ambition. Yes, I do so wish I were a man."

"What could you do if you were a man?" asked Salome, smiling.

"Could I not challenge my critics? This sort of thing." She started up and threw herself into fencing attitude, her left arm flung back, her right as if making a tremendous lunge with the rapier. "Or I suppose that's all out of fashion now—In England at least. This, then: twelve paces; one, two, three—fire!" She had changed her attitude and stood in profile, an imaginary hair-trigger in her outstretched hand.

"But I fear that is out of fashion in England too," said Salome. "And you know, George, you really could not shoot all your hostile critics. You would not desolate the London press?"

George laughed merrily.

"Come now," she said, "I am glad to hear you say something like that; for it shows that you are not wholly out of spirits. But indeed some of the critics are very kind to me. Mr. Levison spoke so warmly of me last week. I know very well who sent him to see me—it was *you*, who are always doing me some good turn. I know he never would have thought of coming to look at me, and to write about me, but for you—such a great literary swell as he is. I can tell you some of our people were very angry and jealous. I saw him in the stalls; and do you know who was with him?"

"No, indeed; who was it?"

. "You surely ought to know. It was your friend Mr. Massie. I saw him the moment I came on, and he smiled, and I could not help recognizing him, and it nearly put me out. You must tell him not to expect recognitions or to claim acquaintanceship under such circumstances. But I like him very much. I think I should like to be such a man. "

" Why such a man ? "

" Well, it is not that he is so very handsome, but he is manly and strong, and has such a fine frank way, and a sweet smile. What bright eyes he has ! Don't you like his eyes ? Ah, yes, you do. But your own eyes look quite weary and worn to-day, as if you had not slept. More than that—they are red too, as if you had been crying. Something, I know, has distressed you. Do tell me—do, dear, dear Madame de Luca, I know you are unhappy ; and I am miserable when I see it."

"Which of us is happy, George? Have you not just been telling me of your own grievances? "

" Yes ; but mine are mere nonsense; they are not grievances that any sensible person would care about. They are only petty spites and vexations; a kind of game-giving that would trouble a woman—there's Shakespeare. These are not the kind of things that would affect you. You are not likely to be cast down because some man does not think as highly of you as you could wish."

Salome smiled sadly and shook her head. George had keen eyes and senses of her own, and did not fail to note the expression which passed like a shadow over the face she was studying.

"Yes," she said, half-soliloquizing, "you are not happy."

" Well, George, I am not very happy—not just now."

" Is it past help, past hope ? "

" Past help, certainly ; past hope, I fear."

" May it be told ; may it be talked of ? My sorrows are always lightened by talking of them."

"This may not be talked of or told; and no confidence could lighten it. It will pass away—perhaps—in time."

"And I cannot help you—in any way? Not in any way?"

"Not in any way."

"Not even if I could partly guess what it was?" This was said in a tone of gentle childlike affection, very tender and full of feeling. Prince Paragon was a true woman.

Salome's cheek flushed, and her eyes did not venture to meet those which were turned upon her. She made no reply for a moment; only shook her head.

"I am a little tired and out of spirits to-day, George," she said at last, "and I exaggerate my trials and see everything in a gloomy light. Things are not going very well, you know, in Italy—and—and—in America."

George was not in the least deceived by the attempt at explanation founded on political difficulties. But she did not pursue the subject.

"Will you sing me something, George,—something bright and vivacious—something like yourself?"

"Delighted, if I can do anything to please you. What shall it be?"

She rattled some lively notes on the piano, and, without waiting for any answer, dashed into some vivacious ballad. But she glanced every now and then over her shoulder anxiously at her friend. Salome still sat at her desk with her forehead pressed between her hands. She was not listening to a note of the music. George did not fail to notice that at every sound of the street-door, at every footstep, every wheel, every dash of a horse's hoofs on the pavement, Salome started, and then sank down again disappointed.

"She expects him," thought the girl; "and he is not coming."

Having finished one song—of which she sang, quite unnoticed, each verse twice over—George straightway called on herself for another, and went on with it unhesitatingly. It was all the same to Salome.

A knock and ring at the door. Salome started up. But the first sound of a foot-step in the hall made her sink down again.

"Don't go, my dear," she said to George, who was rising from the piano. "It is not anyone to see me; it is only the doctor to see Alice, one of my maids, who was hurt the night before last. That is a charming song of yours; pray go on with it."

George began a third ballad. Presently another knock, another eager glance, another expression of disappointment.

"General Lefevre to see Madame," said Clotilde, entering.

"Yes; I will see him," said Salome eagerly. "Show him into the drawing-room.—Don't go, dear: I shall be back presently." This to George.

"O, yes, I must go," said George. "You will have to see many people soon, and you will want me away. But I will soon come to see you again—may I not?"

She kissed Salome affectionately. "Ah," she said to herself, as she received a warm farewell from her friend, "I wish I were a man—at least one particular man—for your sake."

As George left the house, she observed an odd rowdy-looking man at the other side of the street, who, the moment she passed out, began to move as if towards or after her. Was he a beggar? Did he mistake her for somebody to whom he wanted to speak? No matter. The moment he saw her face he dropped behind, and she thought no more of him just then.

She passed through the Park and went along by the railings to see the crowd of ladies on horseback. George, with all her wish to be a man, or perhaps because of it, dearly loved to see a fine woman on horseback. As she walked slowly on, she was aware, as the old ballad-phrase is, of the propinquity of Paul Massie. He was lounging along, listless and weary-looking; his face rather haggard, his dress careless.

George promptly accosted him, and they exchanged some cordial words.

"Why do you linger here, Mr. Massie?" said the girl, after a moment or two; "why don't you cross the Park and go that way?" She nodded towards the north. "Don't you know you are waited for and wished for?"

She spoke not quizzingly or even playfully, but in pure frank and simple earnest.

Paul began to stammer out some reply.

"Now don't pretend you don't know what I mean," she said; "you do know well enough. Why don't you go, or remain away altogether and never go there any more? Don't be offended with me; I think about her; I love her; I would die for her; and what ought not you to do for her?"

"Miss Renville, I only wish I could deserve—I only wish I were worth thinking of."

"Bah! stuff! Who ever said you were worth thinking of—by her? I don't believe any man is worth many thoughts from her. But if she does not think so? I beg your pardon, Mr. Massie; do you know that man, that fellow there, who has just passed us? There—just near that tree."

Paul looked—with the eyes of his body, not his mind. He just saw some hulking, shabby-looking fellow lounging away. The man's back was turned. No, Paul did not know anything of him—at least did not observe him—had not seen his face. Who was he?

"Really I don't know. It's no matter. I thought I saw him a few minutes ago at the door yonder, just as I came out, and he seemed to be watching somebody."

Assuredly if Paul had had his wits about him, even this slight observation would have led him to make some effort to see the man. But he was thinking of something quite different, and George's words made no impression on him.

"Good-by, Mr. Massie. Pray think of what I have said, and forgive me for saying it."

"Forgive you for having been kind and generous ; forgive you for—"

"Well, forgive me in any case ; and good-by."

When George left Salome's house, Salome hastened to receive General Lefevre. She was eager to see him, and yet hardly expected any "news" so soon. "Six months" he had asked for. Even Salome's impatience could not overlook the fact that scarcely so many weeks had passed.

The General rose at her entrance, and made the most profound of bows.

"Dear General, I am glad to see you ; but I don't of course expect—" and she hesitated, and looked expectant.

"Madame, I have had the fortune to fulfil my commission before my time. I know all we can ever know."

"O, how I thank you ! how good you were !"

"Nay, I would of course do my possible to expedite the discharge of the commission ; but chance, not merit, has done it so soon. A Mexican prisoner from Paris, an old friend and follower, fell in my way when least expected ; and from him I know—"

"What ?"

"The fate of Captain Massie."

"Yes, yes ; what of him ?"

"Madame, my old friend is dead."

"Is that certain ?"

"Madame may rely that it is perfectly certain."

Salome was somewhat relieved. She had already heard enough of the antecedents of this Captain Paul Massie to know that no human creature, this side of the Atlantic at least, cared to have him alive.

"Did you learn anything of the facts and circumstances of his death ?"

"Yes ; some little. He had for some time before been in companionship with a person of whom I spoke to you, who came to me on his behalf in New Orleans. Did I say it was in New Orleans he died? Yes, it was. This person of whom I spoke had once been the confidential serving-woman of his wife. Pardon if I tell you these things—such things will happen; he was very wild and reckless at one time."

"Yes; go on, please."

"I believe she was in part the cause of their separation. They had met by chance again after many years, and she was kind to him in his broken fortunes."

"Do you mean his wife?"

"No, no; this woman. His wife he never saw after their separation. He did not know, until after he met with the other woman for the second time in New Orleans, that soon after his leaving his wife she bore a son. He did not ever try to see the son, perhaps feeling .that he had little claim on a son's love after such long desertion of his family, perhaps for other reasons—who knows? But it is certain that before he died he wrote a letter which he wished to be given to the son. The woman was to come to Europe, and she was to bear it. Also she was to see his brother's wife, and to give her a diamond ring which he had long kept. I have often seen such a ring on his finger."

"Pray, General, excuse me for putting such a question, but how do you know all this?"

The General smiled. "My Mexican prisoner has many friends in New Orleans who knew Massie," he said, "and he knows who sent the doctor to attend him in his last illness, and who found the money to send this woman to Europe—without doubt to get rid of her. But I know little more save that he died, and she sailed for Europe. There I have lost her. No doubt she is here, and can be found, if any occasion or need should be for finding her. I question much myself whether she can have anything to communicate to any relative of Captain Massie's, which it would be very agreeable to hear. Perhaps she has already fulfilled her mission. I have my reasons to dread that she came rather to extort money than to fulfil the request of a dying man."

"And so the story ends," said Salome, in a musing way.

"And so the story ends, so far as I can tell it. I would I could tell you more; but this much dries up my sources of information."

"General, I am deeply indebted to you. You have told me all I wish to know. Captain Paul Massie is dead, and there does not seem any end to be gained by reviving his memory in the minds of those who knew him."

. The General shook his head gravely.

"One word, General. Did you happen to hear any thing of *her*—of Captain Massie's wife?"

"Something—very little; vague, and perhaps untrue. It is so long that she is dead."

"But you did hear something?"

"Yes, something. That her husband believed he had found some proofs against her; proofs of want of *sagesse* in fact, and that there was a violent scene, and perhaps even —I am not sure—a duel."

"Her husband! Then was that the cause of their separation?"

"No; whatever of truth was in this, it was after her husband had already deserted her. But remember, all this is rumor and recollection of the vaguest, and whatever happened was done in Mexico, then profoundly disturbed. What I tell you of my old friend's death is exact, and, so to speak, of yesterday; but the other events are—ah, perhaps, near thirty years ago. I think it is certain or probable that there was a quarrel; that is all one can rely on."

Salome thanked the General again for his information. He put no question himself. He must have known quite well that she had more than the interest of curiosity in seeking back into the past of the Massie family; and he could have had no doubt that the Paul Massie now in London was the son to whom a letter had been despatched by the Paul Massie dying in New Orleans. It will be remembered that he had actually seen and read part of a document presumed to be that very letter. But he asked no questions, dropped no hints, formed no conjectures. A true gentleman of the gallant old school, it would never have occurred to him to seek to know anything which was, or seemed to be, anybody's secret. He had taken some pains to procure certain information to oblige a lady,—*voilà tout;* there his share in the business ended. Why the lady sought the information, or what inferences she could deduce from it, he never thought to inquire.

"I need not, General, ask you again to consider our little conversation as entirely private."

"Madame, indeed you need not, on the honor of a very poor gentleman."

"And if I ever can acknowledge your kindness—"

"It is already acknowledged, and far too highly valued."

After he had gone Salome sat down alone, and thought. "This, then, is all." So ran the stream of her reflections. "This is all; and it is nothing. All clew to anything like a solution of the secret is lost. The dead body found—and robbed—upon the Seaborough beach was that of the only person, save one, who could have told us anything. And I fear—I fear enough has been told to warn me off any further pursuit. I fear nothing remains to be found which would bring aught but reproach to the finder. I thought, like a fool, to have bought even his gratitude with a precious discovery. I seem more likely to have exposed him to shame. My folly,—my old, romantic, idiotic folly! And he cares nothing for me; nothing, nothing! He loves that cold inanimate creature, who will coolly marry another man because she is bidden to, and will walk stupidly through her dull life and never think of him or of anything but what she will call her duty. And I, who at my age know now, for the first time and the last, what love really is—I, who would die for him—must plot and scheme to buy his love; and plot and scheme in vain!"

She did not talk all this aloud, or half aloud. Only the heroines of romance and the drama, and occasionally some deaf and decaying old charwomen, thus commune with themselves in audible words. But her heart spoke, and so did her eyes, from which at last there fell some drops of passion, disappointment, and grief.

"No woman on earth," she thought in her bitterness, "is so unhappy as I."

"A lady wishes particularly to speak to Madame," said Clotilde, entering.

"A lady! what lady? Let her give me her name," Salome replied sharply. In all her grief she was vexed to have been found with tears in her eyes.

"She does not wish to give her name, but she begs you will see her. She says she cannot leave until she has seen you."

"Show her in, then," said Salome, in a sort of defiant tone, and quite determined to greet the intruder in a manner which would convince her that she had intruded.

She sat to her desk and affected—indeed, it was pure affectation—to be engaged in writing. The lady was shown in, and the door closed behind her. Salome did not yet look up. When at last she raised her eyes, they met, not without a start, the eyes of Mrs. Massie.

<hr>

CHAPTER XXVIII.

BE SURE THY SIN WILL FIND THEE OUT.

"HAST thou found me out, O mine enemy?"

Salome did not thus accost the visitor who had so unexpectedly intruded upon her, nor did she even think of the words ; but assuredly her face seemed to put some such question, and her heart might have suggested it. She looked bewildered into Mrs. Massie's pale face, where haggard anxiety met her look of surprise, but she seemed unable to speak a word.

"Salome Adams!"

Mrs. Massie spoke.   It was the first time for years that Salome had been addressed by those lips or by that name.

"You are surprised to see me here, and I am surprised to find myself here; but I felt that I must come and see you, and speak to you."

Salome had risen before this; she now motioned towards a chair.   Her visitor took no heed of the gesture.

"I have come to ask you why you persecute me and my family?"

She put the question earnestly and gravely; as a question strictly, and not as a taunt or even an appeal.

"How have I persecuted you?   Why do you accuse me?"

"I have not accused you; I only asked you a question. You are our enemy, and are striving to injure us.   Why? We once were friends."

"*Once*," said Salome with emphasis.

"I was harsh and unjust to you; I know it.   I knew it then; but I could not help it.   Many, many things had embittered me, and rendered me suspicious.   But what if we quarrelled then?—most women do quarrel—why should it have made us enemies for life?   We have both grown older; we have both suffered; we are both widows; more than that—we are bound together, Salome Adams, by a tie you do not dream of, and I have come to tell you of it."

Then she sat down and loosed her bonnet-strings, as if to free her breathing, and threw back her shawl.   Her face was pale as are the dead.

"But why," said Salome, now recovering her composure, and resolving to speak like a woman of the world,— "why do you accuse me of persecuting you?   How could I?   What power have I?"

"You are making yourself the source and impulse of secret inquiries which are designed to bring exposure and trouble upon us.   I know that they come from you; I know that you think you have discovered some secret which gives you power over us ; and I know that you are endeavoring to use it to our injury."

"Then you are wrong," replied Salome coldly. "I have no wish to injure you, or any of you ; but I take a deep interest in one of your family ; I have a strong friendship for him ; and I have reason to believe that while you all cast him out from among you, he has legal rights of which he himself knows nothing, and which give him a heavy claim. I confess—what need of hiding it ?—that I have endeavored to find out and secure those rights ; and I think I have been successful."

"What are the rights ?"

Salome smiled significantly.

"Nay, I don't care to know what is the delusion under which you are acting : enough that it is the most vain of delusions. Salome Adams, every step you take, every question you ask in this most miserable business, is but heaping shame on Paul Massie's head. God help him ! he has no rights. Such unfair dealings as has been done is for his sake, on his behalf; to preserve for him a name to which he has little claim, and to keep him from being an utter outcast. I tell you once again, Paul Massie has no rights."

"Is he not your nephew ? is he not the only son of your husband's brother ?"

"He is not my nephew; he is not the son of my husband's brother."

Salome's face now assumed a startled expression. Mrs. Massie looked fixedly downward. There was a moment's profound silence.

"Then," Salome asked, " of what family is he a member ?"

Mrs. Massie did not seem to hear the question, but she laid her hand softly on Salome's—the first friendly movement made on either side—and asked in a low clear tone,

"Do you love him—Paul Massie ?"

And Salome looked up with calm eyes, although with cheeks no longer bloodless, and replied firmly,

"I do."

"If I had not known it, I could never have come here.
This is the tie between us. Paul Massie is dearer to you
than all the world besides; is he not?"

"He is indeed."

"So he is to me."

Seldom have words so few, spoken in a tone so calm,
produced a more thrilling impression on a listener's ear.
Salome started from her seat.

"Stay, Salome Adams, and listen. Think how I trust
you, you who have been my enemy. To you I tell what I
never before told to mortal but one who is in the grave.
Paul Massie is my son."

Evening was approaching, and Salome sat in gloom—
gloom of heart as well as of atmosphere. The parting
words of he half-distracted woman who had just left her
rang in her ears : "Whatever may happen, let us never
meet again. Forgive me, as you are a Christian woman,
for the weakness which was worse than crime, and has
brought so much misery ; and I forgive you for having
forced this confession on me. It is not right that we should
ever look upon each other again. Do not, O, do not tell
him all!"

Before she went, Salome, saying no word, put into her
hand the ring—the ring whose tiny spark had lighted the
way to the whole disclosure. Mrs. Massie took it with a
new thrill of pain. "It was not mine," she murmured; "it
was my sister's. I wore it sometimes out of folly and
vanity; and I wore it once too often. The night I lost it, it
cost a man his life, and the best of women her reputation and
her happiness. All my wickedness and weakness,—all!"

Weakness which was worse than wickedness ; weakness
which had poisoned many lives for the sake of preserving
one from shame, and had not succeeded even in that ; weakness which had accepted so many sacrifices from more
generous natures. and was ready to the last to suggest and

exact new surrenders and abnegations; weakness full of cruelty; weakness like that which made the woman in the story fling her infant to the wolves to save her own miserable life. The last words of Mrs. Massie to Salome prayed for more secrecy and one final sacrifice of just human claim for the sake of her own ruined life.

Now Salome saw it all. She was enabled, by the fitful light of the half-revelations given to her in gleams and flashes, to read the whole mournful story of that feeble and cowardly life. She read therein of a woman not wholly selfish, not in anywise naturally bad, but too weak to be true, and therefore destructive by her weakness. Too weak to refuse an unsuitable, uncongenial marriage when passionately pressed upon her; too weak to be faithful even to that when the presence of a stronger elective affinity drew her away; too weak even to stand by her sin and atone for it; too weak to refuse the generous, improvident sacrifice of a sister's fame. The retrospect was sickening. Salome tried to turn away from it, and contemplate her own painful and humiliating share in the miserable business.

She had been deluded, self-deluded in great measure; and had well-nigh committed herself and him whom she valued far more than herself to the uttermost folly, to the most shameful exposure. Deep self-reproach stung her heart. She had too generous a nature not to acknowledge with pain and shame the meanness of the motives which first prompted her to spy into the secrets of the Massie family. What had been the spring of her first movements but petty feminine spite and morbid curiosity? She had gone about with menials and vagabonds to discover a secret which now came crushingly on her own head and her own hopes. Refined and purified by her disinterested love, she looked back with bitter regret and self-condemnation on all that she had done. And the end had not yet come.

She arose after awhile from the table at which she had been sitting, and going to her desk took out a faded, wrinkled, stained old rag of paper. She opened it, laid it

on the table, and unconsciously struck her clenched hand
heavily on it, as if she found in it the cause of her folly and
and fault.   It was the letter to which so many an allusion
has been made; the letter found by Halliday on the Seaborough beach; the letter believed to have been written by
the lost and dying outcast, Paul Massie, in New Orleans.

It was addressed, as we know, to Paul Massie—our Paul
Massie.   It ran thus:

"I am dying: and I am conscious of having led an idle
and worthless life.   I neglected and deserted my wife; and
I believe now that I wronged her by suspicions which were
unjust.   But Heaven will bear me witness that I did not
know till lately I had a son.   If I have a son and you are
he, forgive me, and when you can, forget me.   If justice
has been done, you must already have the fortune which,
but for my own folly, I should have had.   The bearer of
this will tell you all, if you want explanation.   If any wrong
has been done you—and there has been long deceit already
—there is a person in England who can put it right: show
her the token I send with this by a sure hand.   She will
know how I got it, and what a price was paid for it.   It has
been a curse so far to every one who wore it; let it be so,
once more to her if it does not remind her that she owes an
atonement to me—and to you.   I cannot feel to you as a
father ought to a son.   I suppose my own wrong-doing and
my desertion of my home are thus punished, and I am
denied, even in death, the sweetness of a natural affection.
You are to me only a name; but I feel that if you have not
been fairly dealt with, and I can help you to your right, I
make some atonement for the past.   I do not sign my name.
If this reaches you, you will know it; if not, then it is
better unknown.   Good-by—and forgive me."

The waves brought to Seaborough strand only a wreck
and a dead woman's body.   The letter and the ring were
found as we know.   One of the strange chances of human
fate brought the bearer and the message to the very feet of

him whom they sought, and brought them in vain. The letter reached Salome.

The inquiry which it suggested revealed the fact that the grandfather of the present Eustace Massie had been offended with both his sons,—the one for his wildness, the other for his sudden and secret marriage; that he had successively banished, as it were, each to Mexico, where the elder fell in love with, married, and soon deserted his brother's sister-in-law; that the younger, Eustace, in some measure redeemed his credit by endeavoring steadily to retrieve the Mexican property. Finally, the father dying left his fortune to his younger son, but only in trust. It was to be divided equally between the "legitimate" elder son of Eustace and the elder son of Paul, after these should have come of age. There was stress laid in each case on the word "legitimate." If only one of the brothers had a son, then to him alone. If neither, to daughters or more distant relatives. Paul the elder was wholly cut off from share of any kind.

And on this false scent had poor Salome gone astray. The word "legitimate," and the uncertainty about the date of Mrs. Massie's marriage, sent her wildly wrong. She now at last reflected that the very audacity which would have been requisite thus coolly to deprive a co-heir of his just rights, and assume that he could never come to know of them, might of itself have warned her of the futility of her speculations. Her quick intriguing genius had only proved an *ignis fatuus*, and led her on a wild chase of a phantom ending in a dreary marsh.

She was not long left to the luxury of her sad reflections. The door soon began to resound with the knocks of visitors. For some time she struggled against the infliction, and pertinaciously declined to see the comers; but the tantalizing interruption to her thoughts occasioned by this very struggle seemed worse than absolute surrender to the oppression. She had, for long years and of her own choice, given up all habit of home life. She could command little more of privacy than a prime minister or the representative of a metropolitan constituency. A weary life that soon becomes where your house-door has to stand as constantly open as that of the good Axylus in Homer—a martyr surely to his hospitality, did we know but all. To a woman—at least to a woman with something better than a mere integument for a heart and a vapor-filled shell or pumpkin for a head—such a life becomes at last the heaviest and dreariest of inflictions. Salome's heart sank within her, and she sickened at the prospect of an evening spent among her ordinary guests. She thought of loneliness as a balm—refreshing as sleep to the weary, as the spring to the dusty wayfarer. Of aught better than loneliness she hardly ventured to think. But if that could be which she now scarcely allowed herself to hope for, how gladly she would give up London and the vanity and nothingness of idle playings at political intrigue; how gladly would she steep her life in the quiet happiness of some secluded home! Thirty years of poverty and hardship and toil and vexation; five or six years of weary, mechanical chase after distraction—was it not time that rest and happiness should come at last? And, indeed, the rest was near.

While Salome at last girt up her energies, and made haggard preparations to meet her guests, Mrs. Massie was already returning to Seaborough, with throbbing head and beating heart and brain all confused. And Sarah Massie was preparing to leave Seaborough to see it no more. And Paul Massie was turning away from the familiar door near Hyde-park, resolved not to enter and greet the mistress of the house, whom we have just seen so sad and lonely. And in an upper room of that house, poor Alice Crossley tossed about sick and anxious, and distracted by shapeless fears. And about the house, in the deepening shadow of the evening,—now in the little lane, or passage, or court at the back, where the wall was so low that a tall man might almost look into the garden; now in the street, on which the front windows looked; now in the portico of an opposite house, the closed shutters of which proclaimed the family out of town; and now in the public-house at the corner—there lurked through all the evening and night the awkward, slouching form of James Halliday. Lapse of days and nights, and disappointment and drink and the thirsty passion for revenge, had wholly developed the wolf-nature in this outcast wretch; and his very shadow had in it something crouching, ominous, and cruel, as it fell upon the pavement.

CHAPTER XXIX.

WESTMINSTER PALACE.

PAUL MASSIE did not act upon the advice of little George the actress. Man's nature is waywardness; and there are few men so docile and good, as at once to accept the boon of affection which all their neighbors seem determined to think they ought to welcome with a grateful heart. In the ordinary course of things, he would probably have gone straightway to Madame de Luca's, but now he felt as if he ought to turn his steps in another direction. The words of Mr. Wynter had produced an unpleasant effect upon him—more, indeed, than he would have acknowledged even to himself. He began to feel ashamed of having his destiny thus cut out for him, without any intervention of his own, or even consultation of his wishes. People who lack natural force of resolution are in the habit of doing something every now and then to convince themselves that they are really independent, and can act with decision; and it generally happens that, when thus prompted, they only do something which shows more than ever their dependence upon the impulse of others. Paul Massie thought he was doing a right thing and a manly thing, in endeavoring to resist, so far, the growing influence of Salome as to remain

15*

away from her side for a day at least; but perhaps beneath all other and better motives was a desire to show to those around him, that he was not literally bound to her and under her spells. After casting some doubting glances therefore in the direction of the house where he was always so welcome, he turned his steps resolutely the other way; and he wished all the while that he could meet her as he went.

Besides, had he not a public duty to perform? Was he not to go down that evening to Westminster to take his seat? Had he not promised Wynter to do so? Of course he had; and Wynter, backed by another friend, was to introduce him to the House. He was to be escorted up the floor of the House between the twain, like a captive between two policemen; and he was to be thus brought to the clerk's table, where he was to take the oaths; and then he was to be solemnly shaken hands with by Mr. Speaker, and so proclaimed to all the world a member of the British House of Commons. Paul was not anxious for the glorious hour. He felt as if he were only playing a part, or trying to play one, for which he was not fitted; nay, he could hardly help at times regarding himself in the light of an impostor. For months back, indeed, he had had this hideous feeling strong upon him, and he sought excitement after excitement to shake it off.

Well, here at all events was the promise of a new excitement for a few hours. He walked rapidly through Hyde-park until he reached Piccadilly, then called a cab, and drove to Westminster, where he felt confident of meeting his friend Wynter, who haunted the House of Commons as faithfully and patiently as one of the government whips.

Now, if this had been a government night—a night, that is, devoted to ministerial business, and when, therefore, the Ministry take good care to keep a House—the course of this story might have been much altered. For Paul went to Westminster fully resolved to remain during the whole of whatever debate, or long succession of debates, might take place, and thus endeavor to discipline his mind into a more business-like and less morbid tone than it had lately owned. If he had stayed there, sitting out whatever wearisome length of talk, there would have been at least one occupant found in the ladies' gallery until a tolerably advanced hour of the morning ; and so, if we had any story whatever to tell, it would, in all probability, have quite a different ending from that which must presently be told.

But it was not decreed that Paul should take his seat that night, or that he should have the gratification of discharging a conscientious duty by listening to a long debate. For this was not a government night, but one of the nights, lately growing fewer and fewer, when ordinary members have the field to themselves, when small politicians put motions on the books, when you ballot for your turn, and, having won your chance, may talk away on your pet theme for hours and hours, if you can only get the House to remain and listen to you. This night there were several such motions on the paper. The son of a peer had a long speech to make about Denmark, Schleswig-Holstein, and the protocol of London ; a ship-owner had to move for papers regarding the treaty of commerce and navigation which had been under negotiation for years back between Great Britain and Guatemala ; there was a resolution to be proposed touching the propriety of reducing the present rate of duty on nutmegs; and there was a proposal for inquiry into the mode of appointing sheriffs for the county Tyrone. None of these subjects unfortunately could lead to anything whatever; and everybody, even the gentlemen about to propose the motions, knew the fact perfectly well. Neither the government nor the Opposition had the slightest interest in keeping a House. Nay, not any one of the gentlemen with the motions had any interest in such an object, except the youthful nobleman who had precedence. For everybody knew that, once he got fairly into his topic, he would keep stammering and muddling over it, making mistakes in dates and names, and going back to set himself right; stopping to hunt through his bundle of papers for some particular quotation or reference, and failing to find it; but in the vain search so mixing up and confusing all his documents, as to render any further search for anything among them utterly hopeless. Everyone knew that he would go on this way for hours, and might, indeed, so go on until the crack of doom, if not pulled up by some accident or influence over which he could have personally no control. Therefore, when this noble youth actually got possession of the House, and rose on his legs to speak, the result was foreshadowed in every face. Members came to the door and looked in, to find out what was going on, having up to the last a faint hope that Lord Rupert de Capulet might have caught a cold, or had to leave town, or lost his manuscripts, or in some other providential way been prevented from attempting his speech. But a glance showed them the drear waste of green leather benches untenanted; another glance showed them Lord Rupert on the Tory benches, pertinaciously and powerfully addressing the Under Secretary of State for Foreign Affairs and the Junior Lord of the Treasury, who represented for that occasion the whole strength of her Majesty's Ministry. So the peeping members fled in despair, and got their carriages or their cabs, and went to the Opera, or the club, or home; and only a few who had some special interest in any of the motions on the paper lingered about the library and the smoking-room and the terrace, impelled by the sternest sense of duty to wait to the last, on the almost hopeless chance of Lord Rupert getting fairly through somehow, and the other business then proceeding. So dismal was the whole affair, that the ladies' gallery, which seems to have a few silken tenants even while poor-rates and main-drainage are being discussed, had this evening but two inmates, and these were Salome de Luca and Mrs. Charlton.

Salome often went to the gallery of the House. She belonged to that class who regard an occasional seat in the ladies' gallery as a part of the season's round of entertainment quite as indispensable as a box at the Opera; and she was never at a loss for friendly offers to put down her name in the book, or to give up their chances in her favor, or to ballot for a seat on her behalf for some tremendously important debate ever so far off. Many days before this it had been arranged that she was to go to the House, if Paul should be returned, the night he went to take his seat, and that Mrs. Charlton, who was still in town, should bring her carriage for her. When the day came, it found Salome little inclined for political debate. Mrs. Charlton's carriage rattled up to the door not long after Mrs. Massie had left —not long after Salome's nerves had been shattered by the revelation which turned her schemes to nothingness. Yet she went. She could do nothing else just then. She could neither write, nor read, nor think. She was glad to find distraction of any kind; and then, if she remained at home, perhaps *he* would not come. Yesterday morning she had avoided him; last night he had not come. Perhaps to-night he might remain away too; and unless she bore with good Mrs. Charlton's company, and quiet, genial, harmless talk, and went to the ladies' gallery, she might perhaps not see him this night.

So she went. But before going she paid a visit of a few moments to Alice, who was somewhat restless, feverish, and frightened — why, Salome could not understand, for she did not seem to be at all seriously unwell, and the medical man spoke very favorably of her condition. Salome's kindly heart found some relief in cheering and comforting the poor girl.

"I don't know what can be the matter with me, madame," said Alice, "but I feel as if something dreadful was going to happen."

"Your nerves are all unstrung, poor child," replied Salome soothingly, as if she were really speaking to a child; "but you are going on admirably, the surgeon says, and you will be up and well in a few days. It was only a little wound—just a scratch. Ah, if you had been where I was a few years ago, you would have seen wounds of a different kind.”

“But it’s not about the wound I was thinking; indeed, ma’am, I don’t care about it. I suppose it’s nothing; but I am afraid of something—I don’t know what; I am afraid that something is going to happen.”

“Nothing can happen, Alice; you are perfectly safe here. What could happen? Foolish girl, if you had only taken my advice and kept within doors a few days longer, nothing would have happened.”

“Ah, it is true; and how good and kind you are to bear with me at all when I acted so badly! And I am here in your room, ma’am, all this while, and you are put out. O, I wish I could get up! I could get up, indeed, madame, and go up stairs.”

“No, no, Alice; the surgeon says you are not to be removed for a day or two; and I do not mind in the least; but do not give way to any foolish fears; you are perfectly safe here.”

“Yes, ma’am; but perhaps there may be danger for somebody else.”

“For whom, Alice? Not for me, I am sure; at least I don’t feel in the least afraid.”

“O no, ma’am, not for *you!* O no! even *he* would not think of harming you.”

“*He!* You mean that wretched man—that unfortunate Halliday?”

“Yes, ma’am.”

“Well, Alice, he is a bad and a wretched man. I hope, perhaps, that, wicked as he is, he did not mean to do more than hurt you. But depend upon it, he will keep far away from this. I feel that I have done wrong in not having taken steps long before this to have him discovered and arrested; but I do not think he will attempt to come in this direction again. Nor even if he did, do I see what harm he could do.”

“But he hates Mr. Massie, ma’am.”

The allusion somehow vexed or offended Salome for a moment.

"Mr. Massie, Alice, can quite take care of himself. I don't suppose he is much afraid of Halliday, or that Halliday would attempt to attack him. Don't keep nourishing these foolish fears. Now I must leave you. I hope every attention is paid to you?"

"O, yes, ma'am; yes, indeed."

"Well, I shall see you again to-night; and I shall probably not be long away. Sleep as much as you can, and don't keep thinking of Halliday, or anything foolish."

So Salome left her patient, a little put out, perhaps, by the girl's foolishness and the perpetual iteration of her recurrence to one subject. She got up as much cheerfulness as she could in order to meet Mrs. Charlton in a genial and appropriate spirit; and the two ladies drove to Palace-yard, where Mr. Wynter, who had secured seats for them, was waiting at the entrance of Westminster-hall to receive them.

"It's a dreadful business," said the senator; "Rupert de Capulet is up, and he's going over the whole story of the Schleswig-Holstein affair, from beginning to end. He's not much further down than the year 1600 now, and he's making a terrible mess of it. He knows no more about it than the man in the moon; and whoever coached him, coached him very badly, or perhaps could not succeed in cramming anything into his head, I shouldn't wonder. *I* tried to cram him once myself; but I couldn't do anything with him. The House will never stand it. There's sure to be a count presently. If Massie came soon, and got introduced, I'd get away from this; for there will be no business done to-night, even if Capulet should get through safely. It's a night given up to bores, I think. I wish Massie would come."

The carrying of the Seaborough election had been an immense triumph to Wynter. He crowed over it all about the House, and took the whole merit of the success to himself. Charlton's interest, Salome's money, the support of Government, and the influence of " No. Popery," he resolutely ignored, and represented the victory as entirely due to his own energy, resource, and presence of mind. He was longing to introduce Paul ; and to go from library to tea-room, and from tea-room to smoking-room, presenting him to members as the member he (Wynter) had made. The returned convict, in Dickens's *Great Expectations*, was not more anxious to gaze upon " his gentleman," than Wynter to contemplate his member of parliament.

The words Wynter spoke to Mrs. Charlton and Salome were spoken in the lone twilight of the ladies' gallery as he leaned over them and handed them to their seats. A forlorn sight was the gallery—empty and gray. A solitary member stretched in the side-gallery just beneath, and trying to go to sleep, pricked up his ears as he heard the rustling of silk, and fixing his eye-glass, endeavored to get a view of the ladies.

" Hallo," said Wynter, peering over, " there's something up ! There's going to be a count. Too soon—too soon ! I want to bring in Massie. I'll see if I can't stop it."

The Speaker's summons to members to come in and take their places was tingling through the House. If within the next minute or so there are not forty seats occupied in the legislative chamber, Lord Rupert de Capulet's grand effort is lost labor ! And the too ambitious youth had counted himself—committed suicide, in a parliamentary sense. For, made angry by the disrespect and indifference which the steadily thinning benches conveyed, he complained, in one unlucky sentence, of the frivolity and want of public spirit which left him to dilate on one of the gravest European questions in a House with hardly a dozen members present. Whereupon the Speaker, who thus found his official attention called to the fact that there were not forty members in the House, rose to his feet, cried out " Order, order !" and proceeded to the usual preliminaries of " counting ; " while the luckless Lord Rupert, dumb-foundered and crushed, sat down amid and upon his piles of papers, pulled his hat over his brows, and waited the fiat of destiny. The fiat presently came, when the Speaker, unable to count more than eight-and-twenty members, announced the adjournment of the House.

Paul Massie had not appeared to take his seat. Salome and her friend left .the gallery. They were presently met by Mr. Wynter, who, failing in his public-spirited attempt to keep a House, now came hurrying up to take charge of the ladies. Salome's eyes sought everywhere for Paul. She felt disappointed and miserable.

"Pity Massie didn't come in time," said Wynter. "Can't be helped now; but I'm very sorry you should be disappointed, ladies. I dare say we shall have a· stirring debate next Monday night, and perhaps that would repay for this sell. I'll see after your carriage, Mrs. Charlton.— Why, here is Massie ! Just the day after the fair, isn't it ? "

For as they approached .the threshold of Westminster-hall, they saw Paul stepping out of the hansom which had brought him down. He had come just in time to be too late for the House, and just in time to meet Salome.

Salome's cheek flushed when she saw him, and she felt as if the eyes of her companions could not fail to discover her emotion.. Her self-control was clearly going, she thought with some sadness. Time was—and that not long since—when the approach of no man could thus have caused her face to crimson and her limbs to tremble. " How is it with me when every noise appals me ? " How is it with a woman when she flushes and thrills at the approach of one man, and of him alone ? "I am like a beaten army," thought Salome, scanning as usual, her own weakness, and scorning it. "I am fast becoming demoralized."

Paul had to undergo some good-humored chaff from his friend Wynter, touching his neglect and want of punctuality in regard to his parliamentary duties.

"A bad beginning, Massie ; and one of your constituents in the gallery too. O yes, it's quite true! I mean Mrs. Charlton. And you won't be long in parliament before you find out that you had much better displease the electors themselves than the electors' wives.—Forgive him this once, Mrs. Charlton; I promise for his more faithful attendance another time."

Paul made such excuses as he could conjure up at the moment. His hearers were not apparently much inclined to deal severely with him. Paul was one of the special favorites of good Mrs. Charlton.

The carriage had not come, and they loitered, first up and down one of the corridors leading from Palace-yard into the Houses, and then along the terrace by the river. Mrs. Charlton leaned on Wynter's arm, and Paul had already given his to Salome. The evening had grown fairer towards its fall, and everything looked bright and glowing after the heavy twilight which reigned under the amber ceilings and painted windows of the House of Commons. A soft summer evening, mellowing beautifully upon the brown square towers of the Lambeth-palace and the dome of the more distant St. Paul's, which, owing to the river's sudden bend, looked as if it were set somewhere in the heart of the Surrey side. The air, the sky, the water, the setting sun, conveyed to the mind of Salome an impression of unwonted and touching beauty. She had not been used to associate the idea of beauty with anything about London, except perhaps a few vistas of the parks; but the scene now before her, so often looked upon, apparently so commonplace, showed strangely fascinating and fair. Doubtless the light that fell upon it was like to that which never was on sea or shore, and came from within; for Salome, at that moment, was almost happy. Seizing the enjoyment of the hour, as a child might, she was delighted to lean on *his* arm again, and to feel the influence of his presence. After the trying scenes and disappointments of the last day or two, it was unspeakable pleasure to walk thus quietly and almost alone by his side; and she enjoyed the present hour, and would fain have entreated it to stay, because it was so fair. Did not Baron Trenck, or some other famous prisoner, declare that, after all, there was as much of happiness in his prisoned days as in any equal length of his life? Because the smallest variations of the day's monotony—the sight of a stray sunbeam, the faint breath of a spring breeze, the efforts of a spider to weave his web, the expected visit of the gaoler,—all these little things delighted the mind, and were as much of refreshment to it as some great and solid gratification would have been to a free man leading an ordinary sort of life in the outer world.

It was in this sense, perhaps, that Salome was now happy. The mere disappointment of not seeing Paul, following as it did on the heels of other vexations, had been so bitter, that the unexpected joy of meeting him was enough to brighten all existence for the hour.

A new feeling too had sprung up in her breast, which strengthened and sweetened her love. Before, she had only loved Paul; now, she loved and pitied him. He was an outcast—a man almost without a name. Secret disgrace hung over him; the story of his life began in shame; his birth was, indeed, his first misfortune. England could be no home to him, if once he came to learn the truth; all thought of pursuing a career there he must abandon. It would be impossible that anyone who loved him could allow him unwarned to remain in England, where so many suspicious eyes were already tracking out his history. Salome thought with bitter compunction of the part she herself had taken in turning those eyes upon him. Well, all this marked him for an outcast. And what passionate woman who loves does not love all the more deeply and tenderly if the object of her affection is likely to be at odds with the world and in disgrace with fortune? Perhaps the ray of a new hope too was beginning to light up Salome's heart. The darker his fortunes, the more must he need, the higher surely must he prize, a woman's disinterested devotion.

In the sky, to which Salome sometimes turned her eyes,

only the latest beams of the sun were now shining. Soon that great light would be gone; but already the faint pale summer moon could be seen growing into distinctness and beauty in the blue heaven. So, after the going down of one hope in her heart, another, paler but purer, was already rising.

What did Paul and Salome speak of, as they paced up and down the terrace of Westminster-palace? Of nothing; at least of commonplace things and people. Even with lovers — acknowledged lovers — the moments when they indulge in the sort of rapturous, passionate, transcendental rhapsodies, which are their ordinary vernacular in books, are rare moments of exaltation. Even passion seldom in life succeeds in flooding over and sweeping away the barriers of conventional speech. And Paul and Salome were not lovers in any sense, unless after the satirical definition which avers that one always loves and the other submits to be loved; so they talked little more than commonplaces, which need not be translated into print. But she was happy, and her presence always was a gladness to him.

"It was a joy to meet her; it was no great grief to part," says Colonel Henry Esmond, when explaining what his feelings were towards his future wife.

It was always a joy to Paul to meet Salome; and if he could bear parting calmly, it must be remembered that he always left her with the expectation of a speedy and easy reunion. Only deep and passionate love makes a separation of twelve hours a misery. Paul was refreshed and brightened for the present hour; his gloom and his scruples and strong resolves alike vanished when Salome took his arm; and he was sorry when at last the carriage came to take her away.

"I shall see you by and by, shall I not?" she said as she was leaving.

Perhaps he seemed to hesitate, for she added, with something of her old tone of genial peremptoriness, "Yes, yes, I must see you; I really have something to say to you;

and there are one or two people likely to come, in whom I think you will feel interested. You must come, in short."

So Paul promised, very glad to be thus decidedly shaken out of his doubts and resolutions.

The ladies drove away, and Paul and Wynter dined together. Wynter was not to be shaken off; and Paul, who on the whole rather liked him, and was never very much addicted to the society of self alone, accepted his companionship unresistingly. Not merely did they dine together, but Wynter announced his intention of accompanying his friend to Madame de Luca's, where, indeed, he was, under ordinary circumstances, always welcome. So, when they had dined and smoked, and talked a little with this fellow and that, and when Paul had received many congratulations upon his success at Seaborough, and answered divers questions as to the probabilities of a petition, they set out to walk towards Hyde-park.

Salome had not counted on Mr. Wynter that night. Indeed she had not counted on anybody except Paul and the one or two persons of whom she spoke—comparative strangers who were not likely to stay long. But Mr. Wynter came; and, as chance would have it, several others came too, and Salome found it almost impossible to exchange six words with Paul. She was now especially anxious to speak to him about Alice, and about Halliday, if of nothing else; for when she returned home she went to see the wounded girl, and found that she had got her brain filled with fantasies and alarming ideas. Alice declared that she had dreamed of nothing but Halliday, and that she knew he meant to kill somebody. Then she fancied that she was about to die. Then she begged of Salome to send for Mr. Paul Massie, declaring that she must see him; and she positively affirmed that she had something to tell him which he ought to have known long ago. Once or twice she said she was sure Halliday was somewhere in the house—hiding—to kill her; and Salome began to think that she was really going distraught with weakness, and fear, and romantic nonsense,

all combined, and so sent at once for the doctor, who came
and pronounced her not seriously feverish, or likely to be
in any dangerous condition. She spoke indeed quite rationally and gently on every subject but the one or two, and
of these in the doctor's presence she did not speak at all ;
so there was nothing to be done, and Salome resolved to
soothe and humor the poor girl as far as she could. Indeed she felt bound to undergo any discomfort on Alice's
account when she remembered how her own eagerness to
tamper in matters with which she ought to have had no
concern was one of the principal influences which had
brought the girl from her village and her parents' home.

But Salome had with all this not a cheerful time of it,
and it is no wonder that she longed for the sunny intervals
of Paul's presence.

She was standing by Alice's bedside when a knock came
which she knew well.   Alice knew it too.

"That is Mr. Massie, madame, " said Alice. "O, how
glad I am !"

"Indeed!" Salome answered rather coldly. "Why
glad ? "

"Because I have been in such fear that Halliday might
meet him or follow him to-night. Will you ask him to see
me, and let me say just a few words to him to-night before
he goes? O, don't refuse me ! I am sure you will not
refuse, for you are so kind ; and if I were to die, and not
see him, I don't know what might happen."

Perhaps, if Salome had followed her first and not unnatu-
ral impulse, her prompt reply would have been, " Stuff and
nonsense !" or some words to a like effect ; but she controlled her feelings, and fell back upon her recollection of
her own copartnership in the girl's folly, and of the impulse
she had given to it ; and she answered gravely and kindly,

"Well, Alice, I will tell Mr. Massie that you wish so
much to see him, and I have no doubt that he will readily
consent. But I would much rather that you put aside all
these thoughts for the present, and took the doctor's word

that you are not in the slightest danger. If you cannot compose yourself to this, there is no harm whatever in what you ask, and I dare say it can be easily accomplished."

As she went to meet Paul, Salome reflected that, once he saw Alice, and that Alice spoke to him, as she seemed likely to do, of Halliday and Halliday's doings, and her own share in them, an *éclaircissement* must be inevitable. One acknowledgment must lead to others, and so much must be known as would compel Paul to seek a final and full revelation. "Then I must speak to-night?" she thought. "Better so than otherwise—better now than later. All I can now do to soften the shock to him is to save him from having to seek the truth elsewhere. He must seek it now; and the worst that could happen to him or to *her* would be to leave him to demand it from the same lips which confessed it to me."

CHAPTER XXX.

CATASTROPHE.

THAT night Salome soon got rid of her visitors. She gave out that she was unwell: indeed she was unwell; but that was not her motive for desiring to be free of company. She had a special reason: Paul Massie learned it soon. As he was about to leave the house in company with Mr. Wynter, M. P., the inevitable and irrepressible, Salome spoke a few words to him in a low tone and in Italian—which, it has already been remarked, was a means of communication quite safe from the comprehension of the British friend of King Victor Emmanuel. The words were imperative: "Come back at once, here, after you have got rid of *him*; I must see you again to-night."

"To-night—here?" asked Paul, as he looked into her face for a confirmation of her words.

"*Si, si*," she added peremptorily; "you are under orders, and you must obey without murmuring."

Paul wondered, but asked no further questions. He walked away with Mr. Wynter, and at last got rid of that gentleman. Then he turned into a by-street, and walked up and down there for a few minutes. Finally he returned to Salome's house. The street was silent and solitary. No evil-boding form anywhere flung its shadow across his path.

The door was opened by Mademoiselle Clotilde, who as usual smiled upon existence in general, and rarely evinced the least surprise at anything. She received Paul as composedly as though it were his first visit that day, and the hour two o'clock in the afternoon. She ushered him into a drawing room, whither presently came Salome rustling down the stairs.

"Good Paul," she said, "good boy, I thought you would come! But I have not brought you back here at this hour to gratify myself; it was only to satisfy the poor creature up stairs. Indeed I had to promise her that you should not leave the house at all. She says she must see and speak to you to-night. She fancies she is dying, poor child, and she evidently thinks death a calamity. Well, well—she is so young."

This was spoken as Paul ascended the stairs with her. Madame de Luca preceded him into the room where Alice lay. She lay neatly and carefully disposed of in Salome's own room, and in a pretty tiny French bed. She looked pale and wild, her hair flung over her shoulders, her arms wandering restlessly. Madame de Luca dragged Paul forward. He took the wounded girl's hand, and murmured some sentences about his sorrow to see her there—his hope that she would soon recover.

"No, no," she said, "I don't want to recover—I don't *now;* and besides, if I did he would find me out again and kill me."

"He!—who?

"Halliday!—Jem Halliday."

Paul started. Madame de Luca motioned to him to express no surprise.

"Take care of him, Mr. Paul," said the girl,—"O, take care of him! He's dreadfully bad, and he swore to be revenged upon you."

"Why, Alice, I never did him any harm."

"No—but—but then he thinks you did. O, don't leave the house to-night!—Don't let him, ma'am! And—and—I wanted to tell you something, but first promise to forgive me."

"My poor girl, what have I to forgive?"

"O, but promise, promise!"

"I do, I do indeed. I promise fully and sincerely."

"Then listen to me, and I'll tell you all."

"Shall I go?" said Madame de Luca softly.

"No, no, ma'am; please don't go. I'd rather you remained; you have been my best of friends : only for you I don't know what might have become of me."

Paul was too deeply agitated and surprised to heed these words.

"Mr. Paul—Mr. Massie—it was I who did it all! It was I who first thought I found out something about you before ever you came to Seaborough. It was I told it to Halliday and set him on; and I got the letter from him, and he gave me a diamond ring. It was I first read the letter, and I knew well enough that he robbed the dead of it as he did of the diamond ring. He set me on to find out all about it; he said we should get plenty of money from you, and he wanted me to marry him. But I would not marry him then, and I told him I would have nothing more to do with him; and then he said he would kill me if anyone found out that we had anything to do with it; and I was frightened and ran away and came here; and that's all. I have made all this unhappiness between you and your family; and Mr. Eustace knows not a word about the whole story, no more than the child unborn. No one knew a word about it but me and Miss Sarah, because we attended

16

Mrs. Massie night and day when she had the fever, and then we heard something strange. She never breathed a word to me—Miss Sarah didn't—nor I to her; but she knew that I was thinking about it; only she never thought that I would make such use of it. And I know something about her which, perhaps, she thinks I don't know, and I should like to tell it; but I must not. O, I have done a great deal of harm, and all because I wanted to have money and to be a lady, and to live in London and—and—well, it's no matter now. I ran away from my father and mother; and now I'm punished. But if I die, you'll tell them I was sorry, very, very sorry, won't you, Mr. Paul? my poor father was fond of you."

Paul was deeply moved. Tears stood in his eyes, and his hand trembled like that of a woman. He tried to speak, but his voice failed.

"My poor child," said Madame de Luca, coming to the head of the bed, and settling the clothes and the hair of the tossing patient, "why do you talk of dying? You will be well in a few days, and you will return and be happy in Seaborough. We can have your father here, if you like, in a day, as soon as you are a little stronger."

"No; I had rather, if you please, not see my father just yet. But O, Mr. Paul, take care of Halliday; he's a desperate man, and he'd do anything. I thought I saw him stealing past that door this very night. Don't go home to-night, please; please don't go home. Say you won't."

"Promise, promise to please her," whispered Madame de Luca in Italian.

Paul promised.

"Now," said the lady of the house cheerfully, "I think we must not talk any more to-night. This poor girl is quite weak and exhausted; she has been upset by some foolish dream, and the surgeon says she must sleep. You are wearied too, Mr. Massie, and must get rest.—You will be better to-morrow, Alice, and then Mr. Massie will see you again."

They left the room, and came down stairs; Paul silent, and quite like one who walks in his sleep.

"Do this poor girl's revelations help you into light?" asked Madame de Luca anxiously.

"Scarcely," said Paul. "They do a little clear up some points which seemed utterly bewildering before; but they confuse and perplex others. Why did I allow that scoundrel to escape, when he must have been within my grasp? O, if I only had the chance again! Let me once come within sight of him, and see if he escape me."

"Don't think of him. He can be found, and shall be found, if it be needful. I think I should rather he escaped and got out of the country. But what of yourself and— and "—she hesitated—" your people?"

"I don't know. I am too confused and bewildered to think of anything but of what an idiot I have been. We must get this poor girl back again to her home. Surely, surely she will not die?"

"O no, certainly not. I am sure not. She is only somewhat feverish, and has had some startling dream about this fellow. All that we can do for her shall be done. At present, she does not seem to me to be in any danger; only her terror of this man paralyzes her."

"Why on earth did she ever come to London?"

"Can you not guess?"

"I cannot indeed. Why did she leave her home to come here?"

"Just because she is a woman and a fool, like the rest of us," said Salome, her eyes lighting up with a sudden and half scornful flash. "Because, having a human heart, she was silly enough to think of loving somebody. I have no patience with such creatures. Why have they not sense and calmness and spirit like me?" she added bitterly.

Did Paul understand her now? He leaned his head upon his hand.

"She said you had been her best friend," he said, suddenly looking upwards.

"Perhaps I have, although not in the sense she thinks. I have kept her here these some weeks back, safe from temptation and danger of every kind. Had she not foolishly ventured out, she might have been safe still."

"Safe here for weeks?"

"'Here, on this ground—Denmark, where I have been cexton—'"

"Here! and you never told me?"

"Nay, that was my secret. I am ashamed and penitent enough now. I too have been meddling in your affairs, as you will presently find, and I have helped to mar what I could not make. You will have little reason to thank me. I meant to serve you, Paul, and I have only done you harm. There, let the whole story be out: 'twas I who tampered in your history, and made all the inquiries, —O, you don't know how many and how!—and terrified your good people until they hate and dread you. Say anything you like to condemn me. I have always been an intriguer, and had my head early crammed with romance and stuff. I thought to make you a hero, and myself your unknown protectress and benefactress. You have come tonight to listen to revelation; then listen to this now." Her voice grew deep and thrilling, her cheeks were red as flame, her eyes had an unmoving light in them as she spoke.

"I do not care what you have done," Paul exclaimed passionately; "all that you did or could do was for the best. You were a friend to me when others cast me away. You have not injured me. What on earth could add to my ruin and shame? But if you had, I welcome the hurt —indeed I do—which comes from the kindly hand of—of a friend."

He took her hand; she withdrew it.

"Listen, Paul; I have more to tell you. I once urged you to stay in London. Now I urge you leave it—tomorrow, if you can. I thought to have made of you a hero restored to his rights and master of a splendid career:

I tell you now that you have no rights; that you are a pauper—a very outcast; that you have not a' penny in the world; that your only hope here is gone, unless you care to accept the alms flung to a ruined claimant—to a misguided poor relation."

"I have long thought it," he said, in a low gloomy tone; "long thought it. Little skill as I have in guessing, yet I have been able this sometime back to guess so much. I am not blind. But why do you tell me this? Why speak of it? Do you exult in my ruin?"

"I do."

She spoke the words with the utmost calmness.

He sprang to his feet and looked wildly at her.

"I do, Paul : yes, it is true. I do rejoice in what you call your ruin. I exult in your being poor, nameless, hopeless. I do, as surely as Heaven hears us. And you know why."

Paul sat down again, and covered his face with his hand.

"Yes, you understand me now. I have had to speak out at last. I am glad of your poverty because I am rich ; of your doubtful name because, since it is doubtful, I may offer to bear and share it. Paul, Paul, I love you, and you know it. See how I unfold my whole heart ; ay, and abase myself before you."

She knelt by his side, took his hand and kissed it passionately.

"I never felt love before," she murmured ; "never, never until I saw you. I would have died for you. O, what I would have given to be young again—to be twenty years younger than I am ! Never should you have known of this—in words at least—had that which I imagined for you come true. But it did not, and cannot ; and now that you are poor and outcast, I may tell you how much I love you, may I not, Paul ? "

She smiled a wild and wan smile, and tried to draw away his hand, and catch one answering gleam of love from his eyes.

He bent over her at last.   "O Madame de Luca—"

"No, not Madame de Luca; call me by my name!"

"Salome, Salome, you are too good, too kind, too generous.   You have been all the world to me, when those to
whom I came cast me off.   What can I say to you?   How
can I accept such a sacrifice?"

"Don't talk to me of sacrifice; I will not listen to it.
You are the only man I ever loved, or could have loved.
I am ashamed of myself for loving you so, and telling you
so.   I thought I could have had the generosity to keep
this to myself, and leave you free to act, and perhaps you
would have loved me of yourself.   Listen, Paul; I will go
anywhere with you, do anything you like, if you will only
not talk of sacrifice.   The sacrifice is yours.   Am I not
growing old and fading?   Nay, look at me."

She stood up, and he gazed at her.   Natural unconquerable coquetry and pride were in her attitude, her eyes,
her tossed and streaming hair.   Paul had never seen anyone so beautiful.   There seemed something wild, weird, and
yet glowing in that lustrous beauty.   If she was not in her
spring, she was certainly in her Indian summer.   No man
could have gazed on such a woman, and heard her say she
loved him, without an enraptured soul.   Paul seized her
hand and pressed it to his hot lips.

"While we both live," he said, "we will not separate."

For a moment neither spoke.

"You will not go home to night?" she then said.   "You
promised Alice that you would not."

"If I may lie upon the sofa until morning," he said.
"It will soon be dawn."

"Remain there," she replied.   "We have no bedroom
to give you.   Alice has been put in my room—to my maid's
great discomfort.   She shall be seen to all night; indeed I
will look after her myself.   I shall not sleep, except perhaps for half an hour in the room which is usually hers.
Good-night, Paul; I shall not in any case see you again
until bright morning, when all the world is astir.   We

are outraging the proprieties a good deal already. But we must not set the household wondering. Good-night."

He drew her towards him and kissed her. This was the first kiss he had ever of his own free motion pressed upon her lips.

"Are you happy?" he asked.

"So happy," she replied, "that I could now, for the first time in all my life, wish to die. I fear to awaken from this happy dream."

Her eyes were calm a moment as they rested on his; then she was gone.

He lay upon the sofa. He ought, one would think, to have been full of anxious, conflicting thoughts, such as scare sleep away. But his senses were outwearied, and refused any longer to sustain themselves. He slept. He dreamed a thousand wild and incoherent dreams in the short hour or two of his sleep. At last he dreamed that some woman—perhaps his mother—came into the room, bent over him, recognized him, and screamed his name. So wild and piercing was the shriek that it seemed to ring in his ears even as he awoke. For he started up, hardly knowing in his excitement where he was. The gray of morning already made half visible the objects in the drawing room. He had not nearly collected his senses when the house rang to another shriek : no dream but a reality.

"Paul, Paul!" rang in his ears. Then a fall and a gurgling groan.

He leaped from the sofa and dashed wildly up the stairs. Rushing upward he passed a room where a light was burning, and where he knew that Alice lay. The French servant came out of that room half undressed and screaming. She sprang up the higher flight of stairs whence the shrieks seemed to have come. Paul rushed past her, nearly flinging her down in his excitement. Not a word was exchanged between them. They reached an open corridor. Before them was a bedroom-door. Inside there was somebody trying to open it. A hoarse voice was heard to say, with an oath: "Damn me, but I thought 'twas Ally!"

The door was locked inside; it was a frail painted thing. Paul's hand and foot drove it in while a man might have breathed. But his furious push displaced an obstacle which lay against it. That object was the body of Salome de Luca, half-dressed, and covered with blood—dead.

The murderer had been bending over his victim. He sprang back when the door gave way. The window behind him, looking into the garden, was open, but he had not time to turn towards it. He drew back, and stood in an attitude of defiance, brandishing a knife.

"Keep away!" he cried. "Don't come near me! I didn't mean to kill her; but I'll kill anyone else that touches of me. I'm as good as a madman."

Paul sprang at him. The murderer struck a savage blow, which Paul caught in his left arm. Then there was a short struggle. The maid who stood on the threshold, aghast and shrieking, declared afterwards that it did not last one single minute. The knife was not used again. It fell clattering on the floor. Neither of the men spoke. Halliday had backed to the window, either with some vague notion of escape, or forgetful of the danger open behind him. Paul seized him with an iron grip; the murderer was a strong man, but he struggled in vain to free himself. Did Paul merely design to secure him, or to slay him then and there? That none, not even Paul himself, might know. The struggling wretch disengaged his right hand by a supreme effort, and struck Paul a furious blow on the face. That was his own death-blow. For Paul instinctively let go his hold, and struck at his enemy a return blow with a force like that of a steam-engine. Hurled against the half-open window, senseless from the paralyzing blow, the man's body went crashing through the frail framework. He fell thirty feet into the garden below.

A second servant had fled screaming into the street.

The surgeon, who was just arriving, a policeman, and an unconcerned passenger, hurried into the house. Surgical aid could do nothing for Salome, nor preserve her murderer for the hand of justice. They laid her beautiful body decently on the bed which she had scarcely occupied. Her maid emphatically refused to allow her mistress's corpse to remain on the floor, that law might come and take heed of it as it fell. She shrieked in wild grief over it, and at last exhausted herself down to a feeble moaning.

But Paul was found in a raving condition. The policeman who first entered the room straightway assumed him to be the murderer, but did not at all like his looks ; and being cautiously unwilling to plunge into danger, hung back on the threshold of the room, and thus allowed the surgeon, who better comprehended the situation, to come forward and take order. Paul was indeed a spectacle to shrink from. His eyes flashed as with the fire of madness. His dark skin, his tossing hair, his wild gestures, his eyes gleaming like those of the serpent, had, when seen in the cold gray light, something peculiarly strange and startling. The policeman afterwards explained his hesitation by confidentially remarking to one of those near him, that the gentleman looked like a wild Indian savage. Perhaps the remark was not utterly meaningless ; perhaps the Indian blood which had sunk into Mexican earth was then at last crying out and asserting its supremacy in the excited veins of Paul Massie.

16*

CHAPTER XXXI.

AUSTRIAN PLOTS.

"EXTRAORDINARY affair that of poor Madame de
Luca," said Shavers, M. P., to Wynter, M. P., at
the Cosmopolitan Club.

"Very extraordinary—very," replied Wynter. "Shocking, dreadful business! I always told Salome de Luca
that she left her jewels and plate and money and things
quite too much about. Kept no man on the premises.
These things get about you know—servants talk of it, and
that sort of thing. Ticket-of-leave man, I hear—seven
times transported for life. I told Grey this morning that
I should put a question to him about it to-night in the
House. 'Be ready, Sir George,' I said, 'for I'm going to
be down on you and on your pets.'"

"But the man is dead, isn't he?" said Shavers.

"Leaped out of the window," replied Wynter, "when
he heard the police coming. Smashed on the pavement.
Sorry he didn't live to be hanged. Grey isn't though, for
it gets him out of a fix."

"Very odd affair altogether," said Shavers, M. P.,
again looking curiously at his friend.

"Very odd indeed," said Wynter, not in the least
disconcerted.

"I hear your friend Massie won't take his seat after
all," remarked Shavers, trying a new tack.

"Stuff!" replied Wynter. "Of course he'll take his
seat. He's cut up of course about poor Salome de Luca;
so are we all. She was deucedly fond of him, no doubt.
But he'll come all right. Of course he'll take his seat."

"Hasn't he been hurt somehow?" inquired Shavers
in a significant tone.

"Not seriously," replied Wynter. "Blow of a stone,

I believe from a Seaborough elector of the opposite side; nothing to speak of."

"Then he wasn't in _her_ house the night of the murder?" said Shavers, coming more bodily to the point.

"Of course he was. Didn't you know? So was I, so was Levison, so were two or three more."

"But not when the murder took place?"

"Not at all. How could he be there? It was at three or four in the morning. Massie and I walked home together that night."

"Deuce you did! People talk such odd things."

"Do they? That's because they know nothing about it."

"Then you really believe, Wynter," said Shavers, growing confidential and bold, "that this was only a common housebreaking-and-murder business?"

"Believe it? Of course I do. Don't I know all about it?"

"You really belief all dat, Mr. Wynter?" intruded Dr. Fleiss, who had just come in. "You really belief dat nonsense? A man like you too dat really knows something of affairs!"

"And pray what do you believe, Dr. Fleiss?"

Dr. Fleiss shrugged his shoulders and looked cautiously all around.

"Mine goot friend, we had better not talk of dese tings too much. She was a brave woman; but I have often told her dere were eyes upon her, and dat she risk far too much. Do you tink the Austrian Government did not always overlook what she did? Do you tink it had not its spies about her? Do you tink it does not watch me— you even, perhaps? So! One day there will be found a dagger in my heart too; and denn Mr. Wynter will say, it is a housebreaker. She was a brave woman, too_brave and too kind; and she loved de Revolution; and now she is dead! Also. Ask your Foreign Office about it. Ask your Civis-Romanus Palmerston! You shall find dere will be no prosecution, no trial; noting of the sort. De murderer is dead, is he? Of course he is—understands itself.

It is not convenient for him to be forthcoming. Ha!
Mind my vorts."

Wynter rarely endured anyone who professed to know
the secret history of anything better than he did. But in
this instance he showed a surprising inclination to adopt
the solution propounded.

"Tell you what, Fleiss," he said, in a tone of sudden
conviction; "there's something in what you say. I'll
change my tactics. I'll put my question to the Foreign
Secretary, and I'll drop a private note to the papers. It's
a capital case against the Austrian Government."

Wynter walked away, as if in a dreadful hurry to put
his threat into execution. Fleiss hung on like grim death
to Shavers, whom he talked into believing that the very
air they breathed was impregnated with Austrian, Prussian,
Russian, and French *espionage*.

Wynter was a good-hearted creature. He knew as little as anybody else what to make of the affair. But he
knew that Paul was in Salome's house at the time of her
murder. It may be that he had formed a conjecture to
account for Paul's mysterious return to the house; and it
is certain that the conjecture he might have formed was
entirely wrong. But he made up his mind that the public
should know nothing about the matter. He attended the
inquest, and gave a full and circumstantial account of the
hour at which he left Salome's house; and he took care to
mention several times the unimportant fact that he was
accompanied in leaving it by a brother member of parliament, Mr. Paul Massie. He suggested privately to the
coroner that it would be only proper to have the name of
the gentleman who, when passing by the house, ran to the
rescue and gave the alarm, kept private. To the coroner
himself he gave a sufficient hint; and indeed there seemed
no occasion for publicity. The gentleman had seen no more
than everybody else—the maid, the surgeon, the policeman.
This discretion, however, as to the other witness, did not
prevent much conjecture in certain circles about the iden-

tity of the gentleman in question. But the general impression was, that it was some very illustrious personage, who simply did not care to have himself, or even his name, mixed up with the witnesses at an inquest. Some people said it was the Duke of Cambridge, others suggested the name of Mr. Disraeli. Dr. Fleiss smiled sardonically when he heard such suggestions, and darkly hinted that it was the Austrian ambassador, who had gone in person to see that the work was accomplished in properly effective style. But Wynter's little stratagem succeeded as far as he wished it to succeed. The general public did not suppose that the individual whose name was freely mentioned by one of the witnesses in connection with the case could be the mysterious personage who turned up at the climax. Therefore, whatever a few suspicious individuals may have conjectured, the eye of common speculation never fixed upon Paul Massie. He had walked home early that night with Mr. Wynter, M.P. ; and there ended his share in the business.

The jury returned a verdict of wilful murder against some person unknown, and likewise found that that person unknown had been killed by falling from a window in the endeavor to escape.

Wynter never propounded his question to the Foreign Secretary ; and the secret share which the Austrian Government may have had in that murder remains unexposed to this day. Dr. Fleiss openly insinuated that fears for his personal safety had alone induced Wynter to desist from following up the track. Dr. Fleiss addressed several letters to the papers on the subject ; but each journal having in turn declined to insert any of them, he denounced everywhere the entire English press as the paid creature of the Austrian Government. He was preparing a pamphlet on the subject, but was discouraged completing it by the fact that the various printers to whom he applied stipulated for a payment in advance as a condition of proceeding to work. Other grievances soon arose. New international and ministerial conspiracies were discovered, and Dr. Fleiss presently forgot the case of Salome de Luca and the purchased press of England.

—◆—

CHAPTER XXXII.

PAUL AND SARAH.

THE first resolution which Paul Massie formed on recovering sense and judgment was to leave England and to return there no more.

He awakened first to consciousness in the house of his acquaintances, the Trentons. Mr. Wynter, M.P., had considerately taken care that those whom he understood to be Paul's friends should know of his precarious condition. "If I had a house and a family myself," said the worthy man, "he should be cared for there; but one can't do much for a poor sick fellow in Albany-chambers." The Trentons behaved with great kindness and promptitude. It is a fact that thoroughly worldly people often have good hearts, and that a passion for gentility does not always exclude every other human feeling. In this instance, as young Trenton was positively to marry Lydia, the removal of poor Paul to the shelter of the Trenton roof seemed in the eyes of respectability quite a proper family sort of affair, and Mrs. Trenton did not incur among her friends a damaging reputation for eccentric beneficence.

For Paul had need of special care. He did not speak a word for hours after his removal from Salome's house and the sight of her dead body. No one at first knew what to do with him. At last the doctors ventured upon a powerful exhibition of chloroform, and then had him conveyed to his lodgings, where next day he awoke—if that could be called awaking—in brain-fever. No gleam of true consciousness visited him until many days after the body of her who so deeply loved him, and whom he had so suddenly and wildly avenged, had been laid to rest under the quiet earth of the grave-yard.

Indeed, at one period the grave-yard seemed to be only waiting to receive Paul himself. But he was well nursed and cared for.

The very day after the inquest, while Wynter was seeing after Paul in Paul's lodgings, and endeavoring to bribe the landlady into contented endurance of a lodger in brain-fever, there was a visitation there of a handsome melancholy lady, who announced herself as a cousin of the invalid's, and calmly declared her intention not to leave him until his recovery—or his death.

Mr. Wynter, being a man of the world, thought that, under the circumstances, it became more necessary than ever to have Paul removed to some other shelter. He learned from the new visitor all about her friends in town; and he urged that Paul should be conveyed, if possible, to the house of the Trentons. Indeed, as the lady obviously shrank from the suggestion, he insisted on acting as the negotiator, and promptly arranged the whole affair.

Paul, still unconscious, was soon transferred to better quarters, where Sarah Massie could at least watch over him unseen by the prying eyes of strangers, and safe from the gossiping speculations of babbling tongues.

She had little heart to enter the Trentons' house; but she would not leave Paul in his danger. So she watched over him and nursed him, and heeded not, although it soon ceased to be a secret to all people, that her feelings, towards him were not merely those of a cousin.

Hers was not a happy part. Except for the womanly delight of watching over the man she loved, she had no happiness. The dread of meeting Eustace or Lydia was always fresh, and never wore off, however frequently she had to encounter each. The one was silently reproachful, the other full of vivacious condolence, comment, and curiosity.   Nor were the utterances of Paul's delirium always consoling to the listener's ears.   Many nights passed away before any name save one issued from his hot lips.   He raved of Salome living and of her as dead.   He wept over her body ; he tore her from the grasp of her murderer ; he saved her, and exulted over her safety ; he call upon her to come back, and vowed that he would always love her.

It was long before he breathed a word which denoted even a vague memory of the existence of her who sat be- side him.   Then gradually she seemed to become a part of his dreams—to be always present to his consciousness.

When the fever of disease had passed away, and the "fever called living" had conquered, the presence of Sarah had so gradually blended itself into his perception, that he felt no surprise on awaking at last to clear consciousness, and seeing her beside him.   He was weak and broken for a long time.   Over-excitement and much exhaustion, culmi- nating in a fearful shock, had well-nigh crushed him. When he first became thoroughly aware of the sweet and tender care which was nursing him, he felt, in his prostrate condition of nerves and strength, less like a lover who finds his mistress beside him, than like a child which awakes from a hideous nightmare, and sees its smiling mother bending over it.   And Sarah, who had always meant to leave him—for ever—before he returned to consciousness, found her presence discovered before she knew of it—and remained.

What of Mrs. Massie ?   Did she not sit by Paul's bed- side ?   No.   She never saw him after their parting at Sea- borough.   She wept over him at home ; and she wrote him a letter, which, when he had quite recovered, he read in silence and alone, and destroyed.   He had evinced no wish to see her ; and they who best understood her knew well that hers was a nature which would at any risk spare itself a shock.   There was no *éclaircissement ;* none whatever. What Paul knew became known to Sarah, whom it did not surprise.   The rest was silence.   Eustace Massie never suspected the relationship that subsisted between him and Paul. He always supposed Paul to have been at one time made the instrument of a stupid money-extorting plot aimed only against the genuineness of Mrs. Massie's marriage; and he ascribed Paul's delusion to the easily-gulled simplicity of one unused to the crafts of British sharpers. And he regarded himself as very magnanimous in so readily endeavoring to forgive and forget the whole transaction.

In other respects Eustace bowed meekly, not without a pang, to fate. He was a religious man, but still a man; a model clergyman, but yet with some of the weaknesses of the human race. The break-up of his plans, the defection of Sarah, had tried him sorely. It was highly fortunate for him that a great theological controversy broke out just then. He rushed into it, eager, like a love-crossed knight of old, to work off his grief by doing battle with the infidels. He wrote letter after letter, and subsequently published the whole of the agitating correspondence in a volume. No ordinary reader would have supposed that the reverend champion who penned those spirited controversial arguments—who ransacked to exhaustion all the Greek and Hebrew texts; who polished so carefully those beautiful periods—could all the time have had his heart smarting with the untheological anguish of disappointed earthly affection. Yet we who know the story may perhaps detect here and there between the lines some little tinge of personal feeling. In that fine passage—some people think it a little of a platitude—about the perishableness of earthly affections and the inevitable disppointment of worldly hopes; in that exhortation to his opponents to lay down all personal pride and become submissive and bow their heads,—there are vague tremulous shades and touches which may hint to the initiated that even in the very thick of the controversy Eustace Massie's mind would wander off occasionally to dwell upon the sharp little trial which had been appointed for himself. But he will recover; nay, he has recovered. He will probably marry yet, and be calmly happy.

Meanwhile, he is not grieved to hear that the cousin whose long-expected visit brought so many strange consequences is soon to go back into the darkness and the Night's Plutonian shore which lie somewhere across the Atlantic. Mexico begins to offer a fresh field for energy and talent; and Mr. Charlton has railway schemes there; and thither is Paul Massie going to push them. After a very few formal sittings, put in to divert attention from recents events, the hon. member for Seaborough has accepted the stewardship of the Chiltern Hundreds; and the Rev. Eustace Neale Massie may return anybody he pleases for that constituency.

This is not a story of sentiment; neither was poor Paul Massie a sentimental man. There shall be no pathetic pictures of his visits to the grave of Salome de Luca; although he stood there many a time, and gave vent to his own deep feelings in his own way. She is buried in Kensal-green; and there was a great concourse of bearded men there on the day of her funeral; and it was with no little difficulty that Charlton and Wynter, having an eye to the prejudices of the British public, averted the delivery of a funeral oration by one of the most eloquent of exiles. Poor Salome's property, for the disposal of which she had made no provision, passed to the old Franco-Irish priest who was her only surviving relative, and who got rid of most of it in the forwarding of schemes to counteract the destinies of United Italy, and to argue with the inexorable on the subject of the temporal power. He did not lament for Salome, whom he had long regarded as the most lamentable of renegades and conspirators. Perhaps the one heart in the world which most sincerely mourned her death was, after Charley Millton's, or after Paul Massie's own, that which throbbed in the little bosom of poor George the actress.

But though Paul Massie was not a sentimental man, yet he had far too much heart even to think of new human ties soon after those which, so nearly formed, were so suddenly broken. His sharpest pain, when he awoke to clear consciousness, was the regret that he had not loved Salome more deeply; that he had not known her earlier; that it had not been given to him to make her happy. He mourned for her, taken so soon from a world that, to her, was full of life and action and brightness. But he mourned with grief unspeakably bitter because he could not help feeling that, only for him, she would not thus and then have died. Many times his agony of grief became almost unendurable, and his wild nature literally swept him away. In his sorrow he undervalued, almost scorned, everything —every human friendship, love, and hope, but the friendship, love, and hope which he persisted in saying had been offered to him when all the world rejected him.

Sarah required some self-control and resignation to listen without outward manifestation of suffering to his wild outbreaks of grief and passion. He spoke to her as freely as if she had been his sister; and it was long before he talked of anything but the generosity, the goodness, the nobleness, the terrible fate of Salome.

Perhaps it is not any disparagement to so good a woman as Sarah to admit that she felt the more sympathy with this deep and stormy grief because throughout the whole poor Paul never ceased to accuse himself of the blackest ingratitude.

" O Sarah," he said one day, after one of the usual outbursts of grief, "I can never be happy; I can never forgive myself."

" Why never forgive yourself, Paul? "

" Because, with all her goodness to me, I had not the heart of a man, and I did not love her as—as—a woman like her ought to have been loved."

Sarah's heart throbbed, but she said nothing.

CHAPTER XXXIII.

THE DRIFTING VESSEL AND THE WRECKER.

ONE bright morning very early, little George made an expedition, or pilgrimage, to Salome's grave. She went to lay a wreath of flowers there, and to relieve her feelings—poor little comic actress and pantomime prince! —by unobserved and copious tears. But when she drew near the grave, she began to fear that she was not to be alone there. For a gentleman was seated, or stretched rather, on the grass beside the little hillock. His hat lay near him ; his hand was over his eyes. When the rustle of the actress's dress announced her coming, he looked up, but did not move from his place. There was something of embarrassment on both sides. The gentleman was yet uncertain whether George was not a mere passer-by, and George was reluctant to approach the grave until he had gone. As he did not seem about to go, she came up. Then he rose from the ground and took up his hat, which he kept in his hand. He was a tall man with long black hair, deep hollow eyes, and worn, lined, handsome face. George had now reached the grave, and his eyes fell upon the wreath she held in her hand. There was a moment's embarrassment : George looked again at the stranger to make sure that it was not some one she knew. No ; she had never seen him before. Their eyes met, and he spoke.

"Did you know the lady who is buried here,—Madame de Luca ? " he asked.

"I did," the girl replied, and her tears were rising ; " I knew her a long time."

A long time ! George was some eighteen years old.

"I knew her too," he said ; "not perhaps a very long time, but long enough to make me remember her for-ever."

"O, she was so good and kind to me!" sobbed poor George. "I loved her; and she was very fond of me."

"*I* loved her too," said wild Charley Millton; "and she was more kind to me than I deserved."

George was used to hearing emotion expressed in tragic tones and fine-sounding words; but there was so deep and genuine a sorrow in the voice and the sentence or two she now heard, that she looked fixedly at the speaker, and opened eyes of wonder.

"I was often at her house lately," she said—hardly knowing what she did say—"and I do not remember seeing you there."

The question was not put in a tone of doubt, but only of mere surprise.

"No—I was away; I was in Italy, and only came back the other day, and saw her but once before—before *this*." He waved his hand over the grave, and for a moment did not venture to speak. Then he said, "My name is Millton, Charles Millton—you may have heard her speak of me."

"O, yes, very often. She showed me your name in Italian newspapers different times, and she told me you were one of her dearest friends."

"She spoke of me kindly?"

"Yes, always kindly—always. More than kindly indeed; she would have spoken kindly of anyone."

He seemed as if about to ask something more, but stopped, and gave up the attempt. Both stood silent by the grave. Then he bowed to George, and turned to go away, but, suddenly looking back, he said: "May I ask your name?"

"My name is Georgina Renville, and I am an actress."

There was so much of seriousness and sadness about every line of his face that George—she could not tell why —assumed that he must be a very religious and puritanical person, and like an honest little girl resolved that he should know the worst at once with regard to the person he was addressing, and then express his horror if he chose.

"I am glad to have had the honor of making your acquaintance," he said, "and I hope we may meet again." She stood indeed on what was to him truly consecrated ground, and he reverenced the little actress because she was laying her flower-wreath on Salome's grave.

He then bowed and went away. But as she left the place, she saw him still waiting among the tombstones. He did not see her. She doubted not that when he found she had gone, he would return to the grave. She walked home to her lodgings in Newman-street, much thinking all the way of the melancholy eyes and deep tones of Charley Millton.

But Charley Millton soon left England again, and was lost to the eyes of his friends for awhile. He has since reappeared. He rose to the surface the moment it became certain that Italy and Prussia were to fight against Austria. He joined the Italian volunteer corps, and served in the exasperatingly short campaign in the Tyrol. He rallied many a fluctuating band of ill-armed, undisciplined youths against the soldiers of the Kaiser. Perhaps Fate could not have dealt more kindly with him than if, as he waved his cap and shouted "*Avanti!*" at some critical moment, she had sent an Austrian bullet through his breast. But the bullets passed him by, and wild Charley Millton still lives.

The news of Salome de Luca's death was not long in reaching even quiet Seaborough. Several copies of the daily papers left London every morning for that community, and therefore of course the story was soon eagerly read ; and all who had ever seen or spoken to the victim of the murder were proud to exaggerate their reminiscences. There were some too who suspected their wretched townsman Halliday of having had something to do with it. Crossley and his wife indeed soon came to know the truth, and did not take much trouble to conceal it. So Halliday became after awhile a sort of local renown of the grisly kind, and glad was the man or woman who could remember anything of what he or she said to or of the outcast the last time he was seen hanging about the public-house doors. His mother had been for some time bedridden in the work-house hospital, and may probably be fortunate enough to die without hearing any of the fearful reports which attached the guilt of murder to her son. Eustace preached an affecting and powerful sermon one Sunday, in which, while of course naming no names, he drew the clear moral of the whole tragedy in a manner which none of his hearers could possibly fail to understand. He attributed the whole calamity to a want of proper religious elevation on the part of the unknown but suspected author of the crime ; and indeed no one can gainsay the fact that a man of properly religious character would never have committed murder. How to infuse true religious principles into the minds of the sort of people who usually keep up the crop of murderers, was a problem which the preacher did not solve.

Mrs. Massie was not one of the first who heard of what had happened. When she did hear of it, was she greatly shocked ? Shocked assuredly ; but very much grieved ? That is another question. Rousseau tells us in his *Confessions* that when he heard of the death of a particular friend, his first impulse was one of gladness ; because there was a certain coat, or garment of some kind, belonging to the friend, which had often excited his envy, and which now he hoped to find bequeathed to him. Yet he insists that he was fond of the friend, and grieved at his death ; but that the first impulse which leaped to the surface of his mind was an impulse to rejoice over the one good thing which the death was likely to do for him. Mrs. Massie was a selfish woman in the passive sense ; endowed with a selfishness indeed which, somewhat like Rousseau's, sprang in great part from constitutional weakness of character, and it would not have been possible to afflict her deeply with any grief which did not concern either herself directly, or some one of the few whom she closely held to her heart.

Therefore, if she had analyzed boldly the sentiment which first filled her when she heard of Salome's death, it would probably have shown itself to be one of relief and hope. There was relief upon her own account—one of the possessors of the secret gone forever! There was hope on another's account, for Mrs. Massie instantly said to herself, "Now he is free—now he can marry Sarah; and they will both be happy; and they will forgive me."

. It would be needless to say that the event had a deep effect upon the character of Paul Massie—a deep and a lasting effect. People fond of interpreting the decrees of Providence might have seen in the gradual development and elevation of his whole nature the specially ordained result which the calamities that fell on him were arranged to bring about. Let us not attempt to conjecture how often or how far one human creature is providentially sacrificed to do good to another. I knew a good man who, having lost a daughter whom he dearly loved, always in after years declared his conviction that Providence had removed her in order that his own moral nature might be elevated and purified by the grief. It was a very sincere sentiment, and seemed pious, and people generally approved of it; and he would have been a bold questioner who ventured to doubt whether a sweet budding girl was cut off, and the heart of a mother broken, merely for the sake of improving the good father's chances of salvation. But without expressing any clear views on the subject either way, and indeed having none such to express, the writer may be allowed to dwell upon the fact that the events, all more or less painful, which culminated in Salome's death, did produce a healthful and elevating effect upon Paul Massie's nature, which, let us hope, is not to be effaced during his life. Reviewing in calmer hours the changes which had taken place since he left Mexico, he could not but see that no small share in such calamities as had befallen was to his own blame. Had he firmly and steadfastly shaped his own course, things must have gone differently

—must, in all human probability, have gone better. He felt that he had played a poor and weak part; and he was acquiring moral sense enough to know that, in another meaning than that of the fallen angel in the great poem, "to be weak is miserable." To be weak in life is to be the source of misery. Little good ever was or can be done by those who do not persistently, like the strong man and the waterfall in somebody's lines, fashion their own channel.

One of the evenings of Paul's convalescence, and when indeed his course of life was beginning to grow clear before him, he sat with Sarah and one of the little Trenton girls. The sun was sinking, and its mild autumnal light fell calm, beautiful, and melancholy on the room. Paul lay on a sofa contemplating the rays, and thinking. His companions probably thought he was asleep.

Suddenly he spoke.

"Sarah, have you ever observed the ships and steamers going up and down a river,—the Thames, for instance,— or in the sea outside Seaborough?"

"No, Paul—at least I have observed them, of course; but I don't know that I ever watched them very closely."

"Well, you may have seen that, however crowded together they may be, yet they pass each other here and there, and get no harm. If you were looking down from London-bridge, for instance, I dare say you might feel alarmed, thinking that every moment some of the vessels going down that narrow miserable stream must run together and destroy each other."

"Yes, Paul, I dare say I should."

She was merely humoring him, and had not the least idea of what he was coming to. The little Trenton girl was listening with open ears and eyes, expecting that some story was about to follow.

"Yet nothing happens, Sarah; or very seldom at least does any accident happen. The same scene may be looked at every day in the year, and for a twelvemonth no collision be seen. Do you know why?"

17

" I suppose because the vessels are well steered."

"Exactly.   Everyone at the helm looks out and takes care to go the way which suits him, and which keeps him out of danger.   But suppose there is one vessel which is drifting.   Suppose the steersman does not trouble himself, or is asleep, and she is allowed to drift down.   What happens ?   She destroys perhaps the course of every vessel in the stream.   She runs against this one, and drives it back upon another ; and this third one carries away the bowsprit of a fourth, and the rudder of a fifth ; and the whole is confusion, and perhaps many lives are lost.   And the man in the drifting vessel may not have meant any harm all the time : he may have been a very good-natured sort of fellow, may he not, wishing well to everyone, very likely ? "

" Yes ; but he ought not to have allowed his vessel to drift.   He must have known what would happen."

" I think he must have been a very lazy, idle, naughty man," said the little girl.

"Sarah," said Paul, " I have been the thoughtless, idle steersman.   I have been drifting ; I have allowed myself to drift.   I have caused the collision ; I have destroyed life."

The little girl started in wonder.   Sarah raised her hand warningly, and endeavored to check the young man's words.

" Yes," he continued, not heeding her attempt at interruption, " I have been looking back, and I see it all only too clearly.   Nothing that has happened lately might not have been avoided, if I had but taken and kept my own course.   My life so far has been only drifting, and I have done nothing but harm.   Please Heaven I will drift no more."

Sarah did not attempt to convince him that he was wronging himself when he charged his " drifting " with any of the misfortunes which had happened.   She thought it better to let him indulge himself in a frame of mind which at least enclosed a healthy and manly resolved for the future. If a woman in love ever can see a defect in the character of the man she loves, perhaps Sarah did think there was some truth in the view which Paul took of his past weakness. Perhaps too, while he was speaking, she thought of a life which, beginning to drift long before he was born, had drifted always, and helped to carry his fortunes and purposes away into ill-omened collisions with existences around him. And Sarah too felt her own moments of self-reproach. Just now she thought herself like the wrecker, who, out of the ruin and death lying scattered on the beach before him, gathers up handfuls of treasure for himself, and runs home with it and hugs it, and is happy. For out of the broken lives and ruined hopes, and the loves that went down in sight of the shore and the port, she was carrying away the means by which to satisfy her own heart, and make her life one of brightness. How should she with sincere lips speak in stern condemnation even of the drifting which had brought about the wreck that was to supply the spoils for her happiness? She nourished this idea for a few moments in silence. The little girl suddenly left the room. The evening was darkening now.

"Paul," said Sarah, in a low tone.

He looked up and answered.

"You spoke of the steersman who allows his vessel to drift and cause collisions, and destroy other ships. You blame him, of course. What do you think, though, of the wrecker, who, when the ships are broken up, carries off as much of the property as he can pick up, and keeps it for himself? Is not he a great deal worse than even the drifting steersman?"

"I don't know, dearest, what you mean."

"You speak of yourself as the one who drifted. But I am worse, a great deal worse—for I am the wrecker."

"Dearest Sarah, how can you say so? What can your meaning be?"

"Ah, you see it, I am sure, only too well. If it be true that you have had any part in causing the wreck of poor Eustace's hopes, and—and—the ruin of others, you at least never meant it, and you lament over it, and cannot forgive yourself that you have had even an innocent part in it. But what can I say of myself? I have seen all this unhappiness, and yet I am selfish enough, like the wrecker, to consent to gather my own happiness out of it. O Paul, I have more, far more, to condemn myself for than you have. I have been cruelly selfish. I am ashamed to confess it, but I have not grieved half so deeply as I ought over all the dreadful things that have happened, because out of the wreck I seem to have snatched your love and my own happiness."

What could Paul say in answer? He could indeed say nothing. He could only draw her towards him and clasp her to his heart. It had indeed this some time been settled for certain between them that they were to play what she now called the wrecker's part, and rescue what sources of happiness they might out of the ruins of the past. But it was not until Paul began to reproach himself for his "drifting," that the image of the wrecker arose in Sarah's mind, and she stood accused of selfishness. Was it selfishness? Not unless love stronger than death—the love which makes us hope and believe that one who has been ours and ours alone this side the grave shall be ours too on the other shore—can be said to deserve the name.

Meanwhile young Miss Trenton had returned to the room, and presently good-natured visitors came to see Paul, who was now quite well enough to be looked upon and talked to; and the lamps were lighted, and the gloomier shadows of the past were banished.

CHAPTER XXXIV

THE LAST.

PAUL MASSIE left England; and Sarah lived only a short time in London. She then removed to a quiet home with some old school-friends on the outskirts of Ghent, and there she taught English to the daughters of substantial Belgian manufacturers.

Alice recovered, but she did not return to Seaborough. She remained with Lydia; was a smart lady's-maid; and held her tongue.

Eustace Massie went abroad after his controversy, and travelled through Italy. His book on "The External Aspects of the Church of Rome" will soon be published.

Fourteen or fifteen months passed away. Sarah has only just received a letter, which concludes thus:

"I am coming, then, by the next steamer. We will go through Germany and Italy before we leave Europe. Can you be happy away from Europe? I think you will like this beautiful place, with its glorious scenery and its tropical air. But if you do not, we will find a home elsewhere. I love Mexico from old association, but I could not continue to love any place which you too did not love. Anywhere, dearest, except in England! I can hardly write these lines, so great is my joy at the thought of seeing you again, and so soon, and of making you my wife—to live with me always!"

And then followed rapturous expressions of love and devotion, which need not be quoted here.

About the same time there came, in the same writing, a few lines to Seaborough House, which were addressed to Mrs. Massie. With a trembling hand the widow opened the paper and read:

"You pledged me to write when I could say I fully forgave you, and not before. At last I write. I am angry and ashamed that so long a time should have passed; but 1 am a bad Christian, bitter of heart, and perhaps even now only softened by the prospect of a great happiness. Forgive you! Yes, indeed I do—if I have anything to forgive who have been the cause of so much misery. You might have been happy, had I never come to Europe. Henceforth you may rest in security. What we know is known only to one other in the world, and will remain a secret always. Good-by. Heaven has dealt with me far more kindly than I expected or ever deserved. I know you will be glad to hear of my happiness. It will add to it if I can think that you too may be happy, and may find in the peace of coming years some compensation for the past."

The writer, in signing himself, began with the word "Your—" But he dashed his pen across it, and simply wrote "PAUL MASSIE."

THE END.